shy girls
can't date
bullies

First Published by Halo & Claws Publishing 2022 as Shy Girls Can't Date at Christmas

SHY GIRLS CAN'T DATE BULLIES

Shy Girls Sweet Romances – Book 2

Copyright © Milly Rose 2025

2nd Edition Published by Halo & Claws Publishing 2025

For information contact: https://hcpbooks.com

Cover Design by Emily Bourne

Ebook ISBN: 978-1-925990-28-7

Paperback ISBN: 978-1-925990-47-8

shy girls can't date bullies

MILLY ROSE

One

There's something both serene and depressing about mornings. I get the house to myself after my dad leaves at 5.30 a.m. to catch the bus to work. Without him around, I can breathe easily. No one is asking if I've done my homework or extra-credit projects.

"Good morning, Mom," I whisper as I touch her portrait on my way through the hallway.

The house is quiet as I sit for my breakfast and retrieve my packed lunch that Dad prepared last night. Dad does his best to be two parents in one. He was once an executive in a fancy office. Now, he's a morning supervisor at a metal fabrication factory. Mom passed away four years ago, and after Dad's extended leave of absence, he couldn't fathom leaving me alone. Since then, every day when I return home from school, Dad greets me at the front door.

I love him for his attention and effort. I just wish things hadn't changed. I wish the daily stress didn't leave me loving the quiet when alone.

Even though the curtains are open, darkness swamps the kitchen. Winter has turned the sunshine lethargic. Yet, my spirits stay high, knowing Christmas is coming soon.

With that thought, I gather my breakfast bowl and glass of orange juice, and move into the living room. After I place them on the coffee table, I move to the switch by the tree. With a quick flick, the Christmas tree and mantle brightens with the twinkle lights I set up last weekend.

I step back and sit on the couch to admire my handiwork. My eyes wander along the tinsel and miscellaneous ornaments from my childhood. Decorating the tree was always something Mom and I did together. I don't mind setting everything up myself. I just wish I had the physical strength to decorate the house's exterior too.

After breakfast, I pack my lunch and cram too many books into my bag. It's the cobalt blue backpack all Ashworth Academy students are required to carry, sporting a large school crest on the front.

Oof.

Maybe I over-packed. It's a little tough to get it onto my back.

With one last check in the mirror, I smooth my loose side-braid and straighten my school uniform. White blouse with navy neckerchief, under a navy school blazer. Below, a thick cobalt and navy tartan skirt which falls below my knees, thick winter stockings, and my shiny black shoes. I guess I look fine. Other girls somehow make this uniform look cute.

When I leave the house, it's not the wintry breeze that sends a chill up my spine. My jaw clenches and a twinge of shame flexes in my gut. Every other house in the cul-de-sac has a glitzy, cutesy, and somewhat cheesy Christmas display. We have a wreath on our front door and some tinsel rounding the banisters and wrapping around the front porch. It's pathetic, and dare I say, embarrassing. I'm just uncomfortable on ladders, and most of the outdoor decorations are too bulky for one person to handle.

The most depressing part of my mornings is the walk to school. Not that I dislike the walk, but it's the time when my serenity drifts away. The more I move toward Ashworth Academy, the closer I am to the loud, hyper, and overcrowded world with my peers. As the wind whips at my face, I must remind myself to breathe. Ugh. At least I live only three blocks from school.

Ashworth Academy is a vast two-story brick building. It's one of the biggest schools in the mountains' area. There is one large gate all the students file through. Every morning I cower, worried I won't get through it alive.

My pace slows to a dawdle as I look for an opening toward the gate. As I tug on my schoolbag, edging it up and redistributing the weight, my eyes drift to the student parking lot. I'm not sure how much it costs to attend this school, but seeing the Ferraris, Mustangs, and Mercedes on display, I'm guessing most kids come from money.

Sometimes I arrive at the same time as the Ashworth siblings' limousine. When they're around, there's a clear entryway into the school because the entire student body treats them like royalty.

My carpooling peers are perky and full of life as they trek my way.

Must be nice.

It's not that I want to feel unhappy. I'd do anything to flick a switch and become an eternal ray of sunshine. That switch would need to become a time machine in order to make that happen. A device to help me prevent the accident that took my mother's life.

Squeezing the straps of my backpack, I push into the crowd entering the gate. I grit my teeth, hoping to keep my balance between the jocks, airheads, and other loners.

I blow out a hard breath when I enter the school grounds. Now, up the steps and into the foyer. There's no way of prolonging it. The surge of the crowd forces me into the building.

Getting to my locker is another story.

The corridors inside Ashworth Academy are wide. In principle, the flow of the large student body should run smoothly. But even Monday mornings can't reduce the hive of activity that bustles through each wing.

I slink to the wall, avoiding others' barging elbows and tripping-hazard feet. Shuffling towards my locker is a slow process. My hushed "excuse me" never registers with anyone. Humiliation colors my face bright red when my backpack lodges between two groups of friends. With both groups deep in conversation, no one budges an inch to set me free. I cup a hand over my eyes as I squeeze myself further along the hallway.

I'm in my senior year, and I've become used to the daily trudge. I wait for the herd to thin out, even when it makes me late for class. When I'm five lockers away from mine, a group of boys huddle in the way. Their boisterous laughter echoes in the hall as they punch each other's arms, and cat-call the pretty girls who stroll past. As I wait out the bell, my backpack slides further down my back, and stress builds between my shoulder blades.

When the bell rings and the hall empties, and the boys move away from my locker. Already fatigued, I drag my backpack along the floor with my foot. With my locker open, I unzip my school bag and sift through the overstuffed contents.

I grab the books for my first two classes and hug them to my chest. As I move through the hall, I try to forget the pressure that comes with a school day. Instead, latching onto the giddiness I felt over the weekend. I haven't been dreaming about my classes. It's what's happening after school that has me excited.

"Do I really have to repeat myself?" a fierce voice echoes in the hallway.

I freeze to a stop. My budding enthusiasm dwindles.

I know that voice.

Everyone at school knows that voice.

Beau Stevenson.

A loud thud makes me grit my teeth. Beau shoves another boy against a locker, holding him by the collar. It's lanky Teddy Wilkins, a quirky guy in our grade. Even though he's close to Beau's height, Teddy cowers on bent knees.

Behind him, Beau has another boy locked at the elbow. Sullivan Hughes winces, struggling to free himself. Beau has them both captured with minimal effort.

Thump.

Sullivan lands against the locker, and Beau clunks their heads together.

"Do you really think I enjoy this?" Beau asks the boys.

The boys' chests heave, searching for a response that will appease their attacker.

Involuntarily, my knees knock together. My brain whirs, figuring out another way to class.

Beau leans into Teddy and yells, "Did you really think you could mess with me? Who do you think you are?"

I hold my stomach, willing the contents to stay inside. Being covered in puke will secure me as Beau's next target.

Oh, wait. Too late.

Beau's head tilts, and his eyes land on me. All the blood drains from my body. Why am I still standing here? *Move, Ava. Move!*

Beau releases the boys, who bolt in my direction. They swoosh past me, and I still can't take my eyes off Beau. He has stunning sky-blue eyes, but they're like an eclipse. It's dangerous to look directly at them. My insides spiral, and I pant shallow breaths. His hand brushes through his blonde hair, which waves back and to the side. He has a casual calmness as he strolls in my direction. His frame broadens as he smooths down his blazer.

There's no argument regarding Beau's attractiveness. He's a ten, but that's part of his game, like a siren luring in fishermen. If someone didn't know all the horrible things he's done during high school, I wouldn't blame them for wanting to ogle this boy.

He nods at me with a sense of familiarity, and my teeth chatter. When he passes, I exhale hard, like a vice grip has released my lungs. I swipe the loose hair off my perspiring face, and hurry to class. I fan my face, hoping not to be a sweaty tomato when I open the classroom door.

"Ava," my teacher, Ms. Hart, says as I enter the classroom. "Nice of you to join us."

"Sorry," I mumble, making my way to my seat.

I plonk down as Ms. Hart regains the class's attention. I fix my braid to the side, swiping sleek sweat off the back of my neck. As I do, I find Hilary Wong giving me side-eye.

I give her a small smile, remembering the friendship we once shared. Hilary and I were in two clubs together last year. During that time, we got along well. However, when those after-school activities ceased, so did our middling friendship.

I'm hoping to ignite that spark this afternoon. Hilary and I both signed up for the Christmas dance committee. We might not chat in classes, but I'm hopeful things are brighter during the committee meetings.

"I want you to start your new assignment this week," Ms. Hart says to the class.

As groans reverberate around the classroom, I do my best to ignore everyone. I open my binder and flip through the pages. Inside this small pink faux-leather binder are all my ideas for the Christmas dance. With all the extra studying, I'm usually ahead of my lessons, so I sneakily add ideas during classes. If my dad ever found out, he'd be livid, but I just can't help myself. All November I added checklists, drawings, mind maps, and mood boards. My ultimate dream is to become the committee chairperson. It's a guaranteed way to make my ideas shine. But, oh boy... Do I have enough confidence to share them with the group?

An assignment sheet lands on my desk as Ms. Hart continues to address the class. "You are to interview someone according to the assignment outline," Ms. Hart says, and I pass the wad of assignment sheets to the next desk. "Your interviewee must be someone outside of this class, and you must complete the interviews before Christmas break. You can use the time off to analyze your interviews and write your report."

"Homework over Christmas?" Franky Romano complains. "You've got to be kidding."

Ms. Hart smiles. "Or you can finish the assignment before the break for extra credit. Your choice."

As more grumbles emit from the class, I already know I'll be getting that extra-credit. Not that I'm proud of being a goody goody, but it's what my dad wants. He seems so happy when I excel at school.

I lose myself in my ideas binder and soon the school bell rings. A collective swell of relief fills the room as I pack up my things. Before I stand, I wait for the herd of students to pass my desk.

"Ava?" Ms. Hart says, moving to my desk.

I stand. "Yes?"

"Do you understand the assignment?" she asks.

My brow furrows, not understanding why she's asking me. I'm one of the top students in the class. "Yes."

Ms. Hart tilts her head, looking me square in the eyes. "You need to analyze your interviewee. That means not only what they say, but it's their body language and facial cues. Keep your head up, observe, and look them in the eyes."

I gulp, shrinking in front of her.

She taps my shoulder and smiles optimistically. "You'll be fine, Ava. I just want you to pay attention and not miss anything. Sometimes, the things people don't say are most important. It can make for interesting analysis in a report."

I nod, trying hard not to frown.

"Okay," Ms. Hart says, stepping to the side. "You'd better run along."

"Thank you," I say, feeling defeated as I trudge out of the classroom.

I hug the wall and wait for the corridor to clear. Ms. Hart thinks I'm too shy to do well on the assignment. I've studied psychology intensely and understand body language. The biggest problem will be finding someone to sit for the interview.

I suck in a breath as I push off the wall. Instinctively, I keep my head low. I don't want another run-in with Beau Stevenson. He's back from his recent suspension and already causing fights. It's a mystery why he hasn't been expelled. Some students talk about him like he's a legend because he can win fights when outnumbered. But overall, everyone fears him.

"Ava?" a voice calls. I search for it, and my friend Ciara paces toward me. "What are you doing?"

"Huh?"

"I'm on my way to study hall," Ciara says as she lands in front of me. "Don't you have economics now?"

"Oh, yeah," I say, wincing as I rub my forehead. "I'm a little out of it."

She pats my shoulder. "Well, cheer up. We have our committee meeting this afternoon. That's something to look forward to."

I smile. "I am excited about that."

"You're lucky you're so smart," Ciara teases as her bob swishes by her ears, "otherwise you'd always be in detention for being late to class."

I push off the wall with a sigh. "I know. It's just that I saw Beau before, and it rattled me."

She gasps. "*Dang.* He's back already."

"Yep, watch out."

"Thanks for the tip."

As we walk down the hall, I ask, "Would you let me interview you?"

"Interview me?" Ciara questions. "What for? The school paper?"

"No, it's for my psychology class."

"Oh, no way," Ciara says, almost disgusted. "I'm not doing anything psych-related."

"Why not? It's just a few questions."

"No way. It's the same as you taking my diary and reading it to your entire class. Forget it."

I pout, taken aback. "Oh, okay."

Ciara turns the opposite direction at the end of the hall. "I'll see you later."

I nod, somewhat deflated. "Yep. See you then."

I don't have the greatest track record for keeping friends. Ciara was kinda my only option for this interview. It'll be embarrassing being unable to start the assignment because I have no one to ask.

Two

My stomach sloshes about like an old boat on a turbulent sea. After my last class and the hallway has sufficiently emptied, I grab my backpack and coat from my locker and head to the second floor library. My heart thuds with every step until I enter the rear meeting room.

"*Ha*. Look who decided to turn up," a vindictive voice greets me.

Great. It's Whitney James. My academic rival and grade-A pain in the butt.

"Being late isn't a good look, is it, Mr. Riley?" Whitney jabs, turning her attention to our teacher.

Mr. Riley sighs, with one hand in his pocket and the other flattening his tie. "Okay, kids," he begins, "let's all be civil. It's senior year, and you've all been through a lot. It's time to pull together and put on the best Christmas dance Ashworth Academy has ever seen."

Mr. Riley's enthusiasm squashes a chunk of my nerves. I pull out my binder out of my backpack and look for a free seat at the table. With a bright smile, Ciara taps the space beside her. Unfortunately, it's on the corner between her and Whitney. There's a free spot on Ciara's left, closer to Mr. Riley, but I don't want to be obvious. I know Whitney would love to make a snide comment about me avoiding her.

As I sit beside her, Ciara's dark brown bob swishes as she bounces in her seat. "We've been waiting for this since sophomore year," she cheers. "This will be so much fun."

Whitney sits tall with her hands clasped in front and wears a superior smile. Today, we need to elect someone to be in charge. Let's face it. With her booming voice and snide remarks, Whitney will boss everyone around no matter what. I've joined a lot of clubs and committees during high school. Ninety-five percent of the time, Whitney is there to ruin the fun.

"Now, myself and other faculty members are here to assist you," Mr. Riley says, "but, ultimately, this is your baby. You will need clearly defined roles and deadlines. Please go about this democratically. Remember, everyone's opinion is valid."

Whitney snorts and clumsily covers her laugh.

Mr. Riley folds his arms, standing at the table, and peers around at the seven of us. With our backs to the door, Ciara and I sit on the long edge. On the short edge, opposite Mr. Riley, sits Whitney and Lucy Jacobs. Across from me sits Hilary, her footballer boyfriend Marcus, and his teammate Jeff.

"Do you need me to conduct the meeting until you elect a chairperson?" Mr. Riley asks.

Whitney taps her fingers along the table, ensuring every eye is on her. "I think we've got this. Right, guys?"

"I don't want to be in charge," Hilary pipes up. Her arm entangles around Marcus's bicep.

Marcus's ebony skin seems to darken as he grimaces. He waves a flattened hand across his neck, showing he's also out.

"Not me," Jeff blurts. "I'm just here because Marcus dragged me along."

"I can barely organize my study notes, let alone a run sheet for the school dance," Lucy says. "I wouldn't want to wreck it."

I open my binder with trembling fingers and flip to my big ideas mind map. I fumble with the page, turning to my tasks checklist. The tremor spreads through my hand and up my arm. I cough and clear my throat as my face grows hot.

With a purposeful inhale, I close my eyes to settle my nerves. I exhale and repeat. When my buzzing energy eases, I open my eyes. As my view settles on an empty table, my mouth falls open.

Where the heck is my binder?

I look at the space in front of Ciara, and it's also empty. I turn to my right, and my jaw drops lower. Whitney hugs the open binder to her chest. Her steely eyes locked on Mr. Riley.

Is she kidding me? How did she even pull that off?

I pan across the other faces. Lucy looks down and away, avoiding the selection process. The three across from me also have their attention averted.

Did no one see my binder being yanked away? Whitney has her wicked fingers clawed around it. She flips the pages, and her eyes light up at my running checklist.

Whitney lowers my binder, grins, and smooths back her sandy hair. "So, is the verdict in?" she asks. "You all want me as the chairperson?"

"Ciara? Ava?" Mr. Riley questions, looking our way. "Do you want to speak up?"

Ciara shrinks in her seat, her bob swishing as she shakes her head.

The room is dead silent as everyone turns in my direction. My palms pool with sweat, and my face burns. My eyes drift towards my binder, and Whitney presses her hands onto the pages.

My shoulders droop forward, and I turn back to Mr. Riley. With a gloomy frown, I shake my head.

"Congratulations, Miss James," Mr. Riley says to Whitney. "As chairperson, you need to keep in contact with your student body treasurer. She will give you your budget and make sure you keep financially on track."

"She?" Hilary cuts in. "David isn't the treasurer anymore?"

"*Duh*," Lucy replies. "Vanessa Ashworth is back at school. David was only temporary."

"But David is way better," Marcus comments.

"*Shush*," Hilary, Lucy and Whitney scold at once.

"Don't say things like that. What if Vanessa walked in?" Whitney whispers harshly.

"I know I said this is a democracy," Mr. Riley says, smirking, "but please keep the schoolyard politics to a minimum while I'm here."

"Certainly," Whitney says, rising from her seat. "I guess I'd better take over the meeting now. You know, because I'm the chairperson."

Oh boy. I don't think I can survive power-hungry Whitney James with a title.

"You kids will have free rein over how the meeting is conducted," Mr. Riley says. "I'll be working on a lesson plan, but I'm also here to supervise." He pulls his laptop from its bag and frowns. "Oh darn, I left the power cord behind. Can I leave you kids alone for ten minutes?"

"Of course," Whitney says, swatting a hand. "I totally got this."

Mr. Riley leaves, and everyone shifts in their seats, slouching to a more comfortable level.

"First," Whitney says, still standing, "I don't think we should have individual job roles. It's easier working on one thing at a time."

"But Mr. Riley said our first task is to assign everyone a job," Hilary counters.

"There'll be too many deadlines," Whitney argues. "And if everyone works under my leadership, it will be easier for me to track the budget."

Lucy shifts away from Whitney. "So you'll be in charge of everything?"

Whitney rolls her eyes. "*Hello*. I am the chairperson. It's kinda the point."

I blow out a hard breath. I jolt in my seat when everyone's attention aims at me.

"Ahem." Whitney clears her throat. "Did you have something to add?"

"Yeah," Marcus says, his eyes shifting between me and Ciara. "Are you going to speak up? Or what?"

12

"See, guys," Whitney says flippantly, "this is why my leadership is so important."

"So, Ava," Jeff says, his eyes narrowing at me. "Did you have something to say?"

"Well," I say, pointing towards my binder. "That's my..."

"Sorry to interrupt," a commanding voice says, entering the meeting room. We turn to see Vice Principal Franklin standing before us.

Whitney blushes, clasping her hands behind her back. "Hi Mr. Franklin. We were just starting our meeting. Did you need something from us?"

"I'm here to add a new member to your crew," Mr. Franklin says, lifting his arm wide to gesture beside him. When we don't react, Mr. Franklin drops his arm and turns from side to side. "Beau?"

"*Beau?*" everyone gasps in unison.

Beau Stevenson wanders in, one hand resting in the pocket of his trousers, the other scrolling on his phone.

"Phone, Mr. Stevenson," Mr. Franklin says with exhaustion. He holds out his hand, and Beau rolls his eyes as he submits his phone. "You can pick this up from the front office at five o'clock."

"No, wait," Whitney says, stepping forward. "We all worked hard to be here. Plus, we're responsible enough to work independently. Beau is the antithesis of that."

Beau looks at her sideways and furrows his brow. "The anti-what-now?"

Whitney groans and shoots a look at Mr. Franklin. "See?"

"Miss James, I don't need argumentative behavior," Mr. Franklin says authoritatively. "Do you understand?"

Whitney squeaks, taking a step backward. Her gaze lowers and she nods. "Yes, sir."

My eyes flick to Beau, and my knees knock together.

Mr. Franklin pats Beau on the shoulder. "You stick out your time on the committee. It'll go a long way toward upping your grades before graduation."

Beau huffs and rolls his eyes.

"Mr. Stevenson is here because he needs to learn school spirit and work productively with others," Mr. Franklin says. "I'm sure this group will be excellent role models. Now, where is Mr. Riley?"

"He went to his office for a power cable," Hilary says.

"Right. I'll find him on my way out and inform him he has an extra student to supervise," Mr. Franklin says, turning toward the door.

"You're..." Lucy stutters, pointing at Beau. "You're leaving him with us?"

"No students are more appropriate to show a good work ethic than all of you," Mr. Franklin says proudly. "Behave yourself, Beau."

As Mr. Franklin leaves the room, an awkward shift ripples through the group. Beau's eyes move from Lucy to Whitney, and I'm careful to lower my head as he pans my way.

"You can't discourage or distract us from our work," Whitney says to Beau.

With my gaze on the table, I shiver at the sound of Beau's laugh.

"Forget him, Whitney," Jeff says. "Get back to what you were saying."

Whitney groans, shaking out her limbs, which forces my eyes up. She's rattled, and I have to fight my desire to smile. As Whitney composes herself, my urge to smile fades. With a slow thud, Beau draws closer to the table.

A small squeak emits from beside me. Ciara quivers in her seat as Beau pulls out the chair on her left. He sits on the table and uses the chair as a footrest.

"Okay, everyone, as I was saying," Whitney says, trying to ignore Beau. "If we work together, we can get this event up and running."

"What's all this?" Beau asks, leaning across the table in front of Ciara and me.

"Nothing for you to worry about," Whitney huffs as he tilts his head to read the contents of my binder. "We are trying to work."

"This is for the Christmas dance, right?" Beau says, and my breathing falters from his looming presence. "Are these all your master plans?"

"You don't need to help," Hilary blurts, grabbing a hold of Marcus.

Ignoring Hilary, Beau sets a hand on my binder and slides it closer. "Lemme see."

Whitney groans. "Don't touch that."

I grit my teeth hard as Beau flips through my binder. Now, two horrible people have touched it.

"Why can't I look?" Beau asks teasingly. "I'm part of the committee, aren't I? Or is this your secret book?"

"I'm the chairperson," Whitney argues. "I'm in charge of everything."

Beau mumbles a laugh and slides the binder across to me. My heart thumps to a low beat, and my eyes fall to my lap.

"Are you collecting everyone's personal information?" Beau asks.

Whitney huffs. "What are you talking about?"

"Well, if this is indeed your binder," Beau replies, "I was just wondering why the front page says, 'Property of Ava Jones' with her home address and email."

I lift my head to see Whitney's exaggerated eye roll. "Well, sure, the binder is Ava's."

Beau leans across, tapping the binder. "What about the contents?"

"Why are you starting trouble?" Jeff cuts in.

"So, the person in charge brought the most information to the meeting?" Beau says dryly.

"What are you getting at?" Whitney mutters.

"Well, if you're in charge," Beau says, leaning over the table, "you must have the most ideas."

Whitney's pale complexion dulls with a green tinge. Her mouth hangs open, and her eyes are sunken. As Beau straightens his back, Whitney's gaze pans in my direction, amplified by a steely flash of anger.

Gulp.

"Well?" Beau laughs. "Where's your master plan?"

Whitney searches for a comeback as everyone fidgets in order to avoid her pitiful gaze.

"Fine!" Whitney shouts. "They are Ava's plans. Are you happy?"

Beau leans across Ciara, shuts the binder, and pushes it closer to me.

My mouth is desert dry. Between the goosebumps and the sweat, my body fights between being hot and cold. My insides squirm as a growing sickness overtakes me.

Beau's arms fold again. "Are you admitting you've got nothing?"

Ciara's hand wraps around my wrist, and her tremors shake my arm.

"It's more than you've got," Whitney says in a quivering voice.

I firm my arm against Ciara's grip and watch Whitney fidget. Under Beau's scrutiny, her illusion of confidence shatters.

Beau shrugs. "I'm just working out why you're in charge." He turns to Marcus and Hilary, saying, "I would think the top dog would have the top ideas. Don't you?"

Awkwardness shifts amongst the group. Hilary and Marcus exchange glances with Lucy and Jeff, but no words are uttered.

"I only skimmed," Beau says, gesturing to the binder, "but looks like Ava put in the most thought."

My breathing grows louder. Oh gosh, I can't stop it. My chest rises and falls with an obvious heave.

Beau turns to me, but I can't bring myself to meet his gaze.

"Don't you think you can do better than her?" he says in a low tone.

My breaths quicken and hyperventilating is imminent.

"You want it, don't you?" Beau presses.

"Leave her alone." Lucy blurts. "She already said she didn't want it."

"*Ha.*" Beau smirks. "Did you give Whitney your plans on purpose?"

I swallow hard as bile leaps from my stomach. Oh geez. Why must everyone stare so hard? Even looking down, I feel the force of every eye burrowing into me.

I push my hands into my stomach and lift my head. I purse my lips as Whitney's intimidation stare hones in on me.

With a shake of the head, I whisper, "No. She snatched the binder from me."

Everyone was in the room when it happened, but that doesn't stop the gasps and heads turning.

Beau plants his hands on the desk and pivots between each committee member. "If Ava has the big ideas, don't you want her in charge?"

"Ahhs" and "Umms" are replied.

Beau slides off the table and slouches onto the chair. "Unless Whitney kicks butt at being in charge."

Ciara clears her throat. "It could be more productive to set some guidelines."

Marcus coughs and shifts in his seat. "Like Hils said, Mr. Riley gave us our first task, and Whitney dissed the idea."

My fingers twitch, and the hairs on the back of my neck stand on end. Is the group backing me?

Beau laughs and claps his hands. "Well done, Whitney. You are a waste of time."

A pain-stricken sob flies out of Whitney. Her hands smack over her mouth and muffle a wail. She launches from the table and barges her way out of the meeting room.

Silence sweeps the room. Until Beau holds his belly and throws his head back, laughing like he's watching a comedic skit.

My eyebrows push together, heartbroken that Whitney's outburst bothers no one.

Beau stretches his arm behind Ciara and pats my shoulder. "Is that better?"

I shove his hand off me, grimacing. "Ugh."

I ran to catch Whitney after taking a final look at the ignorant group. I slow my pace when I move between the bookshelves. She might not have left the library, so I prick my ears. As I step into the classics section, I hear a faint whimper. In the next row of books, I find Whitney slumped on the floor, her head in her hands and knees pulled to her chest.

I edge closer and lower to the ground. "Whitney?"

As I squat beside her, I gingerly place a hand on her shoulder. Whitney screams and shoves me away.

"Get lost, Ava!" Whitney yells. "Haven't you humiliated me enough?"

"What? I... I didn't..."

Whitney swipes at her watery eyes. "But you enjoyed every second."

I frown, unable to deny it. "You shouldn't have stolen my work."

"Fine, whatever," Whitney fires back. "I don't have any ideas of my own. Are you happy?"

"No, I'm not happy."

"Like it matters. You hate that I'm in charge."

My frown morphs into a scowl. "You weren't leading the group. You just wanted to boss us around."

Whitney shoves me again, sending me onto my butt. She leaps to her feet and yells, "Just leave me alone, Ava! Go take over the committee. See if I care!"

As I push myself up, Whitney storms out of the library, slamming the glass door behind her.

I rise from the floor on shaky limbs. Mrs. Thompkins, the librarian, tampers down her anger at Whitney's erratic exit. With anxiety balling in my gut, I turn in the meeting room's direction. A strained exhale leaves my lungs, and I force my feet forward.

Something deep inside urges me to avoid going back in. What if they blame me for Whitney leaving? They all went along with whatever she said. They can't suddenly be Team Ava.

Then the worst dawns on me. The epitome of high school bullies is inside that room.

Three

I push the door open and enter a stunned silence.

Ciara hangs by the door, obviously getting far away from Beau. "Is Whitney coming back?" she asks.

I shake my head. "She left."

Hilary points to a corner. "She left her bag behind."

"We can leave it in the office for her to pick up tomorrow," Lucy suggests. "I'll text her."

"I can take it," Beau offers. "I need to go to the office and grab my phone."

"No way," Jeff says, throwing an arm out towards the bag. "You're not touching her stuff."

"*Geez*, what's with you, man?" Beau smirks. "Are you hooking up with her?"

"He's just not being a jerk," Marcus interjects. "Unlike you."

"I'm the jerk?" Beau replies sarcastically. "You guys can't deny it's better without her around."

"What's your problem with Whitney?"

Everyone turns my way, falling back into silence. As I stare into Beau's eyes, I realize that the question came from my lips.

Beau's eyebrow raises, and he answers with a lopsided grin.

As Ciara fidgets behind me, I don't take my eye off Beau. Whitney's hysteria plays in my mind, sending furious energy throughout my body. He made her cry. He broke her. How can he stand here, acting like it's no big deal?

Ugh, look at that smile. His lips look fuller when they frame his pearly whites. Even when his smile is sarcastic, it brings out cute lines around his eyes. He even has faint dimples. Dimples are adorable.

Whoa. What am I doing?

My cheeks burn with embarrassment.

This boy is despicable. Why am I thinking about him being cute?

"Ah, Ava?" Ciara murmurs beside me.

"Huh?" I squeak. "Ah, umm…"

Beau snickers, enjoying my awkwardness.

"This is crazy," Hilary whines. "Even if she's bossy, at least Whitney took charge. Ava, are you ready to be the chairperson? Because you know no one else wants to do it."

I move closer to the table. As my heart rate steadies, I nod. "Yes, I can do it."

Ciara sidles up beside me, and her fidgetiness reinvigorates my nerves.

"So…" Lucy draws out the word. "What should we do?"

I latch my hands behind my back to hide the tremors. "What we should have done. Assign everyone a specific role."

"Whitney said we shouldn't split up jobs," Jeff says. "We should work on everything together. Doesn't that make sense? It would be quicker."

Marcus snorts. "You're just saying that to avoid being in charge of anything."

"No, we won't be split up," I say as my voice wavers. I spy my binder, and my forehead grows clammy. I want to grab it, but it's on the other side of Beau. "Umm… It's in my binder."

Beau slides the binder across the table, and I wait for his hand to pull away before I grab it. "Uh, thanks."

With no choice but to show off my trembling fingers, I open the binder and flip the pages. Each flip makes a loud wobbling noise as I shudder the papers. My cheeks grow hot with excessive embarrassment.

"Are you sure about taking charge?" Hilary asks, gritting her teeth.

An involuntary moan hurls out of me when my stomach twists in on itself. Pushing my hand hard into my gut, I force myself to stand upright. I shake my head and force a smile.

"Sorry, I'm okay," I say with phony contentment.

I can't bring myself to look at him, but in my peripherals, Beau folds his arms and his posture slouches to one side. He's not buying my hopeless display.

I flip to the two-page spread in my binder regarding job roles, and turn it to face the group. "See? Everyone gets a role so we can cover all our bases. Someone is in charge of decorations. Another is in charge of promotions and ticket sales. We need someone to organize the entertainment, like a band or DJ. Someone needs to work out drinks and snacks. Like, if we should contact the PTA or get it catered. That's just a start, anyway."

As I spoke, everyone moved to the front of the table to gather around the binder.

"Wow, Ava," Hilary remarks, "you did put a lot of thought into this."

Ciara nudges me. "Why didn't you tell me you had a grand plan?"

I gulp, shrugging like a clueless dope.

Lucy turns to Jeff and then to me, suggesting, "Perhaps we can break off into pairs to tackle each aspect? That way, no one will get overwhelmed."

I nod. "That's okay with me."

As if on clockwork, Marcus and Hilary bunch together, and Lucy slides close to Jeff.

Beau smirks, turning to Ciara and me with his arms out wide. "Who's the lucky lady who gets me?"

Ciara latches onto my arm. "Ava and I talked about decorating."

Hilary scoffs. "Decorating is the job everyone wants."

Trying to ignore Beau, I reply to Hilary with, "Like I said, everyone will do everything. We just need someone in charge of each section."

"And you're in charge of all of us?" Jeff questions me.

There's the trembling fingers again. But did they ever really stop? "Yeah, I guess."

Jeff then points to Beau and then at Ciara. "Why don't those two pair up, and Ava can float between each pair?"

"That makes sense," Lucy agrees.

"*No*," Ciara squeals in distress, yanking on my arm.

"Perfect," Beau says, reclining in his chair. His hands rest behind his head. "You two girls will be the last pair, and I'll just chill. It'll be the easiest detention I've ever had."

Marcus groans, swiping a hand over his cropped and faded hair. "Why don't you go to actual detention, Beau? We don't need you here ruining the mood."

"Hey, I already got rid of the buzzkill," Beau says with a smirk. "If anything, I've lifted the mood."

"No one thinks you're cool for making Whitney cry," Hilary says, crossing her arms.

"You don't have to be here, Beau," I say, moving towards Whitney's school bag. "I'll take Whitney's bag to the administration office and tell them our meeting is over. That way, you're free to go."

Beau sits up, intrigued. "Are you serious?"

I reach for the bag, and a voice demands, "Don't touch that."

I jolt and turn to see Whitney, her chest heaving, as she stands in the doorway.

"You're back?" Hilary asks in surprise.

Whitney pouts. "I just came back for my bag."

"Whitney, please stay," Lucy says, mirroring the pout.

Whitney blows out a hard breath. "I don't know."

"Come on," Jeff chimes in. "We were all willing to back you as chairperson. We need you around."

My mouth runs dry as I look at the floor. I'm out? Just like that?

"If she stays," Hilary says with caution in her voice, "she shouldn't be paired with Beau."

"Yeah. No way," Marcus agrees.

"Paired with Beau?" Whitney asks, wide-eyed. "Why would I be paired with him?"

"We all agreed to work in pairs," Lucy explains.

Jeff steps away from Lucy and toward Whitney. "I'll stay with you, Whitney."

Whitney blushes. "Okay, thanks."

I pan to Lucy, who tries her best to hide her devastation. She tucks her hair behind her ears and slips on a smile. "That's cool. So, I'll go with one of you girls?"

Without a moment's hesitation, Ciara zips across to Lucy. My gut contorts as if it's punched by a clenched fist. Ciara ignores my eyeline, quivering by her new partner.

"That works," Hilary says, nodding at Lucy and Ciara in approval. She turns to me, saying, "Ava, you should be with Beau, seeing as you're in charge."

Marcus turns his attention to Whitney. "Ava is in charge, isn't she?"

Everyone's focus turns to Whitney. Her jaw flexes as her eyes narrow in my direction. "Sure," she replies. "I'd love to see what Ava does as the chairperson."

Oof! There goes the second invisible gut-punch.

"Hang on," Beau says, tossing a thumb over his shoulder. "Wasn't I leaving?"

As I turn to Beau, someone else catches my eye. Mr. Riley jogs toward the meeting room, his cheeks puffing as he pants with every step.

"Mr. Riley?" Jeff questions. "Are you okay?"

Mr. Riley stops in the doorway, catching his breath. "Mr. Franklin told me about our new attendee," he says. "Mrs. Thompkins is concerned about the amount of noise coming from this room. Whitney, is everything okay?"

"It's fine," Whitney says with a shrug. "Ava's now in charge."

A dumbfounded look crosses Mr. Riley's face. "Oh, really? Okay, Ava, is everything going smoothly?"

At this point, my mouth is so dry my tongue sticks to the roof of my mouth. As everyone circles around me, claustrophobia sets in. It's a fight-or-flight moment. No, wait. A suffocate or spit-it-out moment, more accurately.

Mr. Riley steps forward, hands on hips. "Ava? Do you have a handle on things?"

As my brain scrambles to find an answer, time slows down. The lagging ticks of the wall clock slice through the silence, and my heartbeats boom with dread.

Motion in the room comes back to regular speed when Beau steps beside me.

"Ava has us all working in pairs so we can focus on more tasks at once," Beau tells Mr. Riley. "We have our pairs. We just need our tasks."

Mr. Riley's eyebrows lift at hearing Beau's response. "Is that so?"

"Yes," Beau replies. "I'll work with Ava and follow her lead."

Mr. Riley bends his knees to gain my attention. "Can you two work together?"

Oh, for goodness' sake. Can everyone stop crowding me? I'll say anything to make this torture end.

I nod and answer. "Yes. It'll be fine."

Mr. Riley straightens his posture. "Okay then. I'll let you kids continue."

I look around the room and land on Ciara's worry-stricken face. Her rounded eyes flick to Beau. I can't help doing the same. As I lift my gaze to him, Beau sends me a wink.

I look away and fan out my blazer. Oh, *geez*. I'm working with Beau. This isn't good.

"Umm, Ava," Whitney says, gaining confidence from my terrified panic. "We need some leadership here."

I jut my mouth open and close, but my brain still won't give me words to say. As I near the point of blacking out, I feel Beau fidget beside me.

"Weren't you guys listening before?" Beau asks harshly. "Ava said someone needs to be in charge of decorations, tickets and posters, catering, and entertainment." He pauses, flicking out each of his fingers. "That's four. Can't we get it together enough to give each pair a category?"

The boom of my heartbeat simmers down as everyone submissively nods. Beau turns to me, and I look into his amicable eyes. His lips curve into that adorable lopsided grin, and my brain function returns.

I lean over the table and pull a blank sheet of paper from my binder. I rip it into quarters and write a task on each piece.

As I slide the pieces into the center of the table, I mention, "Whoever contacts the PTA about food should also ask them about being chaperones. We have only two weeks to get everything together, and we need to ensure we have some parents available on the night."

"Yikes," Beau says with a grimace. "Not it."

"How do we decide this fairly?" Lucy asks with hesitation.

"Guys, we only get ninety minutes after school to work on this," I say as exhaustion sets in. "We've wasted a bunch of time today. We need to choose now so the rest of the week is productive."

"Jeff and I won't be here tomorrow," Marcus says. "We have football practice on Tuesday and Wednesday afternoons."

Hilary raises her hand, adding, "And I usually go and watch."

"What?" I ask, shaking my head. "But you two partnered up. You can't both ditch."

"For the record," Jeff pipes up, "Marcus and I aren't ditching. We already committed to football."

"It's fine." I sigh. "You boys don't have to be here, but your partners do."

Hilary scoffs. "Whatever."

Whitney snatches a piece of paper off the table. "We'll do tickets and promotions. I'm an ace in my graphic design class, so I can get everything ready while Jeff is away."

"Good work, Whitney," Mr. Riley applauds. "That's what I call being a team player."

Even though it pains me, I smile at Whitney and say, "Thanks."

"Whitney and Jeff, you need to have everything ready by Thursday afternoon to send the files to the printing company on Main Street," Mr. Riley says. "You will have Friday off so you can attend the football game."

Hoots and hollers erupt from the group. Do I lack school spirit because I think watching the game is a waste of time? We could get so much more work done if everyone stayed in the library instead of painting their faces blue and white in preparation to yell at a team running around a field.

Hilary takes another slip of paper. "Marcus and I can take care of food," she says, displaying the paper in front of her. "Both my parents are on the PTA. I can attend a meeting and ask everyone at once." She looks around the group. "Can I add everyone's parents down as chaperones?"

As the rest of the group replies with yeses, I clear my throat with a pathetic reply. "Not mine. My dad doesn't do this kind of thing."

"That's surprising when you're into this organizing stuff," Hilary says.

I bite into my lip, looking down at the tabletop. "I took after my mom."

As silence sweeps the room, Beau cuts through the tension. "Don't mark mine down either."

Marcus smirks. "What a loss."

Mumbled laughter simmers from the group as everyone relaxes again.

Across the table from Lucy and Ciara, I wait for them to pick between entertainment and decorations. I know Ciara has her heart set on decorations, but she was supposed to work with me, not abandon me.

I place a finger on the decorations slip of paper, and slide it toward me. "The bulkier decorations can be heavy. It might be better to have Beau help move things." I turn to him, asking, "If that's okay?"

He shrugs. "Sure."

I look back at the girls, and Ciara's rounded eyes grow watery.

"Once you two organize the music and the photographer," I say, "you can join us in decorating. We also need to make a decorating sign-up sheet for extra volunteers."

Lucy takes the entertainment slip, and she and Ciara agree.

"We have thirty minutes," Jeff says, gesturing at the clock. "We could make plans by splitting up."

"Agreed," Marcus says, leading Hilary by the hand toward the door.

Whitney leaves with Jeff, muttering, "Have fun, everyone."

Lucy suggests to Ciara that they find a table in the library too, and they also leave the room.

Mr. Riley then walks into the library, overseeing where everyone has paired off.

Before it dawns on me, goosebumps prick my skin. I'm alone... with him.

"So." Beau slouches in his seat. "I guess I'm staying."

My stomach flips, and I force myself to sit.

"I already have a plan for the decorations," I say, flipping through my binder as nervous energy runs full force through my body.

"Of course you do," Beau remarks. "Miss Ava Jones has a plan for everything."

A cold sweat runs down my back. His tone has me on edge. As if he's not hatching his own scheme right now. He's only here because Mr. Riley is on watch. While I skim through my notes, Beau turns toward the library. He's waiting for the perfect moment to leave the meeting.

It can't come soon enough.

To pass the time, and to prove I can be a leader, I read aloud my notes to include Beau. He reclines on his seat, cracks his knuckles, and stares at the ceiling. I won't let him discourage me. I'll complete this task on my own if need be.

"Why do you keep telling me all this stuff?" Beau finally blurts. "Wait until we're in the gym. I'll do whatever you want."

I cower, staring at the desk. "Huh?"

"You don't need to include me like I'll have some fantastic input. You've already got this all figured out. We're set."

"We are?" I whisper and turn to see his face. "Does that mean you'll be here tomorrow?"

"*Pfft.* You heard Franklin," Beau scoffs. "I'm stuck with this group until the dance is over."

"I just... I thought you'd try to get out of this tomorrow."

Beau laughs. "If I see a way out, you know I'll take it. But you said you'll need help to carry things."

His bright topaz eyes watch me with a gentle kindness. He's sitting here because I said I'd need help?

Before I can help it, I blurt out, "Why did you stick up for me before?"

"What do you mean?" he deflects. "When I told everyone to choose a task?"

"Yeah. I would have passed out if you hadn't stepped in."

He shrugs. "I could see you were dying in front of everyone."

"That I appreciated, but you didn't need to attack Whitney earlier."

Beau leans in and whispers, "Maybe I had my own agenda."

I jolt, sucking in a breath I hope isn't my last.

"If you are in charge, you have to talk to me," Beau says, slipping into his lopsided grin.

Fighting my need to shiver, I reply, "I guess."

"Because I wanted to ask," his whisper has a sly twist. "Were you the one who ratted me out?"

"What?"

He tilts his head, scrutinizing my face. "You did, didn't you?"

"What? No. About what?"

"It doesn't work out well when people play games with me."

Panic surges through my body. "I'm not playing anything. I don't talk to anyone about you."

Beau slams a hand on his chest and feigns a hurt expression. "*Ouch.* That cuts me deep."

"This is about what I saw earlier?" I whisper. "You and those two boys?"

"Someone said something," Beau says. "There were only four of us there."

I swallow roughly. "It wasn't me. You can't think I wanted you here."

"I don't know," Beau says, his tone turning jovial. "You used to have a soft spot for me."

I huff, busying myself with my binder.

"Do you still catch bugs?" he whispers.

Searing pain shoots through my brain as I get a flash of a memory. I grit my teeth, wincing as the vision disappears.

"Well?"

My shoulders lock with tension. "Don't."

"What? It's a simple question."

I slam a hand on my binder and groan. "Just don't."

"Okay, good job everyone," Mr. Riley calls, walking between tables in the library. "It's five o'clock. Time to pack up."

"Thank goodness," I murmur, shutting my binder and sliding out of my seat.

Before I can stand, Beau leans forward and places his hand on the back of my seat.

"I didn't mean to upset you," he says. "Some memories came back while I was with you. Didn't you get any?"

"No," I say firmly as I stand. I hug my binder to my chest and move to my bag. "I was too busy feeling tense and frightened to ever remember something good or fun about you."

I stuff the binder into my bag and move out of the meeting room.

"Frightened?" I hear Beau say in the meeting room.

I wave to the others on my way out. Unfortunately, hurried footsteps gain on me.

Four

"Hold on, wait up!" Beau calls behind me.

His footsteps follow as I jog away from the library. This stupid heavy bag makes a fast getaway impossible. With all my might, I stuff my binder into my open bag. My efforts are futile as I move down the stairs. Inside, three heavy textbooks leave no space for me to jam in one more thing.

"You weren't serious back there." Beau reaches out and grabs my shoulder. "You're not scared of me."

I jerk away from him, and my bag goes flying. Books, papers, and my pen case scuttle around the immediate area. With a groan, I lower to the ground.

"Let me help," Beau says, kneeling beside me.

"Just leave it."

A herd of footsteps rushes down the stairs. I glance at the feet and recognize the hushed whispers of the dance committee. Whitney's mocking laughter is the ultimate cherry on top.

I guess because Beau is here, no one stops to help. At least, I hope that's why they all walked away.

"Are you okay, Ava?" Ciara's mousy voice asks as she follows the others. "I'd help, but I have to be home right away."

I'm too mortified to answer, so I wave in response.

"Bye," she squeaks, and disappears down the hall.

"Psychological evaluation?" Beau reads aloud. He's skimming my assignment guidelines. "*Sheesh*. Are you seeing the school shrink?"

I snatch it away from him. "No, it's my assignment. I have to interview someone."

"Yuck," he retches. "I'd rather talk to the PTA."

Furiously, I stack my textbooks and force them into my schoolbag.

Beau picks up two of my notebooks. "That's a lot of books. How'd you carry them in the first place?"

"It's fine. I've fit more than this before."

"You seem really agitated."

I grab my notebooks from him and scoop up the rest of the papers. "I'm fine."

Still shoving everything back into the bag, I move toward an exit.

"You'll lose everything again," Beau says, following me out.

"Please, just leave me alone." Hugging the open bag, my shoulders bunch high and my head buries low.

"I have to get my phone from the admin office." Beau halts. "Can't you wait so we can talk?"

Talk? I just spent over an hour with this guy. What could he possibly want?

My pace quickens, and I almost slip on an icy step. Thankfully, I keep my balance in my urgency to get away from Beau.

From the school gate, I look over my shoulder. *Phew*, he's gone.

I drop my bag to the ground and rearrange the contents. When it finally zips, I hoist it onto my back and set off home. The swirling icy breeze always makes breathing more difficult, but today is especially labored. This afternoon included too much close contact with Beau Stevenson. I don't know how I will survive more afternoons like that. Plus, it'll be worse now. Everyone is paired off, leaving me alone with him!

As I clear the second block home, an engine revs behind me. I tilt my head and watch a black GT Mustang roll beside me.

The tinted window lowers, and Beau appears. "Don't you think it's too cold to walk home?"

I fold my arms around me and bury the lower half of my face in my scarf.

"Get in," he calls. "I'll give you a ride home."

"No, thank you," I call back, keeping my eyes on the footpath.

"Ava, it's freezing."

"I'm fine. I always walk."

The car pulls to the side, parking behind me.

"Can you stop acting this way?" Beau calls, slamming his car door shut.

I would run if I didn't worry about slipping over.

"You're not scared of me," Beau says, catching up to me.

I flinch as he appears alongside me.

"Flinching?" he says sarcastically. "Really?"

An overwhelming mixture of confusion and annoyance boils inside me. "Why are you tormenting me?"

"Huh? I just helped you become the leader of the dorks. I thought you'd consider that a prize, not a punishment."

I grab the straps of my backpack and yank it higher to allow faster movement. "Look, we're partnered up in the committee. We will have time to talk. Can't you leave me alone outside of school?"

"You're struggling with that bag. Why don't you let me carry it for you?"

"Why? So you can have a good laugh by throwing it in a trashcan?"

I quicken my steps through this last block that leads to my cul-de-sac. I just need to get inside the safety of my house.

"There you go again." There's a layer of hurt in his words. "When have I done anything to you?"

"Stop trying to confuse me." I keep my focus on the slippery cement. "I know all the stories about you."

Beau stops walking. "Yeah, and none of them involve you."

My pace slows as I work out what he's saying. I grit my teeth and look over my shoulder at him.

"Hey," he says, gesturing ahead. "Why doesn't your house have any Christmas lights?"

My brow furrows. "Huh?"

"Your house is the only one with no decorations. What happened?"

I slam my hands onto my hips. "Why do you care?"

"It's just weird. Your house was always the brightest in the neighborhood."

I turn and walk away. "Well, that was a long time ago."

It's a relief not to hear footsteps behind me. I glance over my shoulder and see Beau moving toward his car. By the time I'm walking around the cul-de-sac, the car roars down the suburban street.

I pass Mrs. Yates's house. My neighbor, Mrs. Guthrie, sits on the front porch with her. Both sip from steamy coffee mugs.

"Hello," I say with a wave.

"Oh, Ava," Mrs. Yates replies, rising from her seat. "How are you, dear?"

"Well, thanks," I reply. "And you both?"

"Fine, thank you, dear," Mrs. Guthrie says, hanging over the porch railing. "Did you see that Mustang drive by?"

I grow paler in the chilly breeze. "Yes. Why?"

"Was that Beau Stevenson?" Mrs. Yates cut in. "We haven't seen him since he was twelve-years-old."

I bite into my lip as a weird sense of guilt ripples in my gut. "It was him."

Mrs. Guthrie chuckles. "Did nostalgia set in? He's probably curious about the old neighborhood."

"I heard he became a bit of a problem child," Mrs. Yates says.

That's putting it mildly. "Umm, yep."

"You have nothing to do with him nowadays?" Mrs. Yates asks, scrutinizing me.

I shake my head wildly. "No, no way."

"Dear, how's your father?" Mrs. Guthrie asks.

The question makes me pause. I pull myself together, answering, "He's fine."

"Good," the ladies reply in unison.

I wave, wishing them a good evening, and carry on towards my house.

"How's your father?" The question rattles around in my head. When my mother was alive, the neighborhood was like one big extended family. It's as if her death also killed the community.

I trudge along the garden path home, unlock the front door, and call out, "Hi Dad."

"How was your day?" he calls from the kitchen.

"It was fine," I say, sliding off my bag and hanging up my coat.

Dad emerges from the kitchen with concern on his face. "Your tone doesn't sound fine."

I push for a smile and meet his eyes. "No, it was. It was my first committee meeting."

Dad smiles back. "That's great. You'll help make the school look as spectacular as this home."

My gaze pans around the living and dining rooms. The fully loaded tree, the nativity scene on the sideboard, and the candles and tinsel on the mantel have me smiling.

Dad takes another step towards me. "Who else is on the committee?"

"Ciara," I blurt.

Dad nods his approval. "They'd be silly not to include her. She's a great girl."

"Yep."

"Who else?" Dad presses.

"Hilary Wong, Lucy Jacobs, and two boys from the football team."

Dad looks at me incredulously. "Footballers? That's a strange addition."

"Hilary wanted to bring her boyfriend along."

Dad frowns. "Oh, I see."

"Yep."

"That's a small group."

I nod, pursing my lips. "Mhmm."

"No one else?"

If I tell him Whitney is on the committee, he'll give me that disapproving look. I can't even imagine the expression if I mention Beau's name. Actually, his face would just be red from sheer yelling.

I give him a side hug and kiss his cheek. "That's all, Dad. It was a good afternoon."

He pats my back. "I'm glad you had fun."

"I became the chairperson."

"Ava! That's fantastic," he cheers. "Why didn't you lead with that?"

I blush, rubbing my forehead. "There was just a lot of discussion. A lot to wrap my head around."

"It's not too much work, is it?" he asks. "It won't impede your studies?"

"No, Dad."

"Okay, then. Why don't you hit the books while I work on dinner?"

I nod, moving up the hall. I stop by the framed photo of my mother and smile, running a finger over her hair.

"Hi Mom," I whisper. "I'm home."

I continue on towards my bedroom and toss my bag inside. I plonk onto my bed, fling myself backwards, and stare at the ceiling. Today I got what I wanted. I became the chairperson, yet I feel deflated and deceitful. Did I get the position fairly? I hate that Beau set the pieces in motion and bullied Whitney to the point of crying.

I tilt my head to view my desk, where three open books lie in wait. A sigh pours out of me. All I do after school is study. That's why clubs and committees are so important to me. They're the only social outings I get.

I shift off the bed and slip off my blazer. I yank my books from my bag and toss them onto my desk. Melancholy washes over as I oversee the mass of study notes and annotated books collaging the desktop. I roll my shoulders in tight circles and step away from the unappealing mess.

My interaction with Beau frazzled my brain. He saw my name in my binder and stuck up for me in front of Whitney. He listened to me during the meeting and spoke to the group when I couldn't.

My fear surprised him.

I massage my forehead and open my closet. I kneel before it and dig into the items at the bottom. Behind the shoes and board games is everything I hid from my fragile heart.

As I gaze at a round, green plastic piece, Beau's voice echoes in my head. *"Do you still catch bugs?"*

I yank the plastic item from the back of my closet. My frown sags until my jaw hurts. As I stare at the kid's toy bug catcher, my heart aches.

I stand, carrying it to my desk. "Nope, not doing this."

I stuff the plastic bug catcher into the trash can under my desk. I've blocked out so many childhood memories because it's devastating to replay them. I don't need Beau walking back into my life and reminding me of better times.

I blow out a hard breath and step away from the desk. I pace the soft carpet with my hands pressed to my hips. I tilt my head and glimpse more items at the back of the closet. I step forward as glitter catches my eye. I scoop my hand in and retrieve a lilac photo album with glitter and sequins glued to the front.

I crouch by the closet and open the album. My fingers quirk. I know I shouldn't be doing this. Seeing the bug catcher already set off my anxiety. I sit cross-legged as my mom stares back at me, her arms hugged around a younger me. On the next page, Beau and I explore rock formations on a mountainside. Mom always took us to interesting places, so we'd become more adventurous.

I let the album fall to my lap as I hunch over it. One summer changed everything. I lost my mother and then had to start high school, where my best friend became the enemy of the entire school.

No matter what I felt today when I gazed into his eyes or grew attached to his smile, the boy I knew doesn't exist anymore. He's gone, and he's never coming back.

My finger glides over Beau's younger face. My gut twinges as I stare at that lopsided grin.

Maybe part of him isn't gone?

I chew on my fingernail as Beau's image from on the footpath filters into my mind.

Oh gosh. I'm in trouble.

Five

"I can't believe you were alone with him yesterday," Ciara says, as we walk towards the cafeteria the next day. "How did you survive?"

"I had no choice." It just slips out. I didn't mean to be so blunt with her, but she betrayed me yesterday afternoon.

"I'm sorry," she squeaks. "But I couldn't be left with him."

"It's fine," I sigh. "Like everyone said, I'm in charge, so Beau should be my problem."

She gives me a dubious look. "Do you want to be in charge?"

I shrug, wishing I were more confident. "Yeah."

Ciara pats my back. "It's not fair that any of us are stuck with him."

"There has to be a way to get rid of him." I scan the hall. "Maybe Vanessa Ashworth will have some pull?"

"Do you think so?"

"Her opinion matters around here," I reply. "I'm here to get the dance budget from her, right? Why don't I also ask her about getting rid of Beau?"

"You totally should," Ciara cheers.

"She will be on our side. She'd never let someone like Beau ruin her events."

"I'm so excited," Ciara squeals. "We could be getting rid of Beau!"

We stop at the entrance to the cafeteria and search for Vanessa. After a few minutes, her golden blonde hair bounces into view as she strides through the hall with everyone giving her a wide berth.

I falter as I raise my hand to gain the heiress's attention. I yammer nonsensical sounds and then Ciara elbows my ribs. It startles me, and I step forward. "Vanessa?"

Astonishingly, Vanessa turns our way with a friendly grin. "Hi girls."

My hands tremble. Vanessa is the princess of this school. Not only does her billionaire father provide the jobs for everyone's parents, but her family is also the reason Ashworth Academy exists.

She points at me. "It's Ava, right?"

I nod much too hard, replying, "Yes."

"Sorry," she says with a drained sigh. "I wish I didn't have to re-introduce myself to everyone. I guess I spent too much time overseas and fell out of the Victoria Falls bubble."

"Everyone in this town will always remember you."

"But I used to pride myself on knowing everyone at school," she says with a tight expression. Something in her eyes causes me to feel sad for her.

An idea pops into my brain. I noticed the change in her mood. An observation I need to make for my psychology assignment. Would Vanessa ever sit for the interview? She'd be the ideal candidate, and I'd love to discover something deeper about the Ashworth heiress.

She turns to Ciara. "Uh, sorry, I'm blanking."

Ciara blushes. "Ciara Lennon."

Vanessa giggles and playfully slaps her forehead. "*Duh.*"

"Umm, the reason I got your attention," I say, "is I need the budget from you for the Christmas dance."

Her eyes sparkle as they run over me. "You're the chairperson this year?"

She doesn't think I can hack it? "Yes."

She nods, pulling her phone from the pocket of her skirt. "Good for you. I'll email it to you."

Vanessa opens the school portal app on her phone and searches the directory for Jones.

"I'm glad my mother stayed overseas," Vanessa says, typing on her phone, "or she'd force me onto this committee too."

I frown. Does she think we're lame for doing this?

Her head lifts, and she touches my arm. "Not that it's a bad thing you're planning this event. It's just that I'm running society events at the country club, along with the Christmas festivities at Ashworth Estate. I couldn't bear taking on one more activity. But my mother will think I'm not doing enough."

"That's tough. Will your mother be home for Christmas?"

Her eyes water, but then she blinks them clear. "I really don't know."

"Oh."

Vanessa takes a large breath and shakes her shoulders. "Nevermind. It's all sent. Good luck with the dance."

"Thanks," I say as she veers toward the cafeteria entrance.

Ciara whacks her elbow into me again.

"*Ouch.*"

Ciara's eyes enlarge as she whispers harshly, "Ask her."

"Oh, right." I stand on tippy toes to regain her attention. "Ah, Vanessa?"

She turns around with a flat expression. "Something wrong?"

I flick my eyes at Ciara for reassurance, but she just cowers beside me.

"It's about..."

I'm cut off by Hilary and Lucy bustling toward us. "Oh my gosh, Vanessa, hi," Lucy beams.

"Are you all talking about the dance?" Hilary asks with excitement. "We need to pick your brain."

Vanessa holds her hands up. "Sorry, not getting involved. I didn't sign up for the committee because I already have my hands full."

"But you'd have so many ideas," Lucy pipes up. "You've planned tons of events."

"Sorry, I can't get involved," Vanessa says, wincing. "I'm already stretched too thin."

"*Dang,*" Hilary sighs.

Vanessa pivots between the girls. "But, I guess, if you have ideas and you want a sounding board, we can talk about it sometime."

Hilary and Lucy squeal, grabbing one of Vanessa's arms each as they bounce up and down.

Vanessa giggles and the girls release her, heading inside the cafeteria. Vanessa cups a hand over her mouth, saying, "Bye, girls."

"That was so cute," Ciara pipes up. "Everyone loves you, Vanessa, and any help you can give us will be awesome."

With a sweet smile, Vanessa lowers her hand. "Thanks, girl." Her eyes flick back at me. "Were you saying something, Ava?"

"It's about Beau," I force out.

"Beau?" Confusion contorts her face until realization sets in. "Oh, I heard Mr. Franklin put him on the committee." She traces a finger under her mischievous grin. "How's that going? It'd almost be worth joining the committee to see him in action."

"You'd want to be around him?" Ciara blurts with heavy judgment in her tone.

Vanessa shrugs, the playfulness still curving her lips. "I dunno, he's fun."

"*Fun?*" Ciara and I repeat in unison.

"He was at my welcome home party." Vanessa rolls her eyes, swatting a hand. "It was mostly my father's colleagues and clients. Beau's parents dragged him along, and I was so thankful they did. Those parties at the manor can be beyond stuffy. Beau was like a breath of fresh air. He always avoids those things. Lucky his parents don't make attending mandatory like mine do. Anyway, I just enjoyed his company on a night that should've bored me out of my mind."

"Oh, okay," I mutter, unsure if she's alluding to them becoming more than friends or not.

Vanessa beckons us to follow as she steps into the cafeteria. "Can we walk and talk? I'm starved."

"Sure," I say, following. "Umm. Look, the committee's not happy with him around. We wondered if things would go smoothly without..."

Vanessa cuts me off. "He's not going anywhere."

I halt sharply, and Ciara slams into me from behind.

"How..." Ciara stammers. "How can you be sure?"

"Ashworth Academy will never expel Beau," Vanessa says, continuing to walk between lunch tables. "His mom is an executive in my father's technology division, and his dad donates to the school every three months, which keeps my mother happy."

My eyebrows push together as I search for the logic. "What does that have to do with...?"

"Look, Beau's a rebel," Vanessa replies. "The school's disciplinary department is at a loss with him. They're trying something new. You guys just need to deal with it."

Vanessa moves toward a table, and in my desperation, I storm behind her. "But..."

Vanessa reaches her table, and I skid to a stop. Her friends gush their hellos, and Vanessa waves to everyone seated. Her other hand lands on the broad shoulder of the boy seated beside her. He turns his head sideways, and for a moment I forget how to breathe.

"Oh my gosh," I gasp, grabbing onto Ciara's arm. "She's standing next to Beau."

Ciara inhales rapidly, her tanned complexion turning a paler shade.

"Should we go over there?"

Ciara exhales hard and shakes her head. "Nuh-uh. Abort. It's not worth it."

Vanessa looks over her shoulder as she takes the seat next to Beau. "Are you girls coming over?"

Beau double-takes when he sees me. He stands abruptly and reaches for my wrist. "Are you joining us?"

"What?" I grimace as his hand latches around me.

Beau looks around me and grins. "Come on, Cindy. You can come too."

Ciara's signature gasp sounds behind me, followed by the trampling of hurried footsteps.

Beau laughs. "*Geez.* She spooks easily."

Laughter rounds the table, and my shoulders cramp, waiting for everyone to attack me with insults.

Vanessa stays seated, flicking her sleek blonde hair over her shoulder and setting her eyes to smolder. Oh my gosh, she's so into him.

"Well?" Beau looks at me like I'm dimwitted. "Are you staying?"

My stomach churns, and I shake my hand against his grip. "Let go."

He does, and it causes me to stumble backwards.

"Oops," Vanessa chuckles. "Watch where you're going."

More laughter erupts from the table. As I gather my footing, popcorn and potato chips hurl in my direction. It's impossible to distinguish who throws what. I shoot my hands up over my face to protect myself from the sharp edges of projectile chips. The salty snacks lodge in my hair and jab at my shoulders and mid-section.

When an eruptive slam breaks through the laughter, cutting it into silence, the projectiles cease. I lower my hands and see Beau standing over the table, with a fist rising from the tabletop.

My chest rises and falls in rapid succession. As he turns, I'm too mortified to meet his eyes. I spin on my heels and run from the table. I barge through students and dodge other tables and abandoned chairs. My insides contort with overwhelming embarrassment. Instead of fleeing the scene, I head straight for the cafeteria bathrooms, figuring the closest doorway will be for the best.

I plant my back against the door, puffing and panting. Being the sideshow freak of the cafeteria has me overheating. I don't even understand what happened there. Did Vanessa just watch it all happen? She didn't do anything to stop it. Did she enjoy watching me suffer? So much for the ideal candidate for my assignment.

Why did Beau grab hold of me? He made sure I couldn't run when an arsenal of food was whipped at me? It's just so callous. But do I expect any less? This is what he does for amusement. He tortures people who do nothing wrong for his own kicks.

I peel myself off the bathroom door and move to the sinks. I scowl at the mess of a reflection staring back at me. I pull out my messy braid and shake out my hair.

A flush sounds behind me, and a girl emerges from a stall.

"Whoa," she comments. "What happened to you?"

"Nothing," I grunt, and she takes it as a hint to wash her hands and leave as soon as possible.

When I brush all the salty remains off my school uniform, I huff at the reddened face staring back at me and turn towards the door. Waiting it out won't make life any easier.

I push the door open and step into the cafeteria.

"Hey," Beau says, leaning against the wall by the bathroom door.

I jump backwards, considering whether to stay in the bathroom for the duration of lunch.

Beau tilts his head towards the lunch line. "Are you getting food?"

I wave my hands in front of me, side-stepping toward the cafeteria exit. "No, stay away from me."

"I'll walk you to the line," Beau offers, "so no one messes with you."

I back away further. "No way. I'm not falling for that."

Beau pulls himself off the wall with a grunt. "You know, I'm trying to be nice here."

"Just leave me alone," I say, and glance over at Vanessa's lunch table. Everyone has turned in their chairs, watching what decision I make. I look away and mumble, "Just what I thought."

"Suit yourself," Beau says, moving back toward the table. "Go hungry."

My chin drops as he walks away. A voice inside my head urges me to run, but I'm stuck in place. His words hurt in an unexpected way. Almost like I wish he'd turn around.

Snap out of it, Ava.

I force myself out of the cafeteria and hurry along the hallway. I run toward the auditorium, toward the alcove in an adjacent corner. It's my quiet place, away from laughter and ridicule.

"Hey," Ciara calls, throwing an arm out to stop my fiery pace.

Dejected, I pull off to the side.

"Is she serious?" Ciara says, wall-hugging with me. "Vanessa says there's no way to get rid of Beau."

I fold my arms across my middle. "I don't want to talk about it."

"I thought Vanessa would take the planning committee seriously and be on our side," Ciara continues to ramble.

"Can you stop?" I blurt, slamming a fist against the wall.

Ciara mutes with her mouth wide open.

"That was a crappy thing to do, Ciara," I pout as the betrayal bruises my heart.

Noises emit from her mouth, but nothing resembling actual words.

"You ditched me in the cafeteria. How could you do that?"

She sucks in her bottom lip, and her eyes grow glassy. "I thought you'd be right behind me."

I roll my eyes hard. "Beau grabbed hold of me while the whole table threw food."

Ciara gasps. "They did what?"

"You just left me," I moan. "You're supposed to be my friend."

"I'm sorry. It was fight or flight. I knew something bad would happen, so I ran. I don't know why you didn't."

"You could have helped me get away," I argue. "You just let him grab me."

"It wasn't like that," she whines.

"Whatever," I sigh. "Let's sit apart during classes. I need some time away from you."

"Don't be like that, Ava."

I recoil at her touch and walk away. "Just leave me be."

Six

I kept my word and avoided Ciara. I kept my head down in the classes, cringing at the simmering laughter of kids who witnessed the lunchtime event.

When the last bell rings, my afternoon ritual kicks in. I hang back until the other students leave. In the hallway, I wall-hug until the area clears out. It's the easiest way to navigate through this massive school. Otherwise, my classmates would barge into me, eager to escape their educational environment.

I dump the contents of my locker into my backpack and heave it up the flight of stairs to the library. When I join the group, it feels so much smaller without Marcus and Jeff's broad bodies taking up space. And... hey, wait a second...

No Beau.

I look behind me. He's nowhere in sight.

Could it be?

Did Vanessa reconsider?

I drop my bag with the others, pull out my binder, and join Ciara, Whitney, Hilary, and Lucy at the table. Everyone's body language stiffens, dreading Beau's arrival.

"Sooo," Hilary drags out the word. "Has anyone heard if he's coming?"

A chilling unease sweeps across the table.

Lucy fidgets in her seat. "Maybe he's not allowed to be here today. Because the boys aren't here."

"I doubt it," Whitney says flatly. "I'd love that to be the case, but it's a dumb reason."

"Positive thinking, Whitney," Hilary says, brimming with pep. "If we all think good thoughts, maybe he won't show up."

Ciara raises her hand. "I'm up for that."

Hilary turns to me and asks, "Have you heard anything?"

I shake my head. "No. He is part of the committee until the dance happens."

Whitney groans. "Ugh. Great."

"*Positivity*," Hilary hisses.

"I think it's important we work on our individual tasks," I say, trying to put my leadership hat on.

"About that," Whitney says, tapping her fingers along the table. "We've forgotten a huge component of planning the dance."

"What's that?" Lucy asks.

"*Duh*," Whitney replies, like it's obvious. "Picking a theme."

I squint at her in confusion. "A theme? We don't need a theme. It's a Christmas party."

"Yeah, but what kind?" Whitney continues. "Is it Winter Wonderland, Ugly Sweater Party, Santa's Workshop?"

"We can't do anything that clashes with the winter formal," Hilary adds.

"I don't think we need a theme," I say, my voice wavering.

"We want it to be a good event, don't we?" Whitney asks with thick sarcasm.

"Can't it just feel like a neighborhood Christmas party?" I suggest, feeling like the smallest person in the room.

"Oh, no way," Lucy says under her breath. Her eyes set on the window opposite her, causing everyone to swivel and gaze into the library.

Vice Principal Franklin strides towards us. Behind him dawdles the boy no one is delighted to see.

A collective huff and groan erupts from the group as Mr. Franklin opens the meeting room door.

"Hi kids," Mr. Franklin says with a grin. "Mr. Stevenson apologizes for being late. He promises to stay with the group and not leave the school grounds again."

Beau enters the room with a bemused expression.

"You need to straighten up," Mr. Franklin says to him. "If you work hard, you could get back on the wrestling team."

"You want to reward him after he just came back from suspension?" Whitney blurts.

Beau straightens his tie. "They need their star team member back."

"Take a seat, Beau," Mr. Franklin says commandingly. "I expect everyone to get along amicably. Mrs. Thompkins at the front desk will monitor things until Mr. Riley gets here."

Beau pulls out a chair a good distance from the table and flops down.

"Okay, happy planning," Mr. Franklin says, making a quick getaway.

"Were you all fretting I wouldn't make the meeting?" Beau teases.

Hilary groans, crossing her arms. "You think being here is a joke?"

Beau smirks. "It's a little funny."

Lucy tugs on Whitney's blazer. "We should call Mr. Franklin back and protest this. There's got to be somewhere else they can stick him."

Whitney gives Beau a glaring side-eye. "Yeah, like cleaning gum off the cafeteria tables."

"Done that a few times," Beau says, brushing off his shoulder. "It doesn't take long these days."

"Ugh. I can't believe Mr. Franklin brought you back here," Hilary moans.

"My bad. I tried to give you guys what you wanted," Beau says, panning around our faces. "None of you want me here."

His gaze lands on mine last, and lingers.

I gulp in response, fidgeting as I escape his pointed stare.

I look down at my binder and pick at the edges. "We should get back to work."

"Yes," Whitney says with a clap. "We need to nail down a theme."

"We don't need a theme." I'm still not game to look up.

"Uh, yes we do," Whitney sneers. "We want people to be excited. I started designing the tickets last night. I had to stop because I had no inspiration."

I open my binder and flip through the pages until I land on my aesthetic mood boards. "You need inspiration for Christmas?"

I look up in time to catch Whitney's disgusted expression. "I don't want your clippings from some magazines. I've already started a Pinterest board everyone can follow."

"I don't know why you're making this so difficult," I say, grinding my teeth to keep from scowling. "It's Christmas. It doesn't need over-thinking."

"So, we just do something lame, like your neighborhood party idea?" Whitney replies with a vindictive chuckle.

From the corner of my eye I catch Beau shifting in his chair and leaning in.

"We need a theme," Lucy pipes up. "It'll make the dance more memorable."

"I agree," Hilary says. "I can already see the posters and tickets looking super cute when tied into a theme."

Is she for real? There's no theme. She's picturing tickets with Christmas designs on them.

"If it's so important, Whitney," I say, curling a hand into a fist, "Why didn't you bring it up when you were the chairperson?"

Whitney flicks her hair and looks down her nose at me. "I barely had a chance before everyone turned on me."

I uncurl my hand and press my palm into my twisting stomach. Oh gosh. Is this where everyone votes Whitney back in?

"What do you think, Ciara?" Whitney asks, leaning over the table.

Ciara fidgets under Whitney's stare. She looks at the other girls and then her glassy eyes hit me.

She sucks in her lip, and then blurts, "A theme would be fun."

I slump in my chair as if she just slapped me across the face.

"See," Whitney cheers. "Told ya."

Beau clears his throat, and any gloating in the room disappears.

"Umm," he begins in a low, calm voice. "Isn't Ava in charge?"

A silent awkwardness drifts around the table. Whitney squirms in her seat. I'm guessing she's fearing a repeat of when Beau sent her out of the room in tears.

I can't let that happen again.

"It's fine," I blurt. "A theme is a great idea." I pull out my pen from inside my binder. "How about I write down some ideas?"

"Everyone should be involved in the decision," Hilary says, standing from her seat. "I say we skip the meeting until Marcus and Jeff can join us."

"No, we all have to stay." My voice cracks from my lack of authority. "There's a reason committee and commitment are derived from the same word."

Hilary plonks down with a huff. "This is lame. I've never missed one of Marcus' practices."

"He'll still run and throw a ball without you," Beau teases.

"Shut up." Hilary groans. "You're just jealous of him because they banned you from football since sophomore year."

Beau stifles a laugh. "Yeah, I'm so jealous I can't spend months groping other guys' butts."

Hilary screws up her face. "But you'll wrestle round on the floor with them?"

"This isn't helping," I mutter.

It's enough to get some attention. Beau and Hilary stop their bickering and turn to face me. Lucy, Whitney, and Ciara also face me. I notice the sadness stirring inside me. It must be all over my face.

I point the pen at the note paper. "Can you guys call out suggestions? I'll write them down, and we can vote. We can't wait for the boys to vote. Our first priority is sending the posters and tickets to the printers."

Soon enough, I have a list of seven suggestions.

The North Pole / Santa's Workshop

Ugly Sweater Party

Ice Palace

The Nutcracker and Sugar Plums

Gingerbread Lane

Christmas Around the World

Candyland

"Any favorites?" I ask, drawing a candy cane under my list.

"Ugly sweaters crack me up," Lucy says with a giggle.

"No," Hilary complains. "I wanna dress cute, not ugly."

"What about childhood Christmas stories?" Whitney says. "It could make for the cutest graphics."

"That might be hard to decorate." I draw my pen down the list. "Why don't we do the North Pole? I know from last year there're tons of traditional Christmas decorations in the storerooms. Plus, I have an idea for the photography backdrops. People can have portraits taken against a maze of Christmas trees."

I turn my binder towards the rest of the group. The two-page spread displays my aesthetics to transform the gym for the dance. Behind the image of cutely decorated tables are pictures of different style Christmas trees. It'd be super romantic for couples to wander through together.

"Whoa," Hilary hums. "You really thought this stuff through."

"I want this to work." For some reason, tears build behind my eyes. "Whitney needs to finish the promotional designs by Thursday at the latest. Without tickets and posters, there's no dance."

Lucy raises her hand. "I vote for the North Pole."

Hilary nods. "Works for me."

Whitney sighs, looking off to the side. "Fine, whatever."

"I like it too," Ciara says, standing. "Lucy, should we work on our task?"

Lucy stands. "Sure. Ava, can we have your mood board to help describe what we want to the photographer?"

I gladly tug the pages from my binder and hand them over. "Of course."

The two girls leave the room, finding a table for themselves.

Whitney stands and moves to her bag. She pulls out her laptop and heads for the door.

"Can I help?" Hilary asks, chasing Whitney. "I'm booked in at the PTA meeting, so we've got time to bounce ideas."

Whitney agrees, and they leave for a shared table.

Beau slides his chair closer to the deserted table. "Do I stay?" he asks in his deep, calm voice.

I shrug, scribbling a star on the corner of the page. "Do whatever you want."

"I didn't ask you to stay at lunch so those guys would do that to you," he says, and it causes me to dig the pen deeper into the page. "I put a stop to it."

I stare at the oddly shaped star. "It doesn't matter."

"Shouldn't I be helping you do something?"

"Why would you want to? They already caught you trying to ditch the meeting."

"Sure, if I can get out of this crap, I'm gonna give it a shot."

It hits me like a personal attack. "This crap?"

Beau slumps against the chair. "This isn't exactly my idea of fun."

"Then let me do this myself."

"But I want to talk to you."

I clench my jaw and set my eyes on the page.

"I don't care what we talk about, I just want to talk."

My mind flicks back to when we were alone yesterday. "You want to talk because you think I'm a tattle-tale."

"Yeah. I wanted to know if you held a grudge." He reclines on his seat, arms folded and his chin angled upward. "But maybe I'm the one holding a grudge now."

My eyebrows push together. "Why?"

"You're the mean one," Beau says, "not me."

A puff of air shoots out of me from the shock.

"That's right," Beau says, tipping his seat back to the proper position. "You're mean to me, Ava Jones."

Squinting, I rub the throbbing space between my eyebrows. "How so?"

"You won't give me the time of day," Beau replies. "I just wanted to talk. That's the reason we're not friends. You're the one who shut me out."

I scoot my chair away from him. "That's not the reason we're not friends."

"Yes, it is," he says adamantly.

The back of my neck grows hot and tension wraps around my spine like a heavy galvanized chain.

"You know why I needed space," I mutter, stopping the memories from resurfacing.

He leans forward, whispering, "Of course I do. But I didn't expect when we started high school you'd still push me away."

I turn to him and my irritated eyes grow watery. "And I didn't expect when I was ready to bring my best friend back into my life, I'd find him bullying other kids."

Beau's lips press together, and he leans back in his chair.

"I was in my own world for most of freshman year," I admit. "It was dark and isolating. I looked for you at school, and I didn't realize how much I'd blocked out. Everyone was scared of you." I swallow hard. "I was scared of you."

"I would've stopped what I was doing if you wanted to talk."

I swallow hard as a knot forms in my chest. "No one could stop you. That's why you've got the reputation you have now."

Beau raises an eyebrow. "And you think I'm proud of that?"

I shrug. "Why else do it?"

He smirks, but there's something phony about it. "Guess you still know me pretty well."

The meeting room door opens, and Mr. Riley swings his body into the room. "Everything all right in here?"

I nod, replying, "Yes, thank you."

"Good," he replies, stepping back into the main library. "Call out if you need me."

Beau taps his fingers along the table. "What's with your dad making you walk home from school?"

I clench my jaw, refusing to dignify the question with an answer.

"I know you live close to the school," Beau continues, "but it's freaking winter. It's freezing. How can you stand walking every day?"

"I just do," I mumble through gritted teeth.

"You walk to school as well?" Beau asks with an air of shock. "*Geez.* I would be an icicle all day. Won't he buy you a car?"

Frustration gets the better of me. "I don't want to drive a car!"

"Whoa." Beau's hands fly up. "No need to snap. I was just asking a simple question."

"Well, why don't you use your brain," I say, succumbing to the misery lying under the surface. "I don't drive, and my dad doesn't drive. We avoid cars."

I'm met with tense silence. Beau's chair creaks as he fidgets, finding a response.

I turn away from him. "Forget it."

"I didn't think," he murmurs. "Your mom... Yeah, that makes sense. I'm sorry."

My insides crumble when hearing his words. It would be nice if things were civil. But the past is too ugly. I pick up a pen and make angry scribbles on my note paper. "Surely there's somewhere else you can be."

"Huh?"

"Like you said, this is your detention," I say, unable to contain my dismay. "You're kept here against your will, while dorky me is here because I actually thought it'd be fun."

"You're not a dork for thinking this is fun."

I slam my pen down. "You called everyone here 'dorks' yesterday."

"Okay, fine," Beau surrenders. "I do think it's lame and everyone here is uptight. But you're into this stuff, so I'll help you."

"What about your grudge against me?"

He shrugs. "What grudge?"

The glint in his eyes seems genuine. No, there has to be another angle. I need to stay on my toes. I've seen how he operates. He's a brute with a snarky response to everything.

Beau smirks. "Why are you watching me like I'm about to attack?"

"Why do you ask things like that when I'm aware of your reputation?"

"Can't you just wipe the slate clean while we're stuck together?" Beau whines. "Come on. I've done nothing bad since I came into this group."

"Excuse me?" I ask like I've misheard. "The first thing you did was humiliate Whitney in front of everyone. You went on the attack."

Beau rolls his eyes. "Good lord, it's Whitney. She practically begs for it."

"Whatever Whitney does, doesn't give you the right to retaliate," I counter. "You can't be nasty to anyone in this group."

Beau makes a cross over his heart. "I promise. If it means we can be civil to each other, I'll leave everyone alone."

Just as I smile, Beau hisses. He leans in and whispers, "Except Whitney. I just don't think I can promise to keep my mouth shut around her."

"What? Why?"

"Come on," Beau says, leaning back. "She's mean to you."

I shrug. "What's that got to do with anything?"

"As if I'll let anything mean happen to you."

I shake my head. "Beau, you don't need to act like my bodyguard just to fulfill a promise."

"But I've always protected you."

I look into his gentle topaz eyes and slump in my seat.

"Anytime someone picked on you," Beau says, "they dealt with me later."

I press my hand into my stomach and swallow hard. "Are you serious?"

Beau's hand reaches out and brushes against my chin. "Even if we weren't talking, I've always cared about you. It pissed me off when you shut me out, but I couldn't erase what we had." His hand drops to his lap. "You were my best friend, Ava."

Before the weight of the emotion registers with me, a tear drops onto my cheek.

Beau frowns. "Are you sad because I bullied those people, or because we're not friends anymore?"

I wipe my face dry and sigh. "All the above. It's just a lot."

Beau sucks in a breath, and blows it out hard. "It's my punishment to be here, but I'll stop acting like it's the worst thing in the world."

I hug my middle, watching the sincerity in his eyes. "Really?"

He smiles gently. "I'll try to make it fun, like you want it to be."

I take the olive branch. "Will you help me sketch out the design for the dance?"

His eyebrows raise with apprehension. "I don't draw."

An easy smile tugs at my lips. "No, that's okay." I slide my binder between us, open to my desired floor plan for the gym. "I envisioned the gym looking like this. I just want to make sure it fits with this North Pole theme."

"Okay, where do we start?"

I tap my pencil against the maze of Christmas trees. "I want this to stay. It'll be so dang cute for photos. Maybe we get some of that white felt that's used for fake snow. You can get reams of it, basically like a carpet."

"Maybe run it around the bottom of the trees?" Beau suggests.

"And we could layer it with leaves and twigs to make it feel real."

Beau runs his finger along the page and then slides his hand under his chin. "Whitney said you wanted this to feel like a neighborhood party."

Already knowing where he's going with this, a shiver runs down my spine.

"Did you want to do something like your mom used to do?" he asks.

I clear my throat and keep my eyes on the page.

"Do they still throw those parties?" Beau asks, digging a little deeper.

I sit back in my chair and face him with a rigid stare. "No."

Beau blinks. "Oh."

"The neighborhood idea is moot anyway," I say, turning my pencil so the eraser points downward. "Instead of having this feel like a tight knit community, it needs to be tweaked as a home for elves, reindeer, and Mr. and Mrs. Claus."

"You want the dance to feel like a home for elves?"

"I wonder if the budget will allow for buying everyone an elf hat?" I ponder aloud.

Beau splutters a laugh. "You're not serious?"

"It could be cute."

"No, it's not cute."

"It's Christmas. Shouldn't it be a little cheesy?"

"Yeah, but I thought the idea was this event wouldn't be lame," he counters.

I drop my pencil and frown. The idea of a specific theme has me frazzled. I just want things to be simple and nostalgic.

"I didn't mean it will be lame," Beau says gently. "Whatever you come up with, I'm sure it'll be awesome." He taps the tree maze. "I think this will look great."

I exhale gradually. "Thanks."

"Like you said, you chose the North Pole because you can tweak your existing ideas."

I tap the food and drinks area. "I was thinking 'barnyard chic' for the tables. Like wooden crates or something. Perhaps they can look more like toy crates?"

"I don't know what 'barnyard chic' means, but toy crates seem very North Pole."

I turn to him with a smile. "Thanks for being my sounding board. I might've balled this up and thrown it out otherwise."

Beau smiles back. "My pleasure."

As I scribble some changes to my sketch, Beau clears his throat, causing my hand to slow.

I look his way as he asks, "Do you want a ride home today?"

I shake my head. "No, I'm fine."

"It's freezing out. Let me drive you."

"No, really, it's fine."

"What if the wind's too strong? Or there's a heavy downfall of snow?"

I snort a laugh and return to my sketch. "It's not my first time walking home in the snow. Thanks for your concern, but I can take care of myself."

Beau mumbles, "Okay," as he watches me continue with my tweaks.

He sits back with his arms folded, and our chat about the floor plan design grows quieter as the meeting comes to a close.

When five o'clock hits, I wait for the others to grab their bags and then stuff my binder inside mine.

"*Geez*," Beau winces, eyeing the contents of my bag. "It can't be necessary to carry all that junk around with you."

"This junk is my schoolwork," I say, forcing the zipper shut.

"It's way too heavy. Seriously, let me drive you."

I hoist the bag over my shoulder. "Don't start again."

"You're that determined to walk?"

I move through the doorway, eyeing him over my shoulder. "I really am. See you tomorrow, if you don't ditch again."

Beau's lips slide into the gorgeous grin as he leans against the doorway. "Oh, don't you worry. I'll be here."

Seven

In psychology class the next day, my binder sits beside my textbook, open to my new design for the gym. I wish I could pump all my energy into ideas for the dance, but my psychology notes keep tugging at me.

When my eyes land on my assignment guidelines, I huff myself into a frown. What am I going to do? I have no one to interview. Ciara said no, and Vanessa doesn't seem like a good fit anymore. Maybe I could ask Lucy? I flick my eyes across the row of desks to Hilary. She might have already asked Lucy.

I'd jump off a cliff before asking Whitney.

I tap my fingers along the desk and I skim over the interview questions. I need someone who isn't in this class. They also don't have to be a student.

Last night, Dad discussed his work day over dinner. He complained about how some workers he supervises don't pull their weight or work as a team. It could be an interesting angle to explore. I doubt he'd say yes. He'd think I want to discuss Mom. I mean, I'd love to, but I know it's hard for him. Sometimes we reminisce about the fun times, but we never delve deeper into our grief.

"Everything okay, Ava?" Ms. Hart asks, stopping by my desk.

I jolt out of my thoughts, sitting upright. "Mhmm. Yes, I'm fine."

Ms. Hart smiles and motions to the assignment sheet. "Have you found your interview subject?"

I press my lips together, figuring out if I should save face and lie. "Umm." I blow out a breath and slump my shoulders. "No, not yet."

Ms. Hart gives me a sympathetic look and pats my shoulder. "Don't be afraid to ask. I know it's difficult to ask friends. Perhaps a neighbor or a relative could help?"

I smile and nod like the thought never occurred to me. "Thanks, Ms. Hart." If only I were still close to my neighbors.

She smiles. "Sometimes it takes some out-of-the-box thinking."

When Ms. Hart moves onto other students, I can't help letting my eyes roll.

When the bell rings, I shuffle behind the crowd toward my last class of the day. Ciara approaches from the opposite end, and we meet at the doorway.

"Hi," she says in a faint whisper, clutching her books against her body. "I've barely seen you all day."

I flick my loose braid over my shoulder. "I was hanging out in an alcove."

"Oh," she replies.

I know avoiding her is super petty, but she hasn't had my back the past few days. I'm not ready to forgive and forget.

Unless...

"Remember how I asked you about that interview?" I blurt out.

Her face tenses in confusion. "Yeah?"

"Have you changed your mind?"

Ciara grimaces like I'm offering her something disgusting to eat. "*Eww.* No. I told you I don't like that psychology stuff."

I swallow a sour lump in my throat. This time I won't be last into class. Without another word, I breeze past her and storm towards my desk.

"Ava?" Ciara whines, hurrying into the classroom. She stops by my desk, lowering herself to whisper, "I'm sorry, but I don't want to."

I place my books on my desk, not giving her the privilege of eye contact. "It's fine."

"Okay," she squeaks, slinking off to her desk.

"Ciara?" Whitney's voice pipes up. "Honey, what's wrong?"

My eyes roll even bigger than they did before. Whitney's false concern sickens me to my core. She doesn't give a crap about Ciara. She only cares about isolating me from my last remaining friend.

Not that Ciara needs any help in that department.

I slink down in my chair for the entire lesson. I want to just zone out. No such luck. Whitney's blathering voice is as obnoxious as ever.

When class is over, and I join the committee, I make a shocking decision. Wanting to avoid Ciara and Whitney, I need an out.

I leave the library with Beau.

Since when is he the better option? But unlike everyone else, he hasn't fought me on my ideas for the dance.

We leave the rest of the group paired off in the library. Ciara and Lucy scour websites for prospective bands, and before Hilary leaves for the PTA meeting, she watches over Whitney's shoulder who messes around on Photoshop.

"I was thinking about you yesterday when I was walking to my car," Beau says. "Those icy winds were blowing so hard they almost knocked me over."

"That's why my shoes have a good grip. I dig into the cement as I walk."

"But you shouldn't have to walk in this weather."

He doesn't fight me on the dance. He needs to do the same about my walking.

"If it's ever horribly bad, I call a taxi. My house is too close for a school bus, and if I want a public bus, I need to walk the opposite way towards Main Street, and it's just not worth it."

Beau and I move to the storeroom to check out what's inside. Mr. Riley organized our keys and asked me three times if we needed supervision. Having him stare at us will only make things more awkward. Our budget allows five hundred dollars for new decorations, and I want to spend the majority on a forest of Christmas trees.

I want to know what we can reuse from last year's decorations. Hopefully, this saves us a good portion of money. I want to ensure we have a good amount of tree ornaments in the same color scheme, shape, and size to feel cohesive and luxurious.

"Is this what you're looking for?" Beau asks, pulling a box off a shelf.

He opens the top and tips it so I can see inside. Glittery red and green baubles stare back at me. I grin and tell him yes. We stack boxes of tree ornaments together for easy access. We're getting an abundance of trees. We will need all hands on deck. I already posted a sign-up sheet for sophomores and juniors to help with decorations. Ciara and I helped the seniors last year, and it was a blast. We will also have faculty members and parents help get the bulk of the work done.

Beau moves to the back of the storeroom, searching for other ornaments we may have missed. He drags a box from the corner. "This is full of twinkle lights. Do you want me to untangle them?"

I wince. "Are they a big mess?"

Beau grins. "Oh, yeah."

"Uh, no, you don't have to untangle them."

He pulls out a bundle of lights. "I don't mind. It has to be done at some point."

"I guess," I reply. "Thank you."

He gives me that ridiculously adorable lopsided grin. "No problem."

I turn away, subtlety fanning the heat from my face. That dang smile. It gets me every time.

To distract myself from my unwanted feelings, I investigate the decoration boxes. It'll take a while to sort through everything. There seems to be a good assortment of sizes and shapes in coordinating colors. I pick up a glittery bauble and smile at the delicate details.

I turn to Beau to tell him things are looking up, but my brain function goes haywire.

Beau pulls a long strand of twinkle lights and coils it around his hand and bicep. Not only does he appear strong, but the fact he's helping make my job easier has my heart fluttering.

When he finishes with the strand of lights, he catches me staring. "What?"

"Oh, no, nothing." As I spin away, a bauble pops out of my grip. It clunks to the ground.

"Hey watch out," Beau warns.

The bauble slides under my foot. Before I can save myself, my foot twists, and I wobble, losing my balance. I shriek as my body flings backwards.

Beau skids toward me. "Whoa."

I fall into his arms as he kneels below me.

"*Phew,*" he whispers. "I got you."

I grit my teeth as a twinge pulsates around my ankle. I shake my head and clench my jaw. "No, something's wrong."

Beau lowers me to the ground with his hand on my back. "What is it?" His eyes meet mine with concern, and then he looks down at my body.

I purse my lips tight as I blink my eyes dry. "I twisted my ankle as I fell."

"Oh crap." He slides toward my feet. "Can you move it?"

Gritting my teeth, I fan my foot from right to left. "*Ouch.* Yes, but it hurts."

"You need to put ice on it," Beau says, examining my ankle. "Is the nurse still here?"

I frown. "No idea."

"Well, we can't wait for it to get worse." He snaps his fingers. "I got it. The cafeteria has freezers. There will be something we can use."

"No one will be there."

Beau smirks. "*Pfft.* That won't stop me."

Beau crouches beside me, holding his arms out.

"I don't know if I can get up," I say, embarrassed.

"Just put your weight on me. You'll be okay."

My hands tremble as I reach for his shoulders. Being this close to him sends my shivers deep into my core. I loop my arms around his neck and his hands plant on my waist.

"Ready?" he whispers. "On three. One, two, three."

I squeak as he lifts me off the ground. As we stand together, I don't loosen my hands. Instead, I lean against him, squeezing my eyes closed and wishing the pain away.

"Are you okay?" he asks. "Will you be able to walk?"

I exhale and turn my body away. I limp my foot out to the side and nod. "Yeah, maybe."

"You shouldn't put weight on it," Beau says, curving his arm around my back for support. "The cafeteria isn't far. I'll carry you."

A blush blazes across my cheeks. "What? You can't carry me."

"Keep a hold of my shoulders." He crouches in front of me. "If you get on my back, I'll carry you across."

My heart pounds as I look down at his tousled blonde hair and strong, broad shoulders.

My teeth chatter. "Are you sure?"

"Sure. Hop on."

I lower myself toward his back and his arms scoop up my thighs. In one effortless movement, Beau hoists me into the air behind him.

"You good?" he asks.

My hands clasp against his chest, and I force my breathing to slow down. "Yes, I'm okay."

Beau leaves the storeroom and I bounce against his back in the hallway. With all my might, I try not to whimper, squeak, or yelp. By the way Beau's head jerks, I can tell he's listening for any signs of pain.

When we enter the cafeteria, I expect Beau to lower me to the ground, but he continues to carry me until we reach the counter. He turns our backs to the space by the register and I lower until my butt hits the countertop.

"See?" Beau says, turning to me with a happy smile. "Told ya I could get you here."

I smile back. "Thanks, Beau."

His smile drops, and he stares at my face.

"What?" I say, unnerved.

His thumb brushes against my cheek, moving a wet sensation against my skin.

"You're in a lot of pain," he says rhetorically.

I move my head back and pat my eyes dry. "Oh, I didn't realize I had done that."

Beau leapfrogs over the counter and moves toward the kitchen.

"What are you doing?" I ask in a panic. "You can't just go back there."

"Chill out," he replies. "I'm just looking for ice."

When Beau disappears, I pat my eyes dry once again. I fan my face to dissipate the heat under my skin. An earthy sandalwood scent wafts off my blazer. As it hits my nose, I blush again. It's Beau's cologne and the residual scent turns my insides gooey.

"Wow, they really don't trust us," Beau says, walking back into the serving area.

"What do you mean?"

He jumps onto the counter and leaps over to stand in front of me. "All the fridges and freezers have padlocks on them."

"Ugh. You're kidding."

Beau looks over his shoulder, panning around the room for another solution. "Ah, here we go. The vending machines will still work."

He moves toward the soda machine and inserts some cash. *Clink, clunk, thump.* He reaches into the collection tray and pulls out a soda can. He walks back and places the soda can against my right ankle.

"Feel better?" he asks with hope.

The icy can stings against my ankle, but dulls the pulsing sensation. I nod. "Yes."

He nods back. "Good. I think you should get checked out. I'll find the nurse."

"I'm okay. I don't need the nurse."

He frowns and his eyes droop. "Will you let me find her, anyway?"

His guilty sadness is like a dagger to my heart. I rub the heel of my palm over my chest and nod. "Okay."

"Keep the can against your foot," he says, backing away. "I'll be as quick as I can."

There's still a thump under my skin, but it minimizes to an annoying niggle. I keep the can close so it can work more magic.

"Well, well, well," an abrasive voice enters the cafeteria. "What a fine leadership example this is."

Whitney strolls into the cafeteria. She winds between tables with Hilary following.

"We were walking this way to gain your valuable guidance," Whitney says in a sarcastic tone, "and here you are, kicking back with a soda." Whitney clicks her tongue, nudging Hilary. "Can you believe this?"

With her arms folded, Hilary scrutinizes my seated position and the soda can. She looks at my right foot and then my left.

"Umm, Whit..." Hilary begins unsteadily. " I don't think..."

Ignoring Hilary's concerns, Whitney doubles down. "Why did you even accept the chairperson position?" she spits. "You don't even care what happens. You just want everyone else to do it for you."

The biting pain between my tender ankle and the crisp temperature of the can have all my attention. Whitney is white noise at this point. Like blocking out a yappy dog in a neighbor's yard.

"Ava, are you okay?" calls Mrs. Whiteborne, the school nurse, who briskly enters the room.

As she makes her way toward me, Whitney steps out of the way. Her mouth hangs ajar as she inspects the situation. Her confidence shatters once Beau enters the room.

Mrs. Whiteborne removes the soda can from my ankle and places an ice pack on the counter. She rests my foot in her hands. "Can you move it, dear?"

"Yes, I can. It's just a little sore."

"That's good," she says, watching my movements. "It's most likely a sprain. You might have some bruising, but I'm sure it'll heal quickly. It was smart thinking to put something cold on it. You should get home and keep your weight off it."

Hilary steps forward, craning her neck to view my foot. "You hurt yourself?"

"I tripped on something and rolled my ankle," I explain, and notice Whitney shrinking into herself.

"We can help in the storeroom," Hilary offers, "if you're going home now."

"I think you should take off," Mrs. Whiteborne cuts in. "It's not worth making the injury worse."

I nod, biting into my lip. "Okay. Hilary, if you could just make sure the storeroom looks neat and lock up. The key is in the lock and needs to be returned to Mr. Riley."

"Will do." She pats Whitney's shoulder, saying, "Come on, let's go."

Without uttering a word, Whitney hurriedly follows Hilary out.

Beau watches the girls leave and lets out a grunt. He rolls his shoulders and moves toward the counter. His expression softens when meeting my gaze.

"Will you let me drive you home today?" he asks with that adorable, lopsided grin.

A happy warmth spreads within me, and I grin. "Sure."

Beau leans forward, and I wrap an arm around his neck. With his help, and Mrs. Whiteborne on the other side, I glide off the counter and my feet gently land on the tiles.

They help me move through the cafeteria, and Beau blurts, "Oh, your bag is still in the storeroom. I'll go get it."

"We will keep moving toward the foyer," Mrs. Whiteborne says.

Beau jogs towards the storeroom, and my heartbeat dances in a happy rhythm.

"So, what did you do?" Mrs. Whiteborne asks, a presumptuous curve to her smile.

I look down at my foot as another wave of embarrassment washes over me. "It was silly. I dropped something, and it rolled under my foot."

She shakes her head. "No, not that. What did you do to Beau?"

"Excuse me?"

"He frantically ran into my office," Mrs. Whiteborne says with a whisper of a laugh. "I've never seen the boy show so much concern."

"I think he just felt guilty."

Mrs. Whiteborne pauses before taking her next step. "Ava. Beau has sent many kids to my nurses' station. Guilt is not a common trait of his."

I swallow uncomfortably.

"I'm bringing it up because I saw him in a new light," she says. "What did you say to calm his aggression? I would never have known he could display empathy."

"I... I don't..." I don't know how to finish this sentence.

"I heard you're chairing your committee," she continues. "It's a mark of a good leader when you have a positive influence on others."

With nothing else to say, I reply, "Thanks."

"Hey," Beau calls, jogging to catch up. "Got your bag."

We wait for him to meet us.

With a pant, Beau skids to a stop, hitching my backpack over his shoulder.

"Where's your bag?" I question.

"*Pfft.* I never carry a bag." He checks out my right foot. "Do you feel okay walking?"

"I'm slow, but I'm okay," I reply, pushing myself away from Mrs. Whiteborne. I know she was only trying to be nice, but she's made me super uncomfortable.

Beau runs a hand through his hair and a small pinkish patch glows on his cheeks. "I could give you another piggyback."

I push a lock of hair off my face. "I'll just limp."

Beau holds out his elbow. I hate that Mrs. Whiteborne's eyes don't waver. Seriously, lady, stop gawking at us like we're on a teen reality show.

As I hold on to Beau's solid bicep, Mrs. Whiteborne says, "Watch out as you step outside. It's getting slippery out there. Do you need help getting to the car?"

"I'm already feeling better," I say, not looking back. "Thank you for your help."

Beau steals a look my way. His eyes narrow, as if wondering whether my foot has stopped hurting. I rock my jaw, hoping he doesn't ask within earshot of the nosey nurse.

When we get to his car, I stay silent as I get in and buckle up. It's beyond weird to be in his flashy car. As he pulls out of the student parking lot, the silence brings awkwardness with it. So I decide to break it.

"Thanks for taking me home. I feel a little guilty for leaving early."

"Don't worry about it. Those girls deserve to hang back and clean up the storeroom."

"What does that mean?"

"I walked in on them talking about you."

I wince. "They were talking about me?"

"Whitney was mouthing off as per usual. She shut her yap when she saw me."

I cross my arms. "She won't let up."

"This is why I can't promise to be nice to her."

"Oh my gosh, what did you do to her?"

He gives me a defensive look. "Nothing. I stared her down so she said nothing else, and then left. I needed to get back to you more than putting her in her place."

"You promise?"

He smiles as he pulls up by my house. "I promise."

I hold on to Beau's arm as I limp along the garden path. When we get to the porch, he tells me to take it slowly as I hobble up the steps.

At the front door, I puff out a strained breath. "Thank you. My key is in the front pocket of my bag."

Beau pulls my backpack off his shoulder and unzips the front pocket. As he holds the bag against him, I dig my hand inside the pocket and retrieve the key.

I give him a thankful smile and thrust the key toward the front door lock. Before the key hits metal, the latch unlocks from the inside. Time slows down, my heartbeat is a dragged thud, and my foggy breath seeps out of me.

The front door opens, and my dad stands before us. His face pivots between us, morphing from mild surprise to menacingly stern.

"What is this?" Dad asks, curling his fists. "Ava? What are you doing with this boy?"

"Dad, he was just helping me," I say, trying to explain before Dad turns manic.

"Get inside." Dad grabs me by the arm and yanks me inside.

I stumble over my feet and yelp in pain.

"Wait, don't do that," Beau shouts. "Her foot..."

"Ava," Dad grunts, tossing me about by my arm. "Why are you with this boy? You said you were at school for your committee meeting."

"I was," I squeak. "I got hurt."

Dad loosens his grip on me. "Hurt?"

Beau dumps my bag by the door and waves the ice pack in front of Dad. "She needs this," Beau tells Dad. "She's hurt."

Dad snatches the ice pack and shoves Beau through the doorway.

"Hey! What gives?" Beau shouts, stumbling onto the porch.

My dad doesn't give a response, except to slam the door shut.

Dad turns around and stomps toward me. "Why are you lying to me?"

"What?" my voice trembles. "I'm not."

"If you were with that boy, you weren't at your committee meeting," Dad argues. "Now tell me where you were."

Tears pool in my eyes as he looms over me. "I'm not lying. He's part of the committee."

"What has happened to you?" Dad says, looking at me with a sickened expression. "Since when do you act this way with me?"

"Dad," I whimper, cowering on bended knees. "I can't stand much longer. My ankle hurts."

The wrinkle lines in Dad's forehead soften and he scoops an arm around me. He guides me to an armchair, and when I sit, he places the icepack on my foot.

"You're home earlier than usual," Dad says softly, examining the foot.

"Because of this," I reply. "The nurse said I should go home."

"With Beau Stevenson?"

"He had a car."

Dad lifts his head with deadly seriousness. "You got in his car?"

My stomach flips and, despite the pain it causes, my knees knock together. I swallow hard. "I couldn't walk home."

Dad stands and watches over me. "Did he do this to you? Did he scare you into lying?"

"He's part of the committee," I whimper. "Mr. Franklin said..."

"Are you telling me," Dad says with a rising volume, "that you've been spending afternoons with Beau Stevenson and not telling me about it?"

I shake my head, tears dripping from my eyes. "It's not like that. We're in a group."

"I know everyone else in the group," Dad says, growing to shouting level. "Or do I? Who else haven't you told me about?"

"We just talk about the event," I argue. "It's not like it's a wild party."

"That's not for you to decide!" Dad yells. "I'm the parent, and I'll decide what you can and can't do!"

Tears pool in my eyes. "Yes, Dad."

Dad blows out a breath and steps into the hall. "I'll get you a glass of water and some painkillers."

I hug my middle. The pain in my ankle is nothing compared to the ache in my heart. A sound pricks my ears, and it registers as the front door opening. As I listen for other noises, Beau creeps into the room.

My eyes grow wide with shock. "What are you doing? You can't be here. He'll go crazy."

Beau rushes towards me and cups my face in his hands. "I could hear him yelling from outside. I can't leave you here with him."

"You have to go," I say, pulling his hands off my face. "It'll be way worse if he catches you."

"I can take it," Beau replies. "I'm not leaving you."

"Go, please," I plead. "He's not far away. He'll hear you."

Beau's eyes round with concern as he whispers, "Does he always treat you like this?"

Dad's footsteps enter the hallway, and panic causes me to shove Beau away. He darts out of the room, but I don't hear the front door. My heart leaps into my throat and pounds like a beaten drum.

"Here." Dad holds a glass of water and two painkillers. "These should help."

"Thanks." I take the pills and wash them down.

"Do you want to stay seated here, or try resting on your bed?" Dad asks, voice lowered to a more compassionate level.

Even though I've sipped some water, my mouth is still dry. Beau's presence is my first concern when making this decision. Perhaps if Dad helps me to my bedroom, it'll then give Beau the time to sneak out of the house.

"I think I want to lie down," I say.

Dad takes the glass of water and sets it on a side table. He then helps me out of the chair and into the hall. I limp beside him, ensuring to glide my fingers over the image of my mother as we move to my bedroom.

Dad helps me lower to the bed and tells me to get some rest. With an appreciative smile, I thank him and recline against the pillows.

Dad leaves the room, closing the door behind him. I stare up at the ceiling and sigh.

"Ava," a voice whispers.

Eight

"Ava." As soon as I hear my name, a hand presses on mine.

I scream my lung capacity and rush my feet towards my body. Beau crawls out from below my bed.

"Ava?" Dad calls, causing Beau to shoot back under the bed. The pink dust ruffle hides him from sight.

I slam a hand over my racing heart and push my legs back down as the bedroom door opens.

"What is it?" Dad asks, leaning into the room. "What's the matter?"

"Nothing," I say, panting. "I tried to move, and it hurt. My bag is by the front door and I thought I should study."

Dad gives me a proud smile. "Don't worry about studying, sweetheart. Just take it easy until dinner is ready."

"Really?"

He nods. "Yes, really. How about I leave this door open and you call out if you need anything?"

"Okay." Wait, there's a boy hiding under my bed. "No, don't."

"Huh?" Dad questions, turning towards the hall.

"Can you shut it?" I ask. "I'm going to get changed and it might take a while."

"Okay, but don't exert yourself. You need to take it easy."

When the door closes, I fall back on the bed with a massive sigh.

"He flips from maniac to doting dad like it's nothing," Beau mutters, sliding out from under the bed. "Living with someone like that would give me a permanent headache."

"*Beau*," I hiss. "What are you doing?"

"I told you," he says, sitting by the bed. "I'm not leaving you alone with him."

"This is my life," I say. "He was only yelling because he saw you."

"Really?" Beau asks, looking deep into my soul. "That was scary, Ava. Does he normally yell like that?"

"No," I say, shifting against my pillows. "He doesn't yell like that because I don't do things that will make him mad."

"Meaning you spend your life walking on eggshells?"

"I'm not like you," I counter. "I don't like to stir up trouble."

"That doesn't mean you let people walk over you or control you."

"We're talking about my dad. I won't defy my dad."

"Until the meetings, you didn't stand up for yourself at school either."

"I was just fed up."

"You took charge. It was cool." Beau grins, resting his elbows on the bed. As his head rests against his hands, something catches his narrowing eyes. "Hey, is that..?"

Beau stands and moves around the bed toward my desk.

I tilt my head, searching for what he sees. "What?"

Under the desk, he digs in the trash can and retrieves my old bug catcher. He holds it like a trophy. "What's this doing in the trash?"

"Oh, I found that the other day."

"Doesn't answer my question."

I lift my hands questioningly. "Why would I keep it?"

"I dunno," he says, placing the bug catcher on the desk. "For the memories."

"I don't need those memories."

"*Ouch*," Beau hisses.

"You should go," I blurt, wanting a subject change. "Won't your parents be expecting you home?"

Beau laughs. "I'm out late most nights. Plus, I usually beat my parents home."

"Really? I remember when your mom worked late. She still does that?"

Beau nods. "Yeah. It's mostly her. Dad stays away from home when he can. I think he hates our house as much as I do."

I stare at the ceiling, searching for answers. "Why did they move in the first place?"

"I've been asking that since the 'for sale' sign went up in our yard," Beau replies, sitting by the bed.

"Didn't your mom quit her job?"

"Yeah, when we moved," Beau replies, resting an elbow on my bed and sliding his head against his palm. "She tried the stay-at-home mom thing, but I guess she hated it. About a year later, she went back to work."

"Oh."

"She wasn't your mom," Beau says with a smile. "I remember when your mom would come over in the evening when mine was still at work. She'd make extra dinner for us and bring it over. She'd even stay until I fell asleep. She was a kickass storyteller."

I giggle, looking at the darkening sky through the window. "Yeah, she was. I always liked when she went to your house. It meant I got to stay up later, waiting for her to come home and tuck me in."

Beau rises from the carpet and sits on the edge of my bed. "I know she was your mom, but I miss her too."

I pat his knee. "I know."

He leans closer, whispering, "What's going on with your dad? I don't remember him being angry like that."

"He just wants to protect me. I'm all he's got left."

"That didn't sound protective. It sounded aggressive."

"That's how everyone describes you," I say bluntly. "Why did you change so much?"

He smooths his hair back and sadness falls over his face. "Because life changed around me."

Stabbing pains attack my heart as he succumbs to melancholy. I forget my sprained foot and scoot forward to wrap my arms around him.

I rest my head against his shoulder and he rubs my back, asking, "Your dad changed after your mom died?"

Tears spring from my eyes as I nod my head.

"I'm sorry that you have to hide your feelings," he whispers. "It tears me up that you're not happy here."

The surge of buried emotion rushes out of its internal barricades. I hold on to him for dear life as an avalanche of sobs hurtle out of me. My body rocks against him, but he holds me with unwavering strength. For years, I've been an academic robot. I did what my dad said because my mom was gone. Even if it meant never having my best friend in my life.

"Ava?" my dad's voice sounds as my bedroom door swings open. "What in the... Take your hands off my daughter! Get the hell out of my house!"

Before I can lift my head from Beau's shoulder, my dad is prying open Beau's embrace. I fling back on the bed as Dad pulls Beau away from me.

With a snotty nose and garbled voice, I yell, "No, Dad! Stop!"

"How dare you defy me, Ava!" Dad yells. "I heard you crying, and never would have believed you were with a boy. And this boy, of all people!"

"Stop!" Beau yells, catapulting himself between me and Dad. "You can hit me all you want. Just don't hurt her!"

Dad takes a step back, startled. He blinks hard and pivots his gaze between me and Beau. And then something happens that freezes my insides. Dad's eyes fill with rage, and he grabs Beau by the collar.

"Out!" Dad yells, pulling Beau off the bed.

"*Dad*," I wail. "Let him go."

Dad drags Beau out of the room. Beau doesn't fight back, only uses his strength to turn back and look me in the eye. His concern is palpable, and then he's thrown into the hall.

My hands claw at bed covers. I'm too afraid to move. My ears prick to every stomp as Beau is forced out of the house. The dread sloshes in my stomach, knowing my dad will rampage his way back into this room.

I blink my watery eyes clear as I stare at my bedroom door. Should I shut it? What good would that do? Should I shut it and barricade it with a piece of furniture? And then what? Never leave my bedroom? Never talk to my dad again?

I pull my arms tight around my knees. Dad's heavy footsteps boom up the hall. The dread wants to unload from my stomach. I force it back down as Dad appears in my doorway.

"There's a strict no boy tolerance in this house, let alone your bedroom," Dad says firmly. "I've told you about boys like him. They take what they want, no matter who they hurt. Don't you understand the trouble he will bring?"

I shiver hard as I utter, "I... I... He was..."

He crosses his arms, and the fury in his eyes has diminished. "What did I walk in on?"

I squeeze my arms tighter and press my chin against my knees. "I was crying."

Dad doesn't budge. "Why?"

A tear drops from my eye and hits my chin. "I miss my old life."

"Don't tell me you want Beau back in your life."

"It's not just him," I whimper. "It's Mommy."

Dad's arms collapse against his sides, and a wounded sigh pours out of him. "Oh Ava," he whispers, moving to the bed. "I'm sorry. You're always allowed to miss your mother."

As Dad sits on the side of the bed, I release my knees and wrap my arms around him.

He strokes my back while he hums.

I pull out of the hug and pat my eyes dry.

"Bringing Beau back into your life won't bring your mother back," Dad says gravely.

I drop my hands from my face and stare at him with offense.

Dad slams a fist on the bed and his face strains with aggression. "Why was that boy in this house? Why on earth were you with him?"

"I told you," I reply with a garbled, snotty voice.

"The school put that boy in your committee?" Dad asks with bitter disdain. "You work hard not to associate with kids like him. Is this true? Because if so, I'm calling your principal."

"*Don't*," I yelp. "He's helping me."

"Why would you need his help?"

I shift on the bed, looking away with a shrug. "Everyone listens to me when he's around."

"Are they listening?" Dad questions. "Or scared quiet?"

"You asked me if there are others in the group who I haven't told you about. Whitney James is on the committee, and Beau stopped her from tormenting me. You can't get him removed from the group."

"You know how I feel about that girl. This is why you want him around so badly?" Dad crosses his arms. "No. I think it's best if you leave the committee."

"No, Dad!"

"There needs to be repercussions for all this deception."

"That's not fair!"

"I don't want you around these bad influences."

"We can't get rid of them," I argue. "Ciara and I had already talked to Vanessa Ashworth about kicking Beau out. We suggested he go to regular detention, but Vanessa said the school wants to try something new with him. It's a decision that comes from the Ashworth family."

Dad's jaw rocks, and he folds his arms. "Beau's parents made some kind of deal. I bet his father still forks over cash to keep that no-good-boy in school."

I press a hand into my twisted gut and whisper, "Dad?"

He looks up at my eyes. "Yes?"

"When I was younger, you were okay with me being friends with Beau." I stay on edge, waiting for him to snap. "What if I never pushed him away? What if we always stayed friends?"

Dad strokes the side of my face. "But you wouldn't have."

My eyebrows knit together. "How do you know?"

"As soon as he started shoving other kids around, you would have walked away."

I frown and nod. "That's true."

"Did you tell him I've hit you?"

My eyes grow wide and I gasp. "What? No?"

Dad nods with a solemn expression. "Okay."

"Why would you ask..."

"Because he leaped in front of you, like he was saving you. Besides, the day I lost your mother, I've never felt more crushed."

I rub the space on my chest over my shattered heart. "Oh, Dad, I'm sorry. I promise, I didn't say anything. I don't know why he assumed anything. I promise."

Dad pats my shoulder and gives a gentle smile. "You should get some rest. Do you need any more ice for your foot?"

I shake my head. "No, it's fine."

Dad moves away from the bed, saying, "I'll get a start on dinner."

"So, I can stay on the committee?"

His frown twitches like it wants to morph into a smile. "Yes, sweetheart."

"Okay." Despair weighs down on my entire being as his sad footsteps disappear down the hall.

My phone buzzes inside my pocket. When I retrieve it, there's a notification from the school portal app. *New message from Beau Stevenson.*

My hands tremble around the phone. I unlock the screen, but don't look at the message. Instead, I delete the app.

I slide my legs off my bed and gingerly step onto the carpet. I wince as a dull pain shoots up from my foot. I creep towards my desk and take my laptop back to bed. I curl up, logging into the school portal and opening Beau's message.

"Is everything okay? Should I try to get back into the house? Do you need help?"

I almost want to laugh at his panic. The thought of my dad being dangerous is ridiculous, but Beau's concern warms my heart.

"No, I'm fine. Dad and I talked, and now he's making dinner. I think it's best that he doesn't see you again."

"I didn't fight him for your sake, but I didn't want to leave you."

"Thanks for helping me home. I'm sorry for how it all ended."

"This app isn't great. Maybe I should get your number to text you."

"No, I can't use my phone. My dad might find out we're talking."

"What do you mean?"

"He has a parental control app on his phone so he can see what happens on my phone."

"What the hell? That's so creepy!"

"It's not creepy. He had it installed when I first got my phone as a safety thing. He never looks at it because I'm so boring. But with you in the picture, he might look again."

"You need that app taken off. You're letting people control you."

Says the boy, who does the complete opposite. He uses terror to control everyone else.

I push the laptop off my lap and brush my hands over my face. I sigh, exhausted, and fling myself backwards to stare at the ceiling.

What am I doing? Yes, we were once friends, but that doesn't make him magically likable again.

I sit up, pulling off my blazer, and the bug catcher catches my eye. I stare at the oddly shaped plastic device, and a smile tugs at my lips.

I pull the laptop closer and type, *"Do you still have your bug catcher?"*

"I just pulled it out of my closet."

"I only caught cool bugs because you took me on adventures. I was never brave enough to do it solo."

"My bugs only lived because you convinced me not to kill them."

I relax into the ease of typing over talking. "Someone had to stop you from yourself."

"It's a little funny how your dad reacted. It's not like it's the first time I've been in your bedroom."

I tug at my shirt collar, and then move my fingers back to the keyboard. "We're not little kids anymore."

"Ain't that the truth?"

"Things were easier back then."

"Yeah. I certainly had more fun. High school kinda sucks, doesn't it?"

I frown and draw a finger over his message. I sigh and reply, "Yeah. It does."

Nine

Before I leave the house this morning, I backtrack through to turn off the twinkle lights strung around the Christmas tree and mantle in the living room. Quietly viewing this display is still my favorite part of the day. Although, if another day ends with messages from Beau, I may have a new favorite part.

Wow!

I can't believe talking to Beau makes me excited. Sure, there's our history. I didn't think we'd get back to a friendly place after so long. And, in the meantime, there's a list of horrible things he's done. Shoving kids' heads in toilets, vandalizing lockers, sending threats through the school portal app, are just to name a few. This is crazy. Dad caught Beau in my bedroom and will never approve of him being in my life.

I pull on my backpack with an almighty grunt. I check out my hunched posture in the mirror. *Geez*, what am I doing?

Without a second thought, I dump my bag onto the carpet and remove half the books. Even though my life revolves around studying, I don't need to carry everything. I have one notebook that's filled with the most important notes from every class. Plus, I've memorized so much. I could turn up at school with no bag at all.

The thought of Dad seeing me return home without my backpack gives me chills. I throw it on my back and head for the front door.

My teeth chatter the instant I leave the house. The wind howls, and powdery snow falls over the street. My shoes crunch against the fallen snow, and I dig my gloved hands into the pockets of my coat. I keep my head down, watching the cement path out of the cul-de-sac until the roar of a car engine steals my attention.

I look up and find an idling GT Mustang just outside the cul-de-sac. My heart skips a beat as Beau steps out of the car.

"Need a ride?" he asks with that gorgeous grin.

I nod enthusiastically. "I don't want to walk in this weather."

"I thought your foot would be the issue."

I shake my head. "It's a little sore, but I don't have to limp."

"*Phew.* That's good news." He opens the passenger-side door. "Your chariot awaits."

I slide my backpack off and move towards him. He takes my bag as he holds the car door open. Surprise takes over his face. "Whoa. It's not as heavy."

I giggle, sliding into the car. "I got fed up."

"Fair enough." He drops the bag into the trunk and moves to the driver's side. "Was everything okay last night?"

"Things were a little awkward between me and my dad," I reply. "Boys aren't allowed, period, and then he finds you in my bedroom with your arms around me."

"I get it. It blindsided him."

"To say the least."

"He made it happen that way," Beau counters. "If he hadn't completely freaked out when we got to your house, I wouldn't have had to hide."

"You shouldn't have snuck back in."

He sends me a wink. "But you're glad I did."

"I liked chatting with you last night," I say softly as a blush heats my cheeks. "It was the first time in ages I didn't pour myself into homework."

"I'm glad you liked talking to me," Beau replies. "Every time I sent a message, I was sure you wouldn't reply."

"Really? Why?"

"Because you've been pretty clear I don't fit in with you anymore. I thought at some point you'd flip out and cut off contact."

"The moment to flip out was when my dad caught you in my room."

Beau sucks in a ragged breath. "Yeah, that was brutal. Despite what he'd do, I didn't want to let you go."

"Really?"

"You were upset. I wanted to make it better. I thought you'd feel worse if I left."

I nervously run a hand over my braid. "I didn't want you to go."

Beau smiles, turning on the ignition.

"I think I missed you," I admit.

Beau puffs a laugh. "What, last night?"

I shake my head. "No. For always."

"Oh," he murmurs. "I've always missed you."

I smile. "Really?"

"Yeah, but we weren't friends anymore," he replies with a shrug. "You were too good for me, and I was dealing with my own problems."

My smile fades, and I shift closer to the door. "I wasn't too good for you."

"You got deep into studying. You didn't have time for me."

"That's not true. You could have studied with me."

"Would you have had fun with me?"

"You know why I put distance between us."

"Yeah, yeah, I know."

I huff, banging my shoulders against the seat. "Why are we arguing?"

Beau sighs. "I don't know. Maybe things aren't meant to be easy between us."

I groan and open the car door. "Then what am I doing here?"

I leap out of the car, landing hard on my foot. Pain shudders up my leg, and I limp toward the trunk.

"Ava," Beau calls, opening his car door. "What are you doing?"

"Open the trunk," I order.

He moves to the back of the car, gesturing to the front. "Get back in the car."

"No. Open the trunk."

"Ava."

I slam a fist on the trunk. "Open it."

"Whoa." Beau lifts his hands in defense. "The car did nothing wrong."

I turn from the car and step onto the sidewalk. "Fine, keep the bag. I don't need it, anyway."

"Ava, stop being so dramatic," Beau says, leaning against the car. "You can't limp your way to school. Let me drive you."

"You don't want to drive me," I argue in a childish tone. "You want things to be difficult between us."

"Ava, it was a silly fight," he says, stepping onto the path. "We have barely spoken in four years. Arguments are bound to happen until we know each other better."

The reasonableness of his words forces me to stop. "Do you want to know me better?"

He laughs, and I'm mesmerized by that lopsided grin. "You're so silly. Of course I do."

As I stand on the snow-littered sidewalk, the only problem is indeed how silly I feel. I made a scene and fled his car. My fingers flex at my sides as I ground into this spot. I can't just walk back over there like nothing happened.

Beau ambles toward me and holds out a hand. "Come on," he says gently.

In a state of confusion, I fidget in place.

"I'm not letting you walk back to the car," Beau says adamantly. "You're already limping, and I don't want you slipping on something icy on my watch."

I cup a hand over my mouth and giggle. "You want to watch over me?"

"Here's a secret," he whispers through cupped hands. "I'm always watching over you."

Before I can respond, I let out a squeal. In one swift movement, Beau lifts me into the air.

I bite into my lip as he cradles me against him. His strong, powerful arms have me back in the car in no time. Embarrassment tugs at me from within. I hope nobody saw that. But I can't help swooning. What an absolute Prince Charming moment.

"Ready to go now?" He leans against the car door with a teasing grin.

I look up, blinking at his kind face. A few days ago, I would've balked at Beau's capability for chivalrous acts. But within twenty-four hours, events happened that made this moment feel... normal.

I smile. "Yep. Let's go."

Beau drives us into the school parking lot, and anxiety writhes inside me as I glimpse the surrounding cars. I clasp my hands together, growing rigid in the seat.

"What's up?" Beau asks, turning off the engine and unbuckling his seatbelt.

"Hmm, nothing," I squeak, eyeing a group of boys walking past the car.

"You don't want to be seen getting out of my car?" he guesses.

I fidget, searching for the right words. "People might wonder why..."

Beau shrugs, opening his door. "Let them wonder."

When he closes the door and moves to the trunk, I force myself to unbuckle my seatbelt.

"Just get out of the car," I whisper. My trembling hand pulls on the door handle.

Beau walks around to my side as I stand on shaky legs. He pulls an arm through the strap of my backpack and hoists it over his shoulder.

"Shall we?" he asks.

I gesture towards the bag. "Yeah, I can carry that."

"It's all right," he says, clutching the strap. "I got it."

Awkwardly, I mumble my thanks. Beau follows as I dawdle between cars toward the school gate.

I reach the front of the parking lot, and a voice calls out, "Ava!"

Hilary moves toward me. "Hi," I say with a wave.

"How's your foot?" she asks, looking down as she meets me on the path.

"Yeah, it's okay, thanks."

"Good." Hilary's eyes lift upward and they widen, staring over my shoulder. "Beau? Wait, you two came together?"

"Uh, I, umm..."

Beau nudges his head my way. "She can't walk to school with a limp. I gave her a ride."

"Oh, that's nice," Hilary says, losing interest. "I wanted you to know the PTA meeting went super well. I have a list of chaperones who are also prepared to cook dishes."

"That's fantastic."

"Hilary," Marcus calls, slinging a backpack over each of his shoulders. "I'm not carrying your bag all morning."

Hilary huffs, retrieving her bag from her boyfriend. "Isn't it great, Ava?" she says. "The boys will be back this afternoon."

Marcus lifts his chin, nodding at Beau. "We'll keep this guy in line."

Beau's frame broadens. "Excuse me?"

I place a hand on Beau's arm. "Beau doesn't need to be kept in line. He's been incredibly helpful."

Marcus spits a laugh. "That'll be the day."

I steady my eyes on Marcus. "It has been *the* day."

"Wow," Beau says in awe behind me.

"As long as you're okay, Ava," Hilary says, tugging Marcus toward the school gate, "that's all that matters."

"Who knew I had a cheerleader?" Beau says I turn to face him.

I'm glad it's a low temperature outside so it hides my blush. "I didn't want him badmouthing you. You've been nothing but helpful at the meetings."

He smiles, looking down, and a long wave of his blonde hair tumbles over his forehead. "Thanks."

"At least Hilary seems on our side," I say with hope.

Beau's expression turns doubtful. "I dunno. She was avoiding her boyfriend getting into a fight with me."

"Oh," I draw out the word. "I didn't think that was her motive."

Beau laughs. "Everyone's got an angle."

I raise my eyebrows and suggest, "Maybe you just think everyone's got a hidden agenda."

Beau continues toward the school gate. The crowd ahead fills me with more nervous activity than usual. I meander behind Beau, and he double-takes at my wariness.

"You okay?" he asks. "Is your ankle too sore to walk?"

I move closer to Beau. "No, I can walk."

Beau pushes into the makeshift line, and a gap moves around him. Why didn't I see this coming? Of course, everyone will give him a wide berth. I've been doing it for years.

We move through the gate without the attack of a wayward elbow or anyone shoving us from behind. When we get to the front steps, Beau bends his elbow and holds it at the perfect height for me to grab. A tight pulsation heats my ankle as I take each step. I grit my teeth on the ascent, and sigh with relief as I enter the foyer.

As if on autopilot, I gravitate toward the wall.

Beau follows. "Is your locker nearby?"

"Ah, no. At the end of the next hallway."

"Oh. I thought because you walked to the side, it was close."

I suck in my bottom lip, feeling like a timid mouse.

He gives me a strange look. "Do you want me to walk with you?"

I brush the loose hair off my face and huff. "I just always wait for the hallway to clear. It's like no one sees me. They stand in my way, or they run into me."

Seriousness crosses his face. "Who does?"

I run a hand over my braid, averting my gaze. "Everyone."

"Well, that's not happening." He moves in front of me and marches toward the people ahead. He bangs a fist against a locker and orders, "Move."

The three students jump out of their skins. In a scramble, they bolt out of the way.

I hurry behind Beau, who continues to clear a path through to the next hallway. I latch onto his wrist and give it a gentle tug. He slows his pace and turns to face me.

"Thank you," I whisper, "but you don't have to scare people for me."

He lifts a palm upwards. "They're moving, aren't they?"

"Only to get away from you," I reply. "They still don't know I exist."

He steps to the side. "You want to go ahead of me?"

As I shake my head, my shoulders hunch forward, and tension camps below my neck.

Beau frowns, folding his arms. "What's that look?"

Sweat beads across my forehead, and my body temperature lowers. "What look?"

"Like you're scared of me again. What gives?"

I lean against a locker, body slumping as my eyes glue to his chest. I just can't look at those eyes.

"I'll just walk away if that's what you want," Beau says, slipping my bag off his shoulder. "But you took it hard when I said things between us aren't easy."

I dig my hands inside my blazer and look at my shoes. "Even if you're scaring other people, it still scares me."

He hoists my bag back onto his shoulder. "Fine. I'll just walk. People will still get out of the way, regardless."

I push off the locker, head still downcast. "Just don't provoke them."

Beau's pace is slower as we walk the last stretch to my locker. He stays beside me like a serious bodyguard.

At my locker, I laugh as I unlatch the lock.

"What?" Beau asks with curiosity.

I look at him, meeting his fantastically blue eyes. "I never get to my locker before the bell rings."

"How can you stand waiting for everyone else to move?" Beau asks, leaning against the adjacent locker. "Is this how you start every morning?"

I bite into my lip and shrug it off. "Pretty much. And it's not just mornings. I wait between all my classes."

Beau's eyebrows raise as disgust twists his lips. "Nuh-uh. No way. You can't seriously let the whole school walk all over you."

A nervous giggle seeps out of me. "I don't. That's why I wait until the coast is clear."

"*Crap*," Beau murmurs. "I didn't realize it was that bad for you."

I take my bag from Beau and slide it into my locker. "I don't think anyone does it on purpose. I'm alone, so the big groups knock into me. It's fine. If I had friends, I'm sure it'd be different."

"You don't have friends?" Beau asks in alarm. "What about everyone on the committee?"

I arrange my locker and pull out a notebook and pen case. "Every time I join a club, everyone is nice and friendly. As soon as it's over, we don't talk anymore."

"So, they pretend not to know you?"

"No. If I wave, they'll wave back. But, I dunno... Maybe I'm not good at keeping friendships."

"We were friends for a long time," Beau says, lips creeping into a soft smile.

"But we lived on the same cul-de-sac and our parents were friends. You were always around, so I couldn't mess it up." I huff and fall into a forlorn frown. "Until I did."

Beau rubs a hand on my back. "Everyone changed that summer. Even my parents were never the same after your mother passed."

I blink back watery tears and look deep into his eyes. "Really?"

He nods, lips pressed tightly as he swallows with apprehension.

I toss my gear back into my locker. "I'm so not in the mood for classes."

"You should blow it off."

"No, I can't skip class."

"Why not?" he counters. "You're always late to class, anyway."

"You noticed that?"

"Yep. And I've noticed you're never in detention, which means you never get into trouble."

"That's the positive of being a good girl."

Beau rubs my shoulder. "Well, good girl, I bet if you don't show up to class, your teacher would mark you as present, assuming you'll turn up later."

I graze my finger over my bottom lip, thinking it over. "It'd be an interesting theory to test."

"I would, if I were you." Beau says, peeling himself off the locker. "But I can't afford to miss any more classes."

"Because you suddenly care about your grades?" I tease.

His expression flattens. "I always care about my grades."

His seriousness gives me pause. Since when? Not buying it.

"Ava," Mr. Riley calls, striding up the hall toward us. "How are you? The girls told me about your foot."

"I'm okay."

He lands before me, eyes downcast. "Are you sure? Do you need to see the nurse again?"

I flick my eyes at Beau and then back to Mr. Riley as his gaze lifts. "Actually, that would be great. I could do with another ice pack."

Mr. Riley nods with concern. "Sure, go ahead."

"Can Beau go with me?"

A dumbfounded look crosses Beau's face.

Mr. Riley's concern increases. "You want Beau to stay with you?"

I lean in with the ultimate sad puppy eyes. "People barge into me, and there's this weird crunch when I walk. I don't want to hurt my foot any worse. People get out of the way when Beau's around."

Mr. Riley glances at Beau and then pouts when he studies my eyes. "You really want him with you?"

I nod, bottom lip quivering.

Mr. Riley sighs. "Okay. Beau, who's your first period teacher? I'll have a word with them."

Ten

"You were amazing," Beau says as we walk towards the nurses' office. "You looked pathetically in need of a hug."

"Is the word 'pathetic' supposed to be a compliment?" I joke.

"Absolutely," Beau replies. "When it comes to lying, you're a pro."

I click my tongue. "I don't enjoy your compliments."

Beau laughs. "Sorry. I'm still surprised you brought me into your lie."

"What can I say?" My insides melt into goo. "I didn't want to miss my chance to get back what we had."

His smile spreads. "Aww, Avie. You wanna get to know me again?"

I tuck a piece of hair behind my ear, feeling my blush prick against my hand.

I put more pressure on my foot, walking normally. "You know, we don't actually need to see the nurse. Remember, it was a lie."

"You knucklehead," Beau teases. "Of course we need to see the nurse. We need an ice pack. On the off chance another teacher sees us, they'll want a reason why we're not in class."

I mumble a laugh. "This is why you're the pro at skipping class."

"I try not to get caught unless I want to be."

I give him a strange look. "Why would you want to be caught?"

Beau steps in front of me, arm stretched to grasp the door handle of the nurse's office. He doesn't answer my question, instead opening the door and gesturing for me to step inside.

We walk into the room and Mrs. Whiteborne double-takes.

"My goodness," she says, moving away from a boy sitting on an examination bench. "You two are together again. Ava, is everything okay with your ankle?"

"Yes," I say, putting more effort into my limp. "I was just wondering if I could get another ice pack? Sorry, I left the last one at home."

"That's okay," Mrs. Whiteborne says, moving towards a freezer. "Just bring it back to me as soon as you can."

"Hi Quinton," Beau says, taking a slow stride toward the boy on the bench. "It's been a while since I've caught up with you."

Quinton shudders, averting his eyes from Beau.

My chest constricts and my hands tremor at my sides. Beau has a long list of regular targets, and this fear-soaked boy seems very familiar with this routine.

Quinton's blazer is off, his shirt is unbuttoned, and he wears a white undershirt. His shirt is peeled back on one side, revealing his shoulder and middle back where two ice packs sit.

"Here you go, Ava," Mrs. Whiteborne says, handing me an ice pack.

"Thanks." I do a terrible job hiding the shake in my fingers.

"Move away, Beau," Mrs. Whiteborne orders. "I know it must be tempting to admire your handiwork, but give Quinton some space."

As Beau steps away, Mrs. Whiteborne removes one of the ice packs. Involuntarily, a gasp leaps from my abdomen, and my hand shoots over my mouth.

A mixture of black, blue, and red bruises clump over Quinton's shoulder and down his back.

I fumble my way backwards. "You did that, Beau?"

He turns his head in my direction, his face pale. "No."

My eyes flick back at Quinton, who stares at Beau. An ugly feeling camps in the pit of my stomach. I leave the room, fighting the urge to be sick. In the hallway, I gasp for a solid breath.

Beau's heavy footsteps enter the space behind me, and I press a hand into my torso.

"That looked bad, huh," he says with mild consideration.

I hold myself upright and turn around. "Bad?" I spit. "How could you do that? Those bruises were so vicious."

"What?" he chokes. "I just told you I didn't do that."

"I saw Quinton's face," I argue, backing away. "There's no question who did that."

The hurt drips off his face. "I thought you wanted to know me better."

I point at the nurse's office. "That interaction reminded me why we haven't been friends in four years."

"Well, believe whatever you want," Beau says, scuffing his shoe against the floor. "But I don't hit smaller kids like that."

A lump balls in my throat, and I wipe my clammy hands against my skirt. "What does that mean?"

Beau shrugs, throwing a thumb towards the office. "I've shoved him, sure, but I've never whacked him so hard to cause those kinds of bruises. Someone else is doing that."

I swallow hard as my stomach flips. "Like, someone at home?"

Beau throws his palms upward. "Beats me. It sucks if he's blaming me for it."

I scrutinize the melancholy in his eyes and my heart throbs. I take gradual steps toward him and meet his eyes in an intense moment of understanding.

"You have to say something," I whisper. "You can't let him blame you for it."

"It doesn't matter," he replies, brushing it off. "Whatever I do will be used against me."

I keep my eyes on him and my mouth stays ajar. I have no words. What he said is true.

He folds his arms, frowning. "I hated seeing you hurt yesterday."

"I'm okay," I insist. "It wasn't a big deal."

"You don't get it." There's a strain in his voice. "I've never thought about other people getting hurt. I get into fights or shove people around purely to get attention. It never dawned on me how they could feel."

"I don't feel like you bullied me yesterday."

He shakes his head. Severity tightens his expression. "I'm not talking about that." He points at the nurse's office. "I'm talking about that. *Crap.* I gotta stop doing that stuff."

"You don't want to hurt anyone anymore?"

He looks at me with glossy eyes. "I never wanted to hurt anyone. It just worked for me."

My mouth falls open. "Oh."

Beau's hand meets mine and slides onto the ice pack. "Isn't that thing freezing your hand?"

"Yeah, kinda."

"Shall we go?" he asks. "I want to be somewhere else."

"There's a quiet alcove by the auditorium," I suggest. "It's usually vacant."

Beau smiles, telling me to lead the way. When we round a corner, my anxiety lowers and I become more relaxed in Beau's presence.

"Beau?" the distinct voice of Vanessa Ashworth calls out.

Further down the hall, Vanessa and two friends walk toward us.

"Hi ladies," Beau says with a wave. "What's up?"

"We ran late, getting breakfast at Village Coffee in town," Vanessa says as she and the girls approach us. "Oh hi, Ava. What are you two doing?"

Beau chucks a thumb in my direction. "She hurt her foot. We just got an ice pack."

"Aww, you're such a gentleman," Vanessa gushes.

Vanessa and her followers pout in sympathy. Having three ultra-pretty girls looking me up and down pushes my panic button. Their hair and makeup are flawless. I have a rushed layer of strawberry lipgloss and a side braid that's already unraveling. Their eyes set to judgment mode.

"I thought I'd be seeing posters up about the Christmas dance?" Vanessa comments, clasping her hands in front.

"Umm, they're, uh..." I falter under her stare. I know what I should say, but the words are jumbling inside my brain.

Beau pivots between Vanessa and me, and then says, "They go to the printers on Thursday, right?"

I clear my throat, muffling something resembling, "Yes."

"Aww," Vanessa says, swaying her body closer to Beau. "Look at you, Stevenson, getting invested in the operational side of the committee. So proud of you."

Beau smirks, running a hand through a wave of his blonde hair. "Everyone just assumes I don't pay attention."

Vanessa giggles. "So, are you saying it's me who has to pay more attention to you?"

"How do you ever resist taking your eyes off me?" Beau asks in a brazenly flirty way.

"Oh my gosh, Vanessa," her friend Hope says with a gigantic eye roll. "Get a room already."

On Vanessa's other side, Sylvie turns up her lip and clicks her tongue. "Uh, no, don't bother."

Beau stifles a laugh, saying to Sylvie, "Nice to see you again too."

Vanessa's grin never fades. She grabs a hold of her friends' wrists and tugs them forward. "Come on, girls, we gotta keep moving." She throws Beau a wink. "Catch you later. Oh, and bye, Ava."

Beau and I continue along the hallway, and I can't help commenting, "Vanessa certainly likes you."

"She has an angle," Beau replies. "My mom works for her dad, and her parents want everything to stay friendly."

"It might be more than that," I mumble, looking down at the floor.

Just like yesterday in the cafeteria, I saw clear signs Vanessa was into Beau.

A laugh sizzles out of Beau. "You're talking about the flirting? I always flirt with those girls. It makes things easier, and it annoys their boyfriends, which is always good sport."

"Good sport?" My skin crawls. "Is everything just a game to you? Is it sport to get me to talk to you again?"

"What? No."

"And then what?" I continue to blather. "Once you get me on your side, you'll turn on me?"

"Turn on you?" Beau repeats defensively. "You're the one using the flimsiest excuses to turn on me."

"You were sitting next to Vanessa when everyone threw food at me."

"And I stopped them all doing that."

"But you were holding onto me."

Beau rubs his forehead, letting out a faint laugh of exhaustion. "Because I wanted you around. Just like now."

I shiver, letting the deluge of emotions take me over. "I know you stopped everyone, but it didn't make it any less humiliating. Plus, Vanessa said nothing. She was too busy having her eyes all over you."

"You know Vanessa didn't throw anything in the cafeteria," Beau says gingerly.

I wave it off. "Of course not. She has lemmings to do everything for her. Like Sylvie and her weird vibe toward you."

Beau smirks. "I took her to prom last year. She wanted to piss off her parents. Apparently, I wasn't a great date."

"Oh."

We move into the alcove by the auditorium. The area is silent because everybody else is in class.

Beau sits beside me on the bench. "That's all I am to these girls, a tool to annoy their parents. If Vanessa is making eyes at me, it's a game to her too."

I bite into my lip, my eyes watering. "I didn't know everyone was playing each other. I thought Vanessa was better than that."

"Do you have a problem with her?"

I huff, hugging my middle. "No, not really. I think she's cool, and I was planning to ask for her help on something." Regret tugs at my heart. "Anyway, I asked her about something else and she blew me off. Then the food thing happened, and I didn't want her help anymore."

"What did you need her help with?"

"I wanted to interview her for my psych class," I reply. "I thought she'd make an interesting subject. But someone else probably already asked her."

"What happened that changed your mind?"

Color drains from my skin. "I don't want to say."

Beau's eyebrows push together as he questions, "Why?"

I blow out a hard breath and blurt, "Because it was about you."

Beau sits back and laughs. "You were trying to get rid of me?"

I frown and nod my answer.

"Well, that's no secret." Beau scratches his head, and the waves of his hair sway. "What would I need to answer if you interviewed me?"

A surprised laugh puffs out of me. "You can't be serious. You don't want to be interviewed."

"Correct, I don't. But you need someone's help for your class."

"Yeah, but..."

"But you would've already asked someone else for help," Beau cuts in. "And I'm guessing you haven't gotten a 'yes' yet."

I shake my head with embarrassment.

He grunts, shifting awkwardly. "Okay, I'll do it."

My fingers creep over my mouth and a silent giggle trickles out. He looks so uncomfortable. "I didn't ask you," I tease.

"If we're getting to know each other again, won't an interview speed things up?" He frowns, eyes shifting left to right. "Unless you're gonna ask messed up things that will only damage our non-existent friendship?"

I giggle, relaxing as he shifts further into anxiety. As he sweats on my answer, I realize how easily I pick up on his physical reactions. Maybe Beau is the perfect subject to write my analysis on.

A grin boosts my spirit. "Okay. If you're into it, I'd love to interview you."

I sneak back to my locker to grab a notebook and pen. My brain works best with analogue systems. Something about writing by hand helps things sink deeper into my brain.

I left Beau behind. If a teacher catches him roaming the halls, the jig is up. When I get back to the alcove, he's reclined against the bench seat. When I pull out the assignment guidelines, his back slides up the wall, tightening his posture.

"I just have four questions," I explain. "Do you mind if I record us on my phone? I'm supposed to make notes on body language and facial cues."

Beau grimaces. "*Eww. Really?*"

I giggle, pointing my pen at his face. "Yeah. Stuff like that."

Beau slumps forward. "Sure. Record away."

I pull out my phone and hit record, setting it down between us.

"Do you ever get in trouble for carrying your phone around with you?" Beau asks.

"No, never."

Beau smiles. "Goody Two-shoes get away with everything."

"There are heaps of advantages when you're a good student," I reply. "You should try it."

"Well, hit me with a question and I'll consider it."

"So, the first one is easy," I say, resting my notebook on my lap. "You need to talk about an activity or project you were recently involved in. And then, explain the level of enjoyment you got from it."

Beau shifts against the bench, a pondering look on his face. "Does that mean something that's over? Or can it still be happening? Because, should I say the dance committee?"

"It's up to you," I reply, studying the thoughtfulness in his expression. "You can answer whatever you want. There's no right or wrong."

"Well, if I were to say the committee, I'd say it was surprisingly not as lame as I expected."

I scribble in my notebook, murmuring, "That's interesting."

"But if I had to answer something that's over," he continues. "It would be the wrestling team. That was something I was good at. And it meant something."

"Didn't Mr. Franklin say there was a chance to rejoin the team?"

Beau smooths back his hair. "Yeah, I guess."

I've noticed he's touched his hair a lot today. Has it always been out of nervousness, or is it when he's confused?

"I want to get back onto the team," he admits, "but it's senior year. Maybe they'll phase me out of any sporting groups."

"Mr. Franklin wouldn't use it as an empty bargaining chip."

"Thanks," he says with a soft smile. "School would be more bearable, being back on the team."

I note down his relaxed demeanor at the thought of being reinstated.

"My next question is, how frequently do you do things that bring meaning to your life?"

Beau rubs under his chin and his jaw flexes. I note his agitation and hesitation before answering the question.

"That sounds like it's about doing positive things," Beau replies.

"I would say so," I reply, pursing my lips as his guard raises.

His hand shifts down, rubbing the back of his neck. "I'm sorry. I don't know how to answer that."

I sit back, trying to rephrase the question. "It doesn't have to be a school thing. What about outside of school? Or at home? Do you have any hobbies that bring meaning to your life?"

His eyes drift to the ceiling as he gradually shakes his head.

I lean forward, searching for any sign of brightness in his eyes. "Something has to light you up."

He looks down, and when his light blue eyes meet mine, they blink several times.

Beau clears his throat, attempting to answer the question. "Before wrestling, there was boxing. It got my aggression out, and I liked following instructions that were actually useful. But did it make my life worth living? No, not really."

"Why were the instructions during boxing training more useful than a teacher at school?"

He shrugs, anchoring his elbows behind him. "They made sense. I think I like when someone acts out their instructions. I can't deal with class instructions that are to learn by reading a textbook."

I make a note that he prefers tangible instructions rather than intangible. "I remember you did martial arts when we were kids."

"Yeah, I tried taekwondo and jiu jitsu at different times," he replies. "They were fun at first. But... I think I have an issue with the self-discipline part."

You think? Oops. I hope that didn't show on my face.

"And they are self-defense classes, aren't they?" I ask.

His face shifts into a more serious expression. For a split second, I swear there is a hint of shame. He chews his lip, and then says, "Yeah, I know the best way to hit someone, and I've used it to my advantage."

My fingers send my pen trembling. "And how does that make you feel?"

"Not good," he blurts. "My life is a sack of crap."

At that, the tremor in my hand stops, and I lean forward. "What?"

Frowning, he rubs his jawline. "That's why I couldn't answer about what brings meaning to my life. My life is worthless."

"*Beau*," I gasp, heart splitting into two. "Don't say that. Every life has value."

Beau shrugs it off. "What's the next question?"

After taking a steadying breath, I read from the assignment page. "Can you describe how supported you feel from those around you? For example, from family, friends, or others?"

Beau's body grows rigid. He turns on the bench, pointing his knees away from me. Tension grows thick in the small space.

I decide to prod him. "You said your parents changed after you moved. What is your home life like?"

He hikes a knee up, hugging it close to his body. "It doesn't feel like home."

I don't reply and instead watch his eyes narrow as he focuses on something inside his head. Raw emotion layers his quiet contemplation. He lets out a gradual exhale and then turns my way. "Our new place has never been home."

As his despondent eyes penetrate mine, I can't help welling up. "I never wanted you to move. It sucked. I was so angry that my parents didn't fight to keep your family close."

"I was always arguing with my parents to stay in our house," Beau says in a low tone. "When the 'for sale' sign went up, when every box was packed, and when the moving truck arrived."

I slouch against the bricks. "It was a crappy start to that summer."

"It's probably the reason my parents don't give me the time of day now."

"Huh?"

"Your question was about how supported I feel," Beau says. "If I were to talk about my parents, I'd say I have zero support."

My face tenses as I make sense of his statement. "But your parents spoil you rotten."

"But they don't look at me or talk to me."

It gives me pause. "They don't look at you?"

His lips press into a line, and he shakes his head. A disheartened frown replaces that gorgeous grin that makes me melt. This conversation's direction builds fear inside me that I won't see that smile again.

I reach for my phone and hit stop on the recording.

Beau gestures at the phone. "Isn't this the juicy stuff you need for your assignment?"

I creep my hand forward, resting it on his knee. "All I care about is what happened to my friend."

Beau cranes his neck, peeking at my assignment sheet. "What was the last question?"

"It stays on this subject line." Heaviness weighs on my chest. "It asks you to discuss your recent feelings about your relationships."

"Oh." Beau sits back, looking away from the paper.

"What's going on with your parents?" My gut cramps, waiting for his response. "They can't be mad at you for not wanting to leave your home. Not after so many years."

His body hunches forward, and his chin rests in his palm. "I just remember starting high school and coming home to a cold house."

I want to ask him to elaborate, but I've never seen him with such hopeless low-spirit. Even as a brutish, mean kid, he has always had an energetic spark. Now, there's a war inside my head. How do I work out which version of him is the lie?

"I'd see you at school," he says, eyes downcast. "You were so sad. I couldn't go to your house after school, and you'd push me away when I'd try to catch you between classes."

I shift in my seat as he takes a pause.

"I'd go home after having no contact with you. Then I'd be around my parents, who alienated me." Intensity builds in his stare. "I became so angry."

I slide my arms around my middle and gulp. I cower beside him, wanting to say something to subdue his mood. Instead, fear renders me mute.

He straightens his posture. "My parents were always arguing when together, or I'd come home and they'd avoid each other. Either way, they ignored my existence."

I mouth the words, "I'm sorry."

"I just felt alone," he admits. "And it's stayed the same. Until now."

A tear drops onto my cheek, and I swipe it away before he sees it.

A gut-wrenching moan rushes out of Beau. He pushes himself off the bench and stands in the alcove. His feet fidget indecisively about which way to turn.

With a quick spin, he faces me, blurting, "I just want to be your friend."

My heart crushes as he sits beside me, and I stare at his devastated face.

"Everything sucks without you in my life." His stare falters, breaking away as he swipes away the pain welling in his eyes. "I don't want to be alone anymore."

My lips part, but I don't have words to speak. I lean forward and caress the side of his face. In front of me, I don't see a bully. He's the boy who, for most of my life, I called my best friend. When I peer into his glossy sky-blue eyes, it wrecks hope of keeping any tears at bay.

The sobs hurtle out of me, bouncing my shoulders up and down as streams of tears cascade from my eyes.

"I'm sorry," I wail. I move my hands up to cover my face, but before they get there, Beau pulls me into his arms. He rocks me against him as I continue to cry, "I'm sorry."

"Don't be," he whispers soothingly. "Don't be sorry."

I struggle to breathe, taking heavy, erratic breaths as I pull my head away from his shoulder.

"No," I say, taking in another heavy breath. I slam my hand against my chest and sniff hard. "I'm sorry for crying."

He wipes a hand across my cheek, and a small smile curls his lips. "Why would you say that?"

"Because you look so sad." I sniff back the mucus in my nose. "I don't want to make this about me."

Beau's hands rest on my shoulders, and he sighs. "But you always look sad."

I frown hard and pull him in close for a tight hug. I bury my face in the nape of his neck, and his hands stroke my back. If I always look sad, I don't want him watching me in true despair.

Overhead, the bell rings through the building, but we don't budge. In our small, quiet alcove, I rock against a boy struggling with his own internal anguish.

Eleven

We pull out of the hug. I wipe my eyes dry with a nervous giggle. "Well, I'm in no condition to go to class."

Beau sighs and flops his head on my shoulder. "I'm not budging an inch."

I laugh softly, smoothing a hand over the long waves flopping over his head.

"Sorry for getting so intense," he murmurs.

"I'm sorry we haven't talked sooner," I say, resting my hand against his head. "I didn't know you were hurting this badly."

His hand brushes my thigh and his head lifts from my shoulder. My hand moves down his head and nestles by his cheek.

"I just hide it better," he says with a pale imitation of his usual smile.

I lower my hand, asking, "Are you ever happy?"

"Yeah, sometimes. I'm not completely fake."

"Good. I'd hate to think I never picked up on anything being wrong."

"It's okay." He shifts, making a small gap between us on the bench. "I get why you avoided me all these years. I was deluding myself. Of course you'd be scared of me after all the things I've done."

"So, the bullying," I say, bracing myself. "Did it start so you could take out your home frustrations on other kids?"

"Mmm," he thinks on it. "It didn't really start like that."

"Could you explain it to me?" I ask. "Because I've never understood how you could change into this person. I want to know what happened to my friend."

"I never meant to take things this far." Beau takes a moment. "Things were so frosty at home. I was bugging my parents about the move, and then your mom died, which shattered our family. You know how much losing your mom hurts, but I think my parents never came back from it. They were like emotionless shells. Well, not totally emotionless. They could still yell and slam doors."

"*Yeesh.*" I shudder. "That's horrible."

"I acted out just to get their attention," Beau adds. "It was freshman year, and all this stuff was changing in my life. I started slacking on my homework to get a rise out of my parents, but they barely noticed. It wasn't until I was caught cheating on a test and my parents were called in to discuss it, that they finally looked at me."

I grit my teeth, preparing for the worst but hoping for the best. "Did it have any positive effects?"

"They berated me and asked how I could ever cheat," he replies. "Even though they were harassing me with questions, it was better than being ignored."

My stomach drops, and a frown digs into my face. "So you did more stuff like that to keep getting their attention?"

He nods. "I guess so. I didn't think I had to continue doing it. I thought they'd get over themselves and everything would go back to normal. The more I got into trouble, the less it was about me. My parents would blame each other. As the arguing got worse, my mom stopped parenting and went back to work."

Anguish wells inside me. "Gosh, Beau, it hurts me you've been so discarded. If people only knew."

He laughs. "If people knew how I was treated at home, I'd be the one bullied."

"What?" I gasp.

"That's how it works," Beau replies. "You pick a weak link. Someone already damaged and an easy target. If people knew my parents didn't love me, it'd be their ammunition."

"They still love you," I whisper, but my hope is wavering.

"No, they don't," he says flatly. "If they loved me, they wouldn't treat me this way."

"Do you see yourself in Quinton?" I ask, picturing the boy sitting in the nurses' office. "Could you tell he was an easy target?"

Beau sighs. "I didn't know about those bruises. Ugh. What if his parents did it?"

My eyes well and I pat them dry before any tears break. "You have to stop bullying other kids. I hate that your home life is a mess. But you can't keep lashing out at people. Please."

He doesn't respond, instead wincing as he rubs the back of his neck.

"Beau?"

Still nothing.

"You say you want to be my friend," I say, the hurt running through every word. "And you know I can't be your friend if you bully other people."

"I know," he grunts.

"So? Can't you promise not to hurt anyone else?"

"No," he blurts. "I can't promise because it just happens."

"You're not a robot."

"I just do things without thinking." His voice gains heat. "I can't say I won't because the times I don't want to do anything wrong, I still do it. I don't want to hurt people. Sometimes... It's like a compulsion. I've gone too far."

The frustration gets the better of me, and I move off the bench seat. "Why did you lure me back into your life? Why open up to me if you won't turn your life around?"

He stands up fast. "Because without you, I'll get worse."

His chest heaves as he stands in front of me, raw and vulnerable. I live with a man who has shut himself off from his community and uses education to show me affection. In the last four years, I'm not sure Dad has ever been honest about his feelings. And now here stands Beau, dripping with honesty, and I'd be crazy to walk away.

"Okay," I say and step closer to him.

I sweep my arms around him and squeeze him in a hug. His body relaxes against me, and with a sigh, he whispers, "Thank you."

"Can we really do this?" I ask, breathlessly.

His head nestles beside me. "Do what?"

"Be friends again after all this time."

"Not if we don't try."

I pull out of the hug and run my hands along the sides of his face. "I just wish nothing pulled us apart in the first place."

"Look, I honestly want to stop hurting people. Nothing rocked me like seeing you hurt." He winces, shaking his head. "I don't know why it never hit me before. I'd grab someone in the hall, hold them by the neck, and watch them squirm. I'd smile and think, *good*. My only priority was getting a spotlight. It never occurred to me how they'd feel afterwards. Tunnel vision, maybe? But seeing Quinton back there... *Crap*. I've been messing with him at school, and then he goes home to..."

I grit my teeth, unable to finish the sentence either.

He takes my hands and clasps them between us. "We can't change what has happened. But we can move forward. Can't we?"

I suck in a breath and nod my head. "Yes, okay. I appreciate that you see others' point of view. I don't get how you never did before. Although, I understand getting lost in something. That's why I always study. It blocks me from everything I'm missing."

Beau lets go of my hands. "Did you want to go to class?"

"I wouldn't be able to pay attention. Besides, the class is almost over."

Beau gestures to the ice pack. "You have a good excuse. You can limp. Plus, you're a good liar."

I groan. "Stop saying I'm a good liar like it's a compliment."

Beau rubs my arm. "Okay, I'm sorry. But still, if you want to get to class, I'll walk you."

"Okay." Before I gather up my things, I ask, "You said something before about not skipping classes. Do you actually care about your grades?"

"Yeah, they're my ticket out of here." When I give him a confused look, he elaborates. "I need to get out of this town."

"Oh."

"If I can't get my parents' attention while I'm at school, I doubt I'll ever see them again."

"You can't be serious."

He shrugs. "Why would I come back to visit? They want nothing to do with me. Besides, going to college is moot. Getting back on the wrestling team might help, but despite how much effort I put in, my transcript will still suck. With all the suspensions, my parents can only do so much. I'm lucky to get help from the Ashworths, but that's contingent on my parents' relationship with them. I try not to mess it up."

My stomach twinges as flirty Vanessa appears in my mind's eye.

"Whenever I see their son in the halls, I take a different direction," he says. "I don't want to chance it. Like I said, sometimes I just can't help what I do."

I stroke his arm. "Maybe if you're happier, you'll lose those compulsions."

He smiles at my hand. "With you around, I'm happy. Tell me, why are grades so important to you?"

I slip my hand off him and turn my body away. "Because it makes my dad happy."

"And?"

"And nothing. There was just so much sadness in my house when Mom passed. When I started doing well in school, he lit up. Soon, it was all we talked about and he doubled down on how seriously he took my education."

"Sounds a little intense."

"That's one way to describe him. He'd blow his top if he knew I was skipping class."

"He won't find out. Come on, I'll walk you to class."

I collect my notebook and pens, along with the ice pack, and lean into my limb as we walk away from the auditorium.

"At least this class doesn't have Whitney in it," I say. "Her presence is the only thing that makes me dread our committee meetings."

"We need another excuse to leave the library this afternoon."

I snap my fingers as an idea flashes in my mind. "I've got an excuse. If you're up for it."

Beau's face brightens with an intrigued smile. "Sure, what is it?"

"Well, we can't decorate until it gets closer to the dance," I reply. "Also, we need to order more supplies to fill the space. They have everything at the party supplies warehouse behind Main Street. Would you like to go this afternoon?"

"I'm down," Beau says. "So you're officially cool with me driving you around?"

"You've been a good driver so far."

"It'll be more fun than sitting around listening to Whitney drone on about being 'the best graphic designer in her class'," Beau asks, imitating a perfectly whiny Whitney.

I cup a hand over my mouth as I giggle. "It'll be a big plus to dodge that."

"It's a deal then."

A happy grin sets on Beau's face, and I can't help mimicking it as we walk down the hall at a casual, easy pace.

As we approach my history classroom, I wave him off, mouthing, "Goodbye."

If I walk into class late, with a limp, and have Beau Stevenson looming over me, he'll certainly get the blame.

I knock on the door and gingerly push it open.

"Ava?" Mr. Filch asks by the blackboard. He walks between the desks toward the doorway. "You're very late. Is everything okay?"

Murmurings from the other kids hum around the classroom, causing my nerves to scatter. Before I perspire to a mortifying level, I lift the ice pack and blurt, "Was at the nurse's office."

Mr. Filch looks me up and down. "Are you okay?"

I nod. "Sore, but yes."

Mr. Filch gestures to the desks. "As long as you're okay. Take a seat."

I limp to a vacant desk, trying my best to ignore the hushed gossip. Over my shoulder, I view Mr. Filch at his desk, grabbing a pen and scribbling something resembling a check mark.

I slouch in my chair with a relieved smile. Attendance still in check.

From the corner of my eye, I spy a hand signaling to gain my attention. With my head low, I turn to the right and find Ciara subtly waving.

My lips press into a glum smile, and I lift my hand in a mediocre wave.

"Are you okay?" Ciara mouths. Her shoulders hunch over, fearing the teacher catching her talking in class.

I nod, and then turn to face the blackboard. My gut twinges as cynical thoughts run through my head. It's just telling that she didn't check in with me last night. Surely she heard from Hilary and Whitney yesterday I left early because I was hurt. How am I to believe her worry is genuine?

Even though she was intrusive, Mrs. Whiteborne's words put things into perspective. I was hurt and Beau put in effort to take care of me. We didn't have a meaningful interaction for years. After a few days, it feels like I have my best friend back.

I sit back in my seat, leaving my notebooks closed as I drown out my teacher's voice. A warmth envelops me as I picture Beau's face. He's been broken all these years. Maybe with my help, he can heal.

Being in this classroom was pointless. The bell doesn't take long to ring. I have nothing to pack up, so I stand from my seat. As everyone surges for the door, Ciara winds past the desks toward me.

"What's going on?" she asks in a rush. "Hilary said you're spending all this time with Beau."

I deadpan her. "So?"

Her mouth falls open. "So? He's super scary. Hilary told me he drove you to school. How could you step foot in his car?"

I shrug, exhausted. "Easily."

"What's with the attitude?" Ciara presses. "Isn't he the reason you hurt your foot?"

I cross my arms, scowling. "No. I tripped on something I dropped."

"I just don't understand what you're doing."

"Of course you don't, because you keep abandoning me."

She rolls her eyes. "Stop saying that."

"No. I don't have to do anything."

"Fine." She sighs. "I just thought you'd want the heads up on Whitney."

The tension in my arms eases, and they unravel. "What do you mean?"

"Apparently, she's falling apart with her task," Ciara replies. "Hilary said she kept deleting any progress she made. She went looking for you yesterday to continue her self-sabotage."

I groan. "Ugh. She has to get it together. Plus, her ego won't let her fail. She's just looking for attention."

"You really think so?"

"It has to be. I won't be at the meeting this afternoon, anyway. Beau and I are ordering more supplies."

Ciara's dumbfounded. "More time with Beau?"

I pick up my notebook, pen case, and ice pack. "Leave it alone, Ciara. I don't need your judgment."

Twelve

"Ready to get out of here?" Beau asks, skidding to a stop by my locker.

As usual, the hallway is almost empty by the time I leave last period.

"I just have to check in with the group." My cheeks hurt from my smile. "I am the chairperson, you know."

"Oh, I'm aware," Beau says, wiggling his eyebrows. "A person would be fairly dense not to realize you're perfect for the job."

I run a hand over my braid and bite my lip. "Thanks. I wouldn't have it without you."

"What can I say?" Beau says with a wink. "I'm not dense."

My stomach flutters and I have an immense urge to fan my face.

Leaving my locker, we make it up the staircase and enter the library. I've never wanted to escape this room before. I never thought I'd want to escape with Beau Stevenson. Again.

I open the meeting room door and enter with a bounce in my step. "Hey everyone."

The group replies with "hi" and waves. Mr. Riley grins, seated at the front end of the table. Lucy and Ciara sit at the rear. Hilary and Marcus take their seats on the long edge, facing the door. Jeff takes a seat opposite, trying to gain Whitney's attention.

Whitney hunches over her laptop, and is the only person not to acknowledge my presence.

"Beau and I are organizing decorating supplies," I tell the group, "but I wanted to check if everyone else is doing okay."

"Well done, Ava," Mr. Riley says behind his laptop. "A good leader always checks in with the group."

Lucy beams beside Ciara, saying, "We secured a photographer."

I clap, bouncing on the balls of my feet. "That's awesome."

"We emailed him your drawing of the tree maze," Ciara says, smiling. "He loves them as portrait backdrops."

I squeal at the good news, and Beau pats my shoulder in congratulations.

"And for the band, we wanted everyone else's opinion," Lucy says to the group. "We contacted a few professional bands through social media, but then Teddy Wilkins heard we wanted a live band for the dance. He wanted to know if his garage band could get the gig?"

"Teddy Wilkins' band?" Jeff questions. "Are they any good?"

Ciara cups a hand over her mouth as she giggles. She nudges Lucy, saying, "Show them the video."

Lucy pulls out her phone, telling us to listen up. She holds it out, and a group of goofy boys in Santa hats play an indie-rock version of "Santa Baby."

The rendition has everyone in hysterics, but also bopping away with the beat. It's fun, uplifting, and puts everyone in a cheery mood.

"I really like them," I say, jittery with giggles.

"Me too," Hilary agrees, and Marcus and Jeff add their approval.

"It's not really professional," Whitney says snobbishly. "But I guess if they're doing it for free, it gives us more money for everything else."

I look over my shoulder and ask Beau, "What do you think?"

Beau twists his lips as the decision gnaws at him.

Oh my gosh. It just hit me. These are the boys I saw Beau manhandling. I swallow hard, and my stomach quivers. This can't be a good idea.

He leans against the door frame and flippantly replies, "Give them a chance, if you want."

I give him an apprehensive look. "Are you sure?"

Beau gives me a nod.

Marcus cuts in. "Everyone likes their stuff. They should get the gig."

I turn back to Lucy with a bright smile. "Tell Teddy they've got it."

Lucy flips her phone around, squealing, "Yay," as her fingers wildly text.

My stomach settles. The boys are truly talented, and hopefully this performance can be some kind of peace offering to show no hard feelings between them and Beau.

Or... I'm just deluding myself.

"So, I know Hilary had great success with the PTA," I say, giving Hilary a smile. I turn to Whitney, who has her back to me. "How are the promotional materials going?"

"They're coming," Whitney mutters, staring at her laptop.

I was expecting her to say something that'd stroke her ego. I flick my eyes to Ciara, worried that Whitney was indeed falling behind in her work.

"Can we see?" I ask cautiously.

Whitney huffs. "There's nothing to see."

"What does that mean?" Marcus comments.

"I've been creating vectors from scratch," Whitney says, a heated defensiveness seeping through her tone. "My name is attached to these graphics, so they have to be perfect."

"You don't need to make them from scratch," Ciara pipes up. She hunches over when everyone turns her way. "Just add some PNGs from a stock image website."

"I'm not a hack," Whitney objects. "Besides, isn't taking other people's work plagiarism?"

Hilary snorts. "There are tons of free stock images online. Why are you being so dramatic?"

Involuntarily, I hunch, secretly knowing why Whitney is overreacting. I move closer to Whitney's laptop, peering over her shoulder. "What have you created?"

Whitney huffs. "It takes a long time. If I'm not happy with an image, I delete it and start again."

I frown at the messy shapes on her Photoshop canvas. "Are there any finished images you haven't deleted?"

"I don't see anybody else creating images from scratch," she replies, avoiding the question.

My eyes narrow at her hostile defensiveness. No one said she needed to create images out of nothing. We just need cohesive Christmas images that comply with our North Pole theme.

Crossing my fingers she has another finished file saved, I back away, asking, "Okay, you'll make sure to send the finished files to the printers by five o'clock?"

"There's no way I'll finish today," Whitney says indifferently.

I stumble over my feet as I come to a halt. "Wait, what?" My mouth hangs open after each word.

"What happened, Whitney?" Hilary asked, panicked. "Yesterday you told me you got this."

"I couldn't finish yesterday," Whitney protests, rearing up in her seat. "After you left, I had to clean up *your mess, Ava.*"

The venom in those last three words shoves the blame onto me.

I squint, shaking my head as I make sense of her defense. "Why did you even look for me yesterday?"

"You're the leader of our group," Whitney spits, crossing her arms.

"So?" I blurt as my posture grows tall and perpendicular. "You had your task, which was based on the computer. Why did you stop working?"

An audible shift ripples around the room as everyone angles themselves toward Whitney, waiting for her response.

Whitney squirms under the group's scrutinizing stares. "It's not my fault!" she yelps. "I'm a perfectionist and no one gave me enough time."

"Isn't it your laptop?" Lucy questions, gesturing at the machine. "Can't you continue working at home?"

Whitney scoffs. "I can't commit all my time to this project. I'm already juggling work from all my classes. I have a standard to uphold, you know."

"Why didn't you ask for more help?" Hilary criticizes.

Jeff leans over the table, asking Hilary, "Why didn't you do more to help?"

Hilary's hand slams onto her chest as her mouth forms an o. "Excuse me?"

"Weren't you supposed to be helping Whitney while I was gone?" Jeff digs.

"Hey man," Marcus cuts in, placing an arm around Hilary. "Not cool. Hilary had her own task too. Which, I might add, she accomplished."

"She only had to talk to some parents," Whitney snipes. "My work is precise, creative, and painstaking."

Hilary stands, hitting a fist on the table. "I didn't just talk to the parents. I also got a quote from Caesar's Catering, who I contacted in the evening. AKA, after five o'clock."

"*Guys*," I plead. "We can't fight like this. If we don't all pull together, there won't be a dance to argue about."

"Ava's right," Marcus says, standing and running a hand along Hilary's back. "If one of us fails, we all fail."

Jeff blows out a hard breath, guilt scrunching his broad frame. "That's what Coach always tells us. *Dang.* I'm sorry, Hilary, for getting on your case."

"Whitney," Lucy pipes up. "I'm sorry for being accusatory, too."

Whitney tightens her arms around her middle, lifts her chin high, and nods her acceptance.

"I'm sorry things got heated too," Hilary says as her body eases by Marcus.

The room grows unsettlingly quiet as all eyes focus on Whitney. My stomach somersaults as I wait for her to utter an apology. If she doesn't get her act together, we're all sunk.

Whitney keeps her face angled high, letting out a passive-aggressive humph.

"Oh, good lord," Beau groans.

Everyone turns to face him as he leans against the door frame.

"Just say you're sorry, Whitney, so everyone can move on," Beau complains.

A disgusted grimace twists on Whitney's face. "I'm not saying sorry to you."

Beau peels himself off the door frame, stepping closer to the table. "I don't want your apology," Beau replies. He motions to everyone else. "But they're all clearly waiting for it."

Whitney's eyes redden as she pans around the group. She stands, clasping her hands over her chest. "I'm sorry, everyone, that I wasn't given enough time to create visually appealing promotional materials."

The air is stale as we take in the defensive statement.

"It's fine," I blurt, pulling everyone's attention toward me. "Guys, we don't need any more excuses. We have to finish so we can get this stuff to the printers. Is everyone in agreement that we work together on this?"

Hilary places a hand on my arm and gives me a sweet smile. "I'm in."

"Me too," Marcus says.

Lucy and Jeff add their support, and I move my attention back to Ciara. She fiddles with her shiny black bob and stammers some quivering sounds.

"Yes," she finally squeaks. Her eyes dart about as the weight of everyone's observance drags her down.

The back of Beau's hand taps against my forearm. "You want to stay?"

I give him a small smile and shrug my shoulders toward the table. "We have to stay."

"We have to get this done," Hilary says with a reddening face. "I'm not working tomorrow night. I already missed two of Marcus's training sessions. I'm not missing the game."

"Kids, don't panic," Mr. Riley says, rising from his seat. "You can handle this. You just need to work together."

"I just don't understand why you kept deleting your progress," Lucy says, glaring at Whitney with aggravation.

Mr. Riley lifts his hands, halting any more verbal jabs. "You need to stop assigning blame. Why don't you check whether you can get an extension at the printers?" Mr. Riley suggests. "Perhaps you can send in the files tomorrow for a Monday morning delivery?"

"Do you want to call them?" Jeff asks Whitney.

Whitney groans. "Why should I call them? I'm not the one in charge."

Before I can butt in, Jeff says, "Who has the phone number? I'll call them."

I pull their information from my binder and give it to Jeff. "Thanks."

Jeff punches the number into his cell phone. "No problem. I gotta put in some effort. This is my task too."

Ciara deadpans at Whitney's laptop. "I can't believe you're so far behind."

"And all of a sudden you're Little Miss Perfect?" Whitney snaps.

I move to the corner of the desk between the girls. "Can we please get over it and help Whitney finish all her graphics in time?"

Whitney raises her hand. "I'm keeping creative control."

"You've had creative control." I look at the mess on her laptop screen. "Maybe you can't handle your own creative vision. I say we come up with a simple concept we can execute well."

"What do you suggest?" Hilary asks as she and Marcus take their seats.

"Uh," I murmur, gaining Beau's attention. I motion my head toward the two empty seats at the adjacent corner.

He nods and moves around the table and takes a seat.

"I have a thought," I say to the group, "if you'll hear me out."

I grit my teeth, bracing for something antagonistic to blast out of Whitney.

Whitney slides her laptop toward the center of the table. "Let's hear it."

"Well, if you want original images for your final product, we have tons of Christmas deco down in the storeroom." I pan around the table. "Why don't we all take photos and send them to Whitney? She could make a collage that borders the posters. And something cute for the tickets."

"IPhone photos?" Whitney grimaces. "That'll look so tacky."

"Not with the good lighting and the right app," Hilary says. "Mr. Riley, do you think it's possible to get a light box from a photography class?"

Mr. Riley steps away from his desk, tapping his phone screen. "I'll check the art department to see if anyone is still there."

As Mr. Riley leaves the meeting room, I settle down in a seat next to Beau.

"So much for getting away from pro graphic designer Whitney," he jokes.

I mumble a laugh. "I know. Maybe we could go to the warehouse tomorrow?"

He smiles. "Sure, I'm up for that."

"There's a lot of whispering going on over there," Hilary comments.

Marcus leans back in his chair to get a better view. "Yeah. Everything okay over there?"

"Why wouldn't it be?" Beau snaps.

Marcus smirks. "Because you're involved."

I put a hand on Beau's arm, stopping him from firing back. "We were just talking."

"Ugh," Hilary groans. "Marcus, this is so boring. Can't you lay off him until he actually does something wrong?"

"Babe, you want me to sit back and wait?" Marcus complains. "This is Beau Stevenson. We all know it's inevitable he'll do something messed up."

Beau slides back against his chair with a groan. "Do you want me to start, Marcus?"

Terrified squeaks erupt from Lucy and Ciara, who cower together.

"Don't go there, Beau," Jeff warns.

"I wasn't going to." Beau throws an arm out, pointing at Marcus. "But he's dying for me to do something."

"I just know who you are," Marcus raises his voice.

"You want to take me down, or something?" Beau asks, feet bouncing by his chair legs, preparing to launch. "Hoping to impress your girlfriend by knocking me out?"

"*Eww*," Hilary winces, lifting her hands up. "That does not impress me. What were you two talking about, anyway?"

"We're ordering decorations from the warehouse in town," I reply. "Instead of doing it today, we'll go tomorrow."

Hilary's mouth drops in utter shock. "No way."

I rear back. "What?"

"You can't go tomorrow," she says, still horrified. "It's game day tomorrow."

Beau snickers. "So?"

Hilary's face screws up, unable to comprehend what she's hearing. "Everyone has to be there to support the team."

"But I never go to games," I say in a small voice.

"*Ava.*" Hilary gasps. "For shame."

Marcus laughs. "Hils isn't on the cheer squad, but she's our greatest cheerleader."

"So, you're seriously not going?" Hilary asks, her eyes watering with sadness. How does a football game mean this much to her?

"No, of course we'll go," Beau cuts in. "How did we blank on the game?"

"You can still forget about it," Marcus says in a gravelly tone.

"I would never," Beau says teasingly. "Nothing makes me happier than seeing you boys slip around a sludgy field."

Marcus rolls his eyes, turning away from us.

Hilary beams at me. "You'll be there, right?"

"I guess," I stammer. "If my dad says it's okay."

"It's a football game," Hilary remarks. "What dad would say no to that?"

I turn to Beau and whisper, "We really need to order those supplies."

He leans in closer. "You said you don't keep friendships outside of committee meetings."

My heart swells. "That's why you want to go?"

He smiles. "You want friends, don't you?"

I bite into my lower lip, my grin growing, and I nod.

"How about we go to the supplies store on Saturday?"

Surprise spreads warm tingles through my body. "You'd spend your weekend with me?"

In an adorably jittery way, his hand runs over the back of his head. "Yeah, if you're up for it."

My fingers play at my bottom lip as I awkwardly spit out, "Would you want to?"

"Sure. I'll be there."

I curl my fingers below my lip and slide my palm under my chin. "Yeah, I'd love to."

He puffs out a nervous laugh. "You can't wait to spend more time with me."

"You promised to make this committee fun," I whisper. "I'm just holding you to it."

Beau breathes a laugh. "Oh, I see how it is."

I slip my fingers over my lips as my shoulders jiggle in a laugh.

Hilary taps my shoulder, and my cheeks burn hot.

I turn to her as she asks, "So, it's a yes on the game?"

"Mhmm." I nod. "Looks like it."

"Then you should come over to my house after school," Hilary suggests, bouncing in her seat. "We could get ready together."

"You really want me too?"

"Sure, why not?"

"Just Ava," Marcus says with a grunt. "I don't want Stevenson anywhere near your house."

"Good lord." Beau groans. "Get over yourself."

Marcus sits up in his seat, flexing his beefy arms. "I'm only protecting my girlfriend."

Beau scoffs. "From what?"

"Can you all stop!" Whitney exclaims, shoving her laptop away from her. "How am I supposed to create the best materials when everyone continues to sabotage me?"

Before I can roll my eyes because she's turning everything around, I'm halted by her body language. Whitney's face grows red, her eyes are blood-stricken, and her hands tremble in mid-air.

"Whoa, Whitney," Jeff says soothingly. "Take a breath."

"It's okay, Whitney," Lucy says. "It doesn't have to be a masterpiece. It's just some tickets and posters that will eventually be thrown out."

Whitney moans. "Thanks. That makes me feel better."

"She's just saying you don't need to get so stressed," Hilary says. "That's what got you into this mess in the first place."

Whitney scowls. "So everything's my fault?"

"We're all staying back to help you," Lucy replies.

My heart pounds to a low beat as Whitney spirals in front of the group. "Whitney, no one wants to attack you. Everyone is here, so we can finish by working as a team."

Whitney's bottom lip trembles as her reddened eyes stare at her laptop.

I gesture at the laptop. "Have you got this?"

Whitney shakes out her shoulders and steadies her fingers over the trackpad. "I can do this. If you guys send the photos, I'll get this done."

Mr. Riley enters the room. "Hilary and Marcus, come with me. Ms. Robins is collecting two light boxes for us to grab at her office."

I collect the storeroom key from Mr. Riley before he leaves with Hilary and Marcus.

"Okay, Beau, Lucy, and Ciara. Let's head to the storeroom and collect as much as we can," I say to the group. "Jeff, you stay and help Whitney. By the time we get back, the light boxes will be set up and ready."

Thirteen

It was a relief when Whitney finally sent the files to the printing company. The afternoon seemed to drag on until I made it home. When Hilary continued to hound me about the football game, even asking me if I had a blue and white outfit to wear, time ran away from me further. I told Beau I'd get home on my own. He didn't want to leave me, but Hilary's motor-mouth didn't leave room for debate.

My dad wasn't happy when I got home later than usual. I dodged his third-degree and didn't rock the boat by asking about the game. Even with Hilary's insistence, I wasn't eager about it. Maybe I won't go at all.

I went to school earlier than usual this morning. My mind was topsy-turvy with clashing thoughts. Beau and I got incredibly close yesterday, but inside the meeting room, the boys took every available swing at him, and the girls flinched in fear every time Beau spoke. Am I supposed to ignore all of that?

It's not that I wanted to avoid him. My mind wasn't clear enough. I'm terrified that if I see him, I'll push him away again. After everything he told me in that interview session, pushing him away might completely break him. I don't want to say or do anything mean. I just need to figure out my true feelings.

Between study hall, the alcove, and extra outings to the library, I didn't see him all day. It felt like a regular school day except for the nagging thoughts lingering in my head.

Another thing that sets this day apart is Hilary sidelining me after last period. Her sharp eyes were very telling. She knew I'd skip the game.

Seriously, why does she care so much?

On the flip side, it's heartwarming she does care so much.

Hilary pulls her car to a stop outside my house. She frowns, panning around the cul-de-sac. "What's up, Ava? Every house has Christmas decorations but yours."

Her words send me squirming.

She turns away from the houses and toward me. "You're so into Christmas and giving the dance a traditional and fun vibe. I assumed your house would be the most bedazzled on the street."

I open the car door, hoping to escape her line of questions. "I decorated the inside of the house."

I leave the car, closing the door behind me. Hilary rounds the car, joining me on the garden path.

She pats my shoulder, saying, "Don't worry about your dad. He won't say no."

My stomach tosses itself about. "You don't know who you're up against. I haven't even mentioned the game to him."

I dig inside the front pocket of my backpack for my house key as we move onto the front porch. Before my hand grips the key, the front door pulls open.

Dad stands before us with a stern expression. His scowl morphs into a smile and relief brightens his eyes. His suspicions have been on red-alert since Beau entered our home.

"Hi girls," Dad greets us. "How was school?"

"It was good." I lace my fingers together, bracing myself for the word no. "But I was wondering if I'd be able to go out tonight."

"Tonight?"

"It's the football game tonight against North Ridge High," Hilary says.

"And?"

I look at Hilary, internally saying, *"See?"*

"The whole group wants to get together to celebrate all our hard work this week," Hilary says sweetly.

Dad's eyes narrow. "The whole group?"

"Well, just the girls," Hilary replies.

"Oh." Dad takes us both in. "No boys?"

I grin, nodding. "No boys."

Dad looks at Hilary. "I thought you insist your boyfriend is always by your side."

"He'll be on the field, Mr. Jones."

"We just want to chill out together," I tell Dad. "I didn't tell you, but we hit a major snag last night."

His face grows stern. "What happened?"

"Whitney totally sabotaged us. That's why I was so late last night." I blow out a breath, looking as innocent as possible. "We really came together as a team and fixed her mistakes. Can I please celebrate with them?"

Dad's expression softens, and a hint of a smile appears. "Your committee is doing well, then?"

Hilary pats my back. "Thanks to your girl's fine leadership. You should be so proud, Mr. Jones."

Dad steps out of the doorway, motioning for us to come inside. "Okay, you can go. But home by nine."

"Thank you," Hilary and I cheer as we enter the house.

I cross my fingers and look at Dad angelically. "Can we make it ten?"

Dad frowns.

Hilary wraps an arm around my neck. "Mr. Jones, I promise to have her home by ten. Pretty please?"

Dad melts. "Okay, ten. Not a second later."

In giggles, I grab Hilary's hand and race her towards my bedroom.

"Dads are such a piece of cake," Hilary says, flopping on my bed. "They're always worried about boys. If you tell them there are no boys, they instantly lower their shields."

"I still can't believe he said yes," I say, dropping my bag and removing my coat. "He doesn't like me going out at night."

Hilary fans a hand through her dark hair, giving me a wink. "It's just my sparkling personality."

I laugh, slipping off my blazer and moving to my desk.

Hilary clears her throat. "Ahem. What are you doing?"

"I just want to add something to an essay."

"Oh, no you don't." Hilary leaps off the bed and turns me toward my closet. "You have to find a cute outfit."

I giggle, lamenting. "Fine."

When I pull open my closet and flick through the hanging items, Hilary pushes ahead with bounding enthusiasm. "Let me."

"I'll wear jeans and a sweater."

"Oh my gosh." Hilary gasps. "What is this?"

She pulls out a red satin cocktail dress.

I push the hanger back in the closet. "That's nothing."

"It's gorgeous."

I slide it back into the closet. "It was my mom's."

"Have you worn it?"

"No, I..." My mother's image floats in my mind and derails my thoughts. "Forget it."

Sensing my rising tension, Hilary drops the subject and searches the rest of the closet. She finds skinny dark denim jeans and a fitted navy sweater with a white star on the front. Pairing it with a blue and white scarf, I'm ready for the sidelines.

As I pull my coat over my outfit, Dad reminds me about the ten o'clock curfew. Now, another thought gnaws at me. I summon all my courage, put on my best puppy-dog eyes, and stand before my dad.

"Umm, Dad," I stammer.

"Yes?"

"Well, before Whitney sabotaged us," I say, wringing my hands together, "I was supposed to go to the party supplies store and organize decorations for the dance."

Dad tilts his head. "And?"

I look over my shoulder at Hilary, and then pout as I look back at Dad. "Can I go tomorrow instead? We are falling so far behind. I don't want to be the reason there's no dance."

Dad shifts his gaze from me, to Hilary, and back to me. "You girls have got a lot on your plate, huh?"

"Nothing we can't handle," I reply. "We just need more time."

Dad takes a moment to think. "Okay. You can go."

I squeal and leap at Dad with a hug.

He laughs, patting my back. "Stay safe tonight."

"We will," Hilary replies as I move out of the hug.

We wave goodbye, leaving the house and filing into Hilary's car.

"I can't go to the supplies store with you tomorrow," Hilary says, buckling her seatbelt. "I already have plans with Marcus."

"Oh, no, that's okay," I say, fidgeting with my buckle. "I just implied it was with you."

Hilary turns on the ignition with a sneaky grin. "What exactly is going on between you and Beau?"

I shrug, turning my attention to the window. "Nothing. I'm just taking advantage of his help."

"Ah-huh." Her tone doesn't buy it.

I chew my lip. "I couldn't let my dad know the truth, could I?"

Hilary laughs. "So you're not as innocent as you seem."

Hillary drives us to an impressive two-story home. The outside is stark white and smattered with Christmas lights and festive decorations. As I follow her to the front door, we pass a large Santa cut-out who greets us with a, "Ho! Ho! Ho!"

"It's so annoying," Hilary says, unlocking the door. "I'm getting ready to unplug its sensor."

"Don't be a Grinch. It's fun."

"Says the girl who has the bare front yard."

Even though it's a large home, the interior has a very cozy vibe. We walk into a toasty living room, heated by a crackling fireplace. Stockings hang from the mantelpiece and every surface houses ornaments of varying sizes.

We walk into the kitchen and Mrs. Wong greets us from behind the counter. "Ready for the game?" Her plump cheeks grow high from her beaming grin.

"You know it," Hilary replies. "Mom, this is Ava."

"Hello, Ava. Is your boyfriend on the team?"

I blush, filled with an embarrassment I don't fully understand. "Ah, no, I don't have a boyfriend."

"No, Mom. Ava has a crush on..."

"*Hilary,*" I squeal.

Hilary laughs, swatting a hand. "Just kidding. Ava's single."

"Aww." I swear there's pity in Mrs. Wong's eyes. "Nevermind, dear. A boyfriend isn't everything."

I nod. "I know that." If I believe my dad, studying is everything.

Hilary takes a can of soda from the fridge and wiggles it at me. "You want one?"

"No, I'm good," I reply politely.

"Hi girls," Mr. Wong asks, striding into the kitchen. "What's happening tonight?"

My gut squeezes and pain wraps around my spine. Is this it? The moment it's all over?

Mrs. Wong gives him a dumbfounded look. "Duh, honey. It's game day."

"Oh, that's right," Mr. Wong says with a bouncy energy. "We should get ready to go."

Hilary groans. "Last time you two showed up, you totally embarrassed me. You're not doing that again. Am I clear?"

Whoa. She just ordered her parents around. Cue the yelled response right about...

Hilary's parents respond in a fit of laughter.

"Don't get yourself all twisted," Mrs. Wong says to Hilary. "We won't embarrass you."

Hilary stomps her foot. "Because you won't be there, right?"

Her dad makes a goofy face. "Sure, we won't be there."

Hilary screeches a moan, grabbing my wrist and tugging me out of the kitchen.

Her parents' giggles trail off as we make our way upstairs.

"Ugh. Sorry about them," Hilary says, opening her bedroom door. "They are mortifyingly lame."

"Are you kidding?" I say, unable to contain my nervous laugh. "Your parents are cool."

She squints at me. "Cool? Were you hit on the head or something?"

I point behind me. "They just joked about you going out tonight and didn't accuse you of doing something wrong."

Hilary walks further into her bedroom. "Wow. Your dad has you tightly wound."

"I'm just saying it could be worse. You're lucky to have two fun parents."

"I wouldn't call them fun, but I get what you mean."

"Wow," I say, looking around Hilary's room. "This is a nice bedroom."

Hilary smiles at the large room with furniture accented in lilac and mauve. "Thanks. It's my sanctuary. I'll just get changed and then we can do our makeup."

"Ah, no. I'm good."

"Come on. It's a night out."

"I don't think my dad would approve."

"You can wipe it off before you get home," she says, removing layers of her uniform. "Your dad never has to know."

I fold my arms and fidget my stance as I peer over her makeup vanity.

"He knows you'll wear makeup to the dance, right?"

I shrug. "That's different. Organized events differ from random nights out. He just doesn't want it to be a regular thing."

"But what if you like makeup? You'll be an adult soon. You can choose who you are and what you look like."

"But I'm not there yet. Right now, it's just easier to play along with his rules."

Hilary winces. "I would not survive a night in that house."

I give her a small smile as she reappears in a new blue and white ensemble. "It's not that bad. He's always home for dinner, and always makes sure I have the right school supplies, new clothes and buys me the latest books. I spend most of my time reading and studying, which is something I enjoy."

"Well, I'm sure you'll do great in college," Hilary says, picking up a makeup brush. "Now, take a seat and I'll bring out those beautiful eyes of yours."

When Hilary finishes my makeup, and moves onto her own, Lucy joins us at the house. She's fretting over her accessories, and wants Hilary to choose which will most catch Jeff's eye.

"Are you sure you want to put all your hopes on Jeff?" I ask as the girls mix and match items. "Not to burst your bubble, but isn't he into Whitney?"

"*Eww.*" Both girls screw up their faces.

"I doubt Whitney will be at the game," Hilary says flippantly. "Lucy can still get his attention before it's too late."

I take in the desperation on Lucy's face. My eyes narrow with worry.

"Hilary brought the boys to the meetings so Jeff and I could get time together," Lucy says. "I won't lose this opportunity just because Jeff has been nice to Whitney. He probably only did it because Beau's around. I should be glad he's so caring toward other people."

"You should keep your eye out for a footballer too," Hilary says, moving away from the accessories. "Then we can all triple-date."

Lucy beams a smile at me. "Yeah, that would be so fun."

"Dominic is single. Wouldn't he and Ava be so cute together?"

"Oh my gosh, yes!"

"Hold up." I throw my hands out. "I'm not looking for a date."

"But the dance is coming up," Hilary replies.

"Yeah, you don't want to go stag," Lucy adds.

"I don't need a date. We're student chaperones."

"Doesn't mean we can't have fun," Lucy says.

"Come on," Hilary says, stepping behind me and playing with my hair. "You're just nervous. I bet you'd have a lot more fun if you let your hair down and spent some time with a boy."

Hilary pulls out my braid and combs her fingers through my hair, letting it fall below my shoulders.

Lucy chuckles. "Yeah, someone other than Beau Stevenson."

I flinch and frown before I can stop myself.

"Oh my gosh, I knew it," Hilary says, stepping around and scrutinizing my face. "You're into him."

"Him who?" Lucy questions apprehensively.

Hilary's eyes widen. "Beau."

I look between the two girls, anxiety hunching my posture. "What? No, I'm not."

Hilary shakes her head, looking at Lucy. "We gotta do something about this. We have to set her up with Dominic before it's too late."

"No." I step back as my heart races. "I don't like Dominic. I don't want to date a footballer."

Lucy frowns. "What's wrong with dating footballers?"

"Nothing. I'm not a project you need to fix."

"Sorry," Hilary replies. "I didn't mean to upset you. I just thought you'd want the help."

"I don't need help. You don't know why Beau and I have been talking." I take a deep breath and look the girls in the eyes. "But I'd like to have friends, if I haven't ruined everything."

Lucy grins. "Sure, we can be friends. Just know, being friends with me means helping me get a date."

I smile back. "I'll help if it's what you want."

"Oh, it's what she wants," Hilary says. "It's all I've heard for months."

"And is Jeff the guy?" I ask. "Or could someone else be more into you?"

Lucy wraps her scarf around her neck and places a cute blue beanie on her head. "I guess we'll have to see what tonight brings."

I giggle. Wow, she doesn't care who it is, as long as she gets her date for the dance.

"I thought Ciara was coming here with you?" Hilary says to Lucy.

Lucy shakes her head. "I offered to pick her up, but she said she had to do something with her mom and she'd meet us at the game."

Yeah, right. I know Ciara and her politeness. Just like me, she never goes to football games. Why would she start now?

"Well, let's get going," Hilary says, throwing on her coat. "I wanna give Marcus a good luck kiss before the game starts."

We pile into Lucy's car because Hilary plans on leaving the game with Marcus. On the way, we get drive-thru burgers. Hilary doesn't want to go inside to eat because she's dying to watch Marcus practice before the game starts. I still don't understand this fascination with Marcus and his practices, but she seems to love it as much as she loves him.

"Should we sit in the stands?" I ask, throwing a thumb towards the stacked seating area.

"I don't know if my voice will carry from up there." Hilary's eyes grow wide as she focuses on the field.

"Chill, Hils," Lucy says, tucking an arm around Hilary's. "Let's sit in the stands for the first quarter. The players will settle into the game."

"Fine," Hilary concedes. "But, I'm warning you, I will yell from up there."

Lucy looks at me with a teasing smile. "I knew I should have brought ear muffs."

We steer a less-than-enthused Hilary towards the stands. They are enclosed, keeping out the weather. Several electric heaters hang from the metal ceiling rafters. It's pretty cozy despite the stiff plastic seats in each row.

Through the entire first quarter, Hilary bounces off her seat. She veers left and right, getting better angles to view the field. She cheers encouragement and congratulations Marcus's way. No matter what she calls out, I'm still lost. Either Ashworth Academy has the ball, or the other team takes possession, or I have no clue what's supposed to happen in order to win.

When the quarter ends, Hilary leaps off the seat. She shimmies across the row, toward the aisle. Lucy and I hurry behind to meet up with her on the ground.

"I don't get it. They were great seats," Lucy says. "Not to mention how toasty it was."

"I just prefer to be closer to the field," Hilary says. "I want to be on his level as he runs the field."

"Why? It's not like you run alongside him," Lucy says, holding back a laugh.

"Ugh. Whatever. You two can go back up."

"No, I want to stick together."

I nod in agreement. "Me too. I'm not following along, anyway."

Hilary gives me a surprised look. "You don't know the rules?"

I smile. "Why does that surprise you?"

"We don't need to know the rules," Lucy says, slinging an arm across my shoulders. "We just need to see cute boys running around."

"Who's got your eye, Lucy?" Hilary asks, wiggling her eyebrows. "Jeff or Dominic?"

"There's three more quarters to decide," she answers mischievously.

Hilary beckons us closer to the field. A few people sit on the fence that frames the grassy area. A melodic giggle pricks my ears, and as we move closer, the source of the sound is in clear view.

Even though I'm staring at her back, there's no doubt it's Vanessa Ashworth. The most stylish senior here. Some of her friends sit along her left, and to her right is the one person I've been subconsciously searching for this whole time.

Fourteen

"I love when it's been snowing before they play." Beau smirks, leaning into Vanessa. "Not only do they slip on the sludgy ground, but the ball grows icy. It either slips out of their hands, or when it's thrown, it's like catching a huge rock."

Vanessa's shoulders jiggle in a laugh. "Oh my gosh, Beau. That's terrible. Do you really think that's funny?"

"Hey, I'm not the only one laughing," Beau says, enjoying her laughter. He smirks and looks away. His eyes enlarge as they connect with mine.

"Ava," Beau puffs my name, almost breathless. He lifts his knees and swivels over the fence, dropping to the ground. He stands in front of me with a happy smile. "I didn't know if I'd see you today."

I hug my middle, unable to hide my growing smile. "Well, Hilary won't take no for an answer."

"Ah. Well, I'm glad she got you here. I was worried when I didn't see you all day."

I play with a lock of hair, twisting it around my fingers. "Umm, yeah. Sorry about that."

He folds his arms and shifts his weight in a fidgety stance. "It's lame to even admit this, but I went by your house this morning."

Guilt clenches my stomach. "Oh, you did?"

"You left early?"

I swallow hard. "Mhmm."

"That's okay. I just thought you'd like a ride to school." He looks me up and down, finding my eyes with a bright smile. "You look freaking gorgeous, by the way."

An instant blush splashes across my cheeks. I touch my brunette waves, and murmur, "You think so?"

He rubs behind his neck. "Yeah. I like your hair out."

"Thanks."

"Not that your braids aren't nice, but I think this looks better."

I smile, loving that he's talking about my hair and not the makeup Hilary forced onto my face. He's wearing a black hoodie under a black jacket, as well as ripped black jeans and black sneakers. A tuft of blonde hair peeks out from under his black beanie. Even though he wears all black, his eyes have never looked more blue. "You look nice too."

He puffs laugh. "Thanks."

"He does look particularly cute tonight," Vanessa's voice cuts in and she leaps off the fence. "Doesn't he?"

Beau fixes his beanie, giving Vanessa a cheesy grin. "I am mesmerizing."

Vanessa laughs, playfully hitting Beau's arm. "Oh, stop." She composes herself, turning her attention to me. "Hi Ava. I was just talking to Beau about my Christmas Eve party and suggested he should give me some tips. I've been hearing stories about how helpful he's been this week."

I nod, taking in the pair standing before me. "He is helpful."

"You don't want tips from me," Beau says, stepping closer to me. "Ava is the brains behind everything. She's the party planner."

Vanessa smooths back her sleek blonde hair. "Wow, I have some competition on my hands. Perhaps I'll hire you one day to coordinate some society events."

I no longer pay attention to what is happening between these two. My imagination runs wild with thoughts of the future. Planning events for the Ashworth family would be a career I'd happily work for the rest of my life.

"Anyway, as long as you'll be in attendance at the party," Vanessa says to Beau, stepping forward to once again touch his arm, "it'll be a great time. You will go, won't you?"

He shrugs and his face strains, trying not to grimace. "I dunno. I said I'd think about it."

"So non-committal." Vanessa turns her attention back to me. "Tell him to come to my party."

Beau's hand slips onto the middle of my back. "If I can bring Ava, it's another story."

"*Oof.*" Vanessa winces like she's on the brink of giving bad news. "Sorry, sweetie. It's a closed invite list. Only Ashworth relatives and executives and their families. Your dad is just middle management, right?"

She says it like I should feel ashamed. "Yes, he chose to step down."

"I'm glad he made the right choice for your family." Her eyes flick between Beau and me. "Convince him for me, will you?"

At that, she saunters back to the fence where her friends sit and chat.

Beau's arms tighten around his middle. "Ah. I don't think she meant how that sounded."

I shake my head. "It doesn't matter. You can hang out with her if you want."

"No, I'm good. She called me over when I got here," he replies. "She's over there with her brother's girlfriend."

I lean around a group of boys who block my view. "Oh yeah, her. She was the talk of the school."

"Yeah, but as usual, all news fades quickly at Ashworth Academy."

I nudge him. "Yeah. Everyone is always onto the next legendary thing Beau Stevenson did."

He splutters a laugh. "Legendary? No one is calling me that."

My eyes widen. "Do you really not know? It's like you have a cult following."

Beau rubs his forehead, frowning. "Well, I shouldn't."

It warms my heart to see him realize how wrong the torment is he puts others through.

"I never wanted a legendary status," he says. "Everything snowballed into bigger and worse things."

Hope tingles in my body. "Snowballs melt."

A smile brightens Beau's face. "That's a positive spin."

"All I want to see is the good in you."

He nudges me. "Is that your Christmas wish?"

I brush the loose hair off the side of my face. "It'd be a miracle if you were no longer known as a bully."

His lips press into a smile and his head tilts. "Do you still think I'm a bully?"

I bite my bottom lip and then sigh. "It's a little soon to forget it all."

He stands taller and nods. "That's fair."

My hand plants on his arm. "I want to, though. I want to forget that part of you."

His hand slips over mine. "I'll try to be better. For you."

My heart pounds to a fast yet steady beat. I rub my lips together, panning my eyes down to his hand. Heat prickles under my skin as my urge to lock my hands with his heightens. As butterflies intersperse inside me, my eyes flick to the side in order to calm my nerves. As my gaze wanders through the crowd, two people bring on a new wave of anxiety.

Frantically, I pat Beau's arm. "Come this way with me."

"Huh? What?"

I turn to him, panic-fueled adrenaline making my eyes pop. I pat his arm harder. "Move away with me."

Without further explanation, Beau takes my hand and allows me to lead him away. We slink into the crowd and move towards the concession stand. I tug on his hand as I hide behind a slide pillar.

"Umm, not that I don't love sneaking away with you," he utters, "but why are we hiding?"

My chest heaves, and I pant as I peer around the corner.

Beau hones in on the uniform and hisses. "Oh crap, Sheriff Lennon is here. You're not hiding from him, are you?"

"Mhmm."

Beau smirks. "Why? Did you change your personality and break a law?"

"You don't see who he's with?" I whisper anxiously. "He's Ciara's dad."

"Sheriff Lennon is her dad?"

"I can't let him see me," I whisper, watching him move through the crowd. "Sheriff Lennon and my dad are good friends. I told my dad I was hanging with the girls, and I don't want him to freak out about us being together. I only hope that Ciara doesn't narc to her dad."

"Would she do that?"

Annoyance flares my nostrils. "She's a squealer. Her dad programmed her that way."

"Well, don't worry. I don't want him seeing me, period. Lennon has it in for me."

I deadpan him. "Has it in for you? That means you did something wrong."

"Why does everyone say that?" Beau leans against the concession stand wall. "Why does it matter if Lennon sees us? There are tons of people here. It's not a story if we're at the same event."

"Sheriff Lennon is Dad's confidant. Dad believes anything he says and thinks he's the world's best parent. Ciara's dad is super strict with her. That's why she's so skittish. He comes home from work and tells her horror stories so she won't do anything wrong."

Beau laughs. "Horror stories from sleepy Victoria Falls? He'd be stretching the truth when his shifts involve confiscating my skateboard and spray can."

My lips quirk. "Not that you were doing anything wrong."

He winks. "Of course not. Since when has your dad been friends with him?"

I sigh, leaning against the wall next to him. "Since Mom's accident. Sheriff Lennon was first on the scene."

"Oh." He pauses for a beat too long. "That makes sense why they're so close."

"Mmm. Yeah."

"And the same with you and Ciara."

"We're close because our parents want us to be friends."

"Does that mean you're not really friends?"

"I've never felt that close to her." I turn and look into his soulful eyes. "I've never had a close friend besides you."

His smile slips to the side and his hand scoops mine. I smile, running my fingers over his. His fingertips are rough in places, and I explore the ridges and bumps of his veiny hand.

"What about the other girls?" Beaus asks. "Don't you want to be friends with them?"

I nod. "Sure. it's just always hard to knock down my walls."

"I get that."

"Maybe it's easier with you because of our history?"

"Even after it's been so long?"

I smile. "Yeah. I mean, you know that. You opened up so much to me."

"I guess I've been waiting to talk to you all this time."

With a happy sigh, I rest my head on his shoulder as the sounds of the next quarter ring out around us.

"The coast is probably clear," he whispers. "Do you want to venture out?"

I snuggle closer to him. "Nope."

He laughs and clutches my hand tighter. "So, your dad is expecting you home after the game?"

"I have a ten o'clock curfew."

"We could get out of here," he suggests. "I could get you home in time. Your dad never has to know you left the field."

My heart pounds with wondrous excitement. "Where would we go?"

He shrugs as a bashful glint sparkles in his eyes. "I don't know. Anywhere."

I lift my head. "I guess we can't very well stay by this wall all night."

"Well, we could," he jokes, "but I don't know how fun it would be."

I bite into my lip, tugging him back into the open. "Wouldn't you make it fun?"

He grins back at me with nervous excitement. As we wander into the cheering crowd, our hands break apart, just in time for someone to yank Beau aside.

"Mr. Stevenson," Vice Principal Franklin says in his deep, booming voice. "Nice to see that school spirit we talked about is kicking in."

I stop behind Beau as he replies, "I'm just here to watch the game. There's nothing else to it."

"I believe you, Beau," Mr. Franklin says. "I've received impressive feedback on you this week. No class disruptions, finishing your homework, and no one has sent you to my office." Mr. Franklin roughly pats Beau's shoulder. "Keep it up. I have faith in you."

As Mr. Franklin walks further into the crowd, my mouth falls open. "Whoa."

Beau turns to me and shrugs. "I know."

I smile brightly at him. "Good work."

He smiles back, giving me a wink. "Thanks."

As we move between groups of people watching and cheering for the football game, I spy on the friends I'm supposed to be hanging out with.

"Where did you run off too?" Hilary asks as I approach.

"Umm." I look behind me and almost trip over my feet when Beau has vanished. I look back at Hilary, Lucy, and Ciara with a dumbfounded expression. "Nowhere."

Disinterested, Lucy turns away and chats to a tall and lanky boy. I recognize him as Teddy Wilkins who wants his band to play at the Christmas dance.

"Hi Ava," Ciara says with a wave.

I remind myself to be nice. "Hey. I saw your dad earlier."

She nods. "Yeah, he dropped me off. He got a call about possible underage drinking, so he's patrolling the area."

My chest constricts. "So he's still here?"

"Probably."

Before I can spiral into panic, Lucy grabs my arm, yanking me forward.

"Teddy has some new Christmas covers ready," Lucy says, bouncing with enthusiasm. "Want to see?"

"Oh, sure," I say, regaining my balance. "Hi Teddy."

"Hey there," he replies, handing me an earpiece. When I secure it in my ear, he hits play on a recording on his phone.

It's a high energy cover of "Jingle Bell Rock." It's electro dance music that conjures up images of sweaty bodies in night clubs.

When the clip finishes, Teddy taps on the screen in anticipation. "So? What do you think?"

"It's a well-made song, but I don't think we need a rave vibe," I say, handing back the earpiece. "It can feel cozy. Like you're home with family and friends."

"Home?" Confusion covers his face. "What are you talking about? The point of a school dance is getting out of the house and having crazy fun."

"It's not prom," I counter. "I just think that the Christmas dance should feel different from other events. Like, I dunno, more wholesome?"

A bunch of screwed up faces stare back at me.

I sigh and slouch in defeat. "It was just an idea. If you want it to have a more electric feel, that's fine. The entertainment isn't up to me, anyway."

"Well, that's not true," Lucy says with a pout. "We have to agree on things together."

"And, technically," Hilary says, wincing, "you are in charge, Ava."

I wave my hands in front. "I'm not a dictator. It's fine. Everyone is allowed an opinion."

"Sullivan and I are still working on things," Teddy says. "When we have everything ready, we can do a quick rehearsal."

"Sounds great," I reply.

Lucy grabs a hold of Teddy's arm, bouncing as she places the earpiece in and hits play on another recording.

Hilary leans in and says into my ear, "I think she's over her footballer crush."

I smile, watching Lucy's eyes twinkle as she gazes at Teddy.

When Hilary's attention pulls back to the field, cupping her hands around her mouth as she cheers for our team, and Ciara joins Lucy in gushing over Teddy's music, I back away, searching for Beau.

"Hey." His breath tickles my ear as his hands land on my shoulders from behind.

I jolt and turn around, bumping my chest against his. "Hi. Where'd you go?"

"I was just hanging to the side. I could still hear you guys. I just didn't want to interrupt," he says. "They look like they wanted to catch up with you. I didn't want every question to be about why I was there."

I brush my thumb across his cheek and gently ask, "You held back because you saw Teddy?"

"I didn't want to start anything."

"What's your beef with him, anyway?"

He shrugs, agitated. "It's a long story."

"We've got time."

"I don't want to get into it." His hand runs the length of my arm. "I'd rather just have a nice time with you."

"And we can't have that if you tell me what happened?"

He blows out a hard breath. "Okay, I'll tell you. Let's just go someplace quieter."

I nod. "Deal."

He takes my hand and leads me away from the crowds. We walk along a path that takes us behind the stand. Watching his tall, casual strides and broad physique has me beaming. Not long ago, this walk would have had me cowering in fear. Now, I'm buzzing with giddiness. Despite the racing thoughts in my head, I know I want to be alone with him. I'm busting to get closer to Beau, and be free from everyone else's distractions.

Beau pushes on a metal door that creaks open and then pulls me inside. We walk underneath the stacked seating and muffled voices. Beau leans against a structural beam, readjusting his beanie. Still clutching his other hand, my thumb rubs against his knuckles.

"It was a little crowded out there," Beau says, looking at my hand in his.

"Yeah," I say with a little shiver. "It's nice to have this empty space."

"Are you cold?" Beau opens his jacket and pulls me in for a hug.

I giggle as his jacket envelopes me. My face rests against the soft material of his hoodie, and I swear I hear the steady thumps of his heart. "Thanks."

Beau mumbles a laugh. "No problem."

He lifts my chin with his thumb and index finger. As I meet his eyes, my lips wet. His hand moves to the side of my face and he tucks my hair behind my ear.

"You were still pushing for a cozy, neighborhood vibe. You really miss the old parties, huh? The neighborhood potlucks your mom hosted?"

I blink my eyes, feeling my lashes moisten. "Don't you?"

His smile is small as he nods in agreement.

"I can't replicate what my mom used to do." A heaviness weighs inside me. "But... I just thought maybe I could bring some nostalgia into this year's Christmas dance."

Beau's hand caresses the back of my head. "Isn't your dad proud of the work you're putting into the dance? Why wouldn't he feel the same way if you organized a street party?"

I shrug in his embrace. "Because it'll remind him of Mom. Even when our neighbors offered to host, he couldn't bear to see a party come to life in our cul-de-sac."

"But it's not fair," Beau murmurs, resting his hand on the back of my neck. "Why should you suffer too?"

"It's hard to remember her," I whisper. "I get where my dad is coming from."

"Me too. But he should also be thinking about you."

"After everything you told me about your parents, you know it's not that easy."

Beau frowns, sighing. As if on instinct, our arms squeeze tighter around each other.

I smile as his chest rises and falls. My hands move along his shoulders and I clasp my hands behind his neck. I lift my head, looking up and into his eyes. They appear darker here.

"Why were you attacking Teddy and Sullivan that day?"

He frowns and then rests his head against mine. "Because I was angry."

I don't respond and instead wait for him to continue.

After a long pause, he adds, "They messed with me and I wasn't going to take it."

It takes me aback. "What did they do?"

He pulls his head back to give me a view of his sincerity. "They hacked into the school portal and manipulated my grades."

My jaw drops. "They did what? How..."

Beau shakes his head, astonished. "No clue how they did it, but I knew they were capable. At Vanessa's welcome home party, she said she had the boys snoop around school files so she could keep updated on what was happening while she was overseas."

"Do you think she gave them passwords or something?"

"Maybe. I just know I need my grades to stay strong or I'm not getting out of this town. I'd rather they beat me up than ever do what they did."

"Why did they do it? Did you provoke them first?"

He winces. "They obviously wanted revenge. Before I got suspended, I sabotaged some equipment in the AV room and it messed up a presentation they were doing. I don't know why I did it, I was just bored. And then I got into that fight..."

"Everyone was talking about that fight," I say, disappointed. "You were against three guys on the football team. They are royalty while games are on. You had to know it'd be headline news."

"Yeah, well, that's what I wanted my parents to be upset about. Not my grades."

"How did you find out your grades had changed?"

"I knew what grades I got before being suspended, and then my parents got notified that I failed two assignments. They were pissed, which didn't faze me, but I didn't plan it. Because I was suspended, I needed those assignment marks, or I'd be screwed. Believe it or not, there's a method to my madness."

"Were your grades fixed?"

His jaws strains. "I'm working on it. After I confronted Teddy and Sullivan that morning, I went to my teachers about the grades. The first teacher didn't hear me out, and instead I got a lecture. That was followed by an even long-winded lecture from Mr. Franklin."

"He said being on the committee could help with your grades."

Beau rolls his eyes. "Not that I'd need it if they'd just fix them. They're holding them hostage until the committee is over."

My heart squeezes and I hug my middle. "You feel forced to be on the committee?"

"Ava, no." His hands land on my shoulders and run down my arms. "Being on the committee has turned out to be the best. How else would I get the honor of being around you?"

I snort a laugh and push his hands off. "Oh, stop."

"Mr. Franklin says my grades will be restored after the school dance. If I can get back on the wrestling team, that'll help too." He huffs, looking off to the side. "Those boys should've known better than to come after me."

"I'm sorry that they messed with you. It sucks you lost grades you worked hard for." I blow out a breath. "But when I saw you grab them both... It was scary, Beau. I wish you wouldn't retaliate like that."

"I don't know any other way to get my point across."

"You just said Teddy and Sullivan shouldn't have come after you. Perhaps practice what you preach."

He blows out a breath, hitting his head against the beam. "*Ouch.* But, ah, I guess you're right, Aves."

I stroke my thumb against his chin. "Of course I'm right."

He looks down at me with a pleased smile. "Last week, if someone told me I'd be this close to you, I'd have called them a liar."

I shiver against him, letting out a faint laugh. "Same here."

"I don't want to do anything to mess this up." A serious strain tugs at his face. "I don't want to push you away."

"Just always be honest with me."

"I've been thinking about leaving Victoria Falls for so long," he whispers. "Now, with you back in my life, I don't feel like running."

"Unless we run away together."

His smile grows ridiculously handsome. Oh boy. I can't stand not knowing what those lips taste like.

His hands press into my back. "Have you ever thought about traveling the world?"

"No, but I think I'd love planning a trip."

"Maybe I don't have to stress about college. Maybe there's another way to get out of here."

"College was my endgame too," I reply. "But it was a finish line to make my dad happy. I've never felt such tingles about my own future."

"Maybe because it's unknown."

I rise on tippy toes and cup his jawline. "I like the sound of unknown."

His arms secure me close, and his eyes watch me with steady focus. "I wouldn't blame you if you thought about a future without me in it."

"Every time we've been together, either alone or with a group, you've stuck up for me." My smile grows as the pitter-patter of my heart gains speed. "Even when I haven't wanted you to, you've had my back. At this moment, I can't fathom pushing you away."

A nervous twitch breaks his focus. "You were scared of me."

I lift higher on the balls of my feet, edging my lips closer to his. "But you're trying to be better."

He gulps, rubbing lips together.

My lips pout and my eyes fall shut. In one fluid movement, I push my lips against his. His hands press into my back, and my arms wrap around his neck. Electricity pulsates throughout my body. As Beau's lips pull apart, sucking against mine, my body feels as if it can lift into the air.

I grip onto Beau's jacket, driving further intensity into the kiss. A hunger takes over me, like I'll be deprived of life if I remove my lips. His arms fasten around my middle back as he lifts my body against his. As our lips remain suctioned together, Beau hugs me close, stepping backward to lean against the structural beams.

Beau slouches against the beam, letting my feet touch the ground. My hand brushes against his cheek as I tease his bottom lip. His arms loosely hug around me, and his hands settle against my low back. His knees bend, allowing me to stand tall and taste every passionate moment of our kiss.

In one long, gradual movement, my lips suck and pull at his full lower lip. With a sensual pop, I release his lip and move down to his jawline. Taking in the earthy aroma of his cologne, I nibble at his jawline as he moans.

As I move away, I'm light-headed. "Wow," I mumble.

Beau anchors himself against the beam. His chest heaves. "Wow."

As his arms release me, I giggle, fanning my face.

I run a hand over my hair, biting into my lip as I grin. "So..." I curl a lock of hair around my index finger. "Do you still want to hang out tomorrow?"

He pushes off the beam and leans into me. "Are you kidding? I can't get enough of you."

I giggle and caress the side of his face. "I can catch the bus into town. The earliest I can get to Main Street on a Saturday is nine-thirty."

"Don't be silly. I can drive you."

"No way. My dad will be home. I can't risk him seeing you."

"Can't you say you're catching the bus but get in my car instead? Your dad will never know."

"Sometimes he walks me to the bus stop. If he insists, there's no getting rid of him."

Beau groans, sending his gaze to the bench seats above. "Ugh. Fine. I'll meet you at Main Street."

I giggle, cupping his face and drawing his eyes back to me. "We'll have all day to pick up where we left off."

A moan sizzles out of Beau. "I can't believe I've kissed you. That was a long time coming."

Surprise takes over my expression. "Really?"

Nervousness creeps over him. "I've wanted to for a long time. You had to know I sneak looks at you whenever I can."

I shake my head, feeling the heat of embarrassment coats my neck. "No. Why would I know that?"

Beau mumbles a laugh, bending his knees and nuzzling his nose against mine. "I guess I always thought it was obvious I was obsessed with you."

My heart throbs. I run my hands down to his shoulder. "You're obsessed with me?"

Beau winces. "I hope that didn't come off as creepy. *Ha.* I haven't stalked you, I've just always looked out for you. I've wanted you back in my life on any level. But kissing you... Man. I never thought this part would come true."

"I never thought I'd be so ecstatic to be kissing you," I say, shaking like a leaf. "But, oh my goodness, I'm so freaking happy we did."

Beau grins, running a hand into my hair. The way his lips pout has me energized. Nervous excitement swells inside me, anticipating another kiss.

Inside my pocket, my phone buzzes. I break out of the spell I share with Beau and retrieve my phone. It's a message from Lucy asking where I am and checking if I still need a ride home.

"Oh boy," I murmur. "Looks like time's up."

Beau's arms curl around me, tugging me closer. "Not if we stay here all night."

I giggle. "I'd love to, but Dad gave me a strict curfew. If I'm home late, I'll have a slim chance of going out on another Friday night."

Beau unravels his arms in defeat. "Okay, we won't risk it."

I lift onto my toes and kiss his cheek. "Thanks."

With my hand still in his, we emerge from beneath the bleachers. As we turn toward the parking lot, I skid to a stop. Inside, my gut squeezes and my legs turn to jelly. Sheriff Lennon's heavy footsteps make their way toward us.

"Ava, sweetie, I didn't see you earlier." The glee in his grin fades as he notices Beau to my left. "Beau Stevenson. Well, this is a surprise."

Beau drops my hand and lifts his in a wave. "Hi Sheriff. Have a good shift?"

"It was fine, son," Sheriff Lennon says. "Did you kids enjoy the game?"

My throat has run dry, so I nod. Oh geez. I think my mouth is hanging open. I hate the way Sheriff Lennon is scrutinizing us like he's analyzing clues at a crime scene.

"Yeah, one team won," Beau jokes.

Sheriff Lennon smiles with a silent chuckle. "Ava, it's been awhile since I caught up with your dad. Tell him I'll stop by tomorrow."

I stiffen as my blood drains to my feet. "Mhmm."

"Have you seen Ciara?" Sheriff Lennon asks. "I can give you a ride home."

I clear my throat, hoping I have volume left in my voice. "Lucy's driving me. They should be headed this way."

"Okay. Get home safe."

Sheriff Lennon waves again, walking toward the stands.

I'm about to plummet to the ground from sheer light-headedness. I cup a hand over my mouth, dry heave, and then race towards the parking lot.

Beau hurries behind me, clutching my shoulder as he catches me on the footpath. Panting, I stop, letting his hands massage the stressed muscles in my shoulders.

"Hey," Beau coos, stroking a circle on my back. "It's okay."

"He saw us," I mumble, staring at the cement path with glassy eyes. "He'll tell my dad."

Beau shushes me, stroking my hair and turning me around to face him.

"There's nothing to tell," he whispers. "He didn't see anything."

I shudder, propping my head against his shoulder.

"Aves," he whispers, pressing his hands against the sides of my face and propping my head up. "It'll be okay. Trust me."

I stare into his eyes, tinted by the night, and find the sincerity I've become accustomed to. I pout, gently closing my eyes, and he reads my thoughts perfectly. With a sensational pressure, his lips envelop mine. I hold onto the front of his jacket, still feeling like I could keel over. Our kiss is short, knowing how easily others could see us.

With a sigh, Beau leans his forehead against mine. "I should go."

I haven't opened my eyes yet, and nod in agreement.

"Keep your laptop on tonight," Beau whispers. "I'll send you a message through the portal."

Beau pulls away from me as footsteps sound behind me. Over my shoulder, Lucy bounds our way.

"Ready to go?" she asks me.

I step away from Beau, telling her yes.

As I follow Lucy towards her car, I meet Beau's eyes in one final act of goodbye. I press my fingers to my lips and then send the kiss in his direction.

As he backs away to his car, a cheesy grin lights up his face. He snatches the invisible kiss and pats it against his heart.

I'm a melting mess inside.

Fifteen

"You don't have to walk me to the bus stop," I say as innocently as possible. "Every day I walk to school alone."

Dad smiles, pinching my cheek. "I know, sweetheart."

I pull my face away, slipping out of his grip. "*Dad.*"

Dad chuckles. "Every kid can't wait for the chance to feel like an adult. I need to go into town, anyway. Why not go together?"

I almost choke as the realization hits me. "You're taking the bus too?"

Dad looks at me strangely. "Why do you look so surprised?"

I rub between my eyebrows, squinting. "Ah, no I'm not. I just didn't realize I'd get to go into town with you."

Dad smiles again, looping an arm around my shoulders. "Aw, there's my girl. It'll be nice to get some extra time together."

"Sure."

"Especially after the hiccups we had this week. I feel like you've been pulling away from me."

"No, I haven't," I blurt, closing off my body language. "Last night was really important for..." I trail off. Bringing up Beau right now is unfathomable.

Dad kisses the top of my head. "As long as the lines of communication stay honest, everything will be fine, sweetheart."

I gulp. "Yes, Dad."

I dawdle my way to the bus stop. Dad repeatedly tells me to pick up my feet. On the bus, I'd totally believe it if someone told me it was a rollercoaster, because my stomach keeps flipping.

My dad spends the trip prattling on about his errands, but I'm too on edge to pretend to listen. Beau is waiting for me at the Main Street bus stop. He'll be standing right by the front door and be greeted by my dad.

I'm dead.

I'll never see daylight again.

Should I just come clean? Will it make the inevitability easier to accept?

Sweat greases my palms. I shudder against the vinyl seat and hug my torso tight.

"Cold, sweetheart?" Dad asks.

"Just a little. I'm fine."

"That's the problem with these sunny days," Dad says, staring out the window at the sky. "Sometimes they end up being colder than the overcast days."

My insides spasm as Dad's eyes stay glued to the window scene. He could see Beau out there. What if he recognizes his car? What if Beau is walking along a footpath?

Oh boy. I cannot handle this. I'm ten seconds away from puking all over myself.

As the bus slows toward our stop, panic has me tapping on my dad's arm.

"What is it?" he says, clutching my hand.

My mind whirs into overdrive. "My friends."

His eyebrows lift with surprise. "Yes?"

"Uh..." I stammer. "I think I see them ahead. Can I get off the bus ahead of you?"

There's a softness surrounding his eyes and a proud curve to his smile. "It's so nice to see you excited to be around the other girls." He leans in, the pride faltering as concern breaks through. "They are treating you well? Are you being excluded or ridiculed?"

I swallow roughly as sweat beads around my hairline. "No, Dad. I just want to catch up with them before they leave for the party supplies warehouse."

Dad scoots off the seat and takes a step back in the aisle. "After you, sweetheart."

I leap from the seat, peck Dad's cheek, and hurry along the aisle. "Love you. See you at home."

It's not the first day I've met Dad, so I know he won't be giving me that much space. He'll want to speak with "the girls" before I leave the bus stop. I just need five to ten seconds to signal for Beau to scram.

Shivering, I hold on to the adjacent seats as the bus comes to a complete stop. Pushing my way forward, my heart cries out. Through the windows, I search for blonde hair and piercing blue eyes.

My heart pounds against my ribs at the sight of him. Beau leans against the bus shelter, arms folded, and one foot crossed behind the other. He looks so freaking handsome. Yet, at this moment, he couldn't be more dangerous.

With my hand positioned on a straight edge, I swipe it across my throat. Inside my head I'm screaming, *"Abort! Abort!"*

It takes a moment for Beau to notice me. At first, he smiles like a kid on Christmas morning. When he notices my less than subtle hand movement, and the fear rampant in my eyes, his expression becomes serious. His eyes narrow at the bus, and he backs away.

As I move down the steps off the bus, breathing becomes difficult. I shove my hands in his direction, hoping he takes the hint to run.

He does. He breaks into a jog, moving farther away from the bus stop.

As Beau runs, I turn around, waiting for my dad to disembark the bus.

"Everything okay?" he asks, stepping off the bus.

"I don't think it was them," I say, hoping he doesn't look around our immediate area.

"Do you want me to wait with you?"

"No, we weren't planning to meet here. We were planning to meet at the warehouse, so I'll walk over there. I guess I just got over excited and thought I saw them."

Dad smiles and wraps his arms around me. "Be safe, okay? I want you to have fun, but I want you to stay vigilant. You know these girls can lead you astray."

"Dad, they're all honor students like me. I'll be fine."

Dad pulls out of the hug, giving me the protective look. "They might be smart girls, but they're boy crazy. That Hilary is one wrong step away from being a bad influence."

"I'll be careful, Dad," I say, stepping backwards. "I promise."

Dad smiles and nods. "Good girl."

My stomach is cramping. I ensure Dad disappears around the opposite corner before I make my way to the party supplies warehouse. I take deep breaths to settle my nerves, but it's hard work against the cold breeze. I rub my knitted gloves together and hike my scarf over my chin, hoping to raise my body temperature. Every step towards the warehouse gets more tiresome. It's like there's a hand gripping my shoulder, tugging me backward. I'm convinced my father is still watching me, burning holes into my back.

As light snowfall tumbles down from above, the large warehouse comes into view. I shiver at the grandeur. I've spent weeks dying to go inside, and now that the moment has arrived, I'm terrified.

My dad is in town and skeptical of what I'm up to. All I want is to decorate the gym with a homey feel. But today isn't just about turning that dream into a reality. Beau is here. The boy I'm not supposed to spend time with. The boy I'm not supposed to be developing strong feelings for. The boy I wasn't supposed to be kissing last night.

As those kisses replay in my mind, my steps hasten. My heart beats faster, pumping blood that fills my arteries with a happy warmth. My lips rub together, trying their best to relive the taste of his lips. I can't believe I get to spend more time with him alone.

My heart skips a beat.

I can't believe he's here.

Beau leans against the entryway, his black beanie sits over his sandy blonde hair. When he spots me, his grin slips to the side. I melt as he pushes off the wall and moves toward me.

"Ah..." Beau draws out the word, throwing his hands up. "What was that about back there?"

"My dad," I respond as humiliation spawns inside me. "He joined me on the bus and I was terrified of him seeing you."

"I can stick up for myself."

"I'm aware."

Beau shifts his weight from side to side. "But that wouldn't be helpful, I guess."

"I didn't want my dad to freak out and force me back home," I explain. "I didn't want today to be ruined."

A pink hue highlights Beau's cheeks as small flakes of snow land on his face. "Would today be ruined if you didn't get to hang out with me?"

I bite into my lip and will my middling confidence to shine through. "Yes."

Beau runs a hand down the sleeve of my coat. "Aww, Avie."

I giggle, cupping a hand over my face. "Shut up."

His hand lowers, grasping mine. "It's okay. I'd be pretty heartbroken if I didn't get to hang out with you today."

I uncover my face to look deep into his soulful blue eyes. "Heartbroken?"

Beau pats his hand over the space above his heart. He flinches and emits a mock grunt of pain. When I giggle at his antics, he steps in close and drapes an arm around me. "Come on," he says. "Let's get out of the cold."

We walk into the warehouse and I'm in awe at the sheer size. The steel-framed ceiling clears thirty feet tall, and despite the galvanized walls, this place is anything but cold. The entrance greets us with small Christmas themed displays, and further back aisles of tall shelving house fun, colorful, and glitzy items. As I peer toward the very back of the warehouse, the corners of my mouth quirk. The green tips of Christmas trees have me so excited, my feet might lift off the ground.

"Can I help you?" asks a woman in a stylish red blazer and A-line skirt. A perfect bun sits on her head, and two dainty bells dangle from her earlobes.

"Yes, please," I reply. "We're here from Ashworth Academy to order supplies for the Christmas dance."

"Oh, yes," the salesperson says, stepping behind a desk. "I was expecting someone to come by earlier in the week."

"We tried," I reply. "Just other tasks got in the way."

The salesperson hands over a clipboard with an order sheet and an attached pen. "There are product numbers listed on the labels. Write down the number and quantity. We'll have them dispatched to the school on Friday."

I take the clipboard, thinking it sounds too easy. "That's all we have to do?"

She nods. "Uh-huh. Write down your name and contact info. That way, if we can't stock your required quantity, we can get in touch regarding alternatives."

"Okay, sounds good."

The salesperson smiles, looking at Beau and me. "Do you need help? Or prefer to look around by yourselves?"

Beau slings an arm around me, replying, "We got this."

I wave to the salesperson. "Thanks for your help."

Beau guides me away from the front desk and we head towards the tall aisles filled with Christmas decor.

"This place is freaking huge," Beau comments.

"Before the committee meetings started, I would dream about coming here."

"*Ha.* Are you serious?"

"Totally," I cheer. "I've had the same ornaments at home since I was a kid. This place has everything. I can't wait to go through it all."

Beau grins, lifting his arm off me. "Well, don't let me stop you. Shop till your heart's content."

I look at him sideways. "Aren't we doing this together?"

"This is your thing. You just tell me how I can help, and I'll be right alongside you."

"Okay, hold this," I say, giving Beau the clipboard. I dip my hand inside my bag and reef out my binder. "I have my master list of everything we need."

Beau mumbles a laugh. "Of course you do."

I skim through the binder and land on the map I drew with Beau when the group set our dance theme. "I'm still working out what crates I want for the food and beverage area."

Beau snaps his fingers and then points off to the right. "What about something like that? They have that kind of rustic look you were talking about."

My heart flutters. Not only because he spotted them, but because he listened and remembered what I said. The crates have a barnyard feel, yet there's something chic about them. As we approach, I notice the smooth edges sanded into the wood. They have a walnut stain, and something stamped across the front.

Beau picks one up and grins. "*Ha.* Look at this."

He turns the box on the long edge. I smile at the words, *"North Pole Shipping Co Special Delivery,"* etched into the wood.

I squeal and clap. "Oh my gosh, they're perfect."

Beau lowers the crate to sit with the others displayed. "How many would we need?"

"They don't look sturdy or large enough to turn into tables. Perhaps we place a few beside the trestle tables? We could wrap some empty boxes as presents and sit them inside as decoration."

"Is your imagination just always running?"

I shrug, setting down my binder and taking the clipboard from Beau. "I dunno. I just like things to look special. My mom always said it's the little details that count."

I mark down the product number and that we need four. We only have so much budget. I need the majority for the trees.

Beau picks up my binder, flipping a page to get to my checklist. "What should we look for next?"

I trace my finger down the list, skipping the items highlighted in pink. Everything marked is already in the storeroom at school, such as themed tablecloths, door wreaths for the entrance, assorted ornaments, and twinkle lights.

I tap the twinkle lights. "Should we get more lights? What if some don't work?"

"After all the effort to untangle them, we should use them," Beau replies. "But on the other hand, you did almost break your leg in their presence."

I smirk. "Just a slight exaggeration."

"If you think we need more lights, then we'll get them."

"I also want to get some hanging garlands. It'd be cute if we could get large, glittery snowflakes," I say as we walk towards the other aisles. "But Hilary said we can't do anything that clashes with the winter formal."

"But Hilary's not in charge of the decorations."

I smile at the playfulness in his expression. "Perhaps we can find something else cute that fits our North Pole theme."

Beau gestures to the tall aisles ahead. "I think they have everything we could think of and more."

I slide my binder back into my bag, and Beau insists on holding the clipboard. He marks down the product code for some cute napkins and paper cups with cartoonish reindeer, candy cane, and Santa designs. We find strings of lights encased in green and red lanterns. We agree they'd make a good background frame for the food and beverage area.

When we get to the assortment of Christmas trees, I'm in heaven. I don't know what drove my fondness for Christmas trees, but something about being amongst a large bunch of them feels like stepping into a magical realm. I tilt my head back, staring up at the tall, wide, and fantastically green specimens.

Beau's laugh breaks me out of my spell. "Do you want a minute alone with them?" he teases.

I turn to him, grinning. "I want them all."

Beau clicks his pen, raising the clipboard. "How many can we get?"

"We want a lot for the maze, right?" I say, wandering along the assortment of trees. "They can't be too bulky. We only have so much room. People will pitch a fit if we take away space from the dance floor."

Beau gestures ahead. "What about those? They're tall but slim."

I walk a little further, finding a design where the branches stretch out a little wider. That way, we won't need as many to fill the space. Plus, there's more room for eye-catching decorations.

Beau lists the product numbers of three designs we like the most. The variety will create a realistic look when they're installed in the gym. We don't get equal quantities to keep with the natural feel, favoring the tall and slim design for most of our budget.

Close by the trees, we find the reams of white felt I had on my list. It'll make for a nice addition below the trees, running around each of them. I also rummage through decorations, finding boxes of pinecones, twigs, and golden berries to place on the fake snow.

Beau picks up a can of fake snow, tossing it in the air with a flick of his wrist and catching it with ease. "Is this on your list?"

I shake my head. "Where would we put it? There are no windows in the gym."

Beau reads the back label. "We could spray it round the door frames."

"Isn't it hard to clean? I don't want Mr. Riley to think we're vandalizing the school."

"*Ha.* You don't like the idea of me with a spray can?"

I bite my lip, apprehensive about my true feelings. "Not really."

Beau tosses the can back on the shelf.

My body seizes. "Did I just make you feel bad?"

He jolts, surprised. "What? No way."

I place a hand on my chest over my heart. "I wasn't implying you would graffiti the school."

He shrugs it off. "Don't worry about it. I won't do anything to ruin the dance. I wouldn't do that to you. I told you I want to be better."

My lips quirk, trying to hold a smile. "Okay."

Beau steps forward and hooks a finger under my chin. "I promise, Ava. I want to be better for you."

As I stare into his kind eyes, noting the way his honesty highlights the bright blue, I can't help but wet my lips. This moment is serene, despite the noise from other patrons and the Christmas carols playing. The intimacy of our closeness and our developing connection have my veins sizzling with electricity. His cologne plays at my nostrils and my hands twitch, ready to soar over his shoulders and into that beautiful head of hair.

Instead, Beau clears his throat and takes a step back.

Huh?

What went wrong?

Didn't he sense it was a perfect moment, too?

What about last night's kisses? Were they a mistake? Or was I more appealing last night? What did I do differently?

Why didn't he kiss me?

He half-turns, tilting his head up and then grasping my hand. "Do you hear that?"

Only the thumping of my heart. "Hear what?"

He turns back with an intrigued smile. "This song? Wasn't it your mom's favorite Christmas carol?"

My fingers interlock with Beau's as my ears prick to the sound of "Holly Jolly Christmas" by Michael Bublé. A cheesy grin stretches on my face, and any cringe-worthy confusion floats away.

"Your dad always annoyed her," I say, holding back a laugh. "He called him Michael Bubbly, and Mom would get so upset."

Beau throws his head back with a laugh. "Oh, that was so funny. Your mom made such a big deal about it."

My heart squeezes and then releases a wave of endorphins. "I love thinking about those moments with her."

Beau tugs on my hand, reeling me in. I push up against him and he raises our linked hands to shoulder level. He tosses the clipboard and sits his other hand snugly under my shoulder blade.

I look at him curiously. "What are you doing?"

"Dancing with you," he whispers, swaying with the beat of the song.

A clamminess sweeps over me. I look over my shoulder. "Here?"

"Sure, why not?"

"People will stare."

His eyebrows lift, and a carefree snort escapes him. "So?"

Hesitantly, my hand lifts and sets down on his shoulder.

Beau presses his forehead against mine. "Don't you want to dance with me?"

I grip Beau's shoulder and tension cements from my neck to my lower back. "I don't want anyone to laugh at me."

"Who would laugh?" he questions. "Besides, I'm here with you. I'll protect you from any meanies."

I sway my body with his, and soon our rhythm bounces along with the happy song. I can't help keeping my eyes off to the side. Whenever someone glances our way, it doesn't last long. They either give no reaction, or they smile and then move on. I breathe out with ease and relax my body against Beau.

Do people really not care? Or has Beau's reputation grown outside the walls of Ashworth Academy? Do people look away because of him?

His hand rubs against my back. "Are you okay?"

"Mhmm."

"You relax and then a moment later you seize up again." He stops moving. "We can stop."

I don't let go, keeping my body close to him. "No, I'm okay. Just thinking."

He sighs. "You're second guessing spending time with me."

"No, I..." I trail off, searching for the right words. I hunch, not wanting to lie to him. "Not too long ago, I was scared of you. Now I'm dancing with you."

His head rests against mine. "Don't you believe I want to change?"

I step back to see his face. "I do. I believe you."

His expression is blank. "So now what?"

My hand moves from his shoulder to the side of his face. "Now I choose to trust you."

I notice his jaw flex and he's holding something back. His lips strain as if he's in pain.

"What?" I murmur.

His eyebrows push together. "I thought I already had your trust."

I lower my hand from his face, my heart plummeting. "I'm sorry. I'm trying to stay positive, but I can't stop the thoughts in my head. The truth is... I really like you, Beau, and want you in my life."

Beau steps away from me and picks up the clipboard. "Should we get back to this?"

"No."

He double-takes at me.

"Schoolwork isn't my focus right now."

"What does that mean?"

I wet my lips. "You might think I'm not into you, but that's far from the case."

The clipboard slips from Beau's grip, and he fumbles to catch it.

"Beau," I say in a sultry tone I didn't know I had. "I want to kiss you."

The most adorable smile curves his lips. "Oh, you do, do you?"

"*Yes,*" I squeak as he moves backwards. "Why do you keep pulling away from me?"

Beau doesn't respond. He taps the edge of the clipboard to his chin and disappears out of the aisle.

I scoff. "*Beau.*"

I break into a jog to find him. I march into the next aisle and find him looking up.

"Uh-oh," Beau says.

I follow his gaze. "What?"

Above us is a cluster of green oval branches with sprigs of waxy berries. Even though I'm practically begging for a kiss, my face still morphs into a brighter shade.

"Mistletoe," Beau whispers, curling a piece of my hair around his finger.

I wish I'd braided my hair, because the back of my neck is so hot and sticky.

Beau winks, lifting the clipboard. "How many should we get?"

"We can't get any."

"Why? Scared there'll be too much kissing?"

I smirk. "Not me, it's the school. It's the one Christmas item explicitly not allowed."

"You're kidding?"

My shoulders jiggle in a silent laugh, and I shake my head.

"Well then," Beau says, smoothing back my hair. "We'd better make the most of our time under this bunch."

I glimpse around us for other people. Somehow, the mistletoe feels like a spotlight. "Here?"

Beau runs a hand through a luscious wave of his hair, and there's a sparkle in his eye as he sports a charismatic grin. "Oh, so you don't want to kiss me?" he teases.

"Stop it." I giggle.

He pops a knee, posing in front of me. "Stop what?"

I bite my fingernail and shy away from him. "Stop looking irresistible."

His smile creeps to the side, highlighting his dimples. "So, you do want to kiss me?"

I sigh. "Oh, shut up and kiss me."

He laughs and leans down as I loop my arms around his neck. We connect under the arch that homes the mistletoe and my toes curl from the first caress of his lips. My fingers run through his soft and polished hair. I smile in the kiss, feeling lucky I get to touch this boy that so many other girls swoon over.

Beau's hands run down my back and sit above my hips. As his suction increases against my lower lip, I lean in, ensuring him I'm fully into the kiss. I wonder if he feels lucky to be kissing me. I'm not exactly on most boys' top ten lists.

Our lips gradually break apart. Beau moans, rubbing his lips together. "*Dang.* I love kissing you."

My heartbeat has ramped up its acceleration, so I pant to catch my breath. "Really?"

"Heck yeah," he cheers. "Your lips are so supple and the way you move them is so sexy."

I cup a hand over my mouth, puffing out a nervous laugh in shock. "Sexy?"

He grazes his teeth over his bottom lip and nods. "Yep."

"No way. No one thinks I'm sexy."

"Good. I don't wanna fight off other dudes."

I giggle. "Stop it. You're so silly."

His arms wrap around my middle, lifting me in a bear hug. "I'm being serious, Avie."

My giggles tumble out of me. "*Eep*! Put me down."

"Why? I like holding you."

"Okay," I say, settling in his strong arms. "Just don't drop me."

He pecks my lips. "Never."

One of his arms slackens against me, and instinctively I tighten my arms around his neck. As he lifts his arm, I don't even slide down an inch. *Dang* this boy is strong.

Beau grabs the mistletoe and unhooks it from the arch. He smiles, holding the branches like a trophy. "We can't hang any in the gym, but that doesn't mean I can't take this one home as a souvenir."

"How much kissing will you be doing at home?"

He lowers me so my feet touch the ground. "Heaps, if you come back to my place."

My insides frazzle. "Your place? Me? With you?"

He smirks. "Yes, Yoda."

I swipe a hand across my brow, dabbing a few beads of sweat. "Oh, I just..."

"I didn't mean to rattle you," he says gently. "I was just hoping we could hang out a little longer."

"Will your parents mind?"

He shrugs. "They won't be home."

The beads of sweat quadruple.

He laughs. "I didn't mean it so we could fool around. They are never home. Like, I dunno. Don't you wanna crash and watch a movie?"

My heart flutters. "What kind of movie?"

"I know you, Ava Jones," he says proudly. "Sappy Christmas movie all the way."

The cheesiest grin stretches across my face. "With the corniest love story."

He winks. "Deal."

"I've never been inside your new house."

"I know. It's weird your parents never helped us move. They used to do everything together."

"It's all a blur. Everything around that time gets mixed in with the black hole of sad memories about my mom."

"I completely get that. Sometimes my whole life feels like a black hole."

I frown.

He smiles, grazing my cheek. "Until you came back into my life."

"Shall we finish up and get out of here?"

"Now look who's dying to go to my house," Beau teases.

"I just don't want to waste another minute."

He leans in, pressing his lips tenderly against mine. When he pulls back, his whisper is like a purr against my lips. "If the kisses keep coming, we won't waste any time."

I rub my lips together, tasting the kiss. "Mmm. Agreed."

"I know we are student chaperones for the dance," Beau says, "but, I was wondering, do you want to go as my date, anyway?"

My heartbeat pitter-patters. "Your date?"

"Yeah. It could be fun."

I glimpse around us and then send my focus to the blue of Beau's eyes. "I managed to dance with you in the middle of the store. I'm sure dancing with you in the gym will be sublime."

His eyebrows arch. "Is that a yes?"

"Yes!" I cheer. "I'd love to."

In a rush, he plants a kiss on me. His tongue traces my bottom lip.

He pulls away, rubbing his lips together. "Mmm. I think I've won the lottery."

Sixteen

Beau pulls into the driveway of an impressive two-story home. An inflatable Santa and Rudolf sit in the snow. Black cables run around the oak tree and along the house. Surely to have an impressive light display at night.

"Your home already reminds me of when you lived in the cul-de-sac," I say, marveling at the sight through my window. "I'm surprised your parents still do decorations after all the stories you've told me."

"Mom doesn't really get involved, but Dad still insists we set up everything each year."

I give him a tender smile. "I think that's lovely."

We exit the car and Beau leads me to the front door. Inside, he whips off his beanie and coat, hanging them on a coat rack. I peel off my gloves and scarf, and then Beau slides off my coat from behind.

"Thanks," I mumble, eyeing the opulence in the open-plan interior. I'd forgotten what expensive tastes his parents had. Whenever I went to Beau's for a playdate, it always felt like I could break something.

"Come on in," Beau says, stepping into the pristine living area.

"This place looks like a furniture store display. Does anyone actually live here?"

He smirks. "Not really. Like I've told you, my parents come home late most nights. When they are home, I'm usually downstairs."

"Downstairs?"

He points to a door. "My bedroom is in the basement. When we moved in, my parents wanted me to have a bedroom upstairs, but the basement has a living area, bathroom, and separate area for my bed. It's a huge space, and I wanted it for myself. I guess because I was so unhappy about moving, they gave it to me."

"Wow. It sounds like your own apartment down there."

He nods. "It is a good escape from my family."

From the back of the house, a thunderous scampering noise surges towards us. In the blink of an eye, a German shepherd barrels toward us.

Beau lowers to the ground, throwing his arms out wide. "Hey, buddy."

My heart hammers as the dog races to Beau, jumping up on him and licking his face.

"This is your dog?"

"Yep. This guy has been my best friend for the past two years," Beau says, kneeling down and lovingly patting the dog. "His name is Bruno."

I summon my courage and reach my hand towards the dog. "Hi Bruno." Bruno licks my hand, causing me to giggle. "He's massive. He's only two-years-old?"

"Yep," Beau says, looping his arms around Bruno's neck. "And don't worry, he said he's fine handing over the best friend title."

I scratch behind Bruno's ear. "Maybe Bruno and I can share the title."

Beau scruffs the dog's fur and then stands up. He clasps my hand and his smile makes me melt. "Maybe you can get a new title."

I bite into my lip, blushing. "And what title would that be?"

Nervousness ripples over his face. "Girlfriend?"

My hand tremors in his grasp. My heart pulses to an electrifying beat, and my knees are ready to give way.

Beau clears his throat and looks away. "I've freaked you out."

Goosebumps prickle over my skin as a mixture of ice and heat runs through my body. My mouth juts open, wanting to give him an answer, but the weight of the title has me stammering awkward noises that lead nowhere.

Beau puffs out a forced laugh. His hand is as clammy as mine as his grip squeezes and then releases. "It's nothing. Forget I said that."

As my hand lowers to my side, I watch him fidget and turn away from me. As he pats Bruno, my heart screams in its thunderous beats for me to say something. Clamminess builds across my hairline as I will myself to speak. Every time I open my mouth, it's like I'm gagged and muffled by an invisible force. I press my hand into my stomach, terrified that the mix of emotions running through me will make me puke.

"I..." It comes out of me shaky and fear-soaked.

Bent over, hugging Bruno, Beau looks up at me. His soft expression is calming and kind. He stands tall and runs a hand along my arm.

"It's okay," he soothes. "I shouldn't have said it. We should just move past it. Yeah?"

Worry crinkles across my face. I don't want to move past it. Or do I? Do I want to be his girlfriend? But what would that mean? Could I really go on every day, hiding this beautiful boy from my father? Could my heart take the lying and sneaking around?

"Ava?" Beau says, caressing the side of my face. "You look like you're spiraling. Take a breath."

"I..." It comes out just as shattered as before.

He hushes me with a gentle hum.

"But I..." It comes out less fragile, and I place my hand over his. "I want to..."

He stares into my eyes with purpose, waiting for me to continue.

I swallow hard, unsure of where my sentence will lead me.

"What?" he whispers, smoothing back my hair. "What do you want?"

"I..." I close my eyes and exhale. "I like you."

An anxious yet happy laugh mumbles out of Beau. I open my eyes to see smile lines framing his eyes.

"I like you too, gorgeous."

Another layer of goosebumps coats my limbs, and I summon all my strength to place a hand on his chest and slide it up to his shoulder.

"I mean..." I'm just audible. "I really like you."

He twirls his fingers inside my hair. His smile grows wider. He stays silent, waiting for me to say more.

A nervous giggle slips out of me. "I just don't know what it means."

Beau's hand slips down my back, and I shiver in the best possible way.

He tilts his head as his eyes fixate on mine. "You don't know what *what* means?"

I massage my hand across his shoulder. "We couldn't be together."

His hand presses into my back, and his strength sends me stepping even closer to him. I bite into my lip as only a slither of air stands between us. His body heat has my goosebumps fading.

"Avie," he whispers, drawing his fingers along my back. "We're together right now."

Sadness creeps over me. Instinctively, I wrap my arms around him, pressing my body against his. He rubs small circles on my back, cooing that it'll be okay.

"It's not what I meant," I complain, melting against his warm body. "Everything will be on the down-low. It'll be too hard to keep lying."

Beau buries his face in my hair. His breath tickles my neck. "Why would we have to lie?"

"Beau," I moan. "It won't work."

"But I love you."

Right then, my heart stops. My lungs seize and my body freezes in place. Love?

Is that the word I heard?

He loves me?

I inhale hard, and my heart pounds, begging to break free from my body. My arms pull back from his shoulders and I peel away from him. His arms loosen their grip around me, allowing me to look him in the eyes.

My mouth opens to utter the word, "What?" But nothing comes out.

My face must say it all because he looks at me with charming sincerity.

"Ava," he says with a quiver in his tone. "I've always loved you."

I manage to shut my drying mouth and awkwardly swallow.

One of his hands moves up my back and then cups my face. "I'm sorry," he says with a growing smile. "I can't hide it anymore."

My eyes well with joyous tears. "You love me?"

I turn to goo as his lips slide into that gorgeous lopsided grin as he nods his reply.

"My body has never dealt with so many feelings." I grab the material of his shirt for leverage. "You have me questioning everything. The only thing I know for sure..."

He waits, but only half a beat. His anticipation gets the better of him when he blurts, "What?"

"I don't want to run from you," I reply, pressing my hands into his shirt until I feel his defined muscular physique. "My heart's beating like crazy, and I know it's because all I can think about is you."

"Is it okay that I said..."

With urgency, I press my lips onto his, hoping the passion in my kiss will be all the reply he needs. Our arms wrap around each other. I hold on to him like I never want to let go. As my lips part, his tongue sneaks into my mouth. It's odd but tantalizing. Tingles rush down my back and my toes curl. My fingernails dig into him, and he moans against my lips.

I pull back, whispering, "Sorry."

The most delicious smile spreads across his lips. "Don't be. I liked it."

I blush, rubbing my lips together. "Oh."

His thumb swipes my cheek. "Who knew Ava Jones was such an amazing kisser?"

I giggle. "I am?"

"I'm addicted to your lips."

With that, I don't hold back. I pout my lips, pressing them against his with a wet slide. I welcome his tongue, giving it a playful flick with the tip of mine. His arms grow tighter around my middle and my feet lift from the ground. I squeak in our kiss as he walks me backward until my back hits the kitchen countertop.

My feet lower to the ground, I lean backwards, and Beau takes the lead. I love how he takes control, lowering his hands against my sides and teasing my bottom lip before he applies more pressure into the kiss.

I give myself over, tilting my head back and only moving my lips in reaction to his. He envelopes my lower lip with a powerful suction that makes my eyes roll backwards.

His kisses move along my cheek and then dip below my jawline. My heart throbs as his lips pinch the skin against my neck. It has me squirming for all the right reasons. The countertop cuts into my lower back, but I'm so enamored with Beau's sensual mouth, the pain numbs to nothingness.

"Oh, Beau," I moan, leaning back against the countertop and looping my arms around his neck. "I want to... I want to try."

His kisses move towards my ear. His warm breath hits my earlobe before he flicks it with his tongue. A sharp moan escapes me, and he sucks against the bottom of my ear.

"Oh crap," I hiss, squeezing my arm around him. "That feels so freaking good."

His breathy laugh hums against my ear.

I unclasp my hands and slide them beside his face. I tilt his head so he looks at me. "I'm yours," I whisper. "I want to be your girlfriend."

"Ava," he whispers, moving his mouth closer to mine.

I meet his lips with feverish need. Our tongues fight for control, and my toes curl when our legs intertwine.

Beau pulls back from my lips and moves his face beside mine. He pants against my neck as he hunches over my body.

I rub my hands between his shoulder blades, asking, "You okay?"

"Yeah," he pants, cupping the back of my head. "You just take my breath away."

"I can't believe how natural that all felt."

He moves back, pulling me off the counter. "So we're really trying this?" he asks. "We're official?"

"I don't know how it'll work," I admit as my face flames red, "but I'm willing to try. I don't want to give you up."

He plants a kiss on my forehead. "You have no idea how happy that makes me."

"Beau." Shaky trepidation rushes through my voice. "About what you said to me."

"You don't have to..."

"I..." I bite into my lip and squeeze my eyes shut. "I don't know why I can't."

"It's okay. You don't..."

"But I think I do." My heart hammers against my ribs. "I mean... I'd have to... The way I feel right now... I..." I open my eyes but wateriness blurs my vision. "It's just..."

Beau strokes my hair. Sadness dulls his eyes, but his small smile brightens his blue irises.

"My dad," I whisper. "Knowing he'll hate this has me paralyzed."

He pecks my cheek, resting his head against mine. "You don't have to say it. I already feel closer to you now more than ever."

I gulp, resting my chin against his shoulder. I wish I could say it. I want to, but love and Beau in the same sentence has me torn. Anytime I think of uttering those three words, my heart flat-lines. There's a powerful feeling in my gut, warning me to keep my guard up.

My body is at war. I want to be with him completely. To be deeply in love. Hopefully, time will help me grow into these feelings. I want the words to glide off my tongue.

Hmm.

My toes curl, reimagining the wonderful sensations brought on by the use of my tongue. I never knew I was capable of that kind of action. But, oh boy, am I glad I am. I can't wait to try it again.

Beau rubs my back and then moves out of our embrace. I smooth a hand against his face, and we exchange happy smiles.

"I know it'll be hard." Beau says, rubbing behind his neck. "You had me hide from your dad earlier this morning."

I draw out a hard sigh. "I know. Would it be terrible if we keep this relationship to ourselves? At least for a little while?"

Beau scoops my hand in his. "We can do that. I mean, I don't know how I'll stay away from touching or kissing you whenever I see you. But, initially, we can keep things on the down-low."

"My dad is scared of me being around any boy. It's not just you."

Beau frowns. "But my reputation doesn't help."

I wince. "No, not really."

Beau pecks my cheek. "Well, I don't care what anyone says. I just want to be with you."

"I don't want you taken away from me ever again."

"You know how we were reminiscing about your mom earlier," Beau says, rounding the kitchen bench.

I follow him. "Yeah?"

He leans against the counter. "Remember her awesome hot cocoa? I've never had one as good as she made it."

"She taught me how to make them." I look around the kitchen. "I practice every winter. I could make you one."

Beau's eyes light up. "Uh, yeah, that would be amazing."

I move toward the pantry. "Okay, let me raid your kitchen."

"Have at it."

I skim the shelves, locating cocoa powder, chocolate chips, vanilla extract, and marshmallows. Beau comments about not knowing half the stuff was in there because his parents don't cook. I find a pan, ignite a burner, and warm the milk on the stovetop. I cross my fingers, hoping I've memorized the ratios correctly as I add the ingredients. Beau watches over my shoulder, making "mmm" noises, so I take it I'm on the right track.

"I don't suppose you have any candy canes lying around?" I ask.

"No dice."

"I guess I'll have to make these another time, adding the special ingredients of whipped cream and crushed candy canes."

"Don't tell me that," Beau whines playfully. "It sounds way too good."

I finish up the gooey, chocolaty drink and pour the liquid into two mugs, stopping halfway to add the marshmallows and extra choc chips before filling to the top.

"That looks epic," Beau says as I hand him a mug.

I clink mine against his. "Cheers."

With a small sip to gauge the temperature, the sweet yet thick liquid glides over my tongue. Pleasure waves run through my body, and I smile as I swallow.

"Yep," Beau says after a slurp, "epic."

I giggle. "I'm glad you like it."

He lifts the mug back to his lips, remarking, "I'm glad Lydie taught you."

I smile as he takes another sip. "Me too."

Beau throws a thumb over his shoulder, pointing out the door to his basement bedroom. "Time for a sappy movie?"

I can't help glancing at the main living room. It's not like his parents will interrupt us if we stay on the first floor. However, I guess he won't get in trouble for having a girl down there if they aren't home to catch us.

"Are you freaking out again?"

I suck in a breath and shake my head. "No. Let's go."

He looks unconvinced. "Are you sure?"

I blow out a breath. "Yes. Lead the way."

Beau opens the door, and it leads onto a descending staircase. I follow him downstairs and land in a well-spaced area. There's a three-seater couch facing a large TV. Beside the staircase is the open doorway of a black and white-tiled bathroom. Next is his bedroom, housing a messy double bed.

At the rear is a sliding door. I smirk, assuming Beau uses this to sneak out and avoid his parents. Next to the TV, are three rows of shelves. Trophies, medals and ribbons lay on display. I cup my hot cocoa and edge toward the shelves, admiring the achievements in martial arts and wrestling. I open my mouth to comment, but behind me, the scampering of Bruno shatters my thoughts as he thunders down the stairs.

As I turn to take in the large dog, he bolts toward me. Before I can step aside, Bruno smashes into me. My mug topples, and a tsunami of hot liquid leaps out. I shriek as it splashes and spills onto my torso. The foamy milk soaks into my shirt and stings against my skin.

"*Bruno*," Beau scolds. He taps the dog on the hind and shoos him up the stairs. "Get out of here, you dumb dog."

As Beau and Bruno trample upstairs, I peel the drenched shirt off my torso. I wring the shirt into a moist clump, but the hot liquid drips onto my reddened belly. I hiss and grit my teeth, unable to bear another second. I yank the top over my head and let it land in a soaked mess on the floorboard.

"*Crap*," Beau yelps, rushing down the stairs. "Are you okay? Does it burn?"

"It stings," I say through gritted teeth.

Beau's hands land on me, turning me around and guiding me into his bathroom. He's swift to act, grabbing a fresh wash cloth and dosing it with cold running water.

He squeezes it and then presses it against my torso. "Here. This should help."

I draw out a slow breath. "*Oof.* That does feel better."

"I can't believe he did that," Beau says, letting go as my hands press over the cloth. "I'm so sorry."

I blow out another breath. "It's okay. It was a shock more than anything. At least the drink wasn't boiling hot."

Beau kneels down, opening the cupboard under the bathroom sink. "There's a gel in here somewhere that's good for burns. I used it last summer when I got a wicked sunburn."

He stands up with the tube in his hand. His eyes run the length of my shoulders to my hips and back. He clears his throat and sets the tube on the countertop.

"I'll let you apply it when you're ready," he says, backing away.

He walks away from the bathroom, fanning out his shirt.

I press the cold cloth against my stomach, asking, "Are you okay?"

"I just never pictured you wearing a black bra. It was getting hot in there."

As I look back at the bathroom mirror, my lips purse as I stifle a laugh.

"I'll get you something to wear," he says, moving toward his closet.

I press the cloth against my tender skin, and then set the damp cloth inside the sink. I crack open the top of the gel bottle and squeeze a portion out as Beau's footsteps near.

I apply the gel to my skin, and my jaw clenches in reaction. Beau steps into the doorway with a pullover hoodie draped over his arm.

"Does it feel better?" he asks with hope.

My lips pout as I take another quick inhale and slow exhale. In the mirror, I notice Beau's eyes following where my hand moves. He fidgets in place, settling against the door frame. His eyes stay fixed on the shower behind me.

"Is any of your skin raised?" he asks with concern. "Like it might blister?"

"I don't think so." I squeeze another splodge of gel into my hand.

As I rub the new gel layer over my skin, another throaty grunt rolls out of Beau. He shifts against the door frame, and I can't help looking his way. My shoulder curves forward, hiding my chin and lower lip as I watch his eyes studying the curve of my back.

He looks up, and embarrassment turns his face a shade of pink. "Sorry. You just look so beautiful."

I giggle, not knowing what else to do. "Thanks."

I lower my eyes to my torso, making sure the gel has coated the reddened area. Beside me, I hear a click. My eyes wander over to Beau, and see his phone in his hand, and the camera lens pointed at me.

My mouth forms an 'o' as I gasp. "*Beau.*"

"What?" He has a guilty yet teasing smile as he slides his phone into his pocket.

"Oh my gosh," I squeal. "Delete it."

"Why?" he says, fighting to hold back his laugh. "I couldn't help it. You just look so good."

"*Beau,*" I whine. "Delete it."

"Oh, come on. No one's gonna see it."

"That's not the point."

He smirks, lifting his shirt and revealing a well-defined pack of abs. "You can take a picture of me."

My mouth falls open, and I feel on fire for a whole new reason. I snatch the hoodie from over Beau's arm and drape it against my body.

Beau winks. "I'll be your model any day."

I mumble a laugh, shoving him out of the doorway. "Hush up."

I yank the hoodie over my head, and my body calms at no longer being on display.

Beau pulls out his phone and holds it out for me. "If you really want the picture deleted, you can do it now."

I lift my hand, staring at the phone. I can't believe the girl I'm staring at is me. She's happy, confident, and relaxed. She has me smiling.

"Just don't have it on your main camera roll," I say, pushing the phone toward him. "Make sure it's somewhere no one else will see it."

Beau looks back at me with sheer surprise. "Are you okay with that?"

I shrug, smiling. "I think I look good."

Beau leans against the back of the couch. "I am sorry, though. First your ankle and now your stomach. I don't want to keep endangering you."

"Neither time was your fault. They were just freak accidents."

"Did you get hurt this often without me around?"

I smirk as I saunter towards him. "I guess I didn't. Why would I? Without you, I was chained to my desk all day."

I land in front of him, and his lopsided grin has me melting. He smooths back my hair and then runs his hand down my back.

"So I set you free?" he asks in an almost gravelly tone.

I place my hand against his neck. "It's scary, but I like it."

He draws in a breath, and before exhaling, pushes his lips against mine. My chest inflates as if he's breathing life into me.

"I'm going to watch you like a hawk," he says, resting his hands against my hips. "They say things come in threes. I don't want a third thing to hurt you."

"I think the rule of three has passed for you and me," I joke. "When we were kids, I'd follow your lead on our little adventures. I had enough scrapes and bruises back then."

Beau lowers his head with a laugh. "*Ha.* So I've already hurt you enough?"

"Again, I don't think it was your fault. I was too clumsy to keep up with you."

He leads me by the hand to the couch. "I'll still be careful with you."

I cuddle against him on the couch, and he switches on the television.

"What do you want to watch?" he asks, flicking through the movie covers on display.

"I don't care. I've probably seen them all before."

He hugs his arm tighter around me. "So, can I give up the pretense and make out with you instead?"

I scoff and playfully hit his chest. "*Ugh.* Beau!"

He laughs. "What?"

I steal the remote from him and press play on "The Princess Switch."

"Aw, man," Beau complains. "Why is every girl obsessed with this movie?"

I rest my head on his shoulder. "Because it's good."

Beau laughs. "Whatever."

I've never felt more comfortable than reclining in Beau's arms. The smell of hot cocoa faintly wafts in the room, yet Beau's earthy cologne is the stronger scent. Seriously, I'm addicted to it. I love the way his breathing not only moves his body but also mine. His strong hand either runs the length of my arm, rests on my hip, or plays in my hair. It's obvious he's not focused on the movie.

Let's face it. Neither am I.

Right around the time Margaret and Stacy meet on screen, Beau's lips lock with mine. My heart throbs and my veins pulsate. I taste the remnants of chocolate on his lips, and it sends me dizzy. I run a hand into his hair, and his arms encircle me. Each of his digits press firmly into the hoodie. It's as if he's touching my skin.

As he kisses me, his weight has me leaning backwards. His arm cradles my back, and I slowly recline, lying down on the couch. Beau's legs intertwine with mine, and his body hovers just above me.

My hands move down his sides, and when they slide back up, my hand mistakenly slips inside his shirt. I graze my teeth against his lip as my hand massages his smooth, taut skin. His kiss lands beside my mouth, missing his target when my fingers dance along his back. There's an urgency in his breaths as I fish my hand out from his shirt. I rub my lips together as his shirt rides up.

His body lowers, and my heart runs at a frantic beat. My arms lock around him as I struggle to calm down. Thoughts of legs, hands, abs, and mouths clutter my mind. Another hot kiss caresses my cheek. I tilt my head up, searching for oxygen. My body temperature sizzles toward boiling point. I writhe under him and gasp for breath.

I rub my hand against the base of his neck and whisper, "Can we slow down?"

Beau pulls up, hoisting himself over me. "Sure."

I lift my hand, resting it on his chest. The rapid beats of his heart pat against my palm.

"Your heart is pounding too?"

He grins. "Of course it is. I'm with you."

My heart expands as awe drifts from my lips. My eyes widen as I stare up at his handsome face.

He loves me.

I can't believe he said he loves me.

My heart squeezes, and guilt sloshes in my stomach.

I can't say it back.

Oh gosh. Why can't I just say it?

Beau frowns. "You look worried."

I rub the space over his heart and smile. "I'm not. I'm happy. I promise."

Beau scoops my hand from his chest and gives it a tender kiss.

He releases my hand, and I scoot out from under him. I fan the hoodie out, and say, "Thanks. It was just getting a little steamy."

Beau smirks. "You're telling me."

I push my hair off my neck and wince at the sticky sensation. "It got hard to breathe."

"It felt like I was seeing double," Beau replies. He wets his lips and sinks lower on the couch. "Knowing what you've got on under my hoodie…"

I fan my face, blowing out a cool breath.

Beau lifts the remote. He gestures at the television, about to say something, but is cut off. The sound also steals my attention, sending us both looking up.

Footsteps sound on the first floor.

I gulp, feeling flushed for a whole new reason.

Beau's parents are home.

Seventeen

"They're not usually home this early," Beau says, turning toward the basement door.

"Will they flip out that I'm here?"

"*Pfft.* As if." Beau smirks as he turns my way. "You're a grade-A student on the honor roll. I'm sure they'll be questioning me about kidnapping you."

I wince, not wanting to say it, but I do regardless. "Should we go up?"

Beau mimics my expression. "Do you really want to?"

No. "Won't it be worse if we stay down here longer while they're home?"

Beau groans. "Okay. Let's go up."

"Perhaps I'll just say hi and then you can drive me home. I'm sure my dad is waiting for me."

Beau pouts. "You want to go home already?"

I pinch his cheek. "Aww, you're so cute."

Beau laughs, jumping off the couch. "Okay, you can go home now."

I follow him toward the door. "Why? Because I called you cute? You are cute."

Beau flexes a bicep. "Excuse me, I'm manly."

"Yes. A very cute man," I tease.

Beau rolls his eyes, but the curve of his lips tells me he loves it.

As we make our way upstairs, he interlocks his fingers with mine. He opens the basement door, and we move into the rest of the house. The lack of movement fills me with more nervous energy.

I follow Beau into the kitchen and I squeeze his hand when I spot his father at the counter. Mr. Stevenson leans over a laptop and scrunches his fingers through his hair.

"Ah, Dad?" Beau says, trying to gain his attention.

Mr. Stevenson doesn't look up and instead waves his hand. "Not now, son."

Beau's eyebrows raise, and he gives me a look as if to say, *"See? Told ya."*

A small plume of relief sets off inside me. The thought of reacquainting with his parents is too much. Especially after spending alone time in his bedroom.

Beau turns toward the doorway of the kitchen. I turn as well, but behind me, Beau's father says, "Lydie?"

I stop and turn around. Mr. Stevenson is white with shock. He shakes his head and brushes a hand over his sandy blonde hair.

"Oh, Ava," he says, pulling out of his shock. "Um, hi. Wow! You look so much like your mother."

"Thanks," I mumble.

"What is this?" Mr. Stevenson's eyes shift from Beau to me. "What are you doing here?"

"My plan was to come in here and reintroduce you," Beau says flatly. "But you made it clear you weren't interested."

Mr. Stevenson huffs. "It's just been a rough day."

Masked by a fake cough, Beau mumbles, "When isn't it?"

Mr. Stevenson rounds the kitchen bench and moves toward us. "So you two are friends again?"

Beau gives my hand a gentle squeeze. "You could say that."

I look at Beau and then at his father. "I hope it's okay that I'm here."

Mr. Stevenson looks me up and down, smiling. "Of course. *Geez,* I just can't believe how much you've changed."

Beau loops an arm around my shoulders and sighs. "Yeah, she's beautiful. What's new?"

An embarrassing blush sizzles across my cheeks and over my nose. I cup a hand over my lips and hold back an anxiety-induced giggle.

Mr. Stevenson shifts awkwardly, wringing his hand together. "How's your father? It's been so long since I've spoken with him."

I force myself to keep smiling. "He's fine. Thank you."

"Good lord, do I need coffee," Mrs. Stevenson's voice approaches the kitchen.

Beau and I pivot toward the doorway, ready for another re-introduction. When Mrs. Stevenson appears, she stops dead. She gasps as if she's choking on her last breath. Her jaw wobbles, ready to drop to the floor cartoon-style, and her eyes are circular with red veins occupying the white space.

Her deathly stare points at me. As the shock wears off, her eyes become narrow and enraged. Her chin lifts and her lips spread, framing a toothy scowl. Her shoulders broaden and a guttural groan reverberates out of her.

"You!" she exclaims, almost spitting the word. Her finger points at me like a dagger as she marches toward me. "How dare you? I've done everything for you, and you dare to set foot inside my house!"

"Whoa, Mom!" Beau yells, throwing himself in front of me. "Chill out!"

Mrs. Stevenson shoves Beau, knocking him backwards into me. "What is she doing here?"

I stumble behind Beau, but we both keep our footing.

Beau turns and wraps an arm around me. "Are you okay?" When I nod, he turns back to his mother with a loathsome stare. "What the hell is wrong with you?"

"Get her out of this house!" Mrs. Stevenson shrieks.

"Kate, please," Mr. Stevenson says, stepping forward and trying to placate his wife.

"And you," Mrs. Stevenson's voice is low and callous when addressing her husband. "You allowed this? You were fine to have this girl in our home after everything we've built here?"

"Kate, it's been a long day," Mr. Stevenson says in a calm voice. He reaches for her shoulder and gestures to the doorway. "Perhaps you should kick back with a glass of wine?"

"Forget this," Beau says, stamping his foot. He holds onto my shoulder, pulling me close, and walking us out of the kitchen.

"Beau," his father calls, but we keep moving until we reach the front door and snatch our coats.

Fury has Beau's hand shaking as he reaches for the door knob. The sweat built up in his hands has him sliding over the metal surface. He grunts with aggravation, pulling at the handle until the door reefs open.

We hurry across the porch and slide down the front steps.

I clasp his hands in our rush to his car. "Oh my gosh, Beau. I'm so sorry."

He reaches into his pocket and fumbles with his car keys. "What? Why?"

"Your parents..." I pant. "They are... That was... Just horrible."

Beau halts and scoops me into his arms. "It wasn't your fault. That's just how they are. They're crazy and hateful. I can't believe my mother screamed at you. I swear, I'm never talking to her again."

I press my hands into his back. "I don't want to come between you and your parents."

He kisses the top of my head. "I've already told you there's a rift between me and them. You did nothing wrong."

I bury my face against his chest. "I was just hoping you were lying about your parents. I was hoping it wasn't as bad as you had said."

Beau rubs a calming circle on my back. "Come on. Let's get out of here."

Beau opens the passenger door for me and then moves around to the other side. When he buckles up, his jaw tenses and a scowl twists his lips. He leans over, muttering, "Oh hell no."

I look out the window and see Mr. Stevenson moving down the front steps and heading toward Beau's car.

Beau throws his arm out like a stop sign. "Don't you go near her!"

My heart is like a beaten ping-pong ball stuck to a paddle. My tongue glues to the roof out of my Sahara-dry mouth, and underneath Beau's hoodie, I'm drenched with sweat.

Mr. Stevenson's hands lift in an act of surrender. "Your mother didn't mean what she said. She's not herself."

"Save it," Beau spits. "I've heard it all before, and I'm still not buying it."

Mr. Stevenson tilts his head, meeting my eyes. "Ava, I hope you're okay."

Before I can answer, Beau slams his foot on the accelerator and the car flies in reverse.

My breathing is ragged the entire drive across town. Beau keeps apologizing for his parents, but the shock of everything that went down turns his words into white noise.

The car drives up the street that leads into my cul-de-sac. My eyes narrow in on my house in case my dad is on the porch. Instead, I spy a navy SUV parked in my driveway. My heart drops to the pit of my stomach when I recognize the car.

I groan. "Oh crap."

"What?" Beau asks, glancing over at me.

I suck on my bottom lip and gesture at my driveway. "Sheriff Lennon is at my house."

"Are you sure?"

"It's his wife's SUV."

Beau slows to a stop just outside the cul-de-sac. "Oh dang. Do you think he's here to tell your dad he saw us together?"

I can't seem to blink. My eyes grow wider by the moment.

Beau rubs my shoulder. "It'll be okay. Don't panic."

I turn to him as terror bubbles up inside me. "Don't panic?"

He deadpans me. "Yes. Why are you panicking?"

I give him an incredulous look. I raise my palm upwards and jut it toward my house. "Because Ciara's dad is in my house. Ciara is a little narc, and her dad loves to dish to mine."

Beau gulps, turning a dull shade of green. "Do you want me to go in with you?"

I blow out an unsteady breath. "No, I don't think that'll help. Plus, we don't need any more yelling after what happened at your house."

I unbuckle my seatbelt and tug on the door handle.

Beau's hand lands on mine. "But if I go in, all the heat will be on me."

"That will guarantee there's a problem. If I go in alone, maybe I can deflect."

Beau leans forward, caresses my cheek, and presses a soft kiss against my lips.

"Send me a message if you need me," Beau whispers, tucking a loose lock behind my ear. "I'll be back in a flash."

I kiss him back, loving the smooth taste and taking in the earthy cologne that lingers around his neck and collarbone.

I pull away and open the car door. "I'll do my best not to panic. Are you going back home?"

He frowns. "No way. I'll drive around for a while."

"Don't drive while you're angry. It can be dangerous."

His jaw flexes and his nostrils flare. "I'll be fine."

I lean forward and drape my hand over the back of his neck. A mournful sigh slips out of me. "No, Beau, I mean it. I can't have another person I love getting hurt in a mindless car accident."

Beau's expression softens and his eyes well. "I'm sorry. I didn't mean..."

I stroke the back of his neck and then pull my arm away. "I know you didn't. Just promise me you'll be careful."

He nods. "I will."

I leave the car and give him a wave. He nods and gives a small smile. He makes a U-turn, and the car takes off at a more conservative speed than at his parents' house.

I wrap my coat tight around Beau's hoodie and march myself towards my house. I keep at a ferocious speed because if I dawdle, I don't think I'll ever get there.

I fumble with the house keys and push open the front door. Chatter bounces out of the living room. My palms and forehead grow clammy and my stomach churns. Is it possible for me to run past the living room and make it to my bedroom without anyone seeing me?

"Ava, is that you?" my dad's voice calls out.

Sprung.

I force my feet forward and scuff my way into the living room. I swallow hard as Dad, Sheriff Lennon, his wife, and Ciara all stare at me. Their wide-eyed, knowing looks are a sure sign they've been talking about me.

I deadpan at Ciara. Does she really think it's acceptable to gossip about me with our parents?

"Sweetie, why don't you sit with us?" Mrs. Lennon asks, tapping the space on the couch between her and Ciara.

"Uh, umm, I..." The clamminess is liquefying into sweat. "I can't. I have homework."

"We won't be here long," Sheriff Lennon says jovially. I don't buy his charm; it has to be a front. "We are meeting with Ciara's grandparents for dinner. You'll have enough time for homework later tonight."

"But..." I stammer. I look at Dad for an excuse. He always wants me at my desk, studying. Today can't be the day he decides to mellow.

"Did you fall behind in your schoolwork because you were out last night?" Dad inquires.

I slouch, folding my arms. I use all my strength to stop my eyes from rolling backwards.

"And you were out again today," Dad says, scrutinizing my face.

"I had to be," I argue. "I told you, Whitney made us fall behind."

Dad steps in close to me. "You are always ahead in your schoolwork. Sitting down with the Lennons for ten minutes isn't the end of the world."

The apprehension seeps into my expression before I can hold it back. "Really?"

"Let me take your coat," Dad says, moving behind me and grasping the shoulders of my coat.

My hands squeeze my coat closed and my arms grow rigid. "No, it's okay."

But Dad's grip is stronger than mine. Before I know it, my coat is peeled away.

"Where did you get this pullover?" Dad questions, walking around me with my coat draped over his arm. "You weren't wearing this before you left the house."

It's like I'm experiencing an earthquake aftershock the way my legs tremble. All the blood drains from my head. I have no power to come up with a good answer. To combat my dizziness, I slide in between Ciara and her mother, plonking down on the couch.

Mrs. Lennon rubs my back, pinching at the fabric. "Did you go shopping today?" she asks kindly.

Ciara's lips pucker and her nose crinkles. "Why does it smell like men's cologne?"

Dread simmers in my gut.

She didn't.

"Ciara informed me about who you've been spending your time with," Dad says, standing in front of his vacant armchair.

I hold my breath, calculating if I can get out of this. Is there any way to convince Dad it's all a lie?

I swing my head to view Ciara. I narrow my eyes, fighting the urge to mouth, *"Why?"*

Ciara's eyes shine in her usual sickly pathetic way.

"Tell me the truth," Dad says in a composed tone. "Were you with Beau today?"

I curl my fingers around the neck of the hoodie, breathing in Beau's scent. I don't want to lie about him. I don't want to keep him a secret. I want everyone to accept my relationship with him.

Dad steps forward, lowering to find my eyes. "Answer me."

I fan out the pullover and fidget in place. I swallow rough, and croak, "Yes."

Dad slaps a hand against his thigh and stands tall as an angry grunt hurtles out of his mouth. "Good lord, Ava. Why?"

"Dad," I whimper. "Don't be mad."

"Mad?" Dad questions. "I'm furious."

"He's not a bad guy," I urge.

"Ava, sweetie," Sheriff Lennon says, leaning forward on his armchair and draping his clasp hands over his thighs. "Beau Stevenson is bad news. I've picked him up a few times for reckless behavior. You're too smart a girl to get mixed up with a bad kid."

Mrs. Lennon pats my shoulder. "We're just looking out for you, sweetie."

I groan, flinching from her touch. "Can everyone stop with all the sweeties?"

"*Ava*," Dad scolds.

I launch from the couch. My chest heaves as I pivot to take in all the faces. "I don't need everyone trying to save me from Beau."

"Why are you doing this?" Dad questions. "You know exactly what kind of person he is."

"He was my friend!" I yell. "And he still cares about me more than anybody else."

Dad looks at me like I'm crazy. "Everyone is here because they care about you."

"No," I say firmly. "Everyone is here for their own agenda. No one asks me how I feel or what I want."

"Sweetie," Mrs. Lennon begins and then clears her throat. "I mean, Ava. We want you to be safe."

"Beau won't hurt me."

Sheriff Lennon shifts in his seat, broadening his frame to gain my attention. "We want to prevent that from happening. Ciara told us you and Beau have been spending a lot of time together in close proximity."

Ciara cups a hand around her mouth as if she's about to tell everyone a deadly secret. "They always make a reason to be alone together during our meetings."

I scoff and fling a finger in her direction. "I had to be with Beau because everyone made me. I wanted to partner with you, but you ditched me for Lucy."

Mrs. Lennon leans across the couch, planting her hand on Ciara's knee. "You forced Ava to be alone with this horrid boy?"

"He's not horrible," I interject. "None of you know him like I do."

Sheriff Lennon stands beside Dad. "It's okay," he says gently. "I know it's confusing to be a teenager, and maybe Beau has said everything you want to hear…"

A shrill groan tumbles out of me. "I can't hear any more of this."

"Ava, we aren't letting this continue," Dad warns.

"Whatever," I mumble, and turn on my heels. I move up the hall with heavy stomps.

"Ava, come back here!" My dad orders, following me up the hall.

"I'm almost eighteen," I fire back. "You can't keep treating me this way."

"You're my daughter. I'll do whatever it takes to keep you safe."

"Keeping me away from him isn't keeping me safe!"

"How can you say that?"

"Because I love him!" It comes out of me like a roar. My throat is inflamed, my cheeks are burning, and my heart is pounding.

But I feel good. I feel really good.

"What?" It hisses out of Dad. He squints, unable to fathom what came out of my mouth. "What did you just say?"

I back away on steady legs. "You can't keep me away from him. I'm in love with him."

My heart is palpitating, but I keep my stare firmly on dad.

"You don't know what that word means," Dad fires back.

"Maybe I didn't because I haven't felt loved in years!" I scream the words, leaving my throat shredded and raw. "But I know exactly what love is when I'm with him."

I back all the way into my room and slam my door shut. My whole bedroom quakes and I fall to my knees, panting. My head throbs and I'm near passing out.

Oh, crap. Did that really just happen?

A jolt of embarrassment spirals through my body, knowing Ciara and her family heard my outburst. It's removed by anger as my fists slam against my thighs.

I wouldn't have had that screaming match with my father if the Lennons minded their own business.

I lift myself off the carpet and wake up my laptop. I open the school portal and tap on my email chain with Beau. Pain ricochets past my knuckles and into my wrists as my fingers stab at the keys. I type my cell number along with *"Call me"* with several exclamation points.

Thirty seconds later, my cell phone buzzes in the front pocket of my jeans.

"Beau?" I say breathlessly into the phone.

"Aves, are you okay? What's happening?"

"Beau, I love you," I say with utter desperation. "I love you so, so much."

There's a brief pause and then an exhale distorts the phone line.

"I love you too," he says in a low tone. "What brought this on?"

I flop backwards on my bed and sigh. "I just screamed it at my dad, so I thought I should tell you."

"Wait, what? You screamed your love for me at your dad?"

"Yep. It was a lot."

"Are you okay? How did he react?"

"Not well. I slammed the door in his face."

"*Dang.* Do you want me to come over?"

"More than anything. But it's not a good idea."

"You sound like you need a hug."

The shakiness in my hand that holds the phone subsides, and my body relaxes. "I do. But talking to you is already making me feel better."

"So Ciara and her dad ratted you out?"

"It was the entire Lennon family here. I was seriously outnumbered."

"That's terrible. I wish I had gone in with you."

"Are you home now?"

"No, I'm still driving."

My heart misses a beat. "Still?"

"I've pulled over," he reassures. "I just can't go home. They always make me feel like this."

"Uncomfortable in your own home?" I ask, sinking into melancholy.

"Exactly. I hate that you understand how this feels."

I sigh, staring at the ceiling. "Why are our parents so messed up?"

"I wish I had the answer."

Three loud bangs thud against my bedroom door.

I squeak and lift myself to sit.

"Ava," my dad calls gruffly. "The Lennons are gone. I want you in the living room. Now."

I squeak against my phone, and Beau's voice whispers back to me, "That didn't sound good."

"Don't come over here," I whisper into the phone.

"How did you know I was thinking that?"

The corners of my mouth curl into a smile. "Because you love me."

"And you love me?" Beau says hesitantly. "Do you really? Or did you say it to get back at your dad?"

"I love you, Beau. Caring about what my dad thought held me back. But I love you. You never really left my heart."

"Call me after. I want to know you're okay."

"I will."

We exchange goodbyes, and then I pluck myself off the bed.

This time I might actually be sick. An acidic taste leaps up my throat as I open my bedroom door. I carefully tread down the hall and into the living room.

My dad slouches in an armchair. He doesn't look up when I enter. He's broken.

The sight of him has me flying into remorse. Tears flood my eyes and I race toward him. I drop to my knees and rest my head against his lap.

"I didn't mean it," I sob. "I know you love me. I'm sorry. I'm so sorry."

Dad strokes my hair. "How am I not listening to you?"

I lift my head and blink away the blur in my vision. "What?"

"Were you just on the phone to Beau?"

I look up at him and guilt slithers inside my body. With a gulp, I answer by nodding.

Dad leans forward, cupping my face. "I hate the idea of you with him. But does being around him make you happy?"

A tear rolls down my cheek. "Yes."

"It wasn't until Beau came back into your life that you admitted how much you missed your mother. Do you think you can't talk about her because of me?"

I gulp, bracing myself. "What do you want me to say?"

"The truth, sweetheart."

His voice is so placid that it eases me into saying, "Yes."

He cups my chin and his eyes water. "I'm sorry, darling. I didn't mean to make you feel like that. It's just hard for me to remember her."

"But I want to remember her."

He nods, sniffing back the tears. "I know. You have every right to reminisce about her."

I lift on my knees, tilting my head in puzzlement. "Why don't you want to remember her?"

"It's complicated."

I frown. "Beau's parents don't seem to want to remember Mom, either."

Dad looks at me sideways. "What makes you say that?"

"His mom screamed at me to leave their house."

Dad rears back. "She screamed at you?"

I nod with shame.

It doesn't compute with Dad. "At you?"

"Yes. She said, how dare I be in her house."

"She has a problem with you," Dad says, shifting into over-protective mode. "My grade-A student daughter. Look at how her son turned out. How does she have the nerve to treat you that way?"

"Do you know what happened with Beau's parents?" I ask in a low tone. "Beau said they barely look at him and they argue constantly."

Dad sits back in his chair and looks off to the side. "I haven't spoken to them in a long time."

"That was the impression Mr. Stevenson gave me."

Dad's eyebrows lift, and he looks back at me. "You spoke with him too?"

"Briefly. He seemed friendly."

Dad scoots forward and clutches my shoulder. "Paul Stevenson isn't to be trusted. I've had a sense his son is headed down the same path. Everything Beau has done over the past few years has proven me right. I don't want you to get hurt."

I shiver at his words. "What did he do?"

Dad takes my hand in his and looks at me with purpose. "Are you sure you want Beau in your life?"

My heart flutters. "Yes, I am."

Dad frowns. "I'm sorry, sweetheart. I just don't trust him."

I want to bring up going to the dance with Beau. But I don't want to rock the boat further. I squeeze Dad's hands, asking, "Can you trust me?"

He leans forward and kisses my forehead. "The only thing that's important to me is keeping you in my life. I couldn't protect your mother, and I don't want to fail again. You're far too precious."

"Mom's death wasn't your fault."

Dad taps the side of his head. "That's not what I hear inside here."

"Oh, Dad." I leap up and throw my arms around him. "You can't blame yourself."

"I love you, sweetheart. You are all that matters to me."

"I know." I sniff hard. "I love you. I'm sorry for yelling at you."

"Me too."

Eighteen

Beau and I texted throughout Saturday night and all of Sunday. We even had a long phone call on Sunday night. We reminisced about our childhood adventures and talked about the classes and teachers we do and don't like. It was kinda mundane, but in the best possible way. Like we hadn't stopped being best friends for the past few years. Talking to Beau about anything lights me up.

I don't even care if my dad sees what Beau and I say to each other. If he didn't think to check the parental control app on his phone before, I'm sure Sheriff Lennon gave him a helpful reminder.

To be honest, I want Dad to read the messages. I want him to see how sweet and caring Beau is toward me. A week ago, I was fearful of Beau too. If I can change my tune, surely my dad can, too.

Beau wanted to come over on Sunday. He didn't push on Saturday night because he could tell how exhausted I was from arguing with my dad. Saturday night was rough in my house. Dad and I were civil to each other. Actually, he was overly adoring. I think it was to keep me on his side. We watched a Christmas movie together, and then I said I was off to bed. I said the light would be on because I was studying. However, the only typing I did was replies to Beau.

It was so hard denying Beau's request to take me away somewhere on Sunday. But I didn't want to give my dad a heart attack. We'd never screamed at each other before. I'd never argued with him before this week. I'd always gone along with whatever he said, because I knew he was doing his best after Mommy died.

I wanted to stay home and work on my assignments. I had to review my notes from my interview with Beau. But I couldn't look at them. They felt too private. Now, after everything we've shared, I don't think I can write a report about him. It feels wrong.

So nothing really productive happened on Sunday. The only thing that gave me excitement was knowing Beau would pick me up before school. We need to hang the posters at prime locations. For maximum effect, we need to get it done before school starts.

The committee agreed to meet at seven-thirty this morning. Getting inside the school is easy because there are a few clubs and teams that practice early.

I ate my breakfast at record speed and dressed in a flash. I bounce on my heels, looking out the front window, gleefully waiting for that black GT Mustang to appear. When it rolls into view, I squeal and lift my bag over my shoulder.

I open the front door and skip across the porch, grinning at Beau, who stands at the other end of the snow-framed garden path. Beau's eyes twinkle against the early morning sun and he steps toward me, lifting his arm.

"Good morning, beautiful," he says warmly. "Let me take that for you."

We meet in the middle of the path, and as Beau slips the bag off my shoulder, I lean forward and press my lips against his. As the weight of my bag falls off me, I lean in closer, smiling in the kiss as Beau's hand settles onto my lower back.

I suck his bottom lip, letting it go with a pop. "Good morning, handsome."

"How are you?" he asks, so close that the words reverberate against my lips.

"Happy," I say, cupping my hands against the sides of his face. "Now that I'm with you."

"How long did your dad stay on the warpath?" Beau asks, his head tilting to glimpse the house behind me. "I had a bad feeling he'd be guarding the house when I rolled up today."

I slide my hands down, resting them on his shoulders. "No, he went to work. Do you think I'd be this happy otherwise?"

He puffs a laugh and eases into his lopsided grin. "I dunno. Wouldn't you be this happy to see me, no matter what?"

I giggle again, shying my face away. Beau catches my chin with a crooked finger and tilts my face back to him. My teeth graze my bottom lip, and I nod.

"Considering I didn't hold back, yelling everything I felt for you at my dad..." I suck in a deep breath. "I guess I no longer have anything to hide."

"Your dad knows everything and you're still alive," Beau jokes.

"Well, not everything," I say playfully. "I didn't give him a blow by blow about every time we made out."

Heat colors Beau's cheeks. "Whoa. I hope not."

I clasp my hands over my face, giggling.

Beau shifts my bag on his shoulder and gestures to the car. "Shall we?"

I link my hand with his and snuggle close. "Yes. Let's go."

Beau lifts my hand and kisses it. "I like holding hands with you."

"Me too."

"I guess I should make the most of it."

"What do you mean?"

He squeezes my hand, guiding me to the car. "You won't want to do this at school."

When he opens the car door and tosses my bag inside, I frown. "Why?"

Beau is jittery as he stands by the open door. "Aren't we on the down-low?"

I step in close, enveloping his lips in a soft kiss. I pull back, whispering, "I told my dad. There's no one else I'm afraid to tell."

Beau's fingers run down the fabric covering my spine. "Are you really okay with this?"

"We made it official, didn't we?"

He grins blissfully. "Yes."

"Then do you believe that I'm okay?"

He nods. "Okay, I believe you."

"I just want to be with you, and I don't care who knows it."

Beau sighs, resting his forehead against mine. "I've wanted to hear those words for so long. I can't believe this is real."

"It's real, Beau. I love you."

He kisses my cheek, wrapping his arms around me. "I love you so much. I always have."

I hold Beau's hand the entire drive to school. My dad would have a conniption if he knew we were doing something defined as unsafe in a moving car. I just can't get enough of this boy.

Beau drives into the school parking lot behind Marcus's car. He parks a few spaces away and Hilary and Marcus walk toward the school gate. When I leave Beau's car, he's quick to drape his arm around me. As we walk towards the gate, his arm lowers until it falls off me. Just in time for Jeff's pickup to enter the parking lot.

As we approach, Whitney jumps out from the passenger side, and Jeff opens the back panel of the tray.

As he pulls out three cardboard poster tubes, I say, "Oh, good. You got everything."

"We said we would, didn't we?" Whitney snaps with her snarky level dialed to one hundred.

"Ease up," Beau says.

"I was worried about the printers," I reply. "There might've been an issue."

Jeff tucks the tubes under his arm. "Nope. No problem. Everything is accounted for."

"Hey!" Marcus calls out. He and Hilary stand, huddle together, by the school gate. "Are you guys coming or what?"

"Hi guys!" a faint voice calls from the distance. Ahead, Lucy exits the school foyer and moves down a few steps, waving. "I've been waiting five minutes already."

"*Pfft.* She's keen," Beau mutters.

We all move through the school gate. Oh my goodness, it's so nice to have the space to move without fear of being squashed or trampled.

Hilary stomps up the school steps with the hood from her coat draped over her head. "Ugh. It's so early."

"Don't be so dramatic," Jeff says with a somewhat hoarse voice. "It's not that much earlier than a regular school day."

"What's with the gravelly voice, Jeff?" Lucy asks with interest. "Party too hard this weekend?"

"Did you expect any less?" Jeff replies. "We won our game on Friday. Of course, the after party continued all weekend."

I frown as I think about Saturday night. When I went home, Beau went for a drive to blow off steam. I look at him, mouthing, "Did you go to the party?"

He gives me a strange look, murmuring, "I was texting you all weekend. You'd have known if I was at a party."

Relief pours out of me. "Oh."

He clutches my hand. "As if I'd go to a party without taking you with me."

I cup a hand over my mouth as a quiet giggle sneaks out.

Hilary lands in the foyer, lowering her hood. Her eyes narrow in our direction. "What's happening here with the cutesy hand holding and whispering?"

"Oh, Ava," Marcus says with disappointment. "Did you really let him con you into dating him?"

I puff out a laugh in shock. "He's not conning me."

Beau smooths a hand over his long styled waves. "Yeah. I'm irresistible without any tricks."

A collective retch circles the group.

I choose to hear it as jealousy and not as revulsion.

Footsteps hurry behind us. Over my shoulder, Ciara rushes up the steps to join the group. She skids to a stop in the foyer as she locks eyes with me. She squeaks and freezes in a rigid pose as her eyes lock on my hand in Beau's.

A proud smile curls my lips as I take in her horrified stare.

Why does this please me so much?

Something about it being plainly obvious that her backstabbing meant nothing. That dropping the bomb in my house only made me closer to Beau.

Her eyes water, and before her guilt can fully resonate, I turn away from her.

Jeff taps the poster tubes in his arms. "We've got the posters in this tube. The other two tubes both have banners inside."

"I guess we should divide up the posters," I suggest. "Shall we start at the cafeteria and break into pairs?"

With everyone in agreement, we move down the hallway. In the cafeteria, I suggest we first check out the creations. Marcus lays down the banner and rolls out the canvas material.

Chills run the length of my body and my hands raise to my cheeks as my smile stretches. With all the last minute images the group took, I'm in awe at how wonderful the final product looks. In a cutesy fashion, Whitney arranged the decorations and wrapped boxes we snapped on a wooden workstation background. It's like we have the perspective of Santa and his elves, hard at work.

I clasp my hands over my chest and sigh. "Oh my gosh, I love this so much."

"It's the freaking cutest Christmas banner I've ever seen," Hilary agrees. She adds a gleeful squeal for good measure.

Lucy claps, peering over the banner. "Ah, I'm in love. I can't believe you pulled this off, Whitney."

Whitney groans with wild irritation. Her nostrils flare as she blurts, "Why are you all so shocked? Ugh. I told you I could handle this."

Jeff squeezes Whitney's shoulder. "Chill. They're giving you compliments."

I still don't understand this relationship. He's so doting towards her even when she didn't show up at his game on Friday night.

I take the shorter cardboard tube from the table and pluck off the plastic lid. "We will need posters placed in the cafeteria, the library, and others scattered around the halls."

I shake the cardboard tube, letting the posters tumble onto the table. I flick my fingers between each poster. "Jeff and Whitney can stay here and work on the banners. The rest of us can take on the other areas. It shouldn't take long at all."

"We'll take the library," Lucy volunteers, linking arms with Ciara.

I turn to Hilary. "We'll divide the hallways between you and Marcus, and me and Beau?"

She nods. "Sure thing."

We each take an even share of the posters. All of them are different and beyond cute. We have cartoonish elves sharing baked goods, decorated trees housing presents, and the last two depict hot cocoa and candy cane images surrounding information about the dance. It will be impossible for anyone not to know this dance exists.

I gather the four posters for Beau and me to hang, and we leave the cafeteria.

"Oh, by the way," Whitney says, offhandedly. "Jeff and I won't be at the meeting this afternoon."

Her flippant tone makes me double-take. "Huh?"

Whitney gestures to the banner. "Well, we're in charge of ticket sales. We will put in more work than anyone else during lunch. We'll have already clocked our time for today."

I roll my eyes, even though I appreciate the after school Whitney-free zone. "Fine. Whatever."

"So, umm..." Lucy stammers. She points between herself and Ciara. "Does that mean we don't have to be there either?"

I raise my palms up. "Have you finished organizing everything?"

"The band's locked in," Lucy replies. She looks to Ciara for backup, but she shies away with her head down. "I guess, if we have to be there..."

"It's fine," I cut her off. "I don't want anyone to feel like they have to be there."

Lucy's eyes widen. "Are you mad at me?"

I clasp Beau's hand and reply, "No. I'm not mad."

"Ava," Hilary blurts. I turn around as she gestures to Marcus. "We need to call PTA members and visit the caterer. We were thinking we'd head out after school instead of sticking around."

I take in everyone around me. "So, everybody is leaving after school?" I take in a breath and nod. "Okay, that's cool."

Hilary's eyebrows lift and her hands clasp together. "Really?"

I smile and grip Beau's hand tighter. "Yep. Totally fine."

As Beau and I enter the hall, he waves the rolled up posters and whispers, "What's up?"

I lean into him and whisper back, "I don't care if none of them show up. It just means more alone time with you."

Beau laughs and plants a kiss on my forehead. "School hasn't even started and you're already thinking about spending more time with me."

I giggle. "Can you blame me?"

"Well, no, I am a stud," he jokes.

I interlock our fingers and pick up the pace. "Come on, stud. Let's get to work."

As we move into the hallway, choosing the best space to hang our posters, Beau comments, "I can't believe Whitney is still so high-strung after her main task is done. Plus, we all helped her complete it, but we gave her all the credit."

"She just doesn't want anyone calling her a cheater."

"It's just an after-school project. Why does she always have to freak out? It was messed up when she stole your binder on the first day. Now she's still acting out."

"Did you know she and I used to be friends?"

Beau throws his head back and laughs like he's heard a joke.

"No, seriously," I say. "By the end of freshman year, I wanted to come out of my shell. You were... Well, we couldn't be friends, and Whitney and I got along during a history class. She started coming over to my house to study with me and my dad seemed to approve."

"Whoa. So what the heck happened?"

"She copied my essay and got found out," I reply. "It was a big thing where both our parents got called in. My dad had watched us studying and seen me explaining the assignment to Whitney. When our parents talked it out, Whitney came clean, erupting in tears. Needless to say, my dad no longer approved and forbade me from being her friend anymore."

"*Geez.* So much for second chances."

"I know, but I was just making friends again. Dad wanted to ensure no one was being cruel to me. He was just being protective. That's why he pushed me to be friends with Ciara. He knew she wouldn't hurt me."

Beau smirks. "No, she just ditches you when things get too scary for her."

"Oh well," I say with a bright smile, "it all led me back to you."

"Aww, Avie," he gushes, pecking my cheek.

We place two posters in hallway C and then turn the corner into hallway B. We find a blank space next to a stretch of lockers. Beau stretches his arms above his head, affixing the top two corners to the wall. I slip under his arms, smoothing my hands over the bottom corners.

"Got it?" Beau asks, looking down at me.

I slide back. "All good on my end."

"Good." He steps back, shaking out his arms.

Behind us, a staffroom door swings open. "Mr. Stevenson," Mr. Franklin calls.

Tension radiates off Beau. His jaw strains and his back grows rigid as he turns toward the voice.

Mr. Franklin grins, stepping into the hall. "Don't look so thrilled to see me."

Beau huffs. "I didn't do anything wrong."

Mr. Franklin beams with pride. "I know. That's why I want to speak with you."

Beau and I exchange glances.

"I'm very happy with the change in you," Mr. Franklin says to Beau, "and so is your wrestling coach."

As if on cue, Mr. Graystone steps out of the office behind Mr. Franklin. Beau chokes. "Coach?"

"Beau, we'd like you back on the team," Mr. Graystone says matter-of-factly.

Beau's eyebrows raise and happiness colors his surprise. "Really?"

Mr. Franklin nods, patting Beau's shoulder. "Yes, congratulations." His eyes flick my way, and then back at Beau. "Keep up the good work."

"Seven-thirty in the morning," Mr. Graystone says. "I want you in the gym for training on Tuesday, Wednesday, and Thursday. Unless you've got more of this decoration stuff keeping you busy?"

Beau hurriedly shakes his head. "No, sir."

Mr. Graystone taps Beau hard on the back. "Good on ya, kid. See you tomorrow morning."

Beau clears his throat and tries to subdue his grin. "Thanks. You will."

Mr. Franklin and Mr. Graystone continue along the hall. Mr. Franklin looks over his shoulder with a wry smile. "Be happy, Mr. Stevenson. You're back on the team."

As they disappear down the hall, I bounce on the balls of my feet and throw my arms around Beau. I kiss his cheek and squeal. "I'm so proud of you."

"Thanks, Aves."

"You told me how important the team was to you. You can do something you're good at, and others applaud you for it."

"Oh man. I can't believe it. But it'll be pretty early for me to drive you to school."

I shrug. "I'm up early every morning, regardless. I don't mind coming here early."

"Any excuse for a cram session?" Beau teases.

I click my tongue. "Yes, my life is that dull."

Throughout the rest of the day, I overheard people in my classes talk about the Christmas dance. The good feelings had me soaring for the rest of the day. Well, that and endless time with Beau.

Seeing as how both our parents freaked out at the sight of us together, the storeroom after school seems like paradise. A secret hideaway just for us. Even though we spent every second between classes, both our study periods, and lunchtime wrapped up together, I still can't get enough of this boy.

After Mr. Riley unlocked the storeroom door and left for his office, Beau and I embraced. I don't know if we've spoken more than ten words, but our lips and hands are plenty busy.

The more we kiss, the further back we trek into the storeroom. With giggles, we fumble around boxes and back into shelves. We nestle behind a row of boxes. My heartbeat pounds as Beau's strong hands run down my sides.

He holds me against the wall, nibbling just below my jaw. His lips wander down my skin and find a spot on the side of my neck. A soft moan pours out of me as the sensation pulses under my skin. The vibrations ripple down my body and I rub my thigh against his.

One of his hands brushes over my hair as his kiss becomes wetter and more intense. I tilt my head back, addicted to every mind-blowing sensation his mouth creates. My fingers claw into his back as another moan gasps out of me.

When my thigh lifts higher, Beau snatches it in his grip. A hot breath steams out of me as his fingers press into my thick winter stockings. His grip lifts me higher against the wall, and I pull my arms around his neck. His body melts into mine and his lips wet more of my skin as they nestle under my earlobe.

I seize his shirt collar with a clenched fist and run my other hand through his velvety hair. As my body temperature skyrockets, I rock against him, tilting my head to graze his cheek with my hungry lips.

Beau's hand on my thigh slips further under. His fingertips are only an inch from my butt. My heart throbs and skin glistens from heat.

"Ava," he moans into my ear.

I crush his collar in my hand. The lilt in his voice when he said my name was too much to handle.

"Oh Beau," I whisper desperately. "Kiss me."

Beau lifts his head, turning his face to mine. His lips magnetically push towards mine when footsteps near the storeroom.

"Anyone in here?" Mr. Riley calls.

Beau's hand slides off my thigh and my hands slip off his shoulders and run down his heaving chest. My eyes are circular as I stare at Beau with an open mouth.

As the storeroom door closes, Beau clears his throat, calling out, "Yes! Sorry, we're in here."

Beau steps back, pushing a hand on my back to help me pull off the wall. I'm so dizzy from what Beau and I were doing. Now, being caught by Mr. Riley has me more lightheaded than I've been.

"Beau?" Mr. Riley says with mild confusion. "Is Ava in there with you?"

"Yes," I say in a shaky voice.

With panic coursing through my veins, I smooth down my blouse and rearrange my skirt. Beau helps straighten my collar, but when his hands move down the front of my blouse, he recoils.

"Nope," he says in a strained voice, stepping away from me.

"What?" I whisper, confused.

"I can't touch you." He turns away. "Or look at you right now. I need a minute."

Still confused, I step my way around the boxes and crates toward the front of the storeroom.

"What are you two doing back there?" Mr. Riley asks. "It's time to lock up."

"We were just packing away some boxes," I say when I find my way into Mr. Riley's view. "Some of them collapsed back there. Beau's just fixing them."

Mr. Riley steps into the storeroom. "Does he need a hand?"

"No," Beau blurts. "I'm coming out."

Smoothing back my disheveled ponytail, I squeeze past Mr. Riley for my blazer, coat, and backpack.

Mr. Riley looks me up and down, noting my attire. "If you two are going through boxes, you should change into your gym uniform."

I smile politely as I fumble with my gear. "That's a good idea."

Beau crashes around the boxes, and comes into view. He pulls the knot of his tie further up, yet his top two buttons are still undone. With his shirt sleeves still rolled up, he smooths back the wild waves of hair.

Dang. How did I ever go so long without kissing and touching this boy?

I throw my bag over my shoulder and hurry out of the storeroom with Beau following. He grabs my hand, pulling me towards him as we rush towards the nearest exit.

Outside, the howling wind sends my skin icy. As my skin prickles against the freezing temperature, I blow out a frosty breath. Beau swoops in and kisses my lips, sending my body temperature skyward.

I giggle as our lips part. "That was exactly what I needed."

"You haven't had enough today?" he says with a devilishly handsome grin.

My shoulders bunch toward my earlobes. "Guess not."

"So, you wanna do something?"

"Yes, but I shouldn't. My dad will be waiting."

Beau whines, "But I can't wait till tomorrow."

I pinch his cheek. "Me neither. But we have to."

He smiles and then presses his lips against mine. "Okay. I'll drive you home."

Nineteen

I can't get it out of my head. I wish it didn't bother me this much. But it left me feeling gross from the inside out.

This morning Beau drove me to school. With plenty of time to kill, I walked Beau to wrestling practice, hand-in-hand.

As we approached the gym, a few boys on the wrestling team were outside talking. My hand cupped inside Beau's grew clammy. My stomach twinged, and I swallowed dryly. My intuition told me to say my goodbyes before moving any closer, but Beau was calm and collected. There was no sense of urgency or danger in his demeanor, so I shook off the ominous feeling.

One boy nudged another, sending all three to look our way. Jared, Michael, and Franky. Three boys who enjoy pointing out flaws and mocking other students. Their eyebrows raised, their lips upturned, and their arms crossed. Their disapproving body language was one hundred percent laser focused on me.

I felt like scum. It was as if Beau should wash his hands after touching me. He should wash his mouth with soap after kissing me.

To these boys, I'm a freak.

Jared lifts his chin, looking at Beau. "What's this all about?"

"What?" Beau replied. "Aren't you happy to have me back on the team?"

"Oh, sure," Franky muttered. "So you can smash my head against the floor again."

"It was your bad luck for resisting," Beau joked.

Michael gestured to me. "You got a new cheerleader, Beau? Or is she helping you pass a class?"

Beau released my hand and slid his hand along my lower back. "Don't be jealous just because my girlfriend is hotter than yours."

All three boys spluttered a laugh, and Michael quipped, "Girlfriend?"

Beau kissed me on the cheek. "Will we catch up between classes again?"

I forced a small smile and nodded in agreement.

"You know, I need help with classes too, Ava," Franky said, stepping forward and reaching his hands toward me. "Can I get a kiss too?"

Beau shoved Franky away and turned him toward the gym. The boys erupted in boisterous laughter, staggering their way into the gym. Beau looked back at me with his adorable lopsided grin and I waved goodbye.

He followed the boys inside and I heard my name tossed around. The laughter was loud, and the sentences were rapid-fired, but I swear I heard "nerd," "frigid," and "dud."

I could have puked right there.

It's now lunchtime, and my skin is still crawling.

I didn't want to hear what they were saying as they walked deeper into the gym, but I'm not deaf. In thirty seconds, they said the most heinous things about me. What else did they say to Beau in the following hour of practice? Hopefully, their coach put a stop to any name calling, having them focus on the task at hand. Although, my whole schooling life, I've had to deal with stupid boys and their loud mouths. They can be impossible to mute.

"Hey," Beau says, grasping my arm outside the cafeteria. "Where were you after second period?"

"Oh, sorry. I stayed back to have my teacher look over my study notes," I lie. "I needed to know I was still on track because I started doubting myself."

Beau grazes his finger under my chin as he grins. "As if you could be off-track."

"Sometimes when other people bring up valid points, it makes me question what I believe," I say as my insides quiver. "Do you ever feel like that?"

Beau frowns, linking his hand with mine as he shrugs. "I dunno. I usually get into fights with people I disagree with and then move on."

My gut flips for a whole new reason. "Oh."

Beau lifts my hand, giving it a kiss. "I don't plan on doing that anymore. I promise you, Ava, I'm on my best behavior now."

And at that, my heart melts into goo and my stomach settles.

He tugs me into the cafeteria. "Come on. Let's get something to eat."

"I'm eager to see the lines for tickets. We totally skipped lunch yesterday."

"I was too busy tasting your lips instead."

I giggle and playfully shove him. "*Shoosh.*"

Beau shoots me an apologetic look. I fan my face and we walk deeper into the cafeteria. With every step, my hand lowers and my chin drops. On one side of the cafeteria, Lucy and Ciara sit behind a table with miserable faces and slumped shoulders. Opposite, Whitney sits alone at her table, scrolling on her phone.

My eyes dart around the room. "Do you see Jeff anywhere?"

He pans around the tables and then lifts a pointed finger. "There he is."

Jeff sits backward on a chair, chatting with people at the table, which includes Hilary and Marcus.

I stamp my foot, and my hands curl into fists. "What are they doing? Do I have to babysit these people?"

"Don't panic," Beau replies. "Maybe they sold so many tickets yesterday that now they get to chill."

I gesture to Lucy and Ciara. "Do they look like they are chilling?"

Beau's jaw tightens as he stares at the girls. "No. They look like death."

I groan as my blood boils. "I'm sorting this out."

I storm toward Whitney with Beau on my tail. "What's going on?" I practically yell it when I land in front of Whitney.

Whitney rears back in her chair, dropping her phone and giving me a disgusted look. "What's your deal?"

"Why is no one buying tickets?" I ask, leaning over the table. "Did you guys sell out in one day?"

"Oh my gosh, relax," Whitney whines. "We have all week."

Beau sighs, rolling his eyes. "How many did you sell yesterday?"

Whitney scoffs. "I dunno. Like, fifteen. It's more than the other girls. I think they sold four."

"Nineteen tickets?" I squeak as irritation festers inside me. "The school has hundreds of students. This isn't even close to cutting it."

Whitney groans. "Why are you getting on my case?"

Beau pulls me back from the table. "Forget this, Ava."

I scrunch my eyes closed, unable to believe what I'm hearing. "Forget it?"

I open my eyes to see Beau marching away from me. Before I can call his name, he weaves between tables with his sights set on Jeff.

He roughly pats Jeff's shoulder. "Hey, what gives, man?"

Jeff scoots his chair back, frowning at Beau. "What's your problem?"

Beau motions to Whitney. "Why aren't you up there selling tickets?"

With a hand pressed into my turbulent stomach, I make my way toward the table.

"There's no one over there," Jeff argues. "When there's a line, I'll go over and help Whitney out."

"*Geez*, relax, Beau," Hilary hisses. "It's not the end of the world. People can buy tickets on Friday."

Beau catches my eye as I approach and he taps Jeff's back. "Nuh-uh," he blurts. "Get up. You too, Marcus."

Marcus lifts his head like he's waking from a deep sleep. "Huh?"

"Get up," Beau orders. "We're selling these tickets. Today."

Jeff and Marcus exchange confused looks, and before they can argue, Beau steps on a chair and then onto the table.

"Hey, what the hell?" Hilary squeaks, grabbing her orange juice from the table.

"Ashworth Academy!" Beau bellows through cupped hands.

Gasps mixed with low murmurings circle the room.

Beaus points to the tables at each end of the cafeteria. "See these lovely ladies at these tables? They are selling tickets to the best Christmas dance this school will ever hold. Why aren't you off your butts and buying tickets?"

I pan the room as kids turn to their friends, shrug, and don't budge an inch.

Hilary elbows Marcus, and then he stands and steps onto his chair. "I know you people can move," he yells over the crowd. "I've seen everyone on the sidelines making noise and getting rowdy. Show some excitement for freaking Christmas."

"Come on," Beau takes over, throwing his arms up. "You won't want to miss the band, the food, and the epic maze of Christmas trees. It'll be like nothing you've ever seen before."

Jeff throws a leg over his seat and moves toward Whitney's table. He throws an arm up, calling out, "Come on, guys, and buy your tickets. Haven't the awesome posters gotten your attention?"

Whitney smiles at Jeff with appreciation.

Beau taps his chest as the crowd moves towards the ticket tables. "Does anyone think I'm a liar? Why would I tell you to buy tickets to something that was lame?"

"Fellas," Marcus booms through cupped hands. "You guys are gonna want to buy you and your ladies a ticket. It'll make an epic date night." He exaggerates a wink. "I promise."

My grin hurts when girls shove their boyfriends off their seats and toward the ticket tables.

Beau claps loudly. "Come on, everyone, I need to see you all moving. I'm not gonna shut up until you're all on your feet."

I have to laugh when the gasps and murmurs are combined with groans. I didn't realize it'd be such a hassle for people to buy tickets.

Hilary moves from her seat. When she passes me, she says, "I'm going to help Lucy and Ciara. Their line is getting long, and I don't want them to get overwhelmed."

"Thank you," I reply as she zips away.

Marcus leaps off his chair and moves to the table with Jeff and Whitney. My heart pounds from all the movement in the cafeteria. The chair screeching, chattering, and stomping off feet.

It's actually happening. All these people will see the magic we create.

Beau cheers from atop the table. "That's what I'm talking about. Fill those lines!"

He jumps off the table, and I rush to him with a hug. "Thank you so much!"

He holds me tight. "No problem. I told you I'd do anything to make this fun."

I giggle as his breath tickles my neck. "Was yelling at our classmates fun for you?"

"It always is," he jokes. "Score. The line for food has died down."

"That's because everyone was scared you'd threaten violence if they didn't immediately buy a ticket."

"That's their issue," Beau says as he walks me towards the food counter. "I didn't breathe a word about pounding on anyone."

"It's not like you have a reputation that makes anyone assume that," I tease.

"*Ouch*," he hisses. "That's cold."

I lift on the balls of my feet and peck his cheek in apology.

We get something quick to eat because we're eager to leave the noise and sneak away to our alcove by the auditorium. Seriously, I haven't made out with this boy all day!

After checking on the ticket lines and ensuring the team has it under control, I almost trip over my feet, leaving the cafeteria. Gosh, these make-out withdrawals are getting to me. I straighten up and spy Vanessa Ashworth approaching from the right.

"Good job in there," Vanessa says, throwing her thumb back at the cafeteria. "You really created some hype."

Beau turns to Vanessa, combing his fingers through his hair. "Oh, you know, just doing my part."

"Well, yesterday, it seemed like nobody was in a rush to buy their tickets," Vanessa replies. "Now just about everyone has gotten in line."

Beau turns back to me with a happy grin. "That's awesome."

I smile back at him, nodding.

"Ah, Beau?" Vanessa says, tucking a piece of bright blonde hair behind her ear. When he turns back to her, she lets out a melodic chuckle. "Umm... Oh, geez, I never do this."

His eyes narrow as he leans in. "What is it?"

Her face flushes with a pink hue. "Beau, would you like to be my date for the dance?"

Beau's eyes round, and his mouth falls open in surprise. "Oh," is all he can get out.

Vanessa giggles, swaying her hips. "I know. I'm being all awkward about it. But, I dunno, it might be fun. Right?"

My breathing becomes shallow and rough as my heart rate elevates.

Does she not see me standing here?

"Well, I wouldn't be much of a date." Beau scratches the back of his head. "I'm on the dance committee, which ties me up as a student chaperone."

Why doesn't Beau acknowledge me? Is he ashamed to admit we're together?

Vanessa swats a hand. "Oh, honey, you know I can get you out of that."

I thought he wanted to be with me, no matter what. Why is he playing with her?

"Well, that's not really the key issue, either," Beau says, cringing. He looks at me with a nervous smile and then turns back to Vanessa. "I kinda already have a date."

As embarrassment spreads over Vanessa, the blush pink on her face morphs into a fiery red. "Oh," she mumbles, taking a shaky step back.

Beau cups my hand. "Yeah, it's new, but Ava and I are dating."

"Dating?" Vanessa utters. She shoots a look at me and then back at Beau. "Like more than one date?"

Oh boy. Pins and needles prick every inch of my skin. My body feels more under attack now than when she didn't notice me.

Beau mumbles a laugh, squeezing my hand tighter. "That's the plan."

"Sorry, I didn't know," Vanessa says, stumbling backwards. "Sorry, I shouldn't have said anything."

"It's okay," I rush, wanting to make her feel better. "I'd never have the guts to do what you just did."

Vanessa frowns, looking Beau up and down. "Evidently, you didn't have to."

Vanessa turns and hurries up the hall with a series of rapid heel clicks.

Beau winces. "*Oof.* That was rough."

I sigh. "I knew she liked you."

"*Pfft*, no way," Beau replies. "I'm telling you, she only wants me to piss off her parents."

"She looked pretty embarrassed."

"That's because she got rejected." Beau places a kiss on my forehead. "Either way, I don't care. I've already got the girl for me."

Warmth spreads through my body, putting my shattered nerves at ease. I lift onto the balls of my feet and plant a dainty kiss on his lips. He kisses me back with hungry energy, pressing his hands into my lower back.

Even though my body urges me to continue the kiss, I push a hand against his chest, signaling for him to pump the brakes. Our lips break apart in a wet slide, and I slowly plant my feet on the ground.

"Speaking of the dance," I say, gliding my hand down his chest. "I want to go to the gym with you. That'll mean giving my dad a heads up about this."

Worry lines creep under his eyes. "Do you want me to ask him?"

I clasp both his hands, inhale deeply, and stand tall on the exhale. "Maybe you could come over for dinner? That way, Dad can see you for who you really are. Not just the guy in some stories."

Beau gives me an unconvinced look. "Do you think he'll let me come for dinner?"

"I told him we're dating and that I love you. He should want to get to know my boyfriend."

A goofy grin plays on Beau's lips. "That's the first time you've called me that."

I blush. "That's what you are, right?"

He caresses my cheek. "Correct, girlfriend."

An electric shiver runs down my spine, and I shake out my shoulders.

Beau rubs my arms. "Are you okay?"

"Yeah. I feel great."

He laughs. "Awesome. So, about dinner. I'll be there anytime you want me. I just don't know how you'll talk your dad into it."

"I do," I say with mock confidence. "I'll tell him that if you don't win him over, I'll break up with you."

Beau's jaw drops. "What?"

I caress his cheek. "Don't worry, babe. You'll win him over."

"Way to put the pressure on," he says, deflated. "You wouldn't really dump me, would you?"

I smile, feeling tingles from the power in my hands. "What do you think?"

"I think you like pleasing your father."

"Not as much as I love you."

"Aww. How sappy," Beau jokes.

I giggle and playfully punch his arm. "Shut up."

"*Ouch*," he hisses, rubbing his arm. "Girl, you don't know your own strength."

"Wait. Did I really hurt you?"

There goes his adorably lopsided grin. He leans down and kisses my nose. "You'll only hurt me if you dump me."

I hold on to the opening seams of his blazer. "We won't let that happen."

Twenty

After another storeroom make-out session, I'm in Beau's car on the way home. Kissing instead of talking cleared my head. It was sorely needed. Not only is Beau driving me home, but I'll be taking him inside my house. Probably a terrible idea that I haven't given my dad a head's up. However, asking my dad for permission would probably result in a no.

I'm shaky as I exit Beau's car. I wait for him to join me before approaching my house. I move behind the car when he seems to take too long.

Beau is looking at my neighbor's house, where Mrs. Yates and Mrs. Guthrie are smiling and waving. Tension mixed with happiness washes over Beau's face, and he waves back.

"Umm. Did you want to say hi?" I ask.

He shrugs. "Should I?"

Before I can respond, the ladies are calling us over.

Beau takes my hand and walks me toward Mrs. Guthrie's porch.

"Aww, this is new," Mrs. Guthrie comments. "I thought you said you had nothing to do with him."

A blush sweeps across my cheeks. "I guess a lot can change in two weeks."

"How are you, Beau?" Mrs. Yates asks. "And your parents?"

"I'm good," he replies. "My parents are fine. And you two?"

Mrs. Guthrie swats her hand. "Same old, same old."

Beau gestures across the cul-de-sac. "What's the family like who moved into my old house?"

"They're nice," Mrs. Yates says. "Lovely young family with two kids."

"But not as neighborly as your family was," Mrs. Guthrie adds. "Does much go on in your new neighborhood, Beau?"

"Nope. Nothing like it used to be here."

"Sadly, this place isn't what it used to be, either," Mrs. Yates says, frowning.

Jitteriness flows through my veins, causing me to pipe up. "What if it were again?"

"What's that, dear?" Mrs. Guthrie asks, leaning over the porch railing.

"Would you two be interested in another party in the cul-de-sac?" I ask, voice trembling. "You know, maybe to celebrate Christmas?"

"We'd be baking like crazy and telling all the neighbors in a heartbeat," Mrs. Yates says, beaming.

"But your father..." Mrs. Guthrie says, tampering down her enthusiasm.

"I know. It was just a thought," I mutter. "Beau and I have been reminiscing about how things used to be."

"If we got the green light," Mrs. Yates says, unable to contain her giddiness, "we'd knock on every door and get everyone excited for a get-together. We'd love to get things festive again, just like Lydie did."

I smile, leaning into Beau. "Thank you both. Anyway, we'd better head inside."

"Have a nice evening, you too," Mrs. Guthrie says, waving us off.

"Same to you," Beau says.

Mrs. Yates waves us off, already whispering party ideas to Mrs. Guthrie.

"They seem eager," Beau says as we walk to my front door.

"I know," I say, wanting to be excited, "but I can't think about this right now. We have my dad to deal with."

Beau gulps, nodding.

I unlock the front door and push it open. "Dad?"

A bead of sweat tumbles down my back. I step into the house, with Beau following. I gulp hard as my heart drops to my stomach.

"How was your day?" Dad calls from the kitchen.

Out of panic, I grab Beau's hand and clamp down on it. He hisses in reaction, but I don't loosen my grip as we enter the kitchen.

"Uh, Dad..." I trail off.

Dad turns from the stove and instantly turns pale. His eyes appear sunken and his cheeks hollow as his mouth hangs open.

I let go of Beau's hand and step closer to Dad. "Can Beau please stay for dinner? I want you to get to know him again."

Dad shakes his head, moving his jaw in preparation to speak.

I cut him off. "Please, Dad. He's my boyfriend, and I'm going to the dance with him."

Dad's eyes shut as he comprehends my words. "Why?" is all he can get out.

When he opens his eyes, I greet him with a demure smile and a shrug. "Because I love him."

"I'll leave if you want me to," Beau interrupts. "But, sir, I really do love your daughter."

"It's no secret I don't want you in my house," Dad says to Beau.

Beau scratches the back of his neck. "I know."

"If you get to know him again," I urge, "you'll like him again."

Dad's frown is ironclad as he sizes Beau up.

"If you don't like me by the end of dinner," Beau says, "then Ava and I will break up."

I shoot a look over my shoulder at Beau. Even though it was my plan, it's still earth-shattering when it comes from his lips.

I turn back to Dad, who's now smiling. "Okay, kids, you've got yourselves a deal."

I squeal and take Beau to the dining room before Dad changes his mind. We sit and chat quietly as Dad continues to cook in the next room. Beau is fidgety and keeps his eyes on the doorway. My excitement at having him over for dinner dwindles as realization sets in. My dad isn't easy to win over.

As the minutes tick over, tension fills the room like thick, invisible smoke, wrapping around my neck to a choking point. My inhales are ragged, and I barely exhale.

Beau's hand lands on my shoulder. "Whoa. You okay?"

I stand, knocking my chair backwards.

"What was that?" my dad calls out.

"Nothing," I call back as I round the table.

"Where are you going?" Beau asks, picking up my chair. "Are you bailing on me?"

I dash up the hall toward my bedroom. "I just need a minute."

I burst into my bedroom and pant heavy breaths. With my hands planted on my thighs, I lean over to catch my breath.

Come on, Ava, pull yourself together. This is what you want. You need your dad and Beau to get along. Otherwise, your relationship is doomed.

I stand tall, and as I do, I spot my childhood album sitting askew on my nightstand. My smile tingles, and I'm drawn over to it. When I pick up the album, I cuddle it. A warm breeze plays in my hair and tickles my skin. I look over my shoulder, expecting to see my mother.

"Thanks, Mom," I whisper as encouragement wells inside me.

With the album still cradled in my arms, I walk back to the dining room with renewed energy.

Beau studies my face from the dining table. "Everything okay?"

I bite into my lip and lift the album. "I have something to show you." I move back to the seat beside him and settle in. "This has pictures of us as kids."

Beau laughs. "No way."

"Wanna see?"

"Sure."

I open the album and slide it closer to Beau. He takes charge of flipping the pages, smiling and cringing at the photographs.

Beau taps a photo. "We're right back where we were."

I look past the tip of his finger to see six-year-old versions of us holding hands. My heart swells, and I fall back against my chair. "Aw, we are so dang cute."

Beau taps another photo and sighs. "I just feel so stupid. I lost so much time with you."

I pout and rub his arm. "I pushed you away."

Beau winces. "But I didn't welcome you back."

We settle into reflective silence as Beau flicks through a few more pages. As I drift into my thoughts, Beau puffs a laugh and then plants his palm over his mouth.

"What?" I question.

He lowers his hand and taps a photo. "Wasn't that our wedding day?"

I snort. "What are you talking about?"

He turns the album at an angle. "Don't you remember our wedding?"

I lean over the photo. We are in a park a block from Main Street. It was my mom's favorite place to take us. Set on a rolling grassy hill with fun play equipment and a large formation of rocks, where most of our adventures took place.

In the photo, I'm wearing a shimmery fairy-inspired dress. My mother bought it for me to play dress-up. Beau is wearing dark jeans and the cutest T-shirt with a tuxedo design on the front. I have flowers in my hair and a few squeezed in my hand. My gut squeezes as the memory pings inside my head.

"Oh my gosh," I murmur, a cupped hand hovering over my mouth. "It is. How did I not remember it?"

Beau pulls out his phone and snaps a photo of the photo. "Maybe marrying me wasn't as special to you as it was to me."

"We had so many fun times in that park."

Beau nods, sliding his phone back into his pocket. "We were so lucky to have your mom to take us."

I swipe under my eye just as a tear breaks. "Yeah. She really did let our imaginations run wild."

"You know, that hill is pretty sick to go sledding on."

"Oh, yeah?"

Beau takes my hand, kissing the back. "We should head out there one afternoon. It could be fun."

"I'm down for that."

Just as the tension dissipated from the room, cue my dad. He stomps his way in and places three plates on the table. Dad sits in front of Beau for the ultimate intimidation move.

I try to avoid the negative energy as Dad's famous creamy lemon parmesan chicken wafts delicious aromas in the room. "Mmm. Smells good, Dad."

Beau nods, picking up a fork. "Yeah, it does. Thank you."

"Mhmm," Dad grunts.

As the clanging and scraping of knives and forks fills the space, the invisible smoke wraps around my throat. Oh my gosh, this is brutal. Any time I look up from my plate, Dad is glaring at Beau. If I glance to my side, Beau continues to fidget and awkwardly chew his food.

My desperation climaxes, and I break the tension. "How was work?"

Dad shifts in his seat, making eye contact with me. "It was fine. Gilroy called in sick again, but McCoy picked up the slack. Seems like the team is starting to work together."

"Finally." I smile. "That's great."

"Is that where you get your leadership skills from?" Beau cuts in. "Mr. Jones, did you know Ava is a great leader?"

"Ava is great at many things."

"No doubt," Beau replies. "You should've seen her today. We walked into the cafeteria, expecting to see long lines for tickets, but it was as if the sales tables didn't exist. No one would be interested in the dance if Ava weren't there."

"That's not true," I counter. "You're the one who got everyone up and moving. I'd never seen someone rally a crowd like that. Dad, he was amazing."

Dad crosses his arms. "Did they move because he threatened them?"

"No," I say firmly. "He hyped the dance. He talked about the band, the decorations, and how it'll make a fun date night. Beau listens. You need to give him a shot."

"I don't need to do anything," Dad replies, but his arms uncross. "So, Beau, you've taken more of an interest in this committee? It's not just an after school detention?"

Beau glances at me and then turns to Dad. "Ava told me it would be fun, so now we make sure it is fun. Together."

Images of us in the storeroom flash through my mind. I smile, unable to hold back my giggle. "We make it so fun."

Awe pours out of Dad. I double-take as he smiles at me. "You look so happy."

I bite into my bottom lip. "I am happy."

Dad turns to Beau. "You've got one dinner to convince me."

Beau straightens up, clearing his throat. "I appreciate you giving me another chance."

"I wouldn't put it that way," Dad says bluntly.

"*Dad,*" I whine. "You just said you were giving him a shot."

"I said he has a chance to convince me. I'm yet to give this relationship a chance." Dad scrutinizes Beau's face. "You remind me of your father."

Beau flicks his eyes my way and then back at Dad. "Is that a good thing or a bad thing?"

Dad sits back in his chair with his hands clasped. "It's an unsettling thing."

Beau flinches, and I pivot my gaze between them.

I clear my throat and say to Dad, "Mr. Stevenson said he hasn't seen or spoken to you in years."

"There are reasons people drift apart." Dad swivels a finger at Beau and me. "You two drifted apart after he showed his true colors."

My feet jitter against my chair legs. "That's not entirely true."

Dad gives me a sympathetic look. "I know you were grieving, but when you wanted him, he wasn't the boy you knew. I remember all the days you came home from school crying and feeling scared."

Beau shifts in his chair, turning to face me. "You cried over me?"

I frown, letting my gaze fall. "It was a lot."

"You didn't trust him anymore, sweetheart. Why should you now?"

Beau clears his throat. "Because now I know she wants me back."

I look up as Dad leans forward with a look of surprise. "It's all about Ava?"

Beau nods. "Of course."

"You started bullying other kids because she pushed you away?"

"What? No," Beau replies. "Ava had nothing to do with that."

"But if you'll stop for her, surely you started because of her?"

"*Dad.*"

"It's okay," Beau says, sitting tall. "I'll answer any of your questions because I want you to accept me as part of Ava's life."

"Why should I trust you with my daughter?"

"I care about her the way I always have."

"You're going to pretend it's four years ago and you're her best friend," Dad replies. "But, in the meantime, you've been the school's resident brute."

"I'm not saying I haven't done bad stuff." He slides his hand over mine. "I now know how I pushed her further away. I won't let that happen again."

"He's better," I reassure Dad, "for me."

"And if Ava's not around?" Dad continues, keeping his eyes locked on Beau. "What then? How will you treat other people?"

"I'm not perfect," Beau answers. "I don't have a magic switch to undo everything. I can't change my personality. But, to be honest, with Ava in my life, I don't notice other people."

"Can't you give him a chance?" I plead, and Dad finally looks my way.

"I'm trying," Dad replies, "but my questions keep getting dodged."

I slam a fist on the table. "He doesn't bully people because I wasn't around for him."

Dad huffs, tilting his head as his eyes dull with hopelessness. "How can you say that?"

Beau fidgets uncomfortably, whispering out the side of his mouth. "Ava..."

"You can't judge him," I say, pulling back from unloading Beau's family secrets at the dinner table. "You don't know what his home life is like."

Dad smirks. "Yes, it must be hard being a spoiled brat."

Beau shrugs, attempting to laugh off the comment. "I do all right. You've seen my car, right?"

Dad's jaw flexes. "You mean the death trap?"

Beau shrugs and sinks lower in his seat. "Look, it's hard to break my habits. Maybe I am dodging questions." He shifts again, rubbing the back of his neck. "I never realized I was hurting people until recently."

Dad frowns. "That seems like a stretch."

"I didn't think about it," Beau replies. "When Ava got hurt, it rattled me. I don't want to make people feel bad or be in pain."

"So you did hurt Ava?"

"*Dad*," I whine. "That's not what he's saying."

"Sir, all I'm saying is most of the time I feel like crap," Beau says earnestly. "I want to do better so I'm not passing on this crappy feeling to other people."

"Hmm," is the only response my dad can muster.

Again, the scraping of cutlery on china plates fills the space. Until Dad's cell rings and he excuses himself from the table. When he disappears up the hall, I collapse with a sigh.

Beau blows out a frustrated breath. "Are you okay?"

"I knew this wouldn't be easy." I smooth a hand over the photo album of our younger selves. "If we'd stayed friends, I think I'd be a different person. You were always a thrill seeker, and being with you gave me confidence. I don't think I'd have turned out so shy. I think I'd be a brat."

Beau mumbles a laugh. "No way. Your parents raised you too well."

"I thought yours had too."

"I need a distraction. What else is in here?" Beau asks, pulling the photo album closer. He skips to a page toward the back. "Aw, it's you and Lydie."

All my effort pours into not tearing up right now. Thankfully, Beau flips to another page.

"Wow," he gasps. "Look how good your house used to look."

It's a two-page spread of our home at Christmas time. There's a wide shot of the entire cul-de-sac. Not to be biased, but our house is by far the brightest and cheeriest. Santa on his sleigh, guided by his reindeer. A momma, poppa, and baby snowman with exaggerated smiles and carrot noses. And too many lights cover every side of the house.

"What has you two so interested?" Dad asks, walking back into the dining room.

"Old photos," I reply.

Dad takes his seat, glancing at the photographs. "Oh, I see."

"You still have all these decorations, sir?" Beau asks.

Dad grows rigid. "Yes. What of it?"

"If you want," Beau says tentatively, "I could set up some of your outdoor decorations."

Dad's eyes narrow. "Set them up where?"

Beau points toward the front of the house. "Outside."

Dad grows wary, like he's interacting with a shonky salesperson. "Why would you want to do that?"

Apprehension elongates Beau's face as he sneaks a glance my way. "Ahh..." He trails off as he turns back to my father. "I just thought if you were too busy, maybe you'd appreciate the help. I hang up the outdoor decorations with my dad every year. I don't mind doing it for you."

Dad's lips press into a firm line. "If we wanted the decorations out, they'd be out."

My stomach churns and my knees bounce, forcing my feet to smack against the chair legs. His use of the word "we" forms a crack in my heart.

236

Beau sits back, craning his neck to glimpse the lights, tinsel, and ornaments scattered around the rooms. "But Ava likes decorations."

"Beau," I warn. "It's fine."

"But every other house..."

"*Beau.*" I sharply cut him off.

"We don't need to prove anything, young man," Dad says curtly as he folds his arms, looming over us.

"Sorry," Beau mumbles, raising his hands defensively. "Didn't realize it'd be such a big deal."

"Well, it's getting late..." Dad remarks, flicking his wrist to view his watch.

"You know, if you did have Christmas decorations in your front yard," Beau says, lowering his head as he taps the table, "you'd be ready if someone threw a party for the neighborhood."

Dad huffs. "What are you going on about?"

I suck in a ragged breath. The exhaustion lingering in Dad's tone is a clear sign he's about to break. I want to avoid him yelling across the table. He's always stubbornly inflexible at the mere mention of a neighborhood party.

"When I lived in the cul-de-sac, there was a Christmas party on the street every year." Beau taps the photo album. "Like in this book."

With white knuckles, Dad's hand crumples a paper napkin. "Well, something changed the year you moved out, didn't it?"

Beau's eyes shine with wateriness. "Lydie was like another mom to me. I still miss her. Doesn't mean we can't have fun like she did."

Dad tosses the misshapen napkin onto his plate, and stands tall. "Fun can get you into trouble." He lifts his plate and steps away from the table. "Excuse me."

Beau's lip upturns as Dad disappears into the kitchen. He rubs his temples, whispering, "It's just a potluck with your neighbors, not a kegger with the football team."

I rest my forehead against his shoulder. "He'll never go for the idea."

"We have to try." Beau strokes my hair and plants a kiss atop my head. "He's put a stop to everybody else's attempts. We need him on side so you can host the party you want."

I lift my head. "He's too set in his ways."

A hopeful smile dashes across Beau's lips. "No, he's not. I'm here having dinner with him. Anything is possible."

"That's true. Miracles do happen."

Beau motions to the kitchen. "We should join him."

"Uh, no. We should let him cool off."

"I've had arguments with parents, teachers, counselors, cops, and shopkeepers," Beau says. "They're all the same. You give them some space, and they come down hard. Right now, your dad is forming the best wording to kick me out of the house and shut down this topic for good."

I frown, pressing a hand into my feeble stomach. "I don't want to ambush him."

Beau clutches my other hand, rubbing his thumb in a delicate circle. "It's not an ambush. It's the rest of the conversation."

"How do you have this much confidence to continue such awkward topics?"

He shrugs. "I dunno. Like I said, every conversation with an adult goes the same. Pretty soon it gets easy to exhaust them."

"You've already exhausted my dad."

Beau smirks. "Nah. I got a little more to go."

"Don't anger him."

He lifts my hand and meets it with a kiss. "I would never. If he wants me out, I'm walking out. As long as you're okay."

I nod. We both stand, holding our plates, and make our way into the kitchen.

"Ah, Dad... Can we talk about..."

"Every time someone comes to me with an idea for a street party," Dad says in a broken tone, "they say they want to honor Lydie's memory."

Shock ripples through me. My dad usually shuts these conversations down by now.

"But isn't that a good thing?" I ask gently.

Dad leans against the counter, staring at his shiny black shoes. "Every time I'm reminded of her life ending, it brings back every horrible, dark thought."

"If we have a party, a celebration, maybe happy and light memories will replace all the nasty thoughts?"

Dad lifts his head. His eyes fill with sadness, yet he summons the courage to smile. "But what if it doesn't?"

"I got excited every time a neighbor wanted to host a party," I say, curling my arm around Dad's arm. "It always sounded fun and like a piece of Mom was coming back."

Dad smooths back my hair. "But it wouldn't be her party."

The threat of a sob tickles inside my throat. "Every time you said no, it was like losing her all over again."

"Oh, sweetheart," Dad coos. "I didn't mean to hurt you. I just feel trapped in a dark void when it comes to your mother."

"I don't want to feel that way anymore," I whisper. "You shouldn't want to either."

Dad's smile becomes more genuine, and his hand brushes the side of my face. "You've become more confident over the last two weeks. More aware of your own happiness. I forgot what you looked like when you shine."

I look over my shoulder at Beau, and then back at Dad. "My heart's been broken about the past. I feel like I'm whole again. Well... almost whole."

"And hosting a party like your mother used to would help you?"

Tears sting my eyes as I nod in reply.

Dad looks past me at Beau. "And you think this boy is good to you?"

My voice is weak as I reply, "The best."

Dad's eyes return to me. "I'll think about the neighborhood party, okay?"

Happiness boosts my smile, and I nod enthusiastically.

Dad looks past me again. "And you."

I gulp as I look over my shoulder at Beau.

"Beau, you have my permission to be my daughter's date to the school dance," Dad says, extending his arm.

Beau grins, shaking Dad's hand. "Thank you, Mr. Jones."

"I'm sure you'll be on your best behavior," Dad replies with a wily grin. "If not, I'll know about it because I'll be chaperoning the dance."

I splutter a choked cough. "Excuse me? Since when?"

Dad meets my eyes, and a kind smile relaxes his face. "Since I realized I have to take a more serious interest in what my daughter likes."

Beau clears his throat. "I promise, sir, even if you weren't there, I'd be a perfect gentleman."

Dad nods. "You'd better be."

I pivot between the two and land on my dad with a bewildered stare. "Umm. Ah, thanks, Dad. Oh my gosh. I'm shocked."

"It's undeniable how happy you are, sweetie," Dad replies. "But I'm still watching him like a hawk."

My shoulders slump. "Can't you just say you approve of him?"

Dad taps a finger to his chin as if thinking about it. "Let's give it sometime. It's our first interaction in a long time."

I have to give it to him. I couldn't run away fast enough after my first committee meeting with Beau.

"Well, I'd better not overstay my welcome and say something stupid," Beau says. He steps forward and takes hold of my shoulder, giving me a kiss on the cheek. "Thank you for dinner, Mr. Jones. And for everything else."

"Take care of yourself, Beau," Dad replies. "Drive carefully."

"Will do," he replies.

"I'll walk you out," I say.

Hand in hand, Beau and I leave for the front door.

"Oh my gosh," I squeal. "He's okay with us dating."

"As okay as a man set in his ways can be," Beau jokes.

"This is huge."

Beau smiles and wraps his arms around me. "I get it, Aves. I'm relieved I'm still standing. I guess it'll take a few more family dinners before I stop pushing your dad's buttons."

"He's prodding you to mess up."

"Like I said, I'm staying on my A-game so I can stay in your life."

We pull out of the hug, and I sneak a kiss on his lips. "Text me when you get home."

"Will do."

Beau leaves, and a warm feeling melts through my body. I lean against the closed front door, and a happy sigh pours out of me. My mind conjures wonderful images of the dance, swaying with Beau on the dancefloor, chatting with my dad, and taking happy snaps in front of an array of Christmas trees.

When I see myself in my mind's eye, I'm vividly wearing one particular dress. Courage spirals inside me, and I rush to the other end of the house. In my bedroom, I rummage through my closet, pulling out the satin red cocktail dress. Every vein in my body electrifies, and I force myself out of the room before I chicken out.

"Daddy?" I cautiously step into the kitchen, finding Dad with his back to me.

"Yes, sweetheart?" He doesn't turn around because he's busy making my lunch for the next day.

I press the dress against me and struggle to get words out.

Dad rolls his shoulders back and turns away from the counter. "Are you still there?"

When he turns all the way around, his jaw drops. The butter knife in his hand clangs to the ground. His eyes wander the length of the dress.

I tuck the hanger under my chin. "Can I wear Mom's dress?"

"Oh, sweetie, I..." His words trail off as he fixates on the dress. "It's a little old for you."

"Please," I whisper, hugging the dress. "I'll be careful with it."

"You might be too cold," Dad says, spinning his wheels for excuses.

"The gym will be heated. Please. I love this dress, and it was one of Mommy's favorite things."

Dad smiles, angling his head. "You'll look so grown-up in that."

I lift onto my toes, grinning. "Is that a yes?"

Happiness beams from him. "Yes, sweetheart, you can wear it."

I squeal, lowering the dress and throwing my arms around Dad. "Thank you! Thank you!"

He chuckles and pats my back. "Hang on a minute. I have something that'll go with it."

I unwrap my arms from around him and step back. Dad moves around me and vanishes up the hall. I drape the dress over my arm and prick my ears, wondering what he's getting.

Dad returns with a small black box in his palm. "This will make your dress complete."

He hands me the box, and I carefully open the lid. Inside, sitting on black velvet, is a brooch, shaped like a snowflake and encrusted in diamantes.

"Oh." I gasp. "It's so pretty."

"It was one of the last things your mother bought." Dad pauses, sniffing hard. "She'd want you to wear it."

I dab under my eyes. "Thank you. I love it."

Twenty-One

Lucy sent a group message through the school portal for us all to meet in one of the music rooms this morning. Teddy and Sullivan want to show off their track list for the dance and are ready to rehearse.

Teddy has an electric guitar strapped over his shoulder, and Sullivan stands behind a keyboard. "We have a bassist and a drummer organized for the night," Teddy explains. "You'll get the same feel just from the two of us."

When the boys play, they're as polished as their videos and recordings. They play a medley of different songs and also tell us they have DJ equipment to play upbeat Christmas carols during their intermittent breaks. This makes Lucy smile, as I'm sure she's hoping to take those opportunities to dance with Teddy. Seriously, I've never seen a girl more smitten.

Well, other than me, when the sight of Beau makes my heart flutter.

The group sounds off feedback to the band. My eyes stay glued to the door. Beau is at wrestling practice, but is to join us when it's finished. It should be any minute now. After last night's success during dinner, I can't wait to wrap my arms around this boy.

Involuntarily, I lift on tippy toes as the door handle turns. My grin soars and I feel like I'm floating towards the ceiling as Beau enters the room.

"Whoa," Teddy says, losing grip of his guitar. "What the hell are you doing here?"

"Umm." Lucy clears her throat. "Beau is part of our committee, and we make decisions as a group."

Sullivan points between Lucy and Beau. "You let this guy into your group?"

Beau lifts his hands defensively. "I was told to come after wrestling practice. I can leave."

"Ugh." Teddy grimaces. "You're back on the wrestling team?"

Sullivan points at me. "You're the chairperson, aren't you? Tell me you won't stand for this guy being in the room."

"*Ha!*" Whitney smirks. "She's dating this guy. God help us with her decisions for the dance. She's obviously got no taste."

"Wow," Beau drags out the word. "It's a wonder you never say what's on your mind, Whitney."

"Wait." Teddy glares at me. "You're actually dating Beau?"

My shoulders rise to my earlobes and my face flashes red. My breathing hastens as every eye lands on me. I can't deny that I really wish Beau was standing right next to me. I feel so exposed without his protection.

Teddy looks at me sideways when I don't respond. "You know you can do better. Don't you?"

"Guys." Marcus throws his hands up like stop signs and marches into the center of the room. "We don't need this getting heated. Yes, Beau is part of the group, and we've all made our peace with it. And don't belittle Ava. Yes, it's weird they're a couple, but leave her alone."

Hilary latches onto my hand, giving it a squeeze. She gives me a confident nod and then looks back at her boyfriend. "Marcus and I talked about how we've been rough on you regarding Beau. We'll stick by you if this relationship is what you want."

Wow. People in my corner. I faintly recall this is what it means to have friends.

Beau smirks, nodding at Marcus. "What about me?"

"You can handle yourself," Marcus says bluntly. "You've got years of experience being confrontational."

"We need our lighting, sound, and projection equipment in working order during our set," Teddy says, chest heaving with panic. He fires a pointed finger at Beau. "We can't deal with him sabotaging our equipment and ruining our performance."

"You guys have got to get over it," Beau says, exhausted. "You're not that special for me to keep coming after, and it'd be lame to pull the same stunt twice. Besides, I won't be anywhere near your precious equipment. Lucy and Ciara are in charge of entertainment. They'll make sure everything is in check."

An angry frown twitches on Sullivan's face. "You don't even care. You ruined all our hard work. You know, no one cared. All anyone talked about was your fight with those linebackers."

"No one is saying that was cool," Jeff says in a placating tone. "You have to know Marcus and I aren't okay with that."

Teddy glares at Jeff. "You're talking about the fight, not what Beau did to us."

"Look, I'm down for the set list you guys have offered," Jeff says, moving toward the door. "But I gotta get going. Are we good here?"

"I liked everything you guys did, too." I move toward Beau and motion toward the door. "I hope you guys can cool off and get excited about the dance. We'll see you at rehearsal on Friday night."

Beau swivels toward the door, taking the hint to leave with me.

"Well, that was awkward," he says when we reach the hall.

I blow out a hard breath. "I was so excited to see you. I didn't even think about how those boys would react."

"I don't care what they say about me, but they better watch themselves. If they say anything nasty about you..."

I cut him off. "You won't do anything. You promised."

"Ugh." He frowns, shifting his weight. "Okay. You're right. Old habits die hard."

I reach for his hand and notice a dark red patch of blood dripping from his knuckle. "Beau," I gasp. I gently clutch his hand, lifting it up and inspecting the cut. "You're bleeding."

"Oh, dang," he says, mildly annoyed. "I thought it had stopped bleeding."

"You cut yourself?"

His lips drag down, and he shakes his head. "Nope. I punched the floor."

I give him a strange look. "You, what?"

He points to his index and middle knuckles. "These two cracked against the floorboards. Hurt like hell."

My eyes narrow, noticing faint bruises that color his hand. "Why did you punch the floor?"

"Nothing," he says, taking his hand away from mine. It doesn't answer the question, but he adds, "At least it wasn't someone's head."

"I guess," I mumble, confused by his response. "Why don't I take you to the nurses' office?"

Beau shrugs it off. "It's not that bad. It'll stop bleeding."

"I can already see bruises appearing. You need ice." I brush the side of his face. "You took care of me. Let me take care of you."

He smiles, looking deeply into my eyes. "Okay. You know I'll take any excuse to spend more time with you."

I smile, leading him away from the music room. In a flash, pain drills into my skull as memories flood my mind. Beau standing by those lockers, holding the boys by the throat. The fear I felt replays in my body, muddling itself with the deep affection I now have for Beau. The mixed emotions are sickening.

I cup a hand over my mouth as I silently retch. Everyone still sees him as a bully. Our vice principal might be proud of his turnaround. But is that so the school can get a wrestling trophy? Is it a mistake to believe Beau can walk away from those boys without provoking them later?

We slow down when we round a corner, and he asks, "Are you okay?"

I clear my throat, gulp, and then an audible retch flies out. "Yeah," I grunt. "Are you?"

He steps in front of me. "You sound sick."

I clear my throat again, patting my chest. "No, I'm okay."

He tucks a piece of hair behind my ear. "I hope so. I don't want you feeling sick. Anyway, I meant it about those clowns back there. Did they hurt your feelings?"

I suck in a breath and bite into my lower lip.

Beau sighs, shifting his weight. "I thought I'd put an end to them meddling in my life. I won't let anyone say anything disrespectful to you."

"We already had this discussion about Whitney."

"And I said I wouldn't put up with her crap. Not when it comes to you."

My heart splinters. "I don't want you to hurt anyone."

"It would only be a threat. I won't hit anyone."

I lift his bruised hand. "And what about this? What made you hit the floor?"

His jawline strains, and he blows out a breath. "Yesterday I ignored the comments, but today I couldn't. I punched the ground beside Franky's head like a warning shot. Now he knows better than to say anything vile about the girl I love."

My bottom lip quivers as my eyes water. "They kept talking about me?"

Beau swipes his thumb under my eye. "It's in the past now."

My gut twists in on itself, causing me to wince. "Doesn't it make you want to break up with me? Everyone thinks I'm a frigid dud."

"Hey," he coos, running his hand through my hair. "Three idiots said things like that. The whole school doesn't think that. And, more importantly, I don't think that."

Even though I'm staring into his heavenly light blue eyes, my frown is immovable. "Really?"

He breaks into a smile, dropping his hand to my shoulder. "Of course. You know that. Besides, I'd think you'd want to run from me. Everyone looks at you like you're crazy for being with me."

"I wish they'd all get a life."

A whisper of a laugh slips out of Beau. "Me too."

I run my hands along the lapels of his blazer. "It scares me when you threaten other people."

"I'm trying to stop," he whispers with a pained expression. "I promise. It took so much willpower to hit the floor instead of his face."

I nod. "You just need to keep walking away. Now, we should get some ice."

He shakes his head. "No, it'll be fine. It doesn't hurt that bad."

"Don't let it get worse. I need you to help me decorate on Friday night."

He pecks my cheek. "Nothing will stop me from helping you."

I grasp his hand, inspecting the knuckles. "Is it really okay?"

"Yeah. The pain will remind me not to lose my cool."

My eyebrow arches with skepticism. "Has that ever worked before?"

"Sometimes," he says, staring at the back of his hand. "Any time I need to focus on an exam or listen to my coach instead of fixating on my parents."

I pout. "I didn't mean to be hard on you. I know your home life is tough."

"I'm not making excuses," he says, lowering his hand. "I just have impulses that are hard to control. To be honest, sometimes I don't want to control them."

A spark of hope brightens inside me. "But you will?"

He smiles, caressing the side of my face. "For you, anything."

I push my lips onto his, and the moment stretches out. Our mouths stay closed during the kiss. The prior tension still lingers around us. I want to believe in him. I want to believe our love is enough.

I hate that I'm still questioning my relationship with him.

For the rest of the day, Beau and I text in classes we don't share. At lunch, we join the others in the cafeteria to help with ticket sales. When Whitney insists she's got it covered, we don't argue, taking the time to be alone together.

By the time I'm in my last class, psychology, the messages from Beau have stopped. We were talking about what we're doing this afternoon. He hasn't responded about where we should meet.

I still hate walking the hallways alone. After the bell rings, I resort to old habits, letting others move ahead of me.

"Ava," Hilary calls out from the doorway. She waves and has a chipper smile. "You coming?"

This is the part where I slap my forehead. *Duh.* I have friends now.

I grab my books and hurry to the door. "Yeah. Thanks."

"How are you going with the assignment?" she asks as we enter the hallway.

"I conducted my interview. I just feel icky about writing the report."

"Why? Who did you interview?"

I clench my teeth, not wanting to say.

"I interviewed Marcus," Hilary says, seemingly ignoring the fact I didn't respond. "He did it begrudgingly. I always get my way with that boy."

"He's head over heels about you."

Hilary nudges me. "Did you interview Beau?"

I blow out a breath. "Yes. He was very honest. I'm not sure I want to share what came out."

"*Dang,*" Hilary cheers. "Sounds juicy. What did he say?"

My mouth falls open. "Hils, I can't tell you that."

Hilary shrugs. "Why not? I'll tell you what Marcus told me."

I cradle my books tighter as my back cramps. "I need to figure out my plan before I can share anything in the assignment."

"Suit yourself," Hilary says, veering off towards her locker. "See you tomorrow."

I wave awkwardly under my books and keep moving forward. My shoulders lock as a group of boys block my way.

"Uh, umm..." I stammer. "Excu... Excuse me."

I keep my head down, moving around the group. I almost trip as a group of girls hurtle past me on the other side. I fumble with my books, sure I'm about to drop them all over the ground. I can just imagine everyone stepping on my hands as I gather them up.

"I'll take those," a voice says. Two strong hands take control of my books.

I look up to see Beau's sparkling eyes and adoring grin.

My shoulders ease with a relieved sigh. "Thank you."

He kisses my cheek. "How are you?"

"Good, now."

"What a surprise to see you tackling the hallways on your own. I'm so proud."

Blushing, I wipe a piece of hair off my face. "Hilary was with me. I kinda freaked out when she left for her locker."

Beau tucks my books under his arm. "Well, I got you now."

"Is she okay?" a sweet voice asks from behind Beau.

Beau steps to the side, and Vanessa appears in view, eyeing me with concern.

"Oh, hi," I stammer.

Beau tosses a thumb over his shoulder, saying, "We were just leaving class together when I spotted you."

"Oh my gosh," Vanessa says, rummaging in her blazer pocket. She holds out a phone in her palm. "Here's your phone."

Beau takes it. "Oh, yeah. Thanks."

Vanessa grins with a flirtatious glint in her eyes. "What would you do without me?"

Beau smirks. "Yeah, you totally saved me."

Vanessa coils a hand around Beau's wrist and squeezes. "Anytime."

Queasiness ripples through my stomach. I glance between the two, who hold their stare for a beat too long.

Vanessa breaks the stillness with a giggle. She unhands Beau and wiggles her fingers in a playful wave.

"See you tomorrow," she says, backing away.

"What was that about?" I ask.

"Oh, she took my phone in class before Ms. Kyle walked past my desk." He blows out a breath, looking up at the ceiling. "I did not need my phone confiscated again."

"You need to learn self-control. You should be able to get through class without looking at your phone."

"*Ha.* Says the girl who can't stop texting me."

"You stopped replying to me."

"And, let me guess, you filled the rest of your time by adding ideas to your binder?" Beau teases.

"At least my activity isn't disruptive."

"Neither is mine. I was just minding my own business."

"You weren't sending someone harassing messages?"

Beau rolls his eyes. "Man, you do that a couple of times. Now that's all anyone thinks you do."

"You've got a reputation."

He draws a cross on his chest over his heart. "I've done nothing like that since being with you."

I draw a cross. "I believe you."

He traces a finger along my jaw. "Besides, it's your fault I was looking at my phone."

I look at him strangely and pat the outline of my phone through the pocket of my skirt. "Why? You didn't text me, did you?"

Beau smirks. "No. I was looking at your picture."

In a snap, all the color drains from my flesh. "You what?"

"It was so lucky Ness took my phone when she did," Beau says, holding back a laugh. "I didn't need Ms. Kyle ogling my girlfriend."

"The photo of me without..." The deafening thuds of my heartbeat are in slow motion. "How could you look at that in class?"

Beau chuckles nervously. "I couldn't help it. I was bored, and I like that picture."

My anxiety spikes. "How could you?"

"How can you blame me?"

I suck in a rushed breath. "Oh my gosh, did Vanessa see it? Beau, that picture is only for you. If anyone else sees it..."

He cuts me off. "No, she didn't see it. I mean, she'd say something if she did. Who wouldn't say something after seeing that picture?" He nudges me. "The words ooh-la-la come to mind."

My mood plummets. "Don't joke. If anyone sees..." I take in a breath and then exhale hard. "If you can't keep the picture to yourself, you have to delete it."

"Aves, I'm sorry. I won't look at it during school again."

I give him an uncertain look.

"If I could erase it out of my mind, I would," he says gently. "But I don't think that'll ever happen."

His lips curl in the most delicious way. My body relaxes in reaction, and I smile back at him.

He winks, whispering in a gravelly tone, "You know I think you're sexy."

I laugh. "Stop it."

"Come on, sexy," he says, grabbing my hands. "Let me take you out on a date."

Twenty-Two

Looking at the photo album last night consumed most of our conversations today. So Beau suggests we head to my mother's favorite park and recreate some of our childhood adventures. We'll just leave off the wedding reenactment from the list of activities.

We trek across the snow-covered parkland and head for the rock formations against the hillside.

"It used to look bigger," Beau comments as we stand at the base, gazing up.

"I wanna see if it's easier to climb now," I say, setting my foot on a rock. "I remember being terrified of climbing as a kid."

"It'll be slippery," Beau says, steadying a hand on my lower back. "Your mom only let us climb in the warmer months. I don't want this to be the third incident of you getting hurt on my watch."

"I'll be fine. You're watching me regardless, right?"

He laughs. "Sure, I'm watching. See how far you get."

My knitted gloves are horrible for gripping icy rocks, but I persevere. I dig my shoes into the crevasses between the rock formations and use my core to lift myself higher.

"Whoa, go girl," Beau says, impressed. "I knew you were strong."

I grunt, pulling myself up higher. I suck in a breath as my gloves slip and tear against a new rock.

"Are you okay?" Beau asks, standing guard.

"*Eep*. Can you help me down?"

He smirks, grabbing hold of my hips. "Sure thing. I got you."

I land on the spongy snow and smile at the pride on Beau's face. "I haven't climbed in a long time."

"You look so pleased with yourself," Beau replies. "I love seeing you have fun."

"Usually, I'd be revising history, or geometry, or something else mind-numbing. I'm so freaking glad to be out of the house."

Beau takes me by the hand and gestures to the snowy ground. We both collapse, lying on our backs and staring up at the overcast sky.

"Imagine how many adventures we could have after graduation," he says. "We could take a year off and go traveling. We can use that time to work out what we really want to do with our lives."

"It'll be like pressing pause," I reply. "But instead of standing still, we make epic memories."

He takes his eyes away from the sky, turning to smile at me. "Yeah. Do you want that?"

I grin, nodding. "I want that."

Beau's arm reaches out, and I move to catch it, but instead he fans out his limbs in true snow angel fashion. I follow his lead, dragging my arms and legs through the snow.

"I bet yours looks better," Beau says, sitting up. "It'll look cuter, anyways."

I grab his collar and pull him back down, roughly kissing his mouth. He pulls back with a pop, and I grin at his surprise.

"I don't care what they look like individually," I say. "I wanna see what they look like when we roll around together."

Beau leans over me, and his voice gets gravelly. "Oh yeah. I see what you like."

He lowers, kissing me with increasing intensity. Who knew things could get so steamy when lying on the cold, wet ground?

As I writhe under him from sheer passion, my hand scrunches on the snow at my side. Before I know it, I'm holding a tight ball. Without knowing what possesses me, I whack it against Beau's neck.

He jerks away from me with a gasp.

I cackle at him, rolling away. "I can't help it."

"Yeah, that's right," he says, gathering snow in his hand, "you'd better move away."

I hold up my hands in defense, throwing a pathetic whine into my voice. "You wouldn't hurt me, would you?"

His shoulders slump. "Don't give me those puppy eyes."

Behind my back, I hurriedly ball a wad of snow. With bad aim, I hurl the snowball in his direction.

His jaw drops. "Ava? Seriously?"

I fall back, holding my belly in laughter.

"You bad girl," he says, laughing.

Before I can sit back up, a snowball thwacks against my chest.

"Ah, no fair," I say, still giggling.

"What do you know about fair?" he asks, crawling beside me. "You play dirty, Ava Jones."

I give him my most innocent expression. "What can I say? I don't get out much. My social etiquette is rusty."

"You'd never let me get away with an excuse like that."

I sit up, planting a kiss on his nose. "Yeah, but I'm cuter than you."

He laughs and kisses my forehead. "Very true."

I look up at the sky and whisper, "I wonder what my mom would think if she could see us now."

"I think she'd be happy for us."

I brush my cheek against his. "I hope so."

He briskly rubs my back. "We should get out of the cold. I know you make epic hot chocolates, but how do you feel about going to a café?"

"That sounds great. We should go to Morton's. They make a hazelnut supreme hot chocolate that is crazy good."

"Mmm yum. I've never had it, but I want it."

Eagerly, we race back to Beau's car and head to Morton's Café on Main Street. Inside the cafe, we walk to the front counter, but Beau halts, forcing me to run into him.

"Oh crap."

"What is it?" I ask, finding my footing.

Beau looks off to the side. "My dad is here."

I hastily look around the space. "What? Really?"

Mr. Stevenson sits in a booth with another man. They're both in business suits and deep in conversation.

"Do you want to go somewhere else?" I ask.

"Yeah. He hasn't noticed us yet. Maybe we can get out undetected."

As we turn from the counter, Mr. Stevenson and the other man stand from their seats. They exit the booth and shake hands. Mr. Stevenson turns our way, locking eyes with Beau.

Beau huffs. "So much for our getaway."

"Hugo," Mr. Stevenson says to the other man. "Meet my son, Beau."

There's pride in Mr. Stevenson's expression as he and his business associate walk our way.

"What a pleasant surprise," Mr. Stevenson says as he lands in front of us.

Hugo, as Mr. Stevenson called him, extends a hand to Beau. "Nice to meet you. Heard many good things about you."

Beau's lip upturns as he shakes the man's hand. "Really? That doesn't sound likely."

Mr. Stevenson chuckles, and I wonder if his business associate can also tell it's fake. Mr. Stevenson shows his colleague out as they talk about the bill.

"No, I'll get the check," Mr. Stevenson says through the doorway. "Thank you for meeting with me."

Beau cracks his neck, wincing as his dad strides toward us.

"Hi, Ava," Mr. Stevenson says. "So lovely to see you again."

"What are you doing in town?" Beau says bluntly before I can reply. "I thought you were working in the city."

"Change of plans," his father replies. "Hugo was in town, so we decided to meet over coffee. How about you two? Can I buy you a cup and ask you about school?"

"School?" Beau repeats in an argumentative tone. "Since when do you care?"

"Please," Mr. Stevenson said flatly, "I'm trying here."

I noticed the strain in Beau's jaw as my ears prick to the flex of his knuckles cracking into a fist.

"Not if you're busy," I blurt to cut off anything hostile from Beau. "We don't want to hold you up."

"Nonsense," Mr. Stevenson says with a happy grin that reminds me of when Beau gets excited about something. "I'm so happy to see you two still together. And Beau, it seems like I never see you."

Beau shrugs. "That's not my fault."

Mr. Stevenson frowns. "I know. I work too late. But we have time now."

I look at Beau and wait. He twists his lips, looking deeply into my eyes. He huffs, tilting his head back and bending his knees in a slump. "Fine," he says, "but if you start in on me, we're leaving."

Mr. Stevenson raises his hands in surrender. "I just want to chat. I miss you, son."

Beau rolls his eyes and takes my hand, leading me to the booth his dad vacated. "Two hazelnut supreme hot chocolates for us."

"You got it," Mr. Stevenson replies, stepping toward the counter to order.

We slide into the booth, and Beau's elbows thud against the table and his head flops into his hands.

Tenderly, I brush the back of his head. "Are you okay? We can still leave."

Beau raises his head and captures my hand in his. "I'm okay. I've got you."

I lean forward and kiss his hand. "Always."

Beau releases my hand when his father approaches the table. He slides down the seat with another huff and averts his eyes when his father slides in opposite us.

"You two look so cute together," Mr. Stevenson says jokingly. "Just like when you were kids. Are you best friends again?"

"We're dating," Beau blurts, looking his dad in the eyes. "Is that a problem?"

"Not for me," Mr. Stevenson replies. He straightens his tie and gulps. "Your mother, on the other hand..."

"She already gave Ava a warm welcome," Beau says coldly.

"She had a poor reaction to seeing you two back together."

"That's putting it mildly," Beau fires back. "I won't stand for either of you saying anything nasty to Ava."

Under the table, I give his thigh a gentle squeeze, hoping to remind him to keep his anger in check.

Mr. Stevenson looks my way. "I suppose your dad isn't taking kindly to Beau."

I look at Beau, smile, and then turn back to Mr. Stevenson. "Actually, Beau came over for dinner last night. Dad gave us the seal of approval."

Mr. Stevenson deadpans at me. "Really? That's surprising."

"You have so much faith in me," Beau says dryly.

"It's not that," his dad replies. "I just wanted to explain your mother's reaction, and I assumed Ava's father would've had the same reaction."

"Don't get me wrong," I say. "My dad wasn't thrilled. The first time he saw Beau in our house, he threw him out."

Mr. Stevenson nods. "That sounds more like it."

Beau crosses his arms. "Wow."

Mr. Stevenson frowns, tilting his head as he stares at Beau. "I just mean, none of us thought you two would be friends again. Let's just say John and Kate were counting on it."

"Why do Mom and Ava's dad care if we hang out?" Beau questions. "I get Mr. Jones doesn't want me around Ava because he thinks I'm a bad influence, but what's Mom's deal? Is she worried about me corrupting Ava too? As if she takes enough notice to care."

A server walks over to our booth, holding a tray with three tall mugs of hot chocolate with whipped cream hats dusted in cinnamon sugar.

Mr. Stevenson thanks the server as she leaves and then fidgets in his seat. "Perhaps this isn't the best place to get into this."

"Get into what?" Beau demands. "There's something you're not telling us. Just give it up."

I cup my hands around the mug. The warmth from the ceramic and heavenly delicious scent wafting from the beverage gives me a sense of comfort. I use the renewing energy to get the words out.

"My dad is giving Beau a second chance," I say. "He's chaperoning the school dance this Saturday. Maybe you and your wife want to join him?"

Something equating to a grimace contorts Mr. Stevenson's face. "I don't think that'd be a good idea."

Beau groans, slamming his back against the booth seating. "Of course not, because it has something to do with me."

"*Beau.*" Exhaustion floods Mr. Stevenson's tone. "Don't be like this. It's not about..."

"Don't tell me it's not about me," Beau cuts him off. "You couldn't care less about anything to do with me. Whether it's at school or not. If I torched this café, you'd yell at me for one afternoon and then go back to ignoring me."

Mr. Stevenson's eyes narrow at his son. "What's the matter with you? Why do you unleash these violent outbursts?"

I clutch Beau's shoulder. "There's nothing wrong with him."

Mr. Stevenson's mouth falls open as he turns my way.

"You need to stop ignoring him," I say firmly. "What happened to you and your wife to make you think it was okay to abandon him?"

Beau's dad locks eyes with me. His eyes shine, welling with tears as he sniffs hard. "You look so much like your mother."

The comment has me break eye contact and slide back in my seat. With a sense of confusion that summons dread from deep within, I turn to Beau. His face is stony, still fighting to keep his anger in check. I flick my eyes back at Mr. Stevenson. "Thanks."

Mr. Stevenson sniffs again. "I loved Lydie. She was more than a friend to me."

A hot stabbing pain cuts into my chest. My hands ball into fists. "What was that?"

Mr. Stevenson rubs his hands over his face and sighs, flopping back against the seat. "We kept it from you kids to protect you. I always thought it would come out. But when Lydie died, it felt too ugly to bring it up."

"Hang on," Beau blurts, scrunching his eyes closed and shaking his head. "What are you talking about?"

Mr. Stevenson lowers his hand, revealing an expressionless face. He looks at Beau, then at me, and then his gaze falls to his untouched hot chocolate.

"Dad?" Beau presses.

Sweat drips from my neck down to my back. My heart slams against my ribs, and my fists curl into tighter, agonizing balls. "Why are you talking about my mother?"

"You two deserve to know the truth," Mr. Stevenson says, his complexion dulled with shame, "especially now that you're in a relationship."

Beau slams a fist on the table, causing all the mugs to quake and spill. Heads turn from other booths, but at this point I couldn't care less if they eavesdrop or gossip about us.

"Enough," Beau demands. "Either spit it out or stop messing with us."

"It's not easy to say," his dad responds weakly. "If it were, you'd already know."

I suck in a ragged breath as tears tumble from my eyes. "What are you saying?" I garble as mucus in the back of my throat entangles with my voice. "Why are you talking about my mother?"

Beau's arms wrap around me, and he pulls me close. As he strokes my hair, I pull away from him, leaning forward. "Tell me!"

"We had an affair," he blurts in a low tone. "We were in love."

I gasp. "*Love.*"

Beau retches, slamming the back of his hand over his ajar mouth.

"You're lying," I sob. My shoulders jiggle uncontrollably as more tears stream down my face.

Mr. Stevenson wipes his eyes. "I'm sorry."

Beau leans forward with me, glaring at his father. "If this is true, how'd it never come out? How could you never tell Mom?"

"I did."

The revelation smacks us both in the face, forcing us to sit back.

Mr. Stevenson clears his throat and takes a sip from his mug. "That's why we moved, son. Your mother didn't want to live near Lydie any longer."

Beau's jaw drops and his cheeks become hollow. His skin pales, and his eyes are almost circular.

I groan, wiping tears off my face. "What are you saying? My dad knows too?"

Mr. Stevenson nods, guilt contorting his facial features. "Yes. Your mother and I told them together."

I press my hand into my stomach, but the tsunami growing inside me won't back down with an internal pep talk. I shove Beau, motioning to his side of the booth. Beau slides out of the booth and steps to the side. I hurl myself off the seat and barrel toward the rear bathrooms.

When I race into a stall, everything I've ever held onto hurls into the toilet bowl. Tears stream down my face as I wipe toilet paper across my mouth. I pull myself off the tiled floor and move toward the sink.

There's a knock on the bathroom door, followed by the sweetest voice. "Avie? Aves, are you okay?"

I grip the edge of the bathroom sink and bend over as ugly cries gulp out of me.

The door swings open, and after two beats, heavy footsteps on the floor tiles hurry toward me. My grip slips around the ceramic sink, and before I collapse from exhaustion, Beau's strong arms secure around me.

His face nestles in my hair, and he kisses the nape of my neck. "It's okay, I've got you."

"Why..." A sob croaks out of me. "Why is he saying these things?"

His hand cups the back of my head as I feel his shoulders pivot. "Is there a window we can climb out?"

"My mom didn't do that," I wail, clawing at his sleeve. "Why would he say she did?"

"Come on," he says gently. "I'll walk you out of here."

Beau walks us briskly through the café. Mr. Stevenson stands by the booth, urging us to come back to the table. Our speed doesn't slow down.

"Please," Mr. Stevenson calls out, leaving the café behind us. "We need to talk this through."

"You just dropped a bomb on us," Beau says, taking his hand off my shoulder. "Why should we hear you out?"

"Because I care about the two of you."

I shiver at the sincerity locked on Mr. Stevenson's face.

Beau groans. "Save it."

"I wanted to make our lives better," Mr. Stevenson says. "The move was the first step."

"The first step into my crappy new life," Beau argues.

"We agreed to make our marriages work," he says. "At least, try to. I promise Beau, I only agreed to move houses to keep our family together. I was dedicated to you and your mother."

"Dedicated?" Beau spits. "All you and Mom do is argue. The only way I get your attention is by getting into fights."

"I'm sorry," Mr. Stevenson pleads. "Your mother didn't want a divorce, and I wanted to make her happy. But as time went on, it became increasingly difficult for her to forgive me. Our rift pulled us apart, and we stopped talking about our marriage, family, and anything else."

Beau throws his hands up. "Is that some kind of excuse?"

"I just want to be honest with you. I've been distant because I didn't think I could ever tell you the truth."

"And what?" Beau scoffs. "You went against Mom so you and I can share a secret? How is that any better?"

Mr. Stevenson sighs, rubbing his thumb and index finger against his forehead. "It's not."

"My parents loved each other," I say, stomping my foot. "Everyone loved Mom because she was part of the community. She wasn't a home-wrecker."

"You're right," Mr. Stevenson says brightly. "She didn't want to break up our families. We came clean and called an end to things."

My face collapses into my hands. "My dad would have told me."

"We all agreed to keep it from you kids."

"Why would you tell us now?" Beau interjects. "Is this a ploy to break up Ava and me?"

"No, I just..."

My teeth chatter as I lower my hands. "My mother had an affair... and then she died."

"She loved you more than anything, Ava."

"No, stop." I scrunch my hands into my hair, and my fingernails scrape my scalp. "My mom's not here to defend herself. You're making it up."

"I'm not doing this to hurt you, sweetie," he says, caressing the side of my face. "I thought you had a right to know."

I recoil from his touch, and Beau pushes between us. "Don't touch her."

Mr. Stevenson stumbles a few backward steps. "I shouldn't have said anything. It's just... Seeing you two together..."

"You should have told us when you put the 'for sale' sign outside our house," Beau fires back. "Are you saying your affair is the reason for my crummy life?"

"What do you mean?" Mr. Stevenson looks at him sideways. "You have a great life. We bought you a new car, new gaming consoles, phones, stereos..."

"I didn't want you to buy me off!" Beau yells. "I wanted my parents to notice me."

I shiver beside my boyfriend, and when I can't halt the trembling in my limbs, I clutch his arm. "I have to get out of here."

Beau presses his hand into the middle of my back. "Why don't you go back to work, Dad? We can go back to ignoring each other."

His dad sighs. "Beau."

"Come on," Beau says gently as he steers me away from his father and toward his car.

"Kids, don't go," Mr. Stevenson pleads, but we don't stop moving away, and he doesn't follow.

The walk to Beau's car is a blur. My head spins when he opens the passenger door and I slip inside. When he turns on the ignition, an ache burrows deep between my eyebrows.

"Talk to me," he says softly as he pulls out onto the road.

"It's like I'm awake in some awful nightmare."

"I know. It's bizarre."

"Your dad said my dad knew... How could he never tell me?"

"Are you going to ask him about it?"

My hands plant on either side of my face as I shake my head. "I wouldn't know how."

"Do you want to talk to him about it?"

I drop my hands and carefully breathe in and out. I turn to Beau, and my eyes well. "I have to know what he knows."

He takes my hand and kisses the back of it. "I'll take you home, and we'll confront your dad together."

My stomach is a feeble mess for the entire drive home. At my house, my legs are weak and unreliable on the way to the front door.

I interlace my fingers with Beau's and clamp down on his hand as we enter my home.

"Dad?" I call out.

"Yeah?"

"Umm, is it okay if Beau stays a little while?"

There's a long stretch of silence. My heart thumps until I hear his footsteps moving from the kitchen.

"Beau?" Dad stares at us from the hallway, a befuddled look on his face. "You want to stay for dinner again?"

Beau turns to me, waiting for me to confront my dad. But as Dad waits for a response, my insides shatter like glass. I squeeze Beau's hand harder, and he lets out a hiss of pain. My eyes water as I stare at my confused dad. How could I bring it up? I can't lash out at him for keeping this secret. He's been my only parent for so many years, and he's always done his best to take care of me.

I'm his number one priority, and I can't bring up this ugliness with him.

"I don't know if he's staying for dinner," I say as a quiver runs through my voice. "We were talking about some stuff for the dance and wanted to finalize our ideas. Do you mind if we sit on the couch?"

Dad gestures behind him. "Wouldn't you rather sit at the dining table where you'll be closer to me?"

I nod my head toward the living area. "Please, Dad?"

Dad huffs, turning back toward the kitchen. "Fine, but arms' length apart. I'll be back in to check on you."

"Thanks," I mumble as I slip off my coat.

As Beau takes off his coat, he gives me an incredulous look. "What was that? I thought we were getting his take on the affair."

An ugly moan flows out of me, and I shuffle my way to the couch.

Beau rushes after me. "Hey. Are you okay?"

I criss-cross my legs on the couch and bury my face in my hands. "Affair," I murmur. "How can I ever say that word to him?"

Beau's arms reach around me as he sits on the couch. His head rests beside mine as I use all my strength not to cry.

"I wonder if this would've come out sooner if my mom were still alive?"

"The sad thing is, if Lydie were alive this whole time, she wouldn't have let me spiral." He stares up at the ceiling, and a tear falls from his eye and rolls toward his ear. He sniffs and rubs the heels of his palms across his eyes, and pulls himself up to sit. "This is stupid. I shouldn't be crying about this."

"It's not stupid," I say in a weak voice. "It's my mom."

His head dips low. "I'm sorry."

He rushes to face me and scoops his hand around my neck. His lips suction against mine, and his intensity dials to eleven. He leans over me, pouring heat into the kiss.

I push my hands against his chest and yank my lips away from him. "No. I don't want to do this now."

He wipes his mouth with the back of his hand. "Sorry."

I blow out a frustrated breath and toss my hair off my shoulders.

"I just want to feel close to you," he admits.

"You're closer than anyone can get. I'm just processing something huge. Being intimate is the last thing on my mind."

His fingers dance along my shoulder. "But it would distract us from the messed up things in our heads."

I flick his hand off me. "No, I don't want to."

"Are you angry at me?"

"What? No."

"I don't want this to pull us apart."

"It won't. Just give me time. Don't you need to process this?"

His hands land behind him, allowing him to recline. "I don't want to think about it. I mean, what if they didn't go back to their spouses? We could've become step-siblings."

I shudder. "*Eww.* I don't want to think about it."

"*See,*" Beau replies. "I told you it gets messed up if you think about it too long."

I sigh and hug my knees. "I had such a perfect memory of my mother, and now it's tainted."

"I guess that's why your dad never told you." A faint smile tugs at the corners of his lips. "And why my dad didn't until now. Neither of them wanted people to remember her in a bad light."

"Then why tell us at all?"

Beau shakes his head, frowning. "Maybe he's leaving my mom and wants me to know the whole truth first."

I release my knees and reach for his hand. "Oh, Beau."

He shrugs. "It's okay. If everything Dad said is true, they should have split up years ago. All the tension at home finally makes sense."

I flick my eyes to the doorway. My ears prick at the clanging sounds coming from the kitchen. "Does it also explain why my dad coddles me and controls everything I do?"

Beau's lips drag down as he scoops his hand into my hair. He leans in, his pouting lips edging their way to meet me in a kiss.

I pull back, pressing onto my stomach. "I'm gonna be sick."

Beau pulls back, startled.

I wince. "Maybe you should go."

His eyebrows lift, and the hurt turns his sky-blue eyes into a darker shade. "Are you sure?"

I nod, slumping forward. "Yeah, I'm beat. I need to shower and get to bed early."

He traces his finger along the underside of my chin. "Okay. I'll keep my phone with me if you want to call or text."

"Thank you. Although, I'll be out as soon as my head hits the pillow."

Beau shakes his head. "I don't see myself getting any sleep tonight."

A tear prickles the corner of my eye. "Oh. Now I feel crappy."

He clutches my hand, giving it a gentle squeeze. "Don't. I can see how exhausted you are. I'm just too wired and overthinking everything."

I swallow uncomfortably. "You're not going to drive around, are you?"

"It clears my head."

"I don't want you to," I plead. "It's too dangerous to drive when you're preoccupied."

"I can't go home."

I look back at the doorway. "I don't think my dad will let you sleep on the couch."

He pecks my cheek and then stands from the couch. "Don't worry. I'll be okay."

"I am worried." I stand next to him, linking my arm with his. "Can't you just go home and watch a movie or listen to music? Your bedroom is already away from your parents."

His thumb brushes against my bottom lip. "Okay, I'll try."

I plant a kiss on his thumb. "Thank you."

I walk him to the front door and pull his coat from the rack. He slides his arms into the sleeves, never breaking eye contact with me.

"I'll be okay." I give him a small smile. "I want you to be okay."

He adjusts his coat against his shoulders and then scoops me into a hug. "We'll get through this together."

I nod against his chest. My stomach spasms with the same urgency as at the café. I retch and mutter, "You'd better go."

He kisses my forehead and whispers, "Okay."

When Beau leaves, another wave of sadness rushes over me. I turn from the door and find my dad in the hallway.

"Did Beau leave?" Dad asks, drying his hands with a dish towel.

I nod, dipping my head low as a watery, sour sensation creeps up my throat.

"Your face is all red," Dad says, making his way toward me. "Have you been crying?"

I wipe my face and shake my head. "It's that time of the month."

Dad stops in his tracks. "Oh."

I force a smile and hug my middle. "I'll be fine. I just need a shower and to hop into bed."

"You don't want dinner first?"

"I don't feel like eating."

"Okay, sweetheart. I'll wrap your dinner and leave it in the fridge for you."

I lean into him, giving him a side hug. "Thanks, Dad."

How could he know about Mom and Mr. Stevenson and say nothing?

I can't believe he knew. I certainly won't be the one to break the news to him.

Twenty-Three

Getting out of bed this morning was an ordeal. Knots seized my back. My head pounded, and my heart shattered.

I have to believe it's all a lie. A sick joke Beau's father is playing on us.

My mother would never turn her back on her family.

She never did.

How dare that man try to tarnish her memory?

Now I'm sitting in second period and haven't taken in a word either of my teachers have said. I dig my pen into the paper, drawing heavy, angry strokes. When the bell rings, I twist my pen so tight it snags a hole in the page.

I close my books and bundle them in my arms. Today I don't care if I bump into anyone else. I hustle my way out of the classroom, cutting off my classmates to reach the hallway. I cut the corner and fly into a broad football player.

Oof.

I stumble backward and fall on my butt. The pain ricochets up my back, and my books sprawl out in front of me.

The football player strolls past, and so do my classmates. As I reach for a book, someone kicks it further away. I drop my arm and hunch over. My downcast eyes fixate on the pattern of my school skirt. Laughter trails around me, and more of my books skid away.

"Hey, drop that!" Beau's voice commands the hallway.

Gasps and whispers circle the crowded space, but none of it matters as Beau lowers to the ground and slides close beside me.

"Some guy had this," he says, placing my binder on my lap.

My heart crushes as a tear drops onto my binder. "Oh."

Beau cups the sides of my face and plants a kiss atop my head. "What happened? Why are you on the floor?"

"I ran into somebody."

"You sound so flat. Was someone teasing you?"

I shake my head, still keeping my eyes on my lap. "I just can't do this. I can't be here today."

"You mean, at school?"

I nod against his shoulder. "I need to get out."

"What about your perfect attendance?" he jokes.

I finally look up and meet his beautiful sparkling eyes. "Screw it."

Surprise shines in his eyes. "You really want to go?"

I nod, letting desperation crease my face.

Beau motions to the hallway. "Let me gather your books first."

I sit against the wall as Beau collects my books. I watch how other kids halt, pivot, or skid away from him. Right now, it doesn't bother me if they think he's scary. To me, he's the only person who gives a damn about me.

"Ava?" my teacher questions as she exits the classroom. "What are you doing on the floor? Shouldn't you be getting ready for your next class?"

I stare up at her. My only response is a couple of blinks.

"Got 'em," Beau says with my books under his arm.

My teacher clumsily steps back, looking at Beau and then at me. "Everything all right, Ava?"

"Yes," I say flatly, and hold out my hand to Beau.

He helps me stand, and I give my teacher a stony glare before we continue along the hall.

"Didn't like your class today?" Beau asks.

"I'm just not in the mood for anyone implying you're scary or I'm in danger around you."

"I don't care what anyone else thinks, as long as we're okay."

I lift his lightly bruised hand. "You don't care, huh? Did anyone make comments at practice this morning?"

He shakes his head. "Nope. I told you I put them in their place."

"I'm sorry I couldn't walk you to the gym." I pout. "It was a bad morning before I woke up."

"It's okay. I would've preferred to show those clowns that their words are meaningless, but I guess we have nothing to prove."

I swallow dryly as my tongue sticks to the roof of my mouth. "I don't want to walk with you as some trophy."

We stop by my locker, and Beau leans against the adjacent one, waiting for me to open the door. "I'm just used to making my choices clear."

I open the locker door and pull out my coat. Beau shoves my books inside, closes the door, and shuts the lock.

"Well, I'm not upfront about things." I puff out a mournful breath. "And I'm fine being this way."

Beau's forehead wrinkles. "Is this about your dad? Aren't you going to talk to him about what happened yesterday?"

I rest against the locker, hugging my coat to my body. "I don't want to."

"It's not easy, believe me, but you can't let this stay in the dark."

I bite into my lip, and my eyes sting. "Why not?"

Beau looks around us, ensuring the hall is empty. "Our parents had an affair," he says in a low voice, leaning close. "We can't let this go. It has to come out into the open."

"Why?" I slam a fist against the locker door. "She's dead. Why do we need to talk about something she did before she died?"

Beau's face draws long, and he sucks back a breath. "Because my parents are still alive."

I stare at him deeply, watching the way his eyes waver with the threat of tears. He sniffs and looks away briefly, blinking his eyes dry.

"We don't even know if it's true," I whisper.

He looks back at me with bewilderment. "What? How twisted do you think my dad is to make up something like that?"

"It's too ridiculous to be hidden for this long."

Beau throws up his hands, backing away from me. "I don't even know what to say."

I push off the locker. "I don't want to argue. I just want to get out of here."

With defeat in his eyes, he nods, holding out his hand for me. I take a deep breath, grasping his hand, and turning towards the front of the school.

Beau smirks. "That's cute."

"What?"

"Are you trying to skip school by walking out the front doors?"

I slap my hand over my forehead. "Ugh. Okay, show me where to go."

Beau takes my jacket and puts it over my shoulders. I slide my hands into the sleeves and take Beau's hand. He turns us in the opposite direction, and we move up the hall.

"Do you want your coat?" I ask.

Beau takes his car keys from his pocket and jiggles them. "Not if we're heading straight to the car."

I nod, noting the clamminess sliding between our hands. My eyes dart between classroom doors, and the thought of them opening has me trembling.

He tilts his head to find my face. "Are you scared?"

"I'm freaking out about being seen by a teacher."

"I can tell by the grip. Do you need to squeeze so hard?"

"Sorry," I mutter, not loosening my grip.

Beau stops in place. "You're twitching, Ava. We don't have to do this. I can walk you to class instead."

"No," I say, shaking off my nerves. "I want to go."

"If you're sure."

I nod. "I'm sure."

Beau gestures ahead. "Cool. We're just going past the teachers' lounge and then through the fire exit."

I halt, sweat beading against my hairline. "What?"

"Trust me."

"The teachers' lounge and a fire escape? You're crazy."

"I know what I'm doing," Beau says, tugging on my arm. "We gotta hustle before the bell rings."

Reluctantly, I follow along. The teachers' lounge? Does he want to get caught? Oh my gosh. Is this worth getting in trouble for? Maybe I can get it together enough to sit through my classes.

Beau sneaks us past the teachers' lounge. The door is closed, and the blinds drawn. We move into an alcove, and Beau pushes on the emergency exit door. I hold my breath, expecting sirens to blare, but nothing happens. Everything is as silent as before.

I blow out a relieved breath and hurry beside Beau. We move into the billowing wind, and my face and hands freeze. We move past a courtyard and the teachers' parking lot until we are off school property.

Beau hits the button on his keys, and the shiny black Mustang beeps its unlocking sound.

"Your chariot awaits," Beau says with a cheesy grin.

We hop into the car, ensuring we aren't visible to anyone who might linger around the area.

"They always block out the windows in the teachers' lounge," Beau says. "They want time away from us, as much as we want to get away from them. And that fire exit door needs to be repaired. I've been using it for a while. It's good until the maintenance staff fixes the alarm."

"I didn't realize it was so easy to escape the school," I say, rubbing my frozen hands together.

"Are you cold?" Beau asks, starting the engine, which blasts the heated air conditioning. He then hits a button on my side of the dashboard.

"I love that your car has heated seats," I say. "How do you feel about this car now? Your dad basically said you're living a charmed life because they spoil you."

Beau sinks down in his seat. "I always knew this car was a replacement for their love. It changed nothing."

I wince. "Sorry."

"Don't worry about it." Beau's smile quirks with a hint of nerves. "So, what do you want to do?"

I rub my hands briskly in front of the air conditioning vents. "I don't know. I'd be happy to sit here until the last bell rings."

Beau wriggles his eyebrows. "And then we can move into the storeroom for a little making out."

I laugh at how cute he looks, and then shake my head. "I don't know if I'm up for that today."

Beau groans. "Ugh. Is this stuff with our parents going to drive a wedge between us?"

"I still want to be with you. There's just so many conflicting thoughts in my head."

He rubs my shoulder. "I know. Believe me, I get it."

"It's just really messed up."

"Tell me about it." Beau sighs, and then a mischievous grin changes his expression. "So... Wanna make out in the backseat instead?"

I giggle heartedly. "You're cute but relentless."

He leans across and pecks my cheek. "That's why you love me."

My hands caress the sides of his face. "I really do."

As his serene and sympathetic eyes connect with mine, I push my lips onto his. My eyes fall shut as the tingles of electricity buzz between us. I wrap my arms around his shoulders and melt into him. We hold each other for a long while. Over the hum of the air conditioning, I make out the rhythmic thrum of his heartbeat.

"We can just stay like this all day," he whispers. "I don't mind."

I suck in a breath as a thought strikes me. "We can't. You need to be in class."

"This is more important. You're more important."

"No, I'm being selfish. You can't afford to be caught skipping school."

"But I want to be with you."

"I'll be okay."

"Are you suggesting I go back inside and you stay in the car?"

I shrug. "Maybe?"

Beau touches the steering wheel. "You could always take it for a spin."

"This doesn't feel like the day I learn to drive a car."

"Fair point. But I don't want to leave you."

"I just want to skip this day and get to tomorrow."

His smile slides to the left. "TGIF."

"It's the day we start decorating." I flop back against the seat, letting my eyes fall shut. "Ah, I can't wait."

"I've almost forgotten about the dance. Last night I kept thinking about how I'd bring up what Dad and Lydie did to Mom. She didn't get in until late. I was lying in bed and heard her footsteps above me. I just can't believe she's known all this time."

I scrunch my eyes tighter. "Can we not do this?"

"What?"

I open my eyes to see his bewildered expression. "It physically hurts to think about it. I can't do this."

"But we're in the same boat. I need to talk about it."

"But I can't even fathom it being true."

He deadpans me. "My dad didn't make it up."

"It doesn't make sense for it to be true."

"Avie, I don't want to fight with you about this."

"I don't want to either. Maybe we should spend some time apart to think it over." I wince, trying to turn it into a smile. "My head hurts. Can I just have some time to reflect before talking about it?"

He leans forward and kisses my forehead. "Of course. The last thing I want is for this to break us apart. Not after how much work it took for us to get together. Will you be okay here by yourself?"

I smile, nodding. "I'll be fine. I'll text you when I go back inside."

"Okay. Just tell me to come back before you go into full panic-mode."

I thank him again as he leaves the car. I relax against the heated seat, and my head decompresses. Without him around, the ugly thoughts slip away. I don't want to hurt him. His feelings are valid. I just can't hear him out right now. I never want to discuss the possibility that my mother and his father were ever intimate.

I skipped all my classes and eventually went home, filling my binder with happy thoughts. I drew stars, clouds, and cartoony angels around my notes. All hellish thoughts were excluded from my brain.

Now, it's Friday. The dance is only twenty-four hours away. I need to laser focus all my attention on the event. I don't care if Beau says we have to get the ugliness out in the open. I'm not doing it. I'm here to have fun, be creative, and lead the team. We've all worked too hard for this, and I won't let a hurtful lie derail this event.

Yes, that's how I'm choosing to feel about what Mr. Stevenson said. I can't bring it up with Beau because I know he doesn't feel the same way. I don't want to tune out my boyfriend, but I can't have such vile thoughts invading my brain.

I smile across the gym at Beau and give him a wave as he climbs a ladder. He, Jeff, and Marcus are streaming twinkle lights around the trees, prepping them for the rest of the decorations. They are weaving the cables below the trees, and later the girls and I will cover them with white felt and decor we got from the supplies warehouse.

The warehouse delivery workers were nice enough to set up the trees in my maze design at the rear of the gym. If you block out the rest of the gymnasium, it's easy to imagine looking out at a magical pine tree forest, hopefully on the way to Santa's workshop.

The banners that hung in the cafeteria have now moved into the gym. Two maintenance workers hung them on a wall where tomorrow we will set up the food and beverage station.

The stage is set near the bleachers. Over there, Teddy, Sullivan, and the rest of their band set up their speakers, cables, and a large projector screen. Lucy and Ciara helped the boys select holiday images and collect well wishes from students for the festive season. All of which will be played on a loop via the projector.

Hilary and Lucy enter the gym, each pushing a trolley cart carrying large boxes. Inside are the decorations that Beau and I sorted into color and shape.

"What are your plans for tomorrow?" Hilary asks me.

I give her a confused look. "What do you mean? I'll be here setting up like everyone else."

Hilary puffs out a laugh and waves her hands. "No, no. I mean after that. Where are you getting ready?"

I'm still confused. "At home."

Lucy links her arm with mine. "You should get ready with us."

Hilary nods enthusiastically. "Lucy is coming over to my place. We're helping each other with hair and makeup. You should join us."

I glance over my shoulder, and then back at the girls. "Is it just the two of you?"

"I haven't asked Whitney," Hilary replies. "We aren't exactly vibing with her."

"Plus, Jeff was supposed to join the committee so he and I could spend more time together," Lucy says, side-eyeing Hilary. "Ugh. I can't believe he's so into her."

"Is it just my imagination," I say playfully, "but aren't you into Teddy?"

Lucy goes bright red and cups a hand over her mouth.

Hilary nudges her, giggling. "You're so smitten."

"So, tomorrow night..." I nervously twirl a finger in my hair. "Is Ciara going to your place?"

"I asked her," Lucy replies, fanning her face, "but she said her mom already organized something."

I try not to let the relief show on my face. "Okay, I'd love to join you guys."

"Will your dad be cool with it?" Hilary asks. "Or do I need to charm him again?"

I giggle. "I'm sure he'll be fine with us doing all the girly stuff. Just the mention of anything feminine sends him running for the hills."

Hilary smirks. "Just like all men."

"Umm, Hils?" I awkwardly lower my voice. "Would you mind driving me home this afternoon?"

"Sure," she replies. "But don't you normally go with Beau?"

"Yeah, I just can't go with him today. It's personal."

"Sounds like something juicy to discuss when we're getting ready tomorrow night," Lucy says, rubbing her hands together.

"No, there's nothing juicy," I reply. "Beau and I are good."

I tell Beau I want to go home with Hilary so I can show her my dress for the dance. I hate lying to him, but I just can't risk our conversation veering back to that ugly topic. I just want to get through the dance. Once it's over, I can talk to him about everything and anything. Right now, I don't have the bandwidth. Heck, I'll just be honest. I don't want to think about it ever again.

The overnight texting with Beau was at a minimum. I reassure him I'm not avoiding him after I explain I'm taking the bus to school. Dad is coming with me to help set up the gym. It's wonderful. He's putting in so much effort as a chaperone. My mom always loved organizing school activities, and it always made Dad feel uneasy to take her place. Perhaps because we have talked about her lately, he feels more comfortable taking the role. Or... Let's face it. He wants to keep an eagle-eye on Beau.

I show Dad around the gym, and he smiles proudly as he tells me how terrific everything looks. As I explain to him how to arrange some items at the food and beverage station, Beau enters the gym. His pace quickens, and guilt swells inside me. I feel awful about building a wall between us. I'm just so on edge about the A-word being brought up in our conversations. I need to make sure he knows I still care about him and wrap him up in a big hug.

I take a step toward him, but halt as he quickens to get to me first.

"Ah, Ava…" His mouth stays ajar as eyes shift toward my father and then back to me.

The dread in his expression causes tension to camp between my shoulder blades. "What is it?"

"My dad…" he utters, and then looks over his shoulder. "He insisted…"

My heart flat-lines for a nanosecond. It makes up for the lost time by beating against my ribs.

Mr. Stevenson waltzes into the gym with a cheerful grin. "I'm here to do my part," he announces.

"Paul?" my dad says in shock.

"Hi John," Mr. Stevenson replies. "I was hoping to have a moment to speak with you."

"No," I blurt, forcing myself between the two. "You can't talk to him."

Dad's hand grips my shoulder. "Ava, it's…"

"You're not on the chaperone list," I say, grappling for a reason to kick this man out of the school.

"Yes, I know," Mr. Stevenson replies. "I haven't been great at acknowledging Beau's school activities, and I want to make amends. This event seems to be really important to him. And with you, too."

"It is important," I fire back. "That's why we can't afford to have it sabotaged."

He studies my eyes. I narrow them as I scowl, telling him I don't want him spreading his lies and upsetting my dad. If my dad has a reason to yell, he also has a reason to drag me away from the gym and keep me home all night.

"Ava," Dad says sternly. He steps around me, giving me a disappointed stare. "We don't talk to people this way."

"It's okay." Mr. Stevenson clears his throat. "I haven't made the best reintroduction into her life."

"What does that mean?" Dad asks gruffly.

Beau grabs his father's arm. "Dad, I think you'd better go."

Mr. Stevenson lifts his hands defensively. "Give me a task to do in a corner. I'll stay out of the way. I promise."

My wavy voice goes up an octave. "No, you can't stay."

Beau tugs at his dad's arm again. "Dad? Come on."

"John, can we just have a minute?" Mr. Stevenson persists.

"Get out of here!" I yell, unconcerned about the fact I'm making a scene.

Dad's shock is threefold. "Ava?"

Mr. Stevenson looks at me with apologetic eyes. He sighs and then nods. "Okay, I'll leave. I'm so sorry for upsetting you."

I slide my hands over my eyes as the threat of sobs impairs my breathing.

"I'm sure tonight will be perfect, Ava," Mr. Stevenson says gently. "You have your mother's touch."

At that, I retch and back away from them. Hilary calls out to me, and I glimpse her and Lucy standing over decorations with concerned faces.

I keep my head down and keep moving toward the rear doors. The icy winds outside numb my feelings. I hug myself, letting the breeze spiral around me. Blinking through the watery blur, I look up at the sky, thinking about my mother's face.

"How could you?" It comes out shattered.

I rest against a wall, taking long breaths in and out. I need to calm down before reentering the gym.

"There you are?" Beau says, rounding the corner behind the gym.

I pull off the wall and melt into his embrace.

"I'm so sorry he turned up," he says, stroking my back. "I tried to stop him."

I want to say he didn't try hard enough, but instead I bite my tongue.

"We need to talk about this," he whispers, and I shake my head against him. "We can't forget it happened. My dad will try again to talk to your dad."

I lift my head and slam my hands onto his chest. "No!" Tears sting my eyes, and my vision of him blurs. "Can we just get through tonight? Please?"

His bottom lip quirks as he peels my hands off him. He keeps a hold of my hand, and his eyes well. "We'll talk about it afterwards?"

"I just can't do it now." I sniff hard, holding back the sob that wants to break. "Please don't make me."

He nods, dropping my hand to wipe his eyes. "Okay. We'll avoid the topic until the dance is over."

I let my tears fall as I drape my arms around his neck. I nuzzle my face against his collarbone and sigh out. "Thank you."

Twenty-Four

It didn't take much to placate my dad. My outburst toward Mr. Stevenson agitated him, but Dad can't deny he also wanted him gone. I told Dad I wanted him to feel comfortable while he stayed and helped. I knew Mr. Stevenson's presence wouldn't allow that. I also gave him the sad puppy eyes, telling Dad of my fear Mr. Stevenson would say something mean to me.

Dad's overprotectiveness was in full-force and he let me get on with decorating without follow-up questions. I should feel bad about manipulating him. But, on the flip side, I'm now getting ready at Hilary's, and Dad has allowed Beau to drive me to the dance. It's hard to feel remorse when things are going your way.

"Hurry up," Lucy says, bouncing in her chair in front of the mirror. "I wanna go."

"Chill," Hilary replies, standing behind her as she twists pieces of Lucy's hair back. "We don't need to get back this early."

"I wanna help the band get the rest of their gear ready," Lucy says, flushing pink. "You know, entertainment is my responsibility."

Hilary giggles. "And so is getting your first kiss."

Lucy rolls her eyes before falling into giggles. "I'm so transparent."

Hilary finishes Lucy's hair and steps back. "Okay, you're done. Happy?"

Lucy bounces off the seat with hyper energy. "Ecstatic."

I stand from the edge of Hilary's bed. "Before you go," I say, holding out my hand. "You both need to help me decide where to put this."

The girls gather around, looking at the item in my palm.

"Aw, that's so pretty," Lucy gushes.

"Is it a hairpiece?" Hilary asks.

I let the light catch and flicker against the snowflake diamantes. "It's a brooch. I was thinking I'd either clip it to the belted sash on my dress or pin it in my hair."

When Hilary says, "Hair," Lucy says, "Belt."

I laugh. "That doesn't help me decide."

Lucy gives me a one-armed hug. "Well, you have my vote. I'll see what you decide at the dance."

She embraces Hilary before zooming out of the room.

"My gosh," I utter. "She can't wait to hang off of Teddy."

Hillary giggles. "I know. I never thought she'd get over Jeff so quickly."

"I'm happy for her."

"Me too. Tell me, was Beau your first kiss?"

"Yes. Are you judging me?"

Hilary pulls me to the chair in front of her tall mirror. "No, not if you really like him. Marcus is the first and only guy I've kissed."

"Wow, that's so romantic," I say as I take a seat.

Hilary beams. "He's my soulmate."

I pause, taking in the statement. "Whoa. That's a loaded word."

"It's how I feel. You don't feel that heartstring pull when you're with Beau?"

"We have an intense connection, but..." Soulmate? Does that word even exist? I thought my parents were soulmates, and then my mom...

"I guess I can tell what you see in him," Hilary says, combing her fingers through my hair. "He's a functioning human being when he's around you."

"Thanks, I guess?"

She pats my shoulder. "You should stick to him like glue. It makes the rest of us feel a lot safer."

I pout, staring at her mirrored reflection. "You're still scared of him?"

"He still did everything in the stories. But I'm happy if no new stories happen because he's infatuated with you."

"That's a lot of pressure on me to ensure *he* doesn't mess up."

Hilary crosses her fingers. "It's the general consensus."

I move off the chair and step further into the room. "I think I'll leave my hair out. Beau likes it better that way, anyway."

"Aw, that's cute."

I force a smile. "Thanks."

She holds out her hand. "Want me to pin the snowflake in your hair?"

I hold the brooch against my torso. "Actually, I think I want it on the belt now."

After a light dusting of makeup, I change into the red satin cocktail dress as Hilary works on her hair. I tie the satin sash around my waist, swivel the bow to the back, and clip the snowflake to the front. Perfect.

"Stunning," Hilary says, smiling in the mirror.

"I can't believe I'm wearing this dress. It feels like my mother helped me get ready tonight."

"Oh, *geez.* I feel so bad," Hilary says in a low voice. "I'm always pushing my mother away because her constant help is smothering. But I wouldn't give it up for the world. I'm so sorry you never got a moment like that with your mother."

"Don't be sorry," I say kindly. "It's no one's fault. It's just a freak thing that took her away from us too early. I can't do anything to reverse it."

Hilary rises from her seat and pulls me in with a tender embrace. "You're so brave," she whispers. "I want to be more like you."

I giggle as we pull out of the hug. "I think I'm becoming more like you."

She laughs, moving back to the mirror. "You don't want that."

There's a knock at the door. When Mrs. Wong's head pops in, Hilary mutters, "Speak of the devil."

"Hi girls. Oh gosh, don't you just look stunning," Mrs. Wong gushes. "Anyway, Ava, your knight in shining armor is here."

Hilary drops her curling iron. "Beau's here already?"

I bounce on the balls of my feet. "Are you cool if I go?"

Hilary waves me off, still dressed in a robe. "Of course, go. Marcus won't be long."

"Thanks, and see you at the dance," I say with a girlish squeal.

Mrs. Wong walks me out, and by the front door, Beau stands ready in a dashing charcoal suit with an emerald satin tie.

"Oh my gosh," I cheer, clapping. "You look so handsome."

"Pass me your phone," Mrs. Wong says excitedly. "It'll make the most gorgeous Christmas card. You two are so coordinated."

I slip my phone out of my clutch and hand it to Mrs. Wong.

When I step closer to Beau, he slips an arm around me, smiling. "Hi."

My shoulders bunch high as I lean against him. "Hi."

After the obligatory photo session, we move outside the house after an onslaught of compliments from Mrs. Wong.

"You look beautiful," Beau says, leading me by the hand to his car. "I wanted to say it sooner, but couldn't get a word in."

I giggle. "I know. Hilary's mom is very chipper."

"She and her husband have volunteered at the food station, right?" Beau says. "I say we avoid that area."

"I'm happy to stay wandering among the Christmas trees all night."

"Oh yes, that's a big must." Beau opens the passenger door for me. "I came here early so we could enjoy it all before everyone else gets there."

I lean in and plant a soft, sensual kiss on his lips. "I can't believe tonight is finally here."

We arrive at the gym, and by the entrance sits the table Whitney and Jeff will man, checking tickets. It's vacant at the moment because we are wonderfully early.

Now that nightfall has taken over, the gym has darkened, making the overhead string lights and hanging garlands pop. The timber floors below glitter and shine, waiting for people to fill the space. And filling out the backdrop are the high pine trees, covered in an array of lights, ornaments, tinsel, and topped with glitzy stars.

"Well done, you two," Mr. Riley says, walking over from the food and beverage station. "This place looks magnificent."

"Thanks," I say, swinging Beau's hand in mine. "I'm so glad it all came together."

Beau gestures ahead. "We're going to check it out before everyone else gets here."

"Be my guest," Mr. Riley says, backing off.

Phew. We don't need another adult cramping our style.

Beau leads me toward the tree maze, knowing it's the part I care about most. The photographer has set up his equipment at the entrance. Lucy stands snuggled against Teddy as the photographer tells them to say cheese.

In a flash, a very cute card-worthy photo is snapped.

"Hi guys," Lucy says, waving at us. "Isn't it nice being here without everyone else?"

I nod. "Our thoughts exactly."

Teddy glares at Beau and then tugs on Lucy's hand. "Come on. I've gotta finish up a few things."

Still bouncy with loved-up excitement, Lucy grins as she's pulled away. "Okay. Bye, guys."

"Bye," I say, as the photographer motions for us to take their place. I look at Beau. "You want to?"

He nods. "Yeah, sure."

Even though Mrs. Wong just took our photo, something about a professional photographer is much more special.

After he takes our picture, the photographer smiles at his display screen. "Nice. You two make a great looking couple."

Beau smirks, smoothing a hand over his luscious blonde hair. "Thanks, man."

I giggle and thank the photographer. I yank Beau away. We stumble through the tree maze, cuddling into each other every step of the way.

"This really does look incredible, Aves. From the snow, pinecones, gold-sprayed twigs and berries under the trees. To the coordinating ornaments and tinsel covering the trees."

"Not to mention the comically large stars on top of the trees," I say, smiling at the crowning achievements. Not all the trees have large stars on top. Some have smaller ones to balance out the scene. I just love how the differently shaped trees fill out the space. A happy sigh draws out of me. I can't believe my vision has come to life.

Beau stops us in the middle of the maze. He digs inside his suit jacket, and then his eyebrows wiggle as he takes out an item. "I brought contraband into the dance."

I giggle heartily at the sight. In the air, Beau lifts the sprig of mistletoe he bought at the party supplies warehouse. "Oh my, you're so naughty."

He holds it above our heads and leans in close. I join him in a kiss, which spreads tingles over my lips. The tingles rush down my body, spreading a thrilling goosebumps sensation that makes me flutter with energized anticipation.

"Oh wow," I whisper, pulling out of the kiss. "That was amazing."

He grins. "And the night's only just beginning."

The rest of the parents and faculty members file in to take on their chaperoning duties. Some mingle around the food and beverage station, and some make themselves comfortable at the festively decorated tables and chairs.

My dad gives me a wave and is quickly accosted by an enthusiastic Mr. Wong who, as a former Ashworth Academy football star, is beaming with school spirit.

Soon enough, a large crowd surges into the gym after displaying their tickets to Whitney and Jeff outside the entryway. They mingle around tables, throughout the tree maze, and across the dance floor.

I squeeze Beau in a hug filled with gratitude. If it weren't for his pep-talk in the cafeteria, we wouldn't have this delightful buzz. I feel blessed to have him by my side.

Beau and I wander through the dance floor and spy Hilary chatting to the PTA members by the punchbowl. She gives them all a thumbs up and then drags Marcus away.

"Time for a little boogie," Hilary cheers as she and Marcus join us.

"I can't believe we pulled this off," I say with a happy squeal.

Hilary flicks her hair. "I knew we would."

I giggle at her sassiness. The surrounding crowd reacts positively to the band, who are putting their all into their upbeat covers. It's a relief, considering they're not the most popular group of boys. It doesn't matter to me, but this is high school, after all. I lean into Beau as we sway in a small, steady circle. It must be the Christmas spirit keeping everyone in a good mood.

As the evening draws on, I can't help but people-watch. I remember watching people during our neighborhood events Mom threw together. There was always laughter, growing friendships, and kindness shared between one another. Around me, friends hug and take group selfies, dates dance together and share intimate whispers. I even overhear people inviting others to join them over the holidays.

As I watch the band in a rock-inspired interpretation of "Hark the Herald Angels Sing," my eyes wander. On the bleachers, Vanessa Ashworth sits with her friends Sylvie and Hope. They all look equally bored. Vanessa's date is one of the preppy boys whose family is linked to hers. Honestly, I do feel sorry for her. She never gets the date she wants. She always seems to do things that benefit her family. It must be isolating. I hope when she was overseas she had some fun, but the rumor is all she did was sit in her chalet and spend time with her tutor.

Marcus and Beau left us early. They didn't want to bop away like crazy people with Hilary and me. But after several songs of "boogying," as Hilary calls it, I feel pooped. She takes me over to the punch bowl to refuel. After gulping down two cups, I am replenished.

"You gotta try these sugar cookies," Hilary says, handing me one from the adjacent food table. "Marcus's mom made them, and they're like little pieces of heaven."

I smile at the cookie. Piped in white icing is a delicate snowflake. I bite into the cookie and a "mmm," purrs out of me.

Hilary nudges me, smiling. "Right?"

"Are you girls enjoying the dance?" Mrs. Wong asks, moving around the table to join us.

"Mhmm," I mumble with a mouthful of cookie.

Mrs. Wong holds out her palm. "Hilary, give me your phone so I can take a picture of you and Ava."

"Ugh, Mom, you're so embarrassing," Hilary says, digging her phone out of her clutch.

She hands the phone to her mom and cuddles into me. I dust off my hands and wipe my face of potential cookie remnants.

I grin widely as Mrs. Wong stares at us through the screen. "You two look so darn cute."

"Thanks, Mom," Hilary says, taking back the phone. She shows me the photo, and it's adorable. "I'll send it to you."

"Thanks."

My dad appears alongside Mrs. Wong, smiling. "Having fun, sweetheart?"

"Yes, Dad. And you?"

Mrs. Wong nudges him. "If I haven't bored him to tears with my holiday plans yet."

Dad chuckles. "No, it's been lovely chatting with you and your husband."

I grin, loving seeing Dad so happy. "Maybe our families can meet up over the Christmas break?"

"I'd love that," Mrs. Wong replies.

Dad nods. "We'll see."

Mrs. Wong latches onto his arm. "Well, now I've got more ideas to rattle off."

Hilary giggles. "You're never getting away from her now, Mr. Jones."

"Hi," a breathy yet gravelly voice says as a hand rests on my arm.

I turn to Beau, grinning. "Hi."

Beau looks at my dad with eagerness. "Mind if I steal her away?"

Dad nods. "As long as stealing her away means staying inside this building."

"Do you want to dance?" Beau asks me. "I mean romantic swaying. Not jumping up and down."

"Hey, there's nothing wrong with jumping when dancing," Hilary cuts in.

My heart thumps to a happy beat, and I lean into Beau. "I'd love to."

I wave goodbye to everyone. Dad gives me an approving look, and I gleefully let Beau whisk me toward the dance floor.

Romantic doesn't begin to describe it. I link my arms around Beau's neck, and his hands sit against my waist. Our dancing is made for a slow song, nothing like what's playing, but I don't care. Being with Beau is literal perfection. I want this moment to stay in my memory bank for years to come.

As my hands stay clasped around Beau's neck, people around us nudge into us. As I look around, everyone's elbowing each other or talking in huddles. As I laser in on what has everyone in a flurry, many people have their phones raised to eye-level. Rumblings emerge and soon elevate into hoots and hollers as people stay glued to their screens.

"What's everyone looking at?" Beau asks, pulling his phone from his pocket.

I unravel my hands from around him and watch the screen with him. He has a notification from the school portal app. With a shrug, he opens the app and views the message.

I gasp at the image in his hand.

It's me.

Someone photoshopped a Santa hat onto my head. The background is removed, and I'm cut off at the torso. I'm wearing a bra with a crimson ribbon photoshopped to a strap. The text beside me reads, "Naughty or Nice?"

The email says it's from the school administration to all students. Every student has this picture?

Before I can comprehend everything, the band fires up with a long electric cord from Teddy's guitar as the projector screen lights with bright white. In a flash, the picture on Beau's phone displays on the large screen for everyone to see. The cheers and wolf whistles are deafening.

"What the..." Beau utters beside me. His fists crack at his sides, and his broad shoulders stiffen.

My soul gurgles to the pit of my stomach. I hunch forward, feeling the hairs on the back of my neck stand on end. I pivot from the screen to the band, who play an eclectic up-tempo version of "All I Want For Christmas Is You" by Mariah Carey.

It's like my brain is short-circuiting. Why is the band still playing? Can't they tell everyone's distracted? Haven't they noticed the static picture on the screen?

Don't they care?

I tap Beau's arm and stammer weakly, "Who did you give it to?"

Beau's eyes shoot in my direction. He has to shout over the music and the crowd. "What?"

"The picture," I quiver, pointing at the screen with a trembling finger. "Who did you give it to?"

His lips pout with sorrow. "No one."

I pan across the laughing and mocking student body. "You took that photo. Who did you share it with?"

He clutches my wrist. "No one, I swear."

I fling him off; the hurt getting the better of me. "How could you? I said you could keep it if no one else saw it."

"Ava, it wasn't me."

"Come on, Ava baby, take it off," Franky slurs as he swaggers toward me.

Michael joins him, waggling his phone, which displays the picture. "Yeah, we want the real show."

I gasp, pressing my hands together. "Oh my gosh, you gave it to them?"

"These clowns?" Beau interjects. "No way. I would never."

"Now we understand what you see in her," Franky says to Beau, followed by raucous laughter.

Beau shoves him, yelling, "Back off!"

"Lay off," Michael says, getting between the two. "It's no secret. She's on display for everyone to see."

Too angry to speak, Beau twists and locks Michael's arm behind him and spins him away. With a forceful kick behind his knee, Michael drops to the ground. My heart hammers as Beau moves back to me. He doesn't realize Franky is following him.

Franky grabs Beau's shoulder and turns him around. Beau latches onto Franky's wrist and twists. The two tussle, trying to get in a punch. My gut clenches, wishing this would all end. It's disgusting that this is over a picture. A private picture no one should've seen.

Franky shoves Beau off him, forcing him into me. I stumble on my heels, fighting to keep my balance. Beau's arm winds back, aiming at Franky. When he misses, he winds up again, this time whacking his elbow into me.

Oof.

I collapse to the ground, landing hard on my butt.

"Ava," Beau says with concern, whipping around to see me on the timber floor.

He holds out his arm to me, and I smack it away. "Ohhs" and "ahhs" ricochet around the crowd, but I don't care. Beau stares down at me with confusion.

I sniff hard as the words come out in a wavering tone. "You said you'd be better."

Beau blinks, and his expression morphs into guilt.

"You get away from my daughter," Dad orders, striding through the crowd.

With a firm grip, he yanks me off the floor.

"Dad," I wince, tripping over my feet.

Mr. Riley follows Dad and urges the crowd to move along.

Hot air flares from Dad's nostrils as he scans the onlookers. He loosens his grip on me, and I stumble to find my footing.

Dad plants a hand on my back, ensuring I'm stable. "Are you okay, sweetheart?"

My eyes well, seeing the phones in everyone's hands. I hiss and look down after I mistakenly glimpse the projector screen with my picture graffitied with crude innuendo.

Beau takes a step forward, but Mr. Riley holds him back. Pointing at the picture, Beau declares, "I didn't do this."

Vice Principal Franklin enters the stage, ordering the band to stop playing. Simultaneously, the projector screen goes dark.

"That's enough," Mr. Franklin says into the microphone. "The dance is now over."

The crowd groans, "boos" and curses at the stage.

"I see you all have cell phones. You can use them to arrange for your parents to collect you if you don't have your own transportation," Mr. Franklin says over the groans. "On Monday, there will be a long discussion about this incident. The perpetrators had better come forward."

Beau pushes past Mr. Riley with urgency. "Ava, I swear I didn't send the photo to anyone."

I sniff hard, but it doesn't stop the shakiness in my voice. "But you took the picture. It was on your phone."

"I'll find out who did this and make them pay."

I step away from him in disgust. I swipe away my tears and clench my jaw. "Make them pay? Do you think that's what I want?"

"Whatever it takes for you to trust me."

Before I can say another word, the crowd closes in on me. I yelp as someone behind me runs their hand down my arm. I squeak and flinch as someone else plays with my hair. As someone tugs on my dress, Beau yanks people away and shoves them aside.

"Stay away from her!" he barks at the crowd.

"Enough of this." Dad takes my hand, leading me away from the crowd.

"Aves," Beau calls in a shattered tone, reaching for me. "Let me help."

"Beau, let her be," Mr. Riley says, placing a hand on Beau's shoulder.

Beau groans, bumping off his hand. "Piss off."

Dad and I move at a hurried pace. More people gossip and point fingers at me along the way. The raised volume in the gym has my head spinning. The picture captured a vulnerable moment. My stomach flips and throat convulses with the imminent torrent of sobs waiting to erupt.

Once we are out of the gym, Dad's grip intensifies around my wrist. He tugs me towards him and whispers gruffly in my ear. "Are you sleeping with that boy?"

A solid gasp shoots out of me. "What? No! It wasn't like that."

"Why would he have a topless photo of you?"

"It was innocent. I swear."

Dad yanks on my arm again, forcing me to move forward with him. "That picture doesn't look innocent, Ava."

We continue towards the foyer, and the icy breeze outside is a welcome relief.

As we jog down the front steps, my name is yelled inside the school. I peer over my shoulder and find Beau barreling out the front doors and racing down the steps.

"Come on, Ava," Dad says, clutching my wrist. "Our taxi is on the way. Let's move to the top of the parking lot."

Beau's hunched body is fragile and broken. My stomach twists in on itself, and the tearing pain sends me to look away.

When we arrive home, Dad shoves me inside the house, slamming the door shut. "Explain yourself."

"Dad... I..."

"Why did he have that picture? What were you doing with him?"

"My shirt was wet!" I yell it out of fear. I clear my throat and lower my voice. "I was changing, and he took the photo as a joke."

"A joke?" Dad says, unamused. "It sure did seem like a lot of people found it funny."

"No one else was supposed to see it," I wail. "It was just between Beau and me."

"Why was he looking at you without clothes on?"

"I wasn't naked. It was just my shirt. I put a hoodie on right away."

It dawns on Dad. A look of miserable disappointment tightens his face. "You were wearing Beau's pullover the day Sheriff Lennon was here."

I swallow hard and summon all my courage to stand taller. "I told you I loved him."

Dad folds his arms, and his eyebrow crooks. "And do you still love him? After this?"

A sorrowful moan pours out of me as I lose the ability to respond.

"He's a bully, Ava," Dad says sternly. "Malice is in his blood. All he'll do is hurt you."

"I don't want to hear this anymore," I say, turning toward my bedroom. "I'm going to bed."

"We're not done here."

"I am," I say with a raised voice. "Your picture wasn't shown to everyone in the school. Now, I'm going to bed."

I stomp toward my bedroom, leaving behind the stunned silence of my father.

Twenty-Five

When I wake up, my eyes are sore and puffy. I know I slept, but my body's not so sure. All my joints are stiff. I think I held myself in a tight ball all night.

My head throbs as I pull myself up to sit. I throw my disheveled hair over my shoulder and pull on a bathrobe. I slide my feet into fuzzy slippers and leave my bedroom. I've never had a greater need for a sugary hot cocoa.

In the hall, I stop and linger by Mommy's picture. I stroke her shiny hair and fixate on her crooked smile.

"I wish you were here," I whisper.

As I shuffle my way into the kitchen, I glance at the clock and see it's 11 a.m. It's far later than I normally sleep. I'm surprised Dad let me get away with it.

"Sweetheart," Dad greets me, entering the kitchen. "How did you sleep?"

I flop into his embrace. "Not well. I'm tired and sore."

He rubs my back, humming. "Just take it easy today."

"Good to see you up, Ava," Sheriff Lennon's voice enters the kitchen.

Like a coiled spring, I leap away from Dad, startled. I pull my robe tighter, blinking at the man.

"Sheriff Lennon just wanted to check in," Dad explains.

"I dropped Ciara off at school and thought I'd see how you were feeling."

"They didn't finish the clean up last night?" I ask.

Sheriff Lennon shakes his head. "No. Mr. Franklin wanted everyone to go home after the dance."

I look at Dad. "I should go and help them."

"No one is expecting you to be there," Dad replies. "Not after last night's atrocity."

Sheriff Lennon gestures to the dining room. "Do you want to sit and chat about it?"

I pivot my gaze between the two men. I want nothing more than to disappear back into my bedroom.

Dad places his hand on my shoulder blade, nudging me toward the doorway. "We were discussing this earlier. We wanted to iron out some details."

My fingers flex at my sides as nervous energy bubbles inside me. "What details?"

"Take a seat with your dad," Sheriff Lennon says with kind eyes. "I'll get you a glass of water."

"Are you hungry, sweetheart?" Dad asks.

I frown, shaking my head.

"Okay," Dad says, walking me out of the kitchen. "Let's take a seat then."

The three of us sit at the dining table. Sheriff Lennon sits a tall glass of water in front of me and asks, "Beau took the picture?"

"Yes, but it was only between us. No one else was supposed to see."

"Is it possible he broke that promise and showed it to someone else?"

I pick at my fingernails as dread simmers in my stomach. "It's possible. The thought keeps nagging in my brain. Somehow, the picture came from Beau."

"Do you think he still holds some kind of resentment against you?" Sheriff Lennon asks, leaning forward. "Is it possible he got close to you with the ultimate goal of humiliating you?"

My chin drops. "You think he was dating me as a sick prank?"

"I wouldn't put it past him."

"He's a bully, Ava," Dad interjects. "In a snap of a finger, he became a model citizen. Doesn't that strike you as odd?"

"No," I say with a wavering voice. "You don't know what he's been dealing with. His home life... Anyway, he straightened out because he finally had someone to open up to."

"So, how did the picture end up on the projector screen and in everyone's inboxes?" Sheriff Lennon pushes.

The question hits me hard, causing tears to stream.

Dad strokes my hair. "We just want you to see the real him. He took a picture of you, and then everyone saw it. He has a history of abusing and humiliating other students. I know you wanted your friend back, but I don't think that's possible."

I pat my eyes dry and wipe my sleeve under my nose. "But you saw him last night," I say to Dad. "He kept saying he didn't do it. Why would he deny it if he did it? In the past, he's always taken credit for the bad things he's done."

Dad blinks and then sits back in his chair. He doesn't have an answer. That means he has some faith left in Beau.

"So there's no need to press charges against him?" Sheriff Lennon asks.

"What?" I gasp.

"Harassment charges? Soliciting non-consensual photos?"

"No," I say firmly. "Beau did nothing wrong."

"I just want to get the facts straight."

"Then find the actual person behind this."

Sheriff Lennon holds up his hands, placatingly. "I didn't mean to upset you. I'm on your side."

"Then can you take me to school?" I ask. "I need to find out what everyone knows."

"I don't think that's a good idea," Dad says protectively.

"Please," I urge. "I can't wait until Monday when I have the entire student body to deal with."

"Are you sure about this?" Sheriff Lennon asks, scooting back his chair.

I nod. "I'll get dressed and brush my hair."

Dad stands. "I'll go with you."

"It'll be easier without you," I admit.

"I'm not letting you walk into the gym where those kids can ridicule you," Dad persists.

"Mr. Riley and other faculty members will be there," I say. "I'll be okay."

"I'll walk her in," Sheriff Lennon says.

I bite my lip and look him in the eyes. "I'd prefer it if you didn't."

It's a miracle I got my way. But now, I wonder if that's a good thing. My heart pounds, anticipating doom. Am I crazy to be walking into the gym right now?

"Ava!" Hilary's voice echoes through the gym. She drops a bundle of twinkle lights to her feet and then bolts toward me. Lucy thunders behind, equally eager to reach me.

Hilary skids to a stop and grasps my hand. "Oh my gosh, we've been so worried about you."

"Are you okay?" Lucy says with saddened, droopy eyes. "I can't believe that happened. I'm shocked, and just... sickened."

Hilary nods. "Agreed. Whoever did that is an absolute pig."

Lucy nods her head to the right. "He swears it wasn't him."

The thump of my heart nears a deafening level as I swivel to view the other side of the gym. Beau is sweeping glitter, paper cups, and other rubbish in piles on the floor.

"He came?" It puffs out of me like a wounded whimper.

The girls nod, stepping to either side of me.

"You don't have to talk to him," Hilary says, cracking her knuckles. "The boys will keep him away from you."

"No, I want to talk to him," I answer.

Lucy links her arm with mine. "Are you sure?"

I nod. "Yes. He's still my boyfriend."

The girls step aside, and I summon all my courage as I walk further into the gym.

"Umm, are you okay?" Ciara's mousy voice asks before I find her off to the side.

I move toward the table she's cleaning and force a smile. "Yes. Your dad stopped by and gave me a ride here."

"Oh." Her eyes water. "I hope that was okay. I told him you'd want space."

"It's okay. I'm glad I'm here so I can find out if anyone knows what happened."

Ciara steps around the table and throws her arms around me. "I'm so sorry. I was so appalled by what happened. It keeps flashing through my mind, so I can't imagine what you've been going through."

I slump my head against her shoulder. "I'm sorry I haven't been talking to you. You were my friend for a long time."

"We stopped hanging out because I wasn't there for you." She sighs. "Maybe if I were, that picture never would've happened."

I pull my head up and step out of her hug. "I still would've dated him. That picture would've happened, regardless."

"I just hate seeing you get hurt."

I swallow hard, nodding.

She winces. "Are you sure you should be here?"

I throw a thumb to the right. "I need to talk to him."

As I turn to the right, Beau is staring straight at me. The broom falls from his hand and his mouth hangs open. He straightens up and walks toward me.

I meet him in the middle, when he says, "I'm so glad you're here. I've been so worried."

He holds his arms out, ready to hug me, but doesn't go through with it.

My knees knock together as I take in his tall, broad frame.

He hunches forward and his concern rounds his face. "Are you okay?"

I grab onto his arm out of necessity as my head spins.

"Avie?"

"Can we sit somewhere?"

"Yeah, sure. Keep a hold of me."

I lean into him, letting him pull his arm around me. By the wall, he pulls two stackable chairs off a pile. We take a seat. Thankfully, everyone else is cleaning away from this area.

"I thought you might not be here," I say.

My hand rests on his. "Why is that?"

"After what happened last night, I didn't think you'd want to help."

"I told you this event was important to me, too. I wanted to help everyone, even if you couldn't be here."

A small smile graces my lips. "That's good to hear."

He laces his fingers with mine and there's a noticeable tremble in his hand. "I was telling the truth. I didn't share that photo with anyone."

I shudder. "Then how did it get emailed to everyone?"

"That's what I want to know. Could someone have hacked me?"

"Why would someone hack you and then use my picture at the dance? Wouldn't they try to humiliate you?"

Beau looks down, deep in concentration. "Not if they're scared of retaliation. Maybe they targeted you to get back at me?"

I push a hand into my squeamish stomach. "This is all so disgusting. I never wanted to get involved in this kind of ugliness. I didn't think being with you would make me a target for bullying."

His hand squeezes mine tighter. "Neither did I. I wouldn't have gotten close to you if I thought it would hurt you."

"It makes me question myself. Like after our first committee meeting, when I ran from you. Maybe that was the best decision I've made in the past two weeks."

His eyes well. "Don't say that."

"I don't know what else to think. I'm just really confused."

His watery eyes stare into mine. "Do you believe I still love you?"

I gulp and take a moment. As jittery energy runs through my veins, I take a breath and nod. "Yes, because I still love you too."

He exhales hard, slumping. "Really?"

I grit my teeth and nod again.

"Oh Ava," he breathes and curls his arms around me. I let my head rest on his bicep and listen to the intensity of my heart.

Someone attacked me. But it can't have been him.

"Is everything okay over here?" Marcus asks as he and Jeff stroll toward us.

I pull out of Beau's embrace and face the boys. "Getting there."

"Did you see the school portal was shut down?" Marcus asks.

Instinctively, I clutch the pocket of my jeans before realizing I didn't bring my phone with me. "Oh, did it?"

Jeff nods. "Yeah. There's a message when you open the app saying it's shut down for internal maintenance. I guess they're upping security. The message also said that any assignments uploaded since Friday have to be turned in as hard copies on Monday."

I scratch the side of my head. "That's not such a big deal."

Jeff smirks. "Maybe not for you. I swung by Whitney's house this morning to bring her here, and she was screaming and cursing at her laptop."

I stretch my neck, viewing everyone in the gym. "Is she here?"

"Nope," Jeff replies. "She was pretty manic. She kept saying how everything was unfair and all your fault."

My hand clutches my chest. "My fault."

Jeff twists his lips as he nods his confirmation.

"We're not blaming you for anything," Marcus says and then side-glances at Beau.

I lean into Beau. "Don't blame Beau either."

"Dude, I saw your face when Ava's picture came on the screen," Marcus says. "You were as shocked as the rest of us. It's clear you care about Ava."

"Thanks, man," Beau replies, rubbing a circle on my back. "It's funny how the Photoshop Pro isn't here after that photo leaked."

"No," Jeff draws out the word. "She wouldn't."

"I can't even think about that right now." My mind whirs, thinking about the school portal being shut down, and my picture being wiped with it. A defeated whimper pours out of me. "The picture isn't gone."

Beau tilts his head. "Huh?"

"Even if they wipe it from the school portal," I say, "it's not gone. It'd be pretty naive not to realize most people would've taken a screenshot."

Beau's arm flexes around me. "If anyone shares it again, they will have hell to pay."

I stand up, looking around the gym. "I guess I should help clean up."

"Don't worry about it, Ava," Jeff says gently. "Why don't you go home and get some rest?"

"Yeah," Marcus says. "You look like you need it."

"But I should help."

"Beau, why don't you take her home?" Marcus suggests.

Beau gingerly touches my arm. "Do you want to go home?"

Jeff cups his hands around his mouth. "What do you think, girls? Should Ava take a breather and go home?"

"Oh, for sure," Hilary calls back.

"We got this, Aves," Lucy adds.

My head spins like I could collapse. I grab onto Beau. "Okay. I'll go."

Beau sets our pace to a dawdle as we make our way to his car. Like a gentleman, he holds the door open for me.

"Do you have some time to hang out?" Beau asks when he takes the driver's seat.

"Umm... Maybe."

"There's so many thoughts spiraling through my head."

"Do you have any clue who'd have sent the photo?"

"Now that I know you're okay, I'll try to put the pieces together."

I flop my head against the seat. "It's just such a mess."

"We could use this time to discuss our parents."

My whole body seizes.

He leans over the steering wheel, looking out the windshield. "I feel like my life now makes sense."

The cramps inside me intensify as I will him to stop talking.

"My dad awkwardly tries to talk to me, but it's my mom I want answers from." He sits back, staring out at nothing. "I still don't know how she feels. Or how she's been dealing with this."

I gulp, concentrating on the lack of air I'm pulling in.

"Or, more accurately, why she hasn't been dealing with it." Beau huffs. "Why did she stay with him just to make our home a living hell? Was it revenge? She could've left and found a way to be happy."

A loud groan erupts out of me, and then I shout, "Stop!"

He jolts in his seat, taken aback by my outburst.

I slam my hands on my head, staring at my lap. "I'm sorry," I whimper. "I just can't. I don't want to talk about it."

"Maybe we don't need to talk about your family. We can just discuss what's going on with mine."

"No!" I slam a fist against my thigh. "If you bring up your unhappy mother, I have to think about my unhappy father."

"No, we don't. I'm just trying to understand why my mom's been so distant over the years. I need to vent. I thought I could do that with you."

"Well, you can't right now," I snap and fling the car door open.

I step out of the car and gulp large breaths of cold air.

Beau opens his car door, stepping out. "Ava, get back in the car."

His voice sounds so exhausted that it aggravates me. "No. I don't have to do anything."

"I'm not ordering you. Just let me drive you home."

I turn to him with folded arms. "And you won't bring up our parents again."

He shrugs with mournful defeat. "I won't push it. You're already upset." He winces, pinching the bridge of his nose. "If I'd never taken that picture. Ugh. Come on, I'll take you home."

The drive home was quiet. When Beau pulled up at my cul-de-sac, I pecked him on the lips and then went inside the house. I hugged my dad and told him I was fine. I took the food he prepared back to my bedroom and didn't venture back out until Monday morning.

Thank goodness I still have people standing by me. Hilary and Lucy are like bodyguards as I brave the school halls this morning.

The entire senior class is called into the gym for an emergency assembly. With narrowed eyes, Vice Principal Franklin watches everyone take their seats on the bleachers. Mr. Riley, Ms. Hart, and other teachers also stand in watch.

I follow behind Hilary and Lucy as we take our seats. The hums of whispers and gossip circles around me. Even though I move into the crowd, I've never felt more on display. I really need Beau sitting beside me. Then everyone would look away, pretending to mind their own business.

We sit near Marcus and Jeff, who stare down my onlookers. It minimizes the amount of eyes on me, but I still feel holes burning through me.

"Has anyone seen Beau?" I say to the foursome.

They reply with shakes of the heads.

I look out onto the empty gym before us. I get flashes of the crowd dancing, surrounded by Christmas decorations. Sickening bile races up my throat, reliving the moment my picture lit up the screen.

All I wanted was a sweet party like my mother would host. It was my one shot, and it blew up in my face.

Ciara bounds up the stairs and sneaks into the space beside me. She clutches my hand and finds my eyes. "Are you doing okay?"

"I'll be better when this is over."

She smiles kindly. "We've got you."

Ciara's dad walks into the gym and shakes hands with Mr. Franklin. A hush falls over the crowd as Mr. Franklin approaches the microphone.

"I am repulsed by the incident that happened on Saturday night," Mr. Franklin says into the microphone. "A senior student was harassed at the Christmas dance. Someone hacked into the school portal to do so. Today's assembly is two-fold. I am here to ask whoever was behind this to come forward. Also, we've gathered you to discuss the seriousness of online bullying." Mr. Franklin gestures to Ciara's dad. "Sheriff Lennon has joined us to inform you about the severe consequences of cyber crime. We are taking this incident seriously, and we will bring the culprits to justice."

Mr. Franklin steps to the side as Sheriff Lennon approaches the mic. "I am helping the school investigate this serious incident. If you were involved in Saturday night's incident, or know of someone who was, please come forward with the information. Most of you are minors, and I don't wish to process you down at the station. Please come clean so the school can conduct disciplinary action. You don't want to deal with me."

Mr. Franklin steps back in front of the mic. "Ashworth Academy does not tolerate bullying and harassment."

"Until a donation is made to the school," someone calls from the crowd.

Sneers and hushed laughter seep out from the bleachers.

"That's enough," Mr. Franklin says heatedly. "I am not tolerating what happened on Saturday night. It made a mockery of the school and the hard work of the committee members."

"We all know which one of them did it," a voice shouts from the crowd.

"If you have information about the incident," Mr. Franklin replies, "come by my office today. We will show leniency to whoever admits wrongdoing."

Sheriff Lennon steps back to the microphone. "Kids, I don't want to downplay the severity of the situation. Someone hacked into the school portal and sent unsolicited photos to minors. Not to mention the photo was of a minor. These are criminal offenses."

Gasps and murmuring simmer throughout the crowd.

I latch onto Ciara and shiver. "Do you think your dad would really arrest someone?"

"He told me the Ashworth family consider it a big security breach," Ciara replies. "Mr. Ashworth told Dad over the phone that if one of his companies was hacked, he'd want a criminal investigation. They want to know if any information was stolen before pressing charges."

"So more could've been done besides sending my photo?"

Ciara shrugs. "Perhaps. They just don't know yet. That's why they shut down the portal to do an internal review."

"Your dad asked me if I wanted to press charges against Beau."

"Do you think he's behind this?"

"No." It comes out less sure than I wanted it to. "I don't know who did it. He took the photo, but..."

Ciara waits for me to continue, but the pause gets the better of her. "But what?"

My lips quirk as I fight against my frown. "I don't know. What is the link between him taking the photo and it being leaked to everyone at school?"

"It can't be good."

I blow out a hard breath. "He said he didn't do it."

"I'm sure they'll find whoever did."

"Imagine being the person whose image was sent to everyone's inboxes," Sheriff Lennon says to the crowd. "Her privacy was violated."

Crude remarks and cringe-worthy laughter erupt behind me. There's nudging and pointing. From the corner of my eye, I note the phones being passed around. My insides contort as I know they are looking at screenshots of me. The hairs on the back of my neck stand on end. They're traced by a slick line of sweat. My fingers vibrate with fear, and my feet bounce against the metal step.

I have to get out of here.

And without another moment of thought, that's what I do. I leap from the seat and hightail it down the steps. Ciara calls out for me, but I keep running until I'm out of the gym.

I slide against the wall, anchoring myself as I hunch over, panting.

"Ava?" Ms. Hart calls, hurrying out of the gym. She moves over to me. "Ava, are you okay? I know this must be devastating to deal with."

"They were all laughing at me," I say through heavy pants. "They were looking at my picture and saying horrible things."

Ms. Hart places her hand on my shoulder. "I'm so sorry, Ava. It's very unfair."

I nudge her off and step away from her. "I just need some air."

She lets me walk away and returns to the gym.

I'm shaky as I amble, directionless, through the halls. It feels like a weight hangs off each shoulder as I scuff my way forward. Ahead, the distinct sound of a door opening and closing grabs my attention.

Walking out of Principal Harvey's office is Beau.

He doesn't notice me as his head hangs low.

The weight drops, and I move toward him. "Hey, where were you?"

He shakes his head as if escaping a trance. "Oh, hey," he says, pulling his arms around me for a quick hug. "What are you doing here?"

"I left the gym. I couldn't take it in there. Why weren't you in there?"

He motions behind him. "I was busy being interrogated. They think I did it."

My chest aches. "Oh."

The moment lingers as we share uneasy glances.

I flex my fingers at my sides. "But you didn't, right?"

Hurt pains his face as his eyes narrow. "No. You shouldn't even have to ask."

"I know. But..."

He clicks his tongue, averting his eyes. "You're just like them. Assuming that because I've done bad things before, I must have done this too."

"No, it's not that."

"If they blame me for this," his voice wavers, "there's no coming back. My grades won't be fixed and I'll be kicked out of school."

"You know I don't want that to happen. I just don't know what to think."

He scuffs his shoes against the floor. "How could you think I'd want to hurt you?"

"I don't." A mournful gasp rushes out of me as I rub the ache from my chest. "It's just someone did, and you're the one who took the picture."

"You still think that low of me?" He tosses his arms out and raises his volume. "Why don't you admit you ratted me out after you saw me with Teddy and Sullivan that day?"

"I didn't do that. I already told you."

Beau nods. "You did. But you're also a really good liar."

Tears pool in my eyes as he stares at me point blank.

"Why are we having this conversation?" he mumbles. "If you think I did it, you obviously don't want to be with me anymore."

I wipe my eyes clear and stamp my foot in frustration. "It's not that. I'm confused. Someone humiliated me in front of the entire school, and somehow it involved you."

"You don't think I want to fix this?" he fires back. "But, in case you forgot, another major thing has happened to us."

I look away, grimacing.

"Our parents had an affair," he says in a serious tone, "and you don't seem to want to discuss it."

I flinch away from him. "Because I don't."

"But can't you see that it's hurting me as much as this photo is hurting you?"

I look back at him with unwavering severity. "It's not the same thing. This wasn't sent to everybody's phone."

"So, how I feel isn't valid?" he asks, emotion draining from his face.

I pause, breathless. I blink hard, taking in his words.

"You never want to talk about it," Beau continues. "You change the subject, or you avoid me entirely. You don't care because everything worked out for you."

I gasp in shock. "What was that?"

"Your dad might be tough on you, but he cares about you. Everything he does is to ensure nothing bad happens to you." Beau taps his chest hard. "Bad things happen to me all the time, but my parents never throw their arms around me. They pushed me away."

A sob croaks out of me as I reply, "That wasn't my fault."

"My mom tried to be a good mom, but the betrayal was too much for her. She went back to work to avoid our home. She never said anything because your mom died. She didn't want to make *your life* hard."

"I... I..."

"Over the last four years, I couldn't work out why my life was so crappy. Now I see it clearly." He backs away, pressing his fingertips against his temples. "It's because of you and your mother. You both have made my life hell."

My mouth falls open, and it takes all my strength to raise my hands to cover it.

He shakes his head and huffs. "I can't look at you right now."

"Wait... What... What does that mean?"

"It means..." A painful sound puffs out of him. "Maybe we shouldn't be together."

He walks away, and my heart shatters. I want to call out to him, but he also feels like a stranger to me. The boy I loved would never talk to me like that.

A tear drops onto my cheek.

Love.

Who am I kidding?

This isn't love.

Screw this.

With purposeful steps, I make my way toward the teachers' lounge. I continue toward the fire exit, and then jog through the teachers' parking lot.

I don't need to hear anymore whispers about me. And I don't need the fact my boyfriend walked away from me swirling through my head as I deal with classes.

311

Twenty-Six

Did Beau break up with me? Is that what happened?

I spent the day at home, reliving my conversation with Beau. If you could even call it that. Beau stormed off so angrily. But not because of the leaked photo. He stormed off because I refused to talk about what happened between our parents.

Ugh. Why should I? It's so ugly and sordid. The woman in the story is not my mother.

As I sit at my bedroom desk, a new thought plagues my mind.

Why would Mr. Stevenson admit he had an affair with my mom? If it was a lie, what did he gain? That day at Morton's Café, he kept remarking how cute Beau and I looked together. They weren't the words of a man trying to break us up.

My fingers flex and my jaw clenches as I listen to the front door unlocking.

No. The man who wanted Beau and me broken up is stepping inside this house.

I stomp down the hall and glare at my father. "Why didn't you ever tell me?"

He gives me an incredulous look. "Tell you what?"

"About Mommy," my voice breaks, "and Mr. Stevenson."

Dad sucks in a breath and his back stiffens. "What are you talking about? And why are you home so early?"

"No deflecting. You don't need to tiptoe around this," I say despondently. "I know the truth."

"What is this? Beau has been telling you lies."

"It wasn't Beau. His dad told us he and Mom were more than friends."

Dad's face is horror-stricken. He tries to utter words to refute the claim, but the shock of this conversation renders him speechless.

"It's the reason the Stevenson's left the cul-de-sac," I say, pushing the conversation forward. "Mommy was still alive then. Why wasn't I told what really happened?"

Dad sighs, rubbing his creased forehead. "Because your mother and I were starting over." He pauses, gaining the strength to continue. "We didn't want to hurt you with something so ugly. We were trying to get back to a good place."

"I don't remember you two being in a bad place," I admit. "Why did she do it?"

Dad shakes his head. "It was so long ago. It doesn't matter now."

"It matters to me," I urge. "I need to understand what happened. Beau thinks his parents don't show him affection because of Mom and Mr. Stevenson's affair. It's affected all of our lives."

"I've strived to never let it affect your life."

"*Bull.*"

He rears back. "Excuse me?"

"I always knew you changed around the time Mom died. You became ultra-strict and overprotective. It wasn't just her death, but it was her affair too. Wasn't it?"

Dad frowns and brushes back my hair. "I didn't want you to turn into her."

I whack his hand away from me. "Why would you say that? Everyone loved Mom. She was a great person."

Dad grimaces. "Yes, everyone loved her."

I tilt my head, confused. "What did you think was going to happen?"

Dad huffs, squeezing his hands into fists. "She had an affair and then she died. I've thought about this for a long time. I can't deny it's connected."

"Are you saying she was punished by a higher being?" I shake my head, dumbfounded. "You think her life was taken because she cheated on you?"

He cups my hands. "All I know with certainty is I would let nothing bad happen to you. I wouldn't let anyone corrupt you and risk you being taken away from me."

"And that came down to my friends, too?" I question, trying to slip my hands away, but his grip is firm. "You got rid of Whitney but forced me to befriend Ciara."

He tilts his head. "Ciara is a good friend."

I rip my hands away from him. "You just like her because her dad is a cop. We were never that close because it was a forced friendship."

"I did what I had to keep you safe."

"Mom didn't die because she had an affair," I say. "She died because of a freak accident. The investigation showed it wasn't her fault. You can't blame her."

"I don't," Dad replies, voice wavering. "I blame myself. I wasn't the best husband. We were fighting for weeks leading up to her death. I wish I could do it over and just tell her I love her."

I slouch. "Oh, Dad."

Dad sighs, patting his eyes dry. "I miss her so much."

"Me too."

"You asked me why I didn't speak about her. Whenever I think back, I remember those bad times in our marriage. I just feel so guilty."

"I'm so sorry," I murmur. "But Mom did so much good. I know she loved you."

He nods. "She did, but she loved Paul too."

"What does that mean?"

"She told me she didn't want to leave our marriage. But she had something special with him, too. I hoped she could forget him and we could be happy again, but I could tell part of her heart still belonged to him."

My lip quivers as I splutter a sob. I fight to hold back the deluge inside me. "If only you'd told me." I tremble. "If I'd known the truth, we could've grieved together. I felt like I could never be honest about how much I missed her. You never let me."

Dad wipes under his eye. "I thought I was doing what was best. I wanted to shield you from the ugliness."

Disappointment coats my face. "The lying made it worse."

He shakes his head. "I didn't see it as lying."

My heart splinters as I look into his sorrowful eyes.

Lying.

I do that too to protect his feelings.

I clear my throat and walk past him. "I'm going to my room."

He doesn't fight me to stay and talk. I move into my bedroom and let every emotion crash over me.

I collapse on my desk chair, and stare at the array of books scattered on the desktop. I place my phone on the desk and look at the recordings app. My interview with Beau is still waiting to be played.

Imagine if I had asked Vanessa to sit for my interview and she had answered those four questions. I'd never have that intimate moment with Beau. Never learned about the hardships he's dealt with for the past four years.

I wouldn't feel as violated as I do now. The thought of glimpsing myself in the mirror when I'm changing wouldn't make me shudder. I wouldn't be looking over my shoulder, wondering who's making snide comments about me.

But I also wouldn't have had a snow fight in the park. Or a magical night at the school dance. Or my first kiss and the many wonderful kisses that followed.

I wouldn't have felt an all-consuming love.

I drop my phone as all the thoughts collide in on themselves. An image of Beau and Vanessa standing together forms in my mind. The way she stared at him, her giggle, their flirty banter.

She wanted him.

And she didn't get him.

Did it make her hate me enough to humiliate me in front of the entire school?

My heart drops to the pit of my stomach.

Oh no!

Vanessa took Beau's phone when he had my picture on his screen. She must have sent it to her phone.

Goosebumps line every inch of my skin as I shiver and turn a pale shade of green.

Oh my gosh. Is she capable of something so heinous? Is she that spiteful and jealous?

I move from my desk and flop onto my bed. I cramp myself into the fetal position and hug my pillow for dear life. As my body rocks, the realization solidifies in my mind.

Vanessa Ashworth was behind this.

The next day I go to school with the sole mission of confronting Vanessa. I sit in economics, repeating my mantra. *I am strong and confident.* And with each passing second, the mantra becomes less believable.

I fidget uncomfortably in my seat. In the corner of my eye, something more restless catches my attention. Whitney is twitchy, playing with her hair, chewing on a pen cap, and tapping her feet against her chair legs. Her eyes flick toward me and she sucks in a ragged breath. Her eyes shoot downward and I watch her chest heave.

Oh my gosh. Guilt has never manifested itself more clearly.

When the bell rings, I rise from my seat, leaving my books behind. I push past other students and cut off Whitney from leaving.

"Move out of the way," she orders.

I press on her shoulder and force her to sit. "We need to talk."

"Ugh. We do not."

"You know exactly what this is about, Miss Photoshop Pro."

"As if," she scoffs. I'd almost believe her if she wasn't turning a shade of green.

"Just be honest with me," I whisper. "Were you involved in the photo or not?"

Whitney scowls. "Get out of my way."

"I know Vanessa had the photo. Did you make the changes to it?"

"Look, Ness cares about me, okay," Whitney whines. "She listened to me complain about you, and she took action."

I swallow, saving myself from retching. "What did she do?"

"She said she had a picture and that if I talked to Teddy, he'd help me spread it."

Nope, can't hold it. A violent retch quakes out of me.

Whitney grimaces. "Uh, gross."

I push the loose hair off my face, taking in a calming breath. "Why did you need to attack me so publicly?"

"Oh, big whoop," Whitney mocks. "As if you two didn't have it coming. I could've been the chairperson if it wasn't for you. Beau made me cry, and no one in the group cared."

I blink back watery tears, clearing my vision. My hand lands on the space over my heart. "I cared."

Whitney frowns, blinking hard. Her bottom lip trembles, and she collects her books. Hugging them to her chest, she stands and barges her way past me.

"You need to say something," I call after her. "You need to tell Mr. Franklin before it is too late."

Whitney stops at the door, glaring at me. "Is that a threat?"

"He said he'd be lenient if you came forward."

She shakes her head. "All I did was make a picture. I didn't spread it."

And with that, she storms out of the classroom.

I walk back to my desk to collect my things. Oh my gosh. A team was out to get me. And for what? Some petty grievances?

My head throbs. I need to talk to Teddy. He needs to explain what I did to encourage such a vicious attack.

After ditching my books in my locker, I splash some water on my face in the bathroom. With three more rounds of my mantra, I make my way to the AV room. One more mantra, and I pull the door handle.

As the door creaks open, I find Teddy and Sullivan inside. They're chatting with other members of their club.

"Ava?" Teddy questions. The quiver in his tone suggests he knows why I'm here.

"Can I talk to you?" I ask.

He shakes his head. "It's not a great time."

"Sullivan?"

Sullivan looks at Teddy and then at me. He chews his lip, thinking hard about his response.

"No," Teddy whispers harshly to him. "We said we weren't gonna do this."

Sullivan stands, moving toward the door. "Let's just hear her out."

"*Sully*," Teddy complains.

When Sullivan reaches the door, Teddy groans, pulling himself up and moving toward the door. I step into the alcove, giving the boys space to join me outside the room.

Teddy closes the door and crosses his arms. "What's this about?"

I deadpan him. "Are you really playing that card?"

"It wasn't about you, Ava," Sullivan says.

Teddy nudges him. "Shut it."

"What wasn't about me?" I ask. "My half-naked image on the big screen? Or sending it to everyone's inbox?"

Teddy sighs. "Fine. It was revenge on Beau."

My stomach turns in on itself. "Excuse me?"

"We can't target him directly," Sullivan says, trying to appear as innocent as possible. "We've tried, and we get beaten up. When we saw how much he cares about you, we had to take the shot."

"That's disgusting," I wail. "I'm not a prop for you to toy with. How could you think this was okay?"

"We just wanted the school to target him," Sullivan replies. "And they do think it's him. He deserves it."

"And I'm just collateral damage?"

"What were you doing dating him?" Teddy asks condescendingly. "We showed you what kind of guy he really is."

"You're blaming me?" My hand clutches my chest as an ache drives deep into my core. "I knew he had that photo. He didn't leak it. You stole it from him."

"We didn't steal it," Sullivan says defensively. "It was given to us."

"And that makes it okay?"

Sullivan's expression droops, and he turns away.

"You should just let this go," Teddy says softly. "You're a good girl. This will all blow over for you. Let Beau take the fall so he can get the punishment he deserves. Just keep the truth between us."

"The punishment he deserves? They've already suspended him for countless things."

"He sabotaged one of our presentations and no one cared," Teddy fires back, heat igniting his stare. "The same day, he fought three linebackers, and that's all anyone talked about. That's what they suspended him for."

"Plus, he attacked us in the hall and all they did was put him on the dance committee," Sullivan adds, shifting his weight uncomfortably.

"Oh my gosh." My insides shatter with utter despair. "It really was over something petty?"

"*Petty?*" the boys yelp.

I wipe my eyes dry, looking down at the floor. "This makes me so sick. You two need to confess to Mr. Franklin."

"Fat chance," Teddy mutters.

"We can't do that," Sullivan adds.

"What you did was wrong on so many levels," I say, unable to quantify my shock levels. "How can you live with this?"

Teddy grabs Sullivan's arm and opens the AV room door. "We're done here," he snaps, and the two retreat into the room.

The slam behind them was completely unnecessary.

Somehow, I keep it together throughout the next two periods as I scope the halls for Vanessa. I knew she wouldn't have gotten her hands dirty, but to pair up three broken people with ugly grudges is beyond belief.

Vanessa struts through Hall C, making her way toward the staircase leading to the library. Before she reaches it, I grab her shoulder and swing her around.

"Hey, get off me," she fusses.

"Why did you do it?"

She scoffs. "Do what?"

"Don't play dumb. You know exactly what I'm talking about. You have Whitney, Teddy, and Sullivan as your little minions."

Vanessa scowls and pushes me off to the side. "Keep your mouth shut."

"You had the boys in your back pocket. And then what? You started conspiring with Whitney?"

"I didn't conspire with anyone. I happened to overhear Whitney muttering to herself in class. She was drawing angry slashes in her notebook. Naturally, I asked her what was wrong. It's not my fault her grievances erupted like a volcano."

"So you set her on a path toward the boys? Did you let them complain to you, too?"

Vanessa huffs, stamping a foot. "I didn't let anyone do anything."

"What did I ever do to you?" I fire back. "Sure, you had a crush on Beau, but that's no reason to—"

"I didn't have a crush," she cuts me off in an unconvincing tone.

I raise my eyebrows and plant my hands on my hips. "Really?"

She rolls her eyes. "I think he's fun. I've made no secret of that."

"I've seen the way you look at him."

"And what of it?"

"Did you really think I'd leave him after what you did and he'd come running to you with open arms?" I question. "When he finds out…"

"*Shoosh.*" She whacks my arms. "No one is finding out about anything."

"What does that mean? Beau's not dumb. He'll figure this out on his own."

"I know." Vanessa's shoulders slouch as she pouts. "Look, I did like Beau. He brought an ounce of fun into my life, and I wanted more. I guess I just want a bad boy."

"That's fine," I say bluntly, "but Beau's my boyfriend. Find your own."

She looks at me blankly. Her chin juts up and down as if subtly nodding her understanding.

"So what are we gonna do about this?"

"You know I can't come forward," she says in a harsh whisper. "I'm an Ashworth."

"That's a cop-out."

"No, it's complicated."

"I don't care what you do," I reply. "I just want your acknowledgement."

She rolls her eyes. "I'm not admitting anything."

"Then I want your help."

Her eyes narrow. "For what? Ugh. Are you asking me to help you get Beau back? Like some grand gesture thing?"

I smirk in disgust. "Umm, no. I don't need you to fix my relationship with him. No, I want to interview you."

She folds her arms, tensing. "Interview me? For what?"

"My psych assignment. I need a subject, and I want it to be you."

"Uh, no. I don't…"

"No, you don't understand," I cut her off. "I'm not asking. You will do this because it's nothing compared to what happened at the dance."

She throws up a hand, frowning. "Okay, I get it. I'll sit for your interview."

"Good. I'll send you an email to set it up."

"The school break is coming up. I really don't have much time."

"I don't need the extra-credit. I'm done killing myself to be top of the class. I can hand the assignment in after the break."

Her eyes twitch, working me out. "You're not getting any dirt out of me."

"Don't worry, you can be as vague as you like," I reply, turning on my heels. "Now, if you'll excuse me, I have somewhere I need to be."

"Whatever." She huffs, clip-clopping toward the staircase.

I don't care what phony answers she gives me. I can't wait to scrutinize every facial twitch and every body quirk as she sits in front of me.

Twenty-Seven

"Oh, Miss Jones," Mr. Franklin says, surprised to see me enter his office. "How are you? I suspect things have been difficult the past few days."

He gestures to a seat in front of his desk, and I take it. "Yeah, it hasn't been the easiest. I'm here to discuss the photo and who did it."

Mr. Franklin leans forward with interest. "You know who did it?"

"Beau didn't do it," I blurt. "I want that to be abundantly clear. He's one person, for certain, you should rule out."

His eyes narrow. "Okay, and what makes you say that?"

"I just know he didn't. People were saying he was dating me as a prank, but that's far from the truth. We were dating for real."

Mr. Franklin lifts a hand. "That's fine, Miss Jones. Okay, you say Beau Stevenson has nothing to do with it. But do you know who does?"

I nod. "There was more than one person. I've already talked to all of them and told them to confess to you."

"Why don't you just tell me now so I can begin disciplinary action?"

"I don't want to be a tattle-tale."

"Miss Jones, please, this isn't kindergarten."

I place a hand on my chest over my heart. "I've already said my piece to them. I feel like I have closure. They'll have to deal with their own guilt and karma. All I care about is you remove Beau from the equation. I promise you, he's innocent."

Mr. Franklin gives me an unsatisfied look. "Are you really not telling me who's behind this?"

I nod.

"But these people admitted fault to you?"

"As much as they were willing to."

"So they might not be who we're looking for?"

I move from the seat to the door. "They will either come clean, or the truth will never come out."

"Miss Jones..."

I don't let him continue and instead leave his office. I keep walking toward the foyer and then off school grounds.

As I pull my blazer tighter around my midsection, it's hard to comprehend the person I've become. I've confronted people with high stakes allegations. I spoke my mind to an adult in an authority position. I've left school early and am making my way toward Main Street. When I get there, I plan on taking a bus toward my boyfriend's house and do my darndest to win back his heart.

The wait for the bus is excruciating. Onboard, my knee bounces impatiently as every stop seems to drag out. But, finally, I arrive near Beau's house. As my destination comes into view, I spy Beau's car parked in the driveway.

I smooth down my school uniform and fling my hair over my shoulders. Shaking out my shoulders, I boost my bravery to step toward the front door. With a trembling fist, I knock on the front door.

No response.

After a few silent moments, I try again.

Still nothing.

I look back at his GT Mustang and bite into my lip. He has to be here.

My gaze falls to the ground. He must be downstairs in the basement. That's why he can't hear me knocking.

I step around the house and get to the tall side gate.

Loud, dominating barks boom from the backyard. The thunderous movements of Bruno the German Shepherd gallop toward the gate.

"*Shoosh, shoosh,*" I whisper, bending down and making eye contact with the dog through the gate. "It's me. It's okay."

Bruno's barks soften, and he tilts his head, inspecting me.

I lift my hand and press the back of it against the gate. "It's okay."

Bruno sniffs my skin, and his excitement grows energetically.

"Okay, boy," I whisper, unlatching the gate. "Take it easy. Let's go see Beau."

Treading against the snow-littered path in his backyard, I feel like a creep. But thinking about seeing Beau has my heart fluttering. I just need him back.

I approach the sliding door outside his basement bedroom and tap on the tinted glass. There's no movement inside. I knock again, this time calling out his name. Impatience consumes Bruno, who jumps up at the door, adding a single loud bark.

When he removes his paws, a slither of warm air pours outside. The unlocked door slides ajar. I press on the handle and slide the door open.

"Beau? It's Ava. Are you here?"

I step into the room and Bruno busts in beside me.

"Hey, boy, you gotta stop barging into me."

I walk toward the couch and pivot between the vacant bed and open bathroom doorway. "Beau?"

The basement is silent, but my ears prick to muffled noises seeping through from upstairs. I tiptoe toward the staircase. The basement door is cracked ajar, and the voices are unmistakable.

Beau is arguing with his mother.

I shoo Bruno out of the basement and close the sliding door. I move back to the staircase and lightly tread on each stair. I curl my hands into fists, focusing on the discomfort. I need a distraction from my delicate stomach.

"I wish your father hadn't opened his mouth," Mrs. Stevenson says.

"Why? You obviously haven't been happy for years," Beau replies.

"I wanted you to have both parents at home."

"So I could listen to you both argue and ignore me like I'm invisible?"

Mrs. Stevenson huffs with exhaustion. "That wasn't the plan."

"There was a plan? Please, Mom, enlighten me."

I stand behind the cracked open door, listening. I can't see either of them, but I can feel the tension rising.

"I thought becoming more like Lydie would help my marriage," Mrs. Stevenson admits. "I fired the housekeeper, quit my job, and planned to be a devoted mother and wife."

"I liked having you home all the time."

"I know you did, honey." Her voice is tender. "But despite making dinner every night, and doing all the errands, I could tell he still missed her."

"But she was dead."

Hearing Beau say those words hits me like a dagger. It's true, but the matter-of-fact nature of the comment stings.

"I couldn't be a stay-at-home parent," Mrs. Stevenson says with regret staining her words. "I needed to get back to my life. Get back to being me."

"Then why didn't you get a divorce?" Anger boils in his tone. "Why did we have such a miserable life? You went back to work and became numb to everything at home. Well, newsflash, I was at home and needed your attention."

"Maybe it wasn't about you!" his mother yells.

At that, I push open the door. The shock keeps me rigid as I stare at the standoff happening between Beau and his mother.

"You!" she yells at me. "Get out of my house, you home-wrecking little..."

"Mom!" Beau cuts her off in a commanding tone.

"You're just like your father," she seethes, glaring at Beau. "You both pick these women over me."

"How could I pick her over you when you're never here?" Beau argues. "You're kidding yourself if you think we have any kind of relationship."

She paces the two steps between them and shoves him hard. "How dare you!"

He stumbles backward, holding out his hands.

"You think your life has been miserable?" she wails, hitting him two more times. "I've been living in hell to provide this home for you."

As her arms continue to flail at him, Beau kneels, sheltering his head with folded arms.

"This family fed into my image at work. Female executives need the husband and the kids, or they're not seen as balanced."

Beau lowers to the ground as hands continue to whack into him.

"How do you think you got the car, the clothes, the concert tickets, and whatever else you wanted from us? Do you think this lifestyle is free? We all make sacrifices."

"Stop!" I yell, horrified. "Stop hitting him."

"Shut up!" she seethes at me.

She looms above Beau with a raised hand. He lowers to the ground, cradling the back of his head in his hands. Mrs. Stevenson blinks at her son. Her chest heaves. Her arm lowers, and she steps back. As she continues to stumble backward, I race forward, skidding by Beau.

I hug my arms around him as he trembles. Soft yet strained sobs sniffle out of him.

Mrs. Stevenson's reddened eyes home in on us. She rakes her hands through her hair and lets out a shrill scream. She turns and thuds towards the front door. The slam of it closing echoes throughout the house.

"Beau," I whisper, holding him tight. "Oh, I'm sorry."

His light sobs whisper out of him as he hiccups unsteady breaths.

"It's okay," I whisper, stroking his hair. "I've got you."

It takes a few moments for his breathing to calm. When he rises, I pull him closer, letting him rest his head on my shoulder. His breath tickles my neck, and the pulse of his heart thumps against my chest.

"What are you doing here?" he asks in a gravelly tone.

I press my hands into his back. "I left school to see you."

He lifts off my shoulder and pulls out of the hug. The sadness on his face makes my soul gurgle to the pit of my stomach. "Why?"

"I found out every person behind leaking the photo," I say, holding his arms. "I told Mr. Franklin you had nothing to do with it."

His eyes are unsteady as they look at me. "Okay." His voice is layered with uncertainty.

"I'm sorry for ever doubting you. I had to find out the truth. I needed to get rid of the divide between us."

His jaw rocks with nervous unease.

I give his arms a small shake. "Beau?"

With a twist of his arms, he removes my hands from him. "Look, thanks for going to all that trouble, but..."

I stare at him with urgency. "But what?"

He lifts his palms upward. "Did you not just see that?"

"What, your mom? Of course I did. I'm so sorry."

"You and me... This'll never be easy."

"But things are better when we're together."

He shakes his head, wincing as his eyes water. "Are they?"

My hands raise and plant over my nose and mouth.

"I wanted nothing more than to be with you," he says with a sniff. "But every single person has questioned my motives and asked if you're insane for being with me. Now my mom..." He closes his eyes and a small sob hisses out of him. "I just can't do this. We can't be together. It won't work."

"But I want to make it work," I blurt desperately.

A tear spills from his eyes. "I'm sorry, Ava. I can't."

He stands and walks away from me. I stay kneeling on the carpet, hunched over my lap, and fight the onslaught of tears.

Abruptly, my cries stop when I hear the shutting of the basement door. I purse my lips closed, get to my feet, and bound for the front door. I race from the footpath to the bus stop.

He doesn't want me.

Being with me isn't worth it.

I'm too hard to deal with.

He doesn't love me.

Twenty-Eight

The next day I went to school on autopilot. I went to my first two classes, but I can't recall anything that happened. During my study period, I wander the halls as an ache builds behind my eyes.

What am I doing here? I just want to be in bed.

I move toward the auditorium, ready to hide away in the alcove. I stop dead. From the corner, I glimpse Beau sitting on the bench seat. The same bench where our interview occurred. The day he first told me about his parents.

An ugly pain buries into my gut.

His mom.

Ouch. The pain expands as images of her abuse flicker through my mind.

I rid the images and instead focus on the boy sitting before me. I hug the corner. He hasn't noticed me. He has a stack of books beside him, a school bag at his feet, and is hunched over a notebook while he writes notes. The creases in his forehead are a mixture of worry and frustration. He told me how hard he finds learning from textbooks.

I nudge a foot forward. I could help him. I could make study notes that are easy to comprehend and memorize.

I scoot my foot back. But he doesn't want me around. He pushed me away. Being with me is too hard.

My bottom lip quivers and I step away before a sob bursts.

He hates me. There's nothing more to it.

I cup my hands over my face as I hurry into the hall. The bell rings for the next period, and I jog before the classrooms burst open.

"Ava!" Hilary calls. She latches onto my arm and yanks me to the side. "I've been wanting to find you all day."

I sniff hard and swipe my eyes. "Not now, Hilary."

"Oh my gosh, it is true," she murmurs. "You and Beau broke up?"

I hiccup two sobs, my chest heaving. "What did you hear?"

"Not any details," Hilary blurts with her hands up in surrender. "No one's gossiping about you. It's just, the group is really worried about you."

I wipe a hand over my eyes again. "They still care?"

"Aww, Ava," Hilary coos, rubbing my shoulder. "We're friends. We care. Even about Beau, if you can believe it."

"Beau doesn't want to be with me," I whimper, hopelessly unable to contain my tears. "I messed up."

"I'm sure that's not true."

I shake my head, my chin dimpling. "You have no idea."

"All I know about is the photo, and we think we know who did it."

I step away from her, averting my eyes. "I don't care about that anymore."

"But you'll want to hear this," Hilary says, getting animated. "Jeff has been trying to talk to Whitney. She keeps clamming up or getting super defensive. Like, more than usual. Jeff said he keeps prodding her, and it's like the guilt is written all over her face."

I move toward the middle of the hall, ignoring the students moving up and down. "I said I don't care."

"But, Ava, we..."

"You're not telling me anything I don't already know," I say, raising my voice. "It doesn't matter. None of it matters. I found it all out, and Beau didn't care. He still doesn't love me."

"But it was your picture," Hilary says, not following. "Why would he be mad?"

"*See!*" I yell. "You don't know anything!"

I march against the sea of students, leaving behind a stunned Hilary.

As the rage inside me dwindles, I bump against other people who veer into classrooms. My direction skews, I dawdle against the wall. Ahead, Ms. Hart opens her classroom door.

She stops, her mouth forming an o as she stares at me. "Ava. Oh my gosh, dear, you look haggard."

I collapse against the wall, too deflated to budge.

She motions to her classroom. "Do you want to chat? I don't have a class right now."

"There's no point," I say flatly. "I can't fix anything."

Ms. Hart smiles kindly. "Come on. You can tell me anything."

"I can't talk about this."

She steps into the doorway. "I can't imagine having my image sent to everyone. I know you must be dealing with some immense feelings right now."

"No, you don't get it, I don't care about the photo. That's how messed up my life is right now."

One more time, she motions to the classroom. I sigh, peel myself off the wall, and walk inside with her.

Ms. Hart sits on the edge of her desk. "I guess your mind must be jumbled with thoughts of who sent the picture to everyone."

I sit on a desk facing her. "No. I know who did it."

Her eyebrows raise. "You do?"

"It wasn't Beau, if that's what you're thinking."

"Did you tell Mr. Franklin who did it?"

I look down at my lap. "No. It's their responsibility to come forward."

"But, Ava..."

"I've already moved on. I don't care about the photo. I liked it before it was stolen." I frown, shifting on the desk. "And then it was used to ruin the dance. I worked so freaking hard on that dance. I wanted it to be fun. Now, all anyone will remember is the photo."

"You shouldn't block your feelings like this. You shouldn't feel shameful about the photo. It's okay to be angry or sad."

"I said I'm over it!" I yell.

Ms. Hart's mouth falls open, stunned.

"I'm sorry," I blurt. "I didn't mean to yell."

"No, it's okay. Just very unexpected."

"Look, there's just other stuff going on that's bigger than the photo. I don't want to get into it."

"Okay. But I'm here to listen."

"It's between me and the person I interviewed for the assignment. It's too personal, so I..." I steady myself to look into her eyes. "I deleted my interview."

"Oh?"

"I just... I couldn't share it. Someone else agreed to sit down with me, but it won't be until after the break. So if that lowers my grade, so be it, because..."

"Ava," Ms. Hart interrupts my rambling. "It's okay. Yes, I said the interviews need to be completed before the break, but under the circumstances, I'm happy to give you an extension."

My shoulders relax with ease. "Really?"

"You've spent four years at this school being an exemplary student. One assignment won't change anything. Your hard work should award you some perks."

A tear teeters over the edge of my eye. "Thanks."

She leans forward. "Anything else you want to get off your chest?"

I purse my lips and shake my head. I push off the table and move toward the door. "I'm not feeling so great. I might call my dad to take me home."

"Okay. You look like you need some rest. Take care, Ava."

I thank her again and leave the classroom.

I don't call my dad, but I leave school early. It's becoming somewhat of a habit.

Although, now I give up the pretense of school all together. The next two days, I don't get ready for school. I leave my bed for the kitchen or the bathroom, and then promptly return. I haven't felt this miserable since my mom died. I prayed I'd never be reminded of the pain.

But this pain is different.

Losing a parent shattered my entire world.

A broken heart has me questioning myself.

If only I'd done things differently. If I'd been more honest or understanding. I wasn't there for him when he wanted to talk about his parents. I left him so isolated that I found him in that horrible situation with his mother.

How could she be so cruel to him? There was so much hatred in her heart. It lives inside her, wanting to let loose on my mother. I guess I'm the next best target.

I know everyone grieves in different ways, and none of us have handled the past few years well, but... Oh my gosh... I hope Mrs. Stevenson has never unleashed on Beau like that before. Did he learn his brutal methods from her? He only told me she ignores him or yells at him when he does something wrong. Was there more to it he never told me about?

We both witnessed the black and blue bruising on Quinton that day in the nurse's office. I squint hard, trying to remember Beau's reaction. Did he see himself in that boy? I remember him saying he'd never hit a smaller kid. Did that empathy come from a shared experience?

I dry heave under the covers.

I really hope I didn't get close to Beau and never realize the level of abuse he was receiving at home. Was his dad oblivious too? I can't imagine how resentful Beau would feel if his dad ignored the violence going on around him.

I take a deep breath and sit up to settle my nausea. Beau was shocked the initial day his mother told me to get out of her house. He didn't seem scared of her. I don't think he was acting. He had already been so vulnerable with me.

I retch again.

Oh please, don't let my memories fail me. I'd hate to have been blind to this.

I pull my legs out from under the covers and sit on the side of my bed. I wake my phone to check what day it is. Saturday 12.34 p.m. At least my dad won't lecture me about school today. Wait, it's past midday? Has he given up? According to my dad, no days are for sleeping in.

Last Sunday, he took it easy on me because of the utter humiliation I felt the night before. I barely care about that stupid photo now. I'm sure everyone's inboxes are filled with juicier pieces of trash gossip. I said what I needed to say to the slime balls behind it and got my closure. It's up to them to repent and serve out their punishments. If they don't come clean, I'm sure the guilt will eat them alive.

It's eating me alive.

Why did I have to be so selfish? Why couldn't I talk to Beau? He was desperate for me to listen to him. Everyone ignores him, and I was supposed to be different. No wonder he pushed me away. I'm as bad as everyone else.

I just wanted to live out a moment as my mother did. To put on an event that the whole community could take part in and have a blast. But I'm nothing like Lydie Jones. She always took the time to listen to those she loved. She always made sure we were heard, protected, and loved. She would have sat down with Beau for hours and listened to every word that poured out of his soul.

I pull my robe around me, slip into the fuzzy slippers, and shuffle my way down the hall. I hug my middle, searching for a flavored tea that will take my anxiety away. As I pick up a chamomile tea bag, a noise grabs my attention. I drop the bag and turn to the kitchen doorway. The noise sounds like a group of people talking and laughing. I deepen my focus, trying to pick out individual voices. What the heck is happening in the cul-de-sac?

I edge towards the front door and move over to the window to view the front yard.

I grab onto the window frame because my knees buckle.

"What the..." It puffs out of me as my eyes adjust to the sight before me. In the middle of our white dusted yard, my dad adjusts a tall and cheery Santa Claus cut-out. Beside him, he has set up a happy Rudolf.

"But dad never..." My words trail off as more wondrous anomalies steal my attention.

From every house in the cul-de-sac, neighbors walk in and out of their houses, carrying supplies with bright smiles and happy dispositions. There are baking dishes, cake stands, and punch bowls being brought to the center of the road. The focal point is two large trestle tables manned by Mrs. Guthrie and Mrs. Yates. They collect dishes and desserts and arrange them in the most eye-catching manner.

"Wait... What is happening?"

Seriously, my brain is not computing. Am I dreaming? Have I gone nuts? Is a memory from my childhood being projected in front of me?

I rub my eyes hard, blink several times, and then look out the window again. The same amazing scene lies ahead of me. It's festive and lively, and my dad is a part of it. Beyond the central tables, cars block access to the cul-de-sac. My mom always had neighbors park at the entry of the cul-de-sac so people could walk on the road without fear of harm.

"Oh, Mom," I whisper. "You would've loved this."

My eyes wander across the cars, and then my heart flutters. A shiny GT Mustang is parked on the left-hand side.

I grip the window frame harder. "Oh my gosh. Oh my gosh. Beau is here. Why is Beau here?" I look down at my robe. "*Crap.* I gotta change."

After I change into a cute outfit, which includes a red-knitted holiday sweater, I brush out my loose curls and bound for the front door. Despite the magically cozy scene having me in awe, standing on the front porch is daunting. There is so much going on.

Thumps come from overhead. I step down from the porch and glimpse a ladder leaning against the house. Oh my gosh! One of my neighbors is affixing Christmas lights to the roof. I really have woken in a dream.

"Sweetheart," Dad says from the lawn. He fixes Santa Claus and then moves in my direction.

I skip down the path and get to him with speed. "I don't understand," I pant. "What's going on?"

Dad's eyes are soft as he smiles at me. "Isn't this what you always wanted?"

"But, I thought..."

"I've denied you your happiness for far too long. Consider this step one in my apology tour."

"That's not fair, Dad. You were caught up in your grief. You were robbed of happiness, too."

"But if we had honored your mother every year with a party, it could've gone a long way in the healing process."

I bite my lip, feeling playful. "Well, it wouldn't be once a year. Mom did host Fourth of July cook-outs, Valentine's Day bake-offs, St. Paddy's..."

"Okay, okay," Dad cuts me off. "I get the point."

I giggle and throw my arms around his neck. "Thank you for this. It's the last thing I expected."

"We wanted it to be a surprise. I hope you're not disappointed you didn't help with the planning."

I pull back, unable to stop my growing grin. "We?"

Dad smiles, gesturing to the right. "That boy doesn't take no for an answer. Not that I took much convincing this time."

I search the mingling crowd, finding Beau helping Mr. Johnson set out a bunch of folding chairs.

Happy tears blur my vision. "This was Beau's idea?"

"He got us all together. He was adamant we were pulling off your idea. When he asked Mrs. Guthrie and Mrs. Yates for help, it was a matter of moments before they had the whole street up and moving." Dad sighs, looking out at the buzzing area. "Seems I was robbing many people of something they loved."

"I'm sorry for putting so much blame on you," I say, tensing as the words flow. "And I'm sorry for not always being honest with you. I thought the white lies or omissions were saving you from getting upset. I don't want you to feel bad about anything over the past few years. We've all been acting less than perfect."

He kisses my cheek and pats my back. "Enjoy the party, sweetheart."

I gaze out at everyone mingling and double-take at a particular individual. "Is that... Mr. Stevenson?"

"He promised to keep his distance from me," Dad says, strained. "But I think life will be easier if I get used to his presence. Especially when our kids seem smitten with each other."

My eyes drift back to Beau. "I don't know if our connection will be as intense as before."

"Go and talk to him," Dad encourages, "before you assume the worst."

I give Dad one more hug with a hefty thank you, and make my way to Beau.

"Hi," Beau says with a wave as he moves away from the group of neighbors. "What do you think?"

"This is the last thing I expected to see when I got out of bed today." Unfortunately, a frown tugs at my expression. "I don't understand what you're doing here."

He scratches behind his neck as a nervous, lopsided grin appears. "I wanted to give you the neighborly holiday party you were craving."

"I thought it was all too hard for you." My head spins, going over our last few interactions. "You said being with me was too hard. Why would you do this for me?"

He brushes his thumb across my cheek. "These past weeks have been hard, but you were right. Life's better when we're together. I just got too overwhelmed."

"That's one way to put it." Ugly images of his mom's attack flood my mind. "What about your mom?"

"I haven't seen her since the day you were at my house."

My mouth falls open. "Huh?"

He sucks in a shallow breath. "I guess she came home late, but I really don't know. She just packed a bag and left."

"Wait, what? Are you serious?"

"There was a note. My dad read it, but I can't. The cliffnotes is she's gone."

I clutch his hand. "She just left? Oh, Beau, I'm so sorry."

His eyes well. "Is it bad that I keep thinking she could've done this years ago?"

My swollen heart hangs with a heavy weight.

Beau gestures off to the side. "I mean, look at my dad. He's trying to be part of the community. He has to give your dad a wide berth, but still, they're both here. Who knows what our lives would've been like if Mom left sooner?"

I caress the side of his face. "It wouldn't have been better. It would have been the same."

His face falls with a dismal frown. "You think?"

"My dad held a grudge against your dad, not your mom. I doubt they would've mended fences. My dad would've held onto the betrayal no matter what. Is your dad doing okay?"

"He seems to be. They haven't been happy for years. He hasn't said it in words, but I think my dad is thankful she's gone." Beau sighs. "Hopefully, if I stay out of trouble, he and I can have a better relationship. I just keep wishing things could've been different."

A small smile brightens my outlook. "Things are different. Before I got out of bed, I was sure I would never be this close to you again. I was so depressed."

"I hope I haven't kept your mood low."

"Being around you only makes my mood high. Even if we're sharing sadness, I'm happy to be close to you."

Beau throws his arms around me and kisses my forehead. "This time, we need to promise to not let anyone get between us."

I plant my hands on the sides of his face. "Be honest with me. Has your mom been hitting you this whole time?"

His eyebrows lift with surprise. "No, she barely notices me. I told you that."

I lower my hands and swallow the ugly sensation creeping up my throat. "I just got scared that..."

"I think you saw my mom let out years' worth of suppressed rage."

"And you thought my dad was the scary parent." I shut my eyes as the compounding thoughts simmer down. "How on earth did you get my dad to go along with this?"

He smiles. "You did most of the work. You talked him into this the night I was over for dinner. Plus, Mrs. Guthrie and Mrs. Yates worked some crazy magic when your dad and I approached them."

A surprised laugh puffs out of me. "You and my dad worked together?"

He shrugs with a humble smile. "Somewhat."

"*Ha*! Amazing."

"He doesn't have to hide in fear that everyone is judging him because of what happened during his marriage."

"Do you think my neighbors knew about the affair?"

Beau shakes his head. "Dad told me our parents promised not to breathe a word. As long as they all didn't make contact after we moved out of the cul-de-sac, they wouldn't break the pact."

"I wish that pact never happened. I can't believe my mother went along with it."

He lifts my chin with a crooked finger. "She did it for us. I'm sure she thought we'd grow up happy."

"If only she could've predicted the future."

Beau looks up at the sky. "I wish you were here, Lydie."

"I'm sure she is." He looks back down at me, and I greet him with a smile. "None of this would've happened if she weren't guiding us along the way."

"Give yourself a little credit. You're the reason the dance happened. You're the reason I got out of bed and talked to your dad and neighbors." He gestures across the road. "And I never would have called those guys if it weren't for you."

I look to where he's pointing and start giggling. Ciara, Hilary, Lucy, Marcus, and Jeff hang around a table. They all laugh as Marcus tries to feed Hilary a cupcake. She leans back like she's playing limbo, avoiding chocolate cake going up her nose.

"I can't believe you called them."

"You said you wanted to maintain friendships after the committee meetings were over."

I shake my head. "I only want to be friends with them if they are friends with you, too."

"Baby steps." He smirks. "Plus, they're kind of on my side after what happened at school."

I am stiff with dread. "What happened at school?"

He stays smiling, easing my tension. "Why don't you let them tell you?"

I shrug. "Okay."

We walk hand in hand toward the others.

"It's so good to see you," Hilary says, wrapping me in a hug. "I was so worried when you had so many days off."

I rub her back. "I'm good. I'm so glad you're all here."

"Well, it's not all the committee," Lucy says, getting in on the hug.

As we pull apart, I glance around. "I can't say I'm heartbroken over Whitney not being here."

"Did you hear she got suspended?" Ciara asks.

My jaw drops. I look at Beau and then back to Ciara. "What?"

"Beau planted a seed in my brain," Jeff says. "When he mentioned Whitney was avoiding the group clean up and being a self-proclaimed Photoshop expert, it kept gnawing at me. Two days ago, I confronted her. She kept dodging my questions, but then yesterday she came clean to Mr. Franklin."

"She, Teddy, and Sullivan confessed as a group. They all got a two week suspension," Lucy says. She winces, shaking her head. "Do I have the worst taste in men or what?"

"Why? Who else did you have your eye on?" Jeff asks.

Lucy's mouth falls open. She looks up at the sky and rolls her eyes. "Oh my gosh!"

"So, those three confessed, and no one else?" I ask.

"You were expecting more?" Hilary asks. "*Geez.* I was shell shocked to find out there were three creeps behind this."

"Apparently, they took full credit," Marcus says. "We're so sorry this happened to you, Ava."

Ciara grabs my hand with a thoughtful smile. "You deserve better than what happened to you."

I squeeze Ciara's hand and look around at the group. "I do have better. I'm so thankful you're all here. Shall we eat too much cake? My neighbors are great bakers."

Marcus raises his hand. "I'm ready to load up."

As everyone moves around the tables in the center of the cul-de-sac, I hang back, looping my arms around Beau's middle. I lean against his chest as his hands run over my hair and down my back.

"Teddy and Sullivan admitted to tampering with my grades," Beau says. "Mr. Franklin fixed everything and notified my dad. They're even better than before because of the committee and rejoining the wrestling team."

"Aww, I'm so happy for you."

"I can't believe those three messed with you," Beau says. "I swear, I'll..."

"You'll do nothing," I say, looking up at him.

His jaw rocks, and then his tension releases. "Okay, yes. I'll do nothing. I've done nothing for the past few days at school. I feel like I have a handle on controlling the compulsions."

"That's an amazing accomplishment to feel better about yourself." I smile at him sweetly. "Retaliating against those three had set everything into motion."

"So, I'm supposed to call it even?"

"It's not a competition. Just let it go and be happy with me."

He squeezes me in a hug, lifting my feet off the ground. "That I can do, Avie baby."

I giggle in his arms. "I love you."

He kisses me softly. "I love you, too."

Epilogue

Christmas Eve

"Are you disappointed not to be at the Ashworth Estate?" I ask Beau as I lovingly comb my fingers through his hair.

"Are you kidding me?" he replies, linking his hand behind my back as we sit on the floor. "Why would I be at that snoozefest when I can be with the most beautiful girl in Victoria Falls?"

I giggle, taking in the warmth from Beau and the glowing, crackling fire beside us. It's late in the evening and we're cozying up in my living room, enjoying the twinkle lights framing the mantle and highlighting the overly decorated tree.

"Who would've imagined a scenario where we get to spend Christmas Eve together?" Beau says and gives me a peck on the cheek. "Both our dads left us alone, and are hanging out with the neighbors next door."

"I still can't believe my dad stayed true to his word about making amends. He'd bottled up so many feelings. I didn't think he'd ever be able to let go."

"I bet seeing you happier spurs him on."

"And I'm happier because you now have a brighter home life."

Relief eases his shoulder as he leans into me. "I never thought my dad and I would have an easy relationship ever again. Who knew he cared so much? He's always asking me about wrestling, or homework, or you."

"I'm last on the list?" I joke.

Beau smirks. "He's probably afraid I'll give details."

I giggle. "*Eww.* Don't."

"Yuck. Never." Beau's eyes wander over the tree. "You know, if we had gone to the Ashworth party, you could have interviewed Vanessa."

"Firstly, she made a point that I wasn't invited. Secondly, I doubt she'd sit for an interview while hosting an event. Thirdly, I kinda would like to crash a party there one day."

"I'll put it on our list of adventures." Beau scoots a present out from under the tree. "In the meantime, do you wanna open?"

I squeal as he hands me the wrapped gift. "*Eep.* Should I?"

"Go on," he urges. "It's close enough to midnight."

I glance at the wall clock and snicker. "And you know as soon as it hits midnight, my dad's gonna come in and tell us to call it a night."

Beau nudges me. "So there's no time to lose."

I smile, unwrapping the present. "Okay." As I peel away the tape and paper, I grin at the label on the box. It's from my favorite stationery store on Main Street. "Oh my gosh, Beau, I love it."

Beau laughs. "All you've seen is the box."

"That's enough evidence to know I'll love it." I open the box and find a soft-touch baby blue A5 size, six ring, agenda binder. It has a snap closer and an array of inside pockets. "It's gorgeous."

"I thought you might want a new binder for planning your next big party," Beau says. "Maybe the prom?"

I hug the binder. "Actually, I think I want to avoid another event with so much high school politics. But I know what I want to plan inside this binder."

Beau smiles, intrigued. "And what is that?"

"Our year off travel plans."

Beau pulls his arms around me. "You still want to do that?"

"More than anything."

Beau looks down at the binder cradled in my lap. "Hey, did you check all the pockets?"

"Huh?"

Beau unravels his arms and leans back, staring at the binder.

With curiosity bubbling inside me, I open it up and dig my hands in the pockets. I gasp as I feel a delicate chain. I pull it out and find a ruby pendant hanging from a silver necklace.

"Beau, it's... more beautiful than... I could ever..."

Beau chuckles and moves behind me to latch it behind my neck. "I'm glad you like it,"

I turn and plant my hands on the sides of his face, pressing a drawn-out kiss on his lips.

"Mmm," he mumbles. "Was that my Christmas gift?"

I pull away to retrieve his present from under the tree. "Only if you don't wanna open this."

"Gimme," he cheers.

I giggle as he unwraps the gift.

Inside, he pulls out a card. He reads the note and then gives me that adorable lop-sided grin.

I touch his hand, saying, "I want you to know I'm not reliant on you for my adventures. I can come up with stuff too."

He holds the card open. "An IOU for rock climbing at Logan's Point. I am so there." He leans in and kisses me. "Thank you, I love it."

I rub my lips together, smiling. "Is that all that's in the box?"

He grins and digs in the shredded tissue paper that cushioned the card. "How did we have the same plan?" He lifts out a chunky silver watch. "Whoa, Ava. This is too much." He clasps it around his wrist. "But there's no way I'm giving it up."

"Good, because I wasn't taking it back. It suits you, very handsome."

Beau traces the pendant. "Just like you. Delicate and passionate."

I loop my arms around his neck and push my lips against his with urgent pressure. Our legs intertwine as we scoot closer together on the carpet. His hands run up and down my back, and I lean further into him, forcing him to recline.

Electricity races through my veins, and my heart throbs as I suck against his bottom lip. My hand sneaks into the collar of his shirt. The sensation of his skin gives me a thrill.

"Ahem," my dad coughs, giving us a warning as he opens the front door.

We spring apart, chests heaving and lips moist.

My gaze lifts to the wall clock. Midnight. Right on schedule.

Thank you

Scan the QR code to get a FREE chapter from Beau's perspective. This chapter picks up after the breakup in Chapter 25.

Stay subscribed to the newsletter to get 20+ bonus scenes from all the books in the series.

SCAN ME!

About The Author

Milly Rose is an animal-loving romance enthusiast with a swoon-inducing book formula. Shy girl + hot guy + first kisses. Her YA sweet romance books will have you falling in love every instalment. Milly Rose is the quintessential shy girl, who you can contact via her mailing list and reply to her monthly email blasts! Milly spends her days vying for her cat's affection, dreaming up her next book boyfriend, and writing a fun meet-cute under candlelight with a lovely brewed cup of tea.

Join Milly Rose's Mailing List
millyrosebooks.com
Follow on Instagram @shy.author.milly.rose
Follow on Tiktok @shy.author.milly.rose

Also By

ALL BOOKS SET IN ASHWORTH ACADEMY

Shy Girls Can't Date Billionaires (Christie & Ash)
Shy Girls Can't Date Bullies (Ava & Beau)
Shy Girls Can't Date Frenemies (Jamie & Milo)
Shy Girls Can't Date Bad Boys (Vanessa & Dax)
Shy Girls Can't Fake Date (Kylie & Parker)
Shy Girls Can't Date Celebrities (Josie & Wyatt)
We Shouldn't Be Together (Tabitha & Kai)